Orchid
&
the Wasp

A Novel

Caoilinn Hughes

HOGARTH

London   New York

Copyright © 2018 by Caoilinn Hughes

All rights reserved.

Published in the United States by Hogarth, an imprint of the Crown Publishing Group, a division of Penguin Random House LLC, New York. crownpublishing.com

HOGARTH is a trademark of the Random House Group Limited, and the H colophon is a trademark of Penguin Random House LLC.

Library of Congress Cataloging-in-Publication Data is available.

ISBN 978-1-5247-6110-3
Ebook ISBN 978-1-5247-6112-7
International edition ISBN 978-0-525-57593-1

Printed in the United States of America

Jacket design by Christopher Brand
Jacket photographs by bauhaus1000/DigitalVision Vectors/Getty (orchid) and De Agostini Picture Library/Getty Images (wasp)

10 9 8 7 6 5 4 3 2 1

First United States Edition

For Paul

*If you programmed your computer by conscious thinking,
you know the nature of your values and emotions. If you
didn't, you don't.*

—AYN RAND

*I constantly felt (as I suppose many an ambitious girl has
felt) a thumping from within unanswered by any beckoning
from without.*

—ANNA JULIA COOPER

*The sea is not less beautiful in our eyes because we know
that sometimes ships are wrecked by it.*

—SIMONE WEIL

1.

The Mediocrity Principle

APRIL 2002

It's our right to be virgins as often as we like, Gael told the girls surrounding her like petals round a pollen packet.

"Just imagine it," she said. "Louise. Fatima. Deirdre Concannon."
She pronounced their names like accusations. She snuck the tip of
her index finger into each of their mouths and made their cheeks
go: *pop. pop. pop.* "I did mine already with this finger," she said. The
girls flinched and wiped their taste buds on their pinafores. "Blood
dotted the bathroom tiles but it wasn't a lot and it wasn't as sore as
like . . . piercing your own ears without ice," she concluded omi-
nously. "And now I don't have to obsess over it like all these morons.
You should all do it tonight. We'll talk tomorrow and I'll know if
you've done it or not."

Tiny hairs on their ears trembled at her inaudible breath like Ju-
liet's. Gravely, she confessed: "Some of you will need capsules all
your life. All the way to your wedding night because of being Mus-
lim or really *really* Christian. Wipe your snot, Miriam. It's a fact of
life. It's also helping people. Boys will think they're taking something
from you, when the capsule cracks. But you'll know better," she said.
"You'll know there was nothing to take."

Gael was eleven. It was her last term of primary school. Perhaps that was why the proposition backfired. The girls were getting ready to fly off to some *other* wealthy, witheringly beautiful leader. But Gael wasn't disturbed by this. She no longer needed a posse. It would be tidier if they fell away than having to break them off.

"Really *really* Christian like your brother?" Deirdre replied. "Isn't he an altar boy?"

Gael rolled her eyes so dramatically it gave her a back-of-socket headache. "He hasn't got a hymen, Deirdre, so he's *ob*viously irrelevant."

Deirdre and Louise's mirth was exacerbated by the fact that Miriam's tears had now formed a terra-cotta paste with the foundation she'd tried on at the bus-stop pharmacy earlier. How much would the virgin pills cost, Becca wanted to know. What would Gael price them at?

"What-*ever*," Gael said. "What does *that* matter? Pocket money is what. Everyone'll want them. Hundreds if not millions of people, Rebecca. So choose." She challenged their noncommittal natures, looking from girl to concave girl. "Well, are you or aren't you? *In?*" She addressed the dandruffy crowns of their heads. Of late, they'd become less worthwhile spending time with. Even playing sports, they didn't want to sweat. Headbutting nothing, the chimney-black sweep of her hair kicked forward and she thrust them off like a sudden squall that separates what's flyaway from what's fixture. *Stupid* girls, she thought as the lunch bell trilled and they straggled toward their classrooms. Back to times tables: the slow, stupid common operations.

Turning her back on the blackboard, she took a bottle of Tipp-Ex from her bag and began painting her nails a corrective white. It smelled of Guthrie's bedroom. Acrid. Concentrated. Tissues fouled with paint from cleaning his brushes. Exoneration. Her little brother: the acolyte. On the ninth nail, she lifted her head from the fumes to find Deirdre Concannon striding into the room alongside the Guidance Counselor, who approached Gael's desk with a blob of tuna-mayo in the corner of her puckered mouth, a mobile phone held out and a polite invitation for Gael to take her depraved influence elsewhere. The number Gael dialed was familiar. Though, as Mum was out of town, it was to be an unfamiliar fate.

◆

Jarleth had sent a car to collect them and take them to his work several hours ago. On the phone, his secretary had informed Gael as to the make of the car and the name of the driver. (Both Mercedes.) There'd been no chastisement thus far, other than an afternoon confined to a windowless meeting-room penitentiary in his office building.

In the same school but two years behind his sister, Guthrie had been encouraged to go home too when his whole class had concluded their postlunch prayer in perfect unison: "And lead us not into temp-tation, but deliver us from evil, Hymen." Gael was already waiting at the school gate when Guthrie had come dragging his satchel-crucifix across the tarmac, in utter distress and confusion.

His blue eyes were red-rimmed as a seagull's by the time he finished his homework under the artificial lights of Barclays' Irish headquarters at 2 Park Place in Dublin's city center, just around the corner (though worlds apart) from the National Concert Hall, where they often watched their mother yield a richer kind of equity from her orchestra.

Guthrie spoke quietly into his copybook. "You always do this when Mum's gone."

"I said I'm sorry."

"But you're not." He made a convincingly world-weary noise for a ten-year-old.

Their mother was Principal Conductor of the National Symphony

Orchestra—one of Ireland's two professional orchestras—with whom she gave some hundred concerts a year, on top of guest conductorships where she might perform eight shows in a week, hold interviews, benefits, meetings, recordings, travel . . . generally returning home prostrate.

Gael searched for Ys in the ends of her black hair. Absently, she said, "How was I to know my idea'd make all the sissies go berserk?"

Guthrie's wispy beige hair kissed the polished pine table where he rested his head on his arm. He was slowly translating Irish sentences from his textbook with his left hand. He was a *ciotóg*. A left-handed person. Meaning: "strange one."

> *Fadó, fadó,*
> A long time ago
> *bhí laoch mór ann, ar a dtugtar Cúchulainn.*
> there was a great ~~hero~~ warrior ~~of the name named~~ called
> Cúchulainn.

He stopped writing and let the pencil tip rest on the page like a Ouija board marker. After a while, he lifted it and moved it to a blank page where he began drawing Cúchulainn in profile, sword brandished. It was a giant weapon with an intricate hilt. Guthrie gave his hero long flowing locks and a chain-mail vest and shin guards. When all the details had been filled in, Guthrie began to add squiggles all around the figure and wild loops in the air—childish in comparison to Cúchulainn's frenzied expression.

"Are they clouds?" Gael asked.

A barely perceptible shift of his head.

"Trees?"

"Waves," he said softly.

"Wait." She considered the sketch anew. "He's in the sea? With those heavy clothes on?"

Guthrie exaggerated the hero's grimace and drew a twisted cloak in place of saying yes. He strengthened the line of the chin and the nostril brackets, for defiance. "He's fighting the ocean."

Watching the pencil go, Gael wondered at this. Cúchulainn battling the humongous Atlantic. An invisible duel, in slow, deliberate motion. Had he no mind for reward or reputation, should he win? Or rescue, should he lose? Maybe he was just proving something to himself; testing the muscle of his character, no thought of audience. There aren't viewing posts in towers of water. No adjudication. Why else would a person take on the tireless sea but to learn the strength of his own current? Guthrie lifted his head to reveal a pale yellow mark where his cheek had been pressed against his forearm.

"That's what it feels like," he said, evenly, erasing some lines from the drawing and brushing the gray rubber scraps to the floor. "The way you get dragged in the white part."

"What feels like that?"

Some moments passed without answer.

"Oh," Gael said, realizing. "That doesn't sound relaxing."

"It's not."

"But you know it's only gravity, dragging you down, right? It's not like, a monster or Satan or anything."

Guthrie seemed to think about this. "It's me," he said.

"The warrior?"

He shook his head and Gael half expected feathers of pale hair to come falling off like when you shake a dead bird. "The one dragging."

"Guthrie! That's *not* a good thing to think. It's not your fault."

Gael said this, though she knew it was a lie to make things livable. Her parents had sat her down a few weeks ago to explain the situation. "Your brother doesn't have epilepsy. He only *thinks* he does," Jarleth had said. Sive had looked dismayed by that explanation and had taken over. "It's called somatic delusional disorder, Gael. I'm sure you'll want to look it up. But what's important is that he's physically healthy," she'd said, "but there's one small, small part of

5

his brain that isn't well. The doctors say when he's older, it might be easier to address him directly about it, with counseling. Right now, he gets extremely stressed and anxious, aggressively so, if we talk to him about the disorder. He thinks we're telling him he's not sick. Which he is, just not in the way he thinks. So it's better for everyone to treat it as what *Guthrie* believes it to be. And that's epilepsy." What Gael took from this was that her brother was too young to understand the truth and it was part of his sickness that he couldn't.

"Guth?" Gael repeated, "It's not your fault."

"Dad says so."

A clout of anger to the chest. "Dad's wrong."

"He's mad at me."

"He's just . . . frustrated to see you break something every time you have a fit."

"It's not on purpose."

"I know."

"I don't control it."

"I know that."

"If it was to . . . If I just wanted to skip PE, Miss McFadden would just let me do extra arts and crafts so long as I don't plug stuff in or use scissors or knives or strong glue, she said I can. Or even something else."

Gael made a shocked face. "She must've been drunk or something. McFadden's a prick."

"She can tell that you think that. You make her mean. She said you're arrogant but I told her you're nicer when you're not at school."

"Who cares about nice."

"She said, 'That's convenient.'"

"It'd be convenient if she got mad cow disease from a burger."

"Don't, Gael." Tears surged in his eyes again. "I *like* her."

"Fine, sorry, I take it back! No mad cow disease for Miss McFadden. She's probably vegetarian, Guthrie, don't cry."

6

"It's not—" he said hoarsely.

Gael took his hand from his mouth, where he was chewing on the outer heel of his palm. "Don't do that. Please tell me what's wrong."

He tried to explain but sobbing hampers syntax. Gael pieced together the howled-out word clusters. Dad had warned him he'd have to be moved to Special School if he kept having fits. "But it's . . . not special . . . special is . . . special . . . means . . ."

"It's a euphemism," Gael said. A word she'd learned recently and learned well.

Guthrie blinked at her rapidly. This was new information. "A what?"

"A euphemism. Here." She took his pencil. "You learn it and say it to Dad if he ever threatens that again. You-fa-mism. It means when one word is just a nice way to say something worse. And it's a lie, Guth. There's *no way* you'd have to move schools."

"Dad wouldn't just say it."

"He doesn't see it as a lie. He sees it as a way to protect you. He'll say whatever he thinks will work, to keep you safe. Does Mum know?"

"What?"

"That Dad said that."

Guthrie shrugged. He was looking at the word Gael wrote in block letters on the page beside his drawing. Underneath the Irish homework. He was catching his breath. "She never said it." He took the pencil back up and began to graze it across the whole drawing, diagonally, hazing it in lead.

"Hey!" Gael pulled the copybook from him before it was ruined. She slapped it shut and slotted it in his schoolbag. It was annoying how often their mother was touring these days. She should be dealing with this. "*Look* at me," Gael said. "You didn't have a fit today. Even with . . . your classmates taunting you . . . like silly little dipshits." She didn't add: because of me.

He turned his face from her, to the door, where money missionaries in drab suits and skull-accentuating hairdos passed by the glass panel.

Gael watched the quiver of her brother's shoulder blades. The handholds of his vertebrae. "Come on, Guth. If he comes in and sees your eyes all red still . . ."

"Those estimates submitted this morning"—their father's voice at the end of the corridor carried in as it would through state-of-the-art soundproofing—"having you on . . . fourteen basis points . . . thirteen too many." With only the length of the hallway to prepare for his arrival, Gael got up and paced the room, checking behind the freestanding whiteboard and testing the wall of locked filing cabinets until one opened. She rooted inside and pulled out a roll of Sellotape. "Quick," she said, twirling Guthrie's swivel chair to face her and biting off a length of the tape. "Stay still."

He pushed back from her. "What are you *doing*?"

Jarleth's voice loudened: "—who they take their cues from. He'll call it how he sees it."

"Trust me," she said, wiping his tears with her thumb, which didn't dry them at all.

"*Stop.*"

"Don't try to talk." She plastered the Sellotape across his chin horizontally, so that his lower lip became huge and half-peeled-back and his pink gums showed like a cranky gelada monkey. "It won't hurt. I promise." She wrestled him to connect another length of tape from his temples to the base of his cheekbones, packing his puffy eyes into a tight squint. Shushing her brother's protestations, she braced against his piddly hook punches and completed the collage of his face. On the chair, they wheeled along the table, spinning as they went: the schlepping planet and its beleaguered moon. The last sticky swath gave him a piggy nose from which mucus-water dribbled, threatening to make the whole composition come unstuck.

The door had opened and Jarleth stood there, refastening his watch, like an actor stepping onto the stage mid–costume change. He considered his progeny aloofly. The lines would come to him in due course, or some midmanager would prompt him. This wasn't an important scene.

Gael had jumped to attention, then felt somewhat abased at having done so. Such obeisance. She bent down, not in genuflection but to rummage through her bag for her pocket mirror. Handing it to Guthrie, she said, "We're playing Who Am I." Jarleth gave her a *Playing, is it?* look. His straight eyelashes pointed at her, then moved to the beverages that had been served to them. A can of Sprite for Guthrie. Sparkling water for Gael, who had asked for coffee, but the receptionist had tucked her chin into her chest and had declared Ms. Foess "very sophisticated altogether takes after her father doesn't she but I don't think your mammy'd be happy if we sent you home all jittery now would she missus?" Gael had given her best *tsk* in reply: the sound of a control-alt-delete command. "If you're going to use third person, commit to it," Gael had said. "I'll have sparkling water. Pellegrino, please."

Guthrie hadn't dared to open the compact mirror to guess who he was supposed to be, but at least the disguise had worked. Horseplay trumped waterworks in their father's eyes.

"It's ten past three," Jarleth said. "Since you two have run out of homework, I'll have to call Carla."

"Oh *Dad*," Gael said. "Don't call *Carla*." To Gael, Carla was the most depressing kind of adult—the kind that sees children as a separate species, blind to the puerility of her own life. Girls' nights out on indisposable income. Deliberately limited vocabulary. Lip-gloss mania. Guthrie didn't like Carla because of her general negligence and bad cooking. Their mother liked her threatlessness.

Indifferent, Jarleth took his mobile phone from the breast pocket of his suit jacket and spun it the right way up like a cutthroat razor. The suit was that classic navy-gray color that exists only on the suit spectrum. It had a muted pinstripe and was paired with a crisp white shirt with sloping collar corners, silver button cuff links (that had been no one's gift to him) and a silver and blue tie patterned with a tight grid. His white-gold Claddagh ring looked attractive against his spring tan. He'd gone out cycling for hours on Sunday after mass and the sun shone down on him, he declared upon return, sanctimonious on his carbon cloud. (He never wore cycling gloves or shaved his legs: the two most effeminate aspects of cycling culture. The spandex was just practical.) In the office, he was a bit like a bride in her gown alongside all the bridesmaids, in that none of his colleagues—even fellow executives—dared to wear the same shade of dominion. It was true, he wore it well. When he stood in the daylight, the high thread count made the suit appear pale blue, though this room had no windows. Today was one of those rare days when Jarleth hadn't matched anything with his eyes, which he liked to think of as green, though they were brown as hundred-euro banknotes dropped in a puddle.

"You dropped something," Gael said, to divert his attention from finding Carla's number. She threw her only banknote onto the carpet as she stretched. There goes Susan's hymen pill deposit.

Jarleth looked at the folded fiver. "Buy yourself a coffee." He glanced at his watch.

"Tell you what," Gael said. Her father preferred propositions to questions. She was well trained to please him. The technique had the opposite effect on her teachers, but parents pay cash and report cards are easily forged. "We'll go to Stephen's Green Shopping Center till you're done." She tilted her head toward Guthrie. "I'll hold his hand."

Jarleth studied her with some seriousness. "You have time to kill because your teachers were too provincial to appreciate your business idea—clever, if low-margin and most certainly age-inappropriate—and now you'd like to fritter away that hard-won time in a shopping center?"

"I've karate at half shix," Guthrie said, or at least that was what it sounded like through the Sellotape matrix. "Buth I can *not go* if itch ease—easiel . . . Thath?"

"Market research?" Gael lifted her shoulders to her ears in a cutesy shrug.

"Walter Lippmann had a great name for the masses that congregate in shopping malls instead of libraries," Jarleth said. "'The bewildered herd.' They trample each other down for discount espresso machines. You've seen it."

"We already have an espresso machine," Gael said.

"There'll be something else you want."

"I might *need* something."

"What do you need? Tell me what you need. What your brother needs." Jarleth strode over to the tabletop phone to dial 1. "If I'd only *known* my children were deprived. Anything, Gael. I'll have Margaret put in an order, whatever it is. Same-day delivery."

"I get the point," Gael said, glancing at Guthrie repentantly, then refocusing.

"What point?" Jarleth thrust one hand into his trouser pocket and pushed his stomach out so that his tie slipped to the side and Gael could see the dark coiled hairs of his lower belly through the slits in his strained shirt. He used his body like this on purpose: the body language of an older, uglier, sloppier man; his form unambiguated by an undershirt. This seemed to make him all the more attractive to women of her mother's age, and younger, Gael had observed of late.

"What's my point, Gael?" He always managed to keep his full lips—the same ballet-shoe color as the rest of his face—relaxed, even when the words coming out of them weren't.

Gael put on her straitlaced voice. "My time's more valuable than the time it would take to walk to Stephen's Green to go shopping."

"Good."

Thankfully, he never said "good girl" like relatives and teachers and strangers. Gael hated the phrase in the way she hated people who mixed chocolate with fruit. A denigrating thing to say. It even had the sound of a gag. *G-g.* A cooing baby sound. Worst of all was *good girl, Gael.* Miss McFadden had paid sorely for that in fourth class.

"What else?"

"Huh?" Gael skimmed her mind for What Else.

The landline phone on the table rang shrilly. Jarleth picked up and listened. "Tell him I'm on a conference call with London. I'll be there when he sees me." He spanked the phone to its cradle, gave a sharp sigh and frowned at Guthrie, then at Gael. "Who is he, then? Picasso's Weeping Woman?"

A grin ripped through her concentration. Gael tapped Guthrie on the knee, where the mirror sat in his palm. He opened it and held it at arm's length to try to take himself in. For a moment, nothing registered. They waited. Then, it came as the kind of wave you see at the last minute and you have no choice but to duck under. His face bulged through the tape and the composition slipped apart, taking all the fine down of his cheeks away with it. The laughter was so against his will that his eyes were going again. Straining to make out what he was saying, soon Gael was at it too and it didn't occur to her to stand outside herself to check for giggling; to alter herself toward the caustic, brusque laughter of men. At last, Guthrie steadied himself and sputtered it out. "Deirdre Concannon," he said.

"Asshole in one!" Gael clapped her hands once. She turned for her father's reaction or reprimand, but he was no longer there and the door was shut.

A taxi arrived soon after to take them home. Jarleth said he'd be late and to use the money on the hall table for takeout. Not to wait up.

◆

Guthrie had no lift to karate. Just bail, Gael told him. But no, Dad would be cross if he didn't go because they'd had a talk and they'd made a pact and it was true that his physical strength was that of a wicker basket. Gael said she'd phone Dad to ask if they should order a taxi, but she didn't make the call, predicting how their neediness would irk him.

No, she didn't feel like being that child. That wasn't what she felt like any longer—there was a mismatch between what she felt and how she looked. She considered her uniform with umbrage. Her red tie lay on the living room floor as a discarded snakeskin, blood side up. Slowly, while thinking, she lifted her navy pinafore by its pleated skirt over her head so that she was standing in her white shirt and ankle socks, absorbing the glut of underfloor heating. There was that feeling again, trilling through her. Along the backs of her knees to the base of her buttocks. Across her scalp. The one that felt a bit like fear, but not. A bit like nausea, but not in her stomach. It felt like the inside. As if a dangerous magnet had made its way through her system—harmless so long as it was unpaired. Was it her womb? Her bladder? Like having had way too much to drink but feeling parched. Being giddy on sugar but wanting to get it by the bagful and bury her tongue into its rough dissolvable crystals. She considered herself in the window, where the reflection was clear because it was dark out and all the lights were on inside. She wore a bra because the mandatory crested school shirts were cheap and the absence of bra straps would be conspicuous. Now and then, she filled the sagging cups with things like chestnuts or Barry's tea bags or bits of sponge or textbook pages folded into squares for when there were tests. Mostly, she left them empty, with just air against her nettle-stung nipples. Boys were impressed by mere semblances. She went upstairs dreamily and put on jeans and a black shirt her mother had bought her for a clarinet exam. (Play the part of a musician and they might forgive that awful upper octave, her mother had said, knowing early where Gael's talent did and did not lie.) It would be cold and she'd need a sweater but nothing warm from her closet looked right when she imagined a police car riding by. The shirt would do.

By playing the video clip at double speed, she was able to watch "How to drive an automatic car" four times before they had to go. If this circumstance was a test, part of the test might have been to devise one's own questions. "I'll drive it up and down the road," she called up the stairs, "to get used to it. Get your stuff ready. You're late."

Guthrie had been watching her attempts to start their mother's car from his bedroom window, and the sound of wipers scraping against a dry windscreen, the lack of indicators when pulling out, the fog lights glaring and the way the car juddered like it was having a conniption of its own were enough to convince him. He ran downstairs and waited until she had stopped safely by the curb, give or take a few meters. Just about to test out reverse, she screamed at the appearance of Guthrie's white face in the dark driver's window, looking up to her. "Everything's different from here!" she said, but he couldn't make sense of it. She found the electric window switch. "Where's your dressing gown?"

"It's not a dressing gown."

"The robe thing."

"It's a karategi."

"If it's in the wash, use my gown."

Guthrie's face was all stretched in laughter one muscle from surfacing. "There's no way I'm getting in that car with you!"

"Why not?" Gael struck her palm on the steering wheel and it beeped. "You have to."

"No."

"I'm a natural."

"Way."

"Just get in. I'll go slow."

"Then we'd die slowly."

"Come on, Guthrie. Please. I'm *sick* of relying on parents."

Confronted by her brother's certitude, Gael saw a lost cause. She groaned and went to switch off the lights but, instead, turned on the screen sprinkler. The neighbor's porch lights came on. Gael fiddled with sticks and buttons and keys until everything was dark and still. That must mean off. Only when stopping had been decided for her did the relief come with a collapsing sensation. So *that's* what adrenaline feels like. Stealing had nothing on driving. "Gimme a minute," she said, recovering. Taking in this new perspective. The trimmed gardens of closed-curtain suburbia. The raked lawns stacked with lifestyle. Lives by rote, the driveway pillars tidy and in place like cairns—Connemara granite by way of China grit—never allowing any poor sod the excuse of having lost his way.

Guthrie opened the door for her and she tried to get out, but the seat belt was still on. So she plonked back into the seat and went mock-slack. Guthrie climbed over her to reach the release and helped her arm through the belt.

He stayed close by her elbow. "You're sweaty."

"That was intense." She pushed the door shut and clicked a button on the key to lock it, but the boot popped open. They both stared at it as if at an ice cream on a pavement.

"Let's watch *Karate Kid*," Guthrie said.

Gael looked back down their street where a car was rolling forward. Was it Dad? She went to wave. No, it sped up and U-turned. Guthrie shut the boot. Slipped the keys from her hand. Pressed the right button to lock up.

"Can we?"

She heard him only vaguely. "Sorry?"

"Watch *Karate Kid*."

"Oh. Yeah."

It was ten forty and Guthrie had fallen asleep on the beanbag. Gael brushed *poppadum* crumbs from his jersey and gently steered him to bed. In his fuddled, interrupted-dream voice, he asked, Is Dad back yet? Shh. Stay asleep. Brush. I need my teeth. What time's it? Shh, Gael said. Half ten. Watch your step. Where's Dad? On his way, she lied. He wants you out for the count, so go straight back to your dream while it's warm. Take off your socks. She tucked the duvet around his small frame and pushed his feather fringe back to blow cool air onto his forehead, the way Mum seldom remembered to do. He let her do it. Age wasn't darkening him. It wasn't rendering embarrassing such gestures. Rather, the opposite. All at once, he sucked in as if on a harmonica and his eyes opened wide. Gael was still there, heavy almost as a woman on his bed. What's wrong? She rubbed the duvet across his chest. What is it? Did you forget your meds? I'll get water. But she didn't budge because, beneath the duvet, she could feel his right hand free itself from the mummying and trace a path from his throat to his navel, left shoulder to right. Sign of the cross. He looked to the window, where a moon offered its ear, in competition. Can you go please? he said.

◆

Gael was lying in the dark on the front-room divan when Jarleth got home. She knew it was well after midnight because she'd heard the twelve muffled dongs from the radio, which Sive had left on low in the kitchen six days ago and no one had bothered to turn off. Gael had been thinking about control and how one gains more of it. Her heart, for example, didn't feel under her command. Though it was muscular, she couldn't clench it. She couldn't suspend it pro tem. She couldn't borrow her mother's vocabulary of the heart; write *ritardando* above the ribs' staff. The heart keeps changing tempo. 4/4.

2/4. 9/8. How could it be refuted? When Jarleth passed by the open door without looking in and headed straight for the stairs, it cut time. And she had to stay there, unmoving, for several minutes before it was even again. *Spianato*.

She got up and climbed the stairs, slowly. The costly kind of oak that doesn't creak. A floral scent lingered along the corridor and in the upstairs landing. Sive rarely kept flowers in the house because of too many things to tend to and because it made Guthrie morose to witness the bloom-wilt biorhythm and because Gael would pick at them until they were not flowers but flowers' infrastructure. These flowers smelled as though they'd gone bad. Like if you pulled them from the vase, wherever it was, the stems would be gooey brown. There might well be things like this around the house that they'd neglected while Sive was away. Things that might have consequences. Like a tap left on.

Not a tap though. A shower. Her father was taking a shower without using the extractor fan. After looking in on Guthrie, whose mouth was agape, famished for sleep, she shut his door firmly. Then she pushed open her parents' bedroom door, slipped in and pulled it quietly closed behind her. Steam burgeoned from the open en suite and the mirror above the sink was fogged. There were sounds of skin slapping and soap alather. The carpet felt deep and plush as she padded across it in her socks, taking the path between the bed and the ottoman rather than roly-polying across the bed, like she used to. The curtains were open and the bedside lamp was on, but there were no neighbors in view. Her strides were deliberate, as though readying for a long jump. There was a grunt as if she had taken the leap, but it wasn't her grunt. There was a throaty moan like when you stretch in the morning, after a too-long sleep, but it wouldn't put her off. Long, silent strides. Sive was tall. That boded well for her children. Face-to-face, Sive and Jarleth were even.

Jarleth was someone who faced things. Just now, he faced the shower faucet. The arm closest to Gael was stretched above his head, leaning against the tiled wall. He was letting the water hit the back of his head and umbrella around him. His right hand was cleaning his groin.

Gael took a seat on the closed toilet. The rotten-iris scent was now overpowered by mint from her father's shampoo, which was a hair growth stimulant. He must let the suds run down his spine, she thought, because there was a line of hair all the way down that pooled in his lower back like lichens on a rock. His thighs and buttocks, though, weren't hairy. They were pale. Paler than she'd imagined. Pale like her. There were distinct tan lines from his cycling gear. The lower half of his legs and arms and the back of his neck were brown. The white, palm-sized hollow of his buttock shallowed when he moved. He did a small squat and reached between his legs to his scrotum, which she couldn't see. Then he took his left arm from the wall and made the motion of washing his hands, though surely they were clean by now. He pushed the knob with his fist to turn the water off, then swiped the excess water from his hair and arms and chest. He turned and stepped out onto the mat in the same motion, and froze.

"I don't like the smell of her."

Gael said this. Her eyes met with his, but she couldn't help them darting down to his engorged penis. It listed from one side to the other and the eye at the end lowered slowly to the floor like a remorseful child. He had just jerked off. It doesn't go limp right away, she would later learn. Her heart was more *tremolo* than *spiccato* and she had that strange not-quite-sickening feeling but she didn't want to make it seem as if she couldn't bear to look, so she let her gaze stay there a moment longer. At his hairy hanging sac like a wasp nest and the heavy penis that seemed alive, then dead as gristle. Her cheeks must be even pinker. Setting her expression like a glass on an uneven surface, she tried to look proud. Disaffected. Jarleth didn't leap for a towel. Whatever way he moved would lose him power. The towel hung halfway between them on the wall. He would have to take a long step forward to reach it. She imagined passing it to him, but this way was better.

"How long have you been there?"

His voice was low. Different. Gael lifted one shoulder.

"Gael. I am telling you now to get out. I'll say it again and I'll say it clearly. Get out."

But she didn't move or speak. Only, with some relief, looked back at his eyes.

"If you ever try to use this moment against me," he said. "If you ever misremember it. If your life takes a bad turn and you need someone to blame and you think of saying that your father exposed himself to you when you were a little girl, I am telling you now to get out. Do you hear me loud and clear?"

"Mmm-hm," Gael said in a jolly kind of hum. "But did *you* hear *me*?"

The muscles in his legs strained against the skin when he stepped forward. Gael got flecked in his water. But she didn't flinch, or draw her hands from where they were tucked under her thighs. The cleaners had been here yesterday so the toilet was squeaky. Jarleth dried himself vigorously before wrapping the towel around his waist. The hair on his belly made the small paunch more agreeable. There was something charismatic about a man's belly fat, Gael discovered, as long as it was covered in hair. Something unapologetic. He wiped the mirror down with a face towel and took a small pair of scissors from the drawer.

"So you've got ideas." He proceeded to trim his nose hair. "Go on. Out with them."

"Are you getting divorced?"

"We're not married. There's nothing to divorce from."

"Are you separating?"

"No."

"Is Mum really on tour?"

"Yes."

Questions. That was her error.

"Mum could be cheating on you too," she said. This made him pause and glance at her.

"We don't police one another."

"You wouldn't care if she was?"

"I would care a great deal, as a matter of fact." He said this curtly, as if it would be a very serious affair.

There was a brief silence and Gael felt in her bones how late it was and how she wouldn't sleep tonight. She asked:

"Which is the commandment to do with adultery?"

Thinking this would make him mad. Violent, even. But he leaned on the sink and smiled. Forgetting who he was with.

"Adultery only applies if a person is married. Think of it as a spiritual loophole. Your mother and I are both committing the sin of being . . . sexually active outside of wedlock. That's because of her. Not me. I've asked her many times to marry me, as you know. Every month, I confess and receive the sacrament of Penance for not being married. Always with the intention of righting that wrong. Always meeting with resistance."

"It must make Mum feel like shit." Gael thought about how removed Sive had been lately. Always working. Or trying "to get things out of the way" so she could get back to work. When she wasn't tending to orchestral matters—studying a score, comparing arrangements—she was composing. But then, hadn't she always been like that? Her truest self wasn't communal.

"Your mother's self-confidence doesn't rely on her being the apple of my eye. We wouldn't be together if it did. Besides, what you don't know can't hurt you."

"What? Yes it can! If you have cancer but you don't know and don't take it out, it can *kill you*!"

Nose hairs neatened, he put the scissors away and turned to face her.

"You have some gumption to address me like this. It's none of your concern, Gael. It's adult business."

"I'm practically a teenager, Jarleth. I can handle it."

"Jarleth, is it?"

Gael shrugged. This was new. It felt good. "It's your name. Your Christian name. And anyway, I knew for a while."

"Is that right?"

"Yeah."

"You just knew it."

"Yeah."

"And who have you told . . . what you 'just know'?" Jarleth's small, brown, hair-housed nipples were hard now and the flesh of his chest and arms had textured to sandpaper.

"No one."

He dipped his head for the first half of a nod. "And that's the way you'll keep it."

Gael stared at him and heard her own breathing, loud. All the condensation from his shower had settled somewhere. It hadn't been extracted, but it wasn't hanging in the air either. What hovered instead in the night-poise were theories.

"I saw you took the car out," he said. "It's parked in the middle of the road."

"I drove it around."

"Good. And did you drive Guthrie to karate?"

Gael didn't let her gaze drop to the floor, though that was the instinct. "He wouldn't let me."

"Let you?" Jarleth said. "You're the older sibling. You're the strong one."

"He values his life more than you think he does!"

"He doesn't know what's good for him."

Gael knew this was wrong. She also knew not to say so.

"If you want to be part of the adult world, Gael. If you want to enter into society. You should accept that things aren't as straightforward as you're taught in the classroom."

"You don't need to tell me that."

Jarleth crossed his cyclist's arms. Gael took her hands from under her thighs and crossed her arms too. It was chilly. "Do you know what I do for a living? To put this roof over our heads."

"Global markets something derivative."

Jarleth laughed at Gael's unintended joke—granted her the benefit of the doubt. "Not anymore, but okay. What I do, Gael, has taught me something no university on the planet could have had on its syllabus. And that is that we have a very simple choice to make. Do we aspire to have worth and influence and risk tragedy; or do we aspire toward love and togetherness and risk that it won't have been enough. You can't have both aspirations be equally weighted."

Gael couldn't respond to this. She didn't know what he was asking.

"Now. Bed. I have an important meeting in the morning."

Gael stood up from the toilet and Jarleth held out his arms for a hug. But Gael felt that there was a contract in the hug and she hadn't read the fine print. She was cold and the hug would warm her, but was it a trick? The thing about love and togetherness and the choice? She brushed past him on her way out and his body felt steely. But once she had passed him and she was at the bedroom door, looking back, she caught his expression in the mirror. A troubled frown.

The house felt as though it were wobbling in the dark. As though its foundations had liquefied. Surely there'd be time to climb out the windows, should they start sinking. Sleep would be impossible, Gael thought, so she made a series of searches on the computer. There was something important she'd missed. Since she was the one who would have to decide and then to live with it in the form of her mother every day of her life, she thought she should have all the information. Thus, at two in the morning she found herself reading the Wikipedia entry on cheating, as if it were a history that could be looked up, summarized and digested. There was one part that felt like information, though, and not just semantics.

"Natural selection favors cheating in the biological markets. If a species can increase its chance of survival by cheating, then that strength is selected for. But cheaters need a whole society of cooperators to exploit. In ecology, cheating is regulated by making their success dependent on frequency. The more cheaters there are, the worse they do. The fewer, the better."

So it was an aspect of nature and it was everywhere. Only most people are none the wiser. Then sleep took her. And that sleep knit up all the black and white and made gray of it. There couldn't only be cooperators and cheaters—that was too reductive. Take the sea. She was neither the water nor the hero nor the sword. Nor a bird sitting on the crest of a wave, awaiting the upchuck of a tumid corpse for the easy meat of his eyes. Nor the fish tossed and roiled by a battle taking place, not at all to do with them. Nor the industry of blacksmiths, fed and fat on heroes' mettle. She didn't know what she was. Black and white were too few. All the grays, too many. It wasn't enough.

2

Sorry Is the Child
FEBRUARY 2003

I

One Friday afternoon a year on, when they were walking to Heuston Station to be babysat by Auntie Ada—who was, those days, *relieving* their parents more often than not—Gael came to know the depth of her brother's conviction.

He had become quieter and quieter, as though he believed that each household had a noise quotient and that, as long as the total noise amounted to the same decibel sum, he could control the Foess household balance by way of his silence.

Gael handled him like a cloth, rinsing, wringing, twisting, hoping to get something out of him—some grime. She was trying to get him to play Cursery Rhymes as they walked. "Just do the next bit. *Mary, Mary, quite contrary, how does your garden grow?*"

"I'm *not* changing cockle shells and you can't make me."

Guthrie was pink-cheeked from withstanding her resolve to have him grow up at her abnormal rate. Even though nature would hold her to being eighteen months older than him, with each passing month it seemed as if an extra year of difference were wedging itself between them.

"Genius!" She mouthed versions over and over to herself to perfect it.

"Don't, Gael."

"With silver bell-ends, cocks, rear-ends and pretty maids all in a row!" She snorted with laughter.

"Stop! That's disgusting."

"That was all you, Guth."

"No it wasn't."

"Yeah so."

"No it wasn't! I was going to say, *Na-na na-na, na-na na-na. Wouldn't you like to know?"*

"Not bad . . . for a barely-eleven-year-old. Less good than mine though. Man, I'd been trying to work in a gardener called José, who uses his hosé to make the garden grow . . . but you beat me by miles. Maybe I don't need to worry about you any longer."

Guthrie had crossed his arms and turned into an open gate to get away from her.

"And now you're trespassing," she said. *"This* is what I call progress."

He swiveled around. "I'm not *trespassing*. This is a *park*. Leave me a*lone*."

Gael could see he was close to tears, so she left him to it. The gated garden had an exit farther along. She moved slowly toward it, running her fingertips along the black railing and relishing the pins and needles produced. She only wanted the best for him. It seemed as if he looked up to her, so she couldn't understand why he wouldn't take her help anymore. He believed everything would go back to normal, soon. Whenever soon was. Whatever normal was. Now that Gael was in secondary school, it was hard to look out for him. He had over a year left in primary school, but even after that, he couldn't join her, as her secondary school was single-sex. Girls became fatuous versions of themselves around boys and she hadn't wanted to deal with all that performance. There were always lunch breaks for meeting lads and being fingered behind suburban evergreen trees. Whereas Guthrie *wanted* to go to a mixed school, for reasons unknown. She did spy pale blue welts on his torso when he stepped out of the shower room in a hand towel, when the bath towels were all in the wash. That probably had something to do with it. His friends were mostly girls—too few to make a pack, so they were no use. Jarleth believed in individual responsibility "to put the civil in civilization": all fights had to be debated in an orderly fashion, ideally with an introduction, a conclusion and a moral revelation. It's cool if he's gay, Gael thought, but then he really needs to know how to strike back or, at least, how to survive a beating.

When she reached the far gate, she saw him standing before a bulb-shaped pond that held on its waters a cast bronze statue. It was the figure of a woman reclining, though longer and more still than a human. She had been weathered green from the rippled roots of her hair to her crossed ankles. Mythical art like that—the exalted mother figure—transfixed Guthrie. He could have stood there for hours, Gael knew, and she calculated how long they had before the next train. Thirty-two minutes. There'd still be time to pick up a chai latte at the kiosk. Auntie Ada made vile tea. Gael reckoned she used hot tap water and mangled three cups' worth out of one tea bag.

They were at Croppies Acre Memorial Park. She'd heard of Croppies before and could make sense of that, but she didn't get the "Acre" bit. This shard of park wasn't an acre, surely. Sive had told her that the statue was named after a character in *Finnegans Wake*: Anna Livia Plurabelle. Good name. Gael wondered if the "wake" had to do with the fact that Anna seemed to be having herself a little lie-down. Females were always sleeping in folklore. Sleeping frigid, never snoring. The sculpture was meant to personify the river Liffey, *Abhainn na Life,* which flows through Dublin Town. It had first been part of a fountain in the city center on O'Connell Street, but it became a target for litter and graffiti and piss. Fairy liquid squirts that sent the water sudsing over the sidewalks as if she were in heat. "Floozie in the Jacuzzi," people called her. "The Hoor in the Sewer." Why did Dublin have to be so scuddy? The city council used the excuse of street renovations to extract her from the mobs and she spent a grim decade recovering inside a crate in a yard at St. Anne's Park in Raheny in the Northside, far as you like from her proud river.

Gael would have told Guthrie an embellished version of this tale; only, just then, he needed to be told something very different.

"Don't. Guthrie!"

But it was too late. He had stepped out onto the water, toward the mother sublime, as if the thin film of scum might hold his weight. One wouldn't have needed to know how to swim in that pond, it was so shallow, and Guthrie could swim, but even so he gasped and flailed, his schoolbag still on his back and loading with water. It tugged him the wrong way down and his moccasin shoes couldn't get a grip on the pond's slimed base, so his arms and chin were the only parts of him above water. The gulping sounds were what disturbed her more than anything. "You sounded like a donkey getting off," she told him after. But in fact, it had sounded of something new to them both: it had sounded of the will to survive, falling short.

It was her first real scare, dragging her brother from the pond. His face was translucent white and unfamiliar—as if the experience had orphaned him and him alone. His eyes were unblinking, like astonished fish eyes beholding the sky for the first time. They shimmered. The sun was breaking through, so Gael emptied his bag and laid all his books out on the grass to drain—an illustrated Bible among them—then she peeled off his clothes, piece by piece, and wrung them out as best she could, trying to fathom what he'd meant by it. She couldn't have upset him that much. "What's going on?" she pleaded, her wrists aching as she labored to dress him again, but the only sound that came from him was of chattering teeth. His arms were widest at the elbow. The plastic buttons of her phone kept failing to register her thumbs clicking Contacts—Dad (Irish#)—Call. *Call.* When she finally managed, she could hear the function in his voice. "I'm in the middle of a meeting, Gael. What is it?"

While they waited, Gael rubbed hard circles on her brother's back, around and around, trying to imprint them into him like the growth rings of a tree.

She eavesdropped from the hallway when Guthrie's words returned to him late that night. With heroic restraint, he asked his father why he couldn't walk across the water. He had as much faith as anyone he knew, he said, quietly. He really believed his faith was so strong that he could walk across the pond's surface, and the Virgin Mother had been there in the middle and she had told him to come to her. The alarm clock on his bedside table measured the pause, like a metronome long after the music has ended.

"Why couldn't I, Dad? Why wasn't my faith strong enough to hold me?"

The delay was too brief for truth to accrue.

"Because believing something will work doesn't make it work," Jarleth said. Then he clicked his tongue, exhaled with mild disgust. "The Lord Jesus walking on water was a miracle."

"But my faith's as strong as it goes. It *is*. So why couldn't I make a miracle?"

The bedroom light switched off. The clacking sound was Jarleth wrenching triple-A batteries out of the alarm clock. He tossed them under the bed, where they spun fitful nonsense orbits like moths.

"There are no more miracles."

II

The seizure came a week later, when Sive returned from a tour in
Poland. The smack on tarmac of airplane wheels and Guthrie's skull
was coincident, as if Guthrie had held it off until her plane touched
down in Dublin. At the trace of burning rubber, his bicycle keeled
over—its front wheel whirling for purchase on the foreshortened sky.
He might have felt closest to his mother in those blowsy, flurrysome
moments, Gael supposed. He might've been able to sense the whyfor
in how she moved.

"You can forget about A&E on a Friday night," Jarleth had said,
inspecting Guthrie's purpling wrist. The fit had toppled him on the
way home, alone, from a classmate's birthday party. (Some bossy girl
Gael vaguely recalled. Bossy girls seemed to like Guthrie. It was
his bone structure; his pearlescent skin; his paranormal potential;
his rawny, elfin, death-dancer beauty. They could judge themselves
against him without suffering true envy's vitriol. It didn't matter who
he liked back. It wasn't his role to do the choosing.) Guthrie stuck
out his tongue for the anti-inflammatory tablets his father allotted.
"It's only a sprain—nothing a few prayers won't cure." Jarleth ad-
ministered the medication. "Wash those down and off to bed with
you." With a glance at his watch, he added, "No waiting up for your
mother."

Gael brought a spare pillow into Guthrie's bedroom and saw that
his ears were pinned for sounds of car tires crunching up the drive.
There must have been thoughts boiling over in him, since Jarleth put
the lid on them last week. Dark and scalding thoughts, befouling his

intrinsic shine. She placed the pillow alongside him and lifted his injured arm onto it:

"Elevation."

He nodded cautiously, as if she'd said: *closer to heaven.*

"Even if Mum gets home right this second," Gael said, "she'll say wait till the morning. Then she'll say wait till the afternoon. You know how she gets when she's been away. It takes her, like . . . a *day* to accept she has a family." The word *responsibilities* occurred to Gael but, like spokes to a bicycle wheel, it used too many syllables for so mundane a meaning. She tapped the top of the moon nightlight on the bed-stand and it glowed meekly. Guthrie contrived a yawn. Gael stood to turn off the main light and then surprised herself by returning purposelessly to the bed. The undissected silence revealed that the alarm clock batteries hadn't been recovered.

"Whoever designed that lamp's a moron," Gael said. Now, Guthrie's eyes were theatrically shut. "The moon's not bright. It only looks bright 'cause the sun's photons bounce off it. We wouldn't even *see* it in the sky if it weren't for the sun. It'd just *be there.* A cold gray lumpy rock in the middle of nothing." Why *had* she gone into his room? The pillow, yes. But . . . was it to introduce this idea to him? Of the nothingness? Lying top-to-tail in her fluffy hotel dressing gown, she felt as though there was nothing beneath her. No bed, no floor, no magma core.

◆

By morning, Guthrie's wrist was an uncooked sausage, stuffed to the split of its sheath. "Grooooooss!" Gael moaned at the limp punch of it, hued sallow as if it had been unbound from sweaty boxer's wrapping after days. She sniffed for putrescence. Panting, he shoved her out of his way to parade it into their parents' room, but the reception he got there was deflating. Their needling came through the walls:

I most certainly will not call Carla (Jarleth to Sive) . . . *boy needs his mother . . . yes Saturday morning . . . we're all bone-tired . . . sitting with him in the . . . think it's broken* (Guthrie to everyone) . . . *something feels loose . . . and really really tight like the blood pressure armband . . . Gael slept in my bed and kicked it . . . I'll give you my whole afternoon, love* (Sive to Guthrie) . . . *Whatever you want to do after we'll do . . . two concerts tomorrow . . . eighteen-hour day yesterday . . . breakfast meetings* (Sive to herself) . . . *mezzo-soprano . . . the record company . . . unseen arrangement . . . on Monday . . . Lyric FM . . . must put together . . . an hour's rest . . .*

Gael pressed a pillow over her head to muffle them. Her lower back had the ache of a fallen arch and she felt the stab of needing to pee, only sharper. Like someone had used a melon baller on her bladder. If she stayed perfectly still, it was less painful. *Just . . . stay . . .*

When she woke again, it was after ten and Jarleth had taken Guthrie for an x-ray. The bed felt mysteriously wet and warm. A bright red slick on the seat of her robe was the culprit. It looked like a tube of cadmium red acrylic had been spread and had hardened—a hint of browning at the edges where it had dried, clumping where it was thickest. "Oh." Gael was the wrong way round on the bed. Not her bed. There was a sound like pacing along the ceiling and muffled music surging . . . from where? Which way? Imagining seagulls racing the crest of a tsunami, she heaved herself from the bed, miraculously unstained. Perpendicular, it was easier to place things. Match consequence to cause.

Queasy and somewhat crazily, she tore off her spoiled robe and underwear en route to the bathroom, where she ditched them in the tub and, with a hand mirror, studied the ripe, slippery brilliance of her newly operational sex. It was the way into the body. Now that was clear. Boys had no such access to themselves. She showered with the gratifying effect of washing out hair dye. The mess of self-betterment. She pushed a tampon in, as she had practiced many times, and slid a blister pack of painkillers into the pocket of her dark, loose boyfriend jeans with a wisdom she had long looked forward to retroactively earning. She thought of who she might phone, but her friends believed she'd had it for years. Forget it. Screw them. She'd get a period pain absence note, take all next week off and return to school with tales of her homage to *Carrie*. Let them envisage her box-office gore.

The attic's retractable stairs were drawn down and Witold Lutoslawski's somber, inwardly dramatic Fourth Symphony issued from the antique gramophone up there. The music kept pausing and repeating the same minute-long section. Sporadic vocals betrayed Sive, lifting and dropping the needle; listening exactingly, as though for the mosquito's infinitesimal *eeeeeeeee*. Wonderful how weird a day was developing, Gael thought. This one would not fit into a frame. It would not be on its best behavior. They were well past that. She made a slice of Nutella toast and held it between her teeth to climb the attic ladder, the ruined robe slung over her shoulder.

Sive had a home office downstairs, as had Jarleth, but this symphony seemingly required rafters. Whenever she came up here, it was to be absolutely alone with the work; when it needed the higher level of concentration conferred by asbestos. The attic's discomposure appealed to Sive—the stupefaction admitted here, but not in the house proper. The cleaners were only allowed to dust it twice a year. Dismayed, they might rescue a few moldy mugs planted like mousetraps among the tackle. A philharmonic of broken instruments, a theater set of cast-off furniture, artworks, Christmas crap, diceless board games, carpet offcuts, stuffed unmarked bin liners, towers and towers of records, a village made of masking tape and cardboard upon which Gael now perched, not wanting to interrupt. But the more the music mausoleumed her mother, the more she doubted the possibility of breaking through.

Leaning in, her hands on either side of the turntable, Sive heard out the conversation between a flute and an E-flat clarinet until cellos introduced their gentle, chordal strokes and a pair of harps stippled like rain. Then, she lifted the needle back an inch to the beginning of the discourse. "What do you hear?" Sive didn't raise her head to ask this. "Love . . . or lament?"

The vinyl coughed into sound again and Gael watched her five-foot-ten mother bent as if over a baby-changing table. She wore cigarette trousers, a long, loose shirt and a forest green, sleeveless duster, like a knee-length waistcoat (that Gael wouldn't wear for a bet, but looked borderline cool, she had to admit). It was open. A built-in belt hung down at the back. Her shirtsleeves were pushed up to the dry, white elbows, which appeared to be rosined. Her graying dark-blond hair was held laxly with a pin.

It was a hard question to answer when offered so little continuity, but the section repeating was at once eerie and graceful. However lightly applied, its colors were dark. "Both," Gael decided.

Sive lifted the needle and placed it down again to hear, then once again, talking over it: "There should be more of the elegy, early . . . the gravity of starting, so close to the end. After all that's gone on. This is a man—Gael, you must go to Warsaw—this is a man whose earliest memory was of visiting his father in a Moscow prison, executed days before his trial; whose brother died in a Siberian labor camp; this is a man who escaped the Germans while being marched to a prison camp and *walked* four hundred kilometers to Warsaw, where he survived by playing Nazi-sanctioned, Soviet-sanctioned music—no notes of dissent, no jazz, no Jewish composers, nothing *atonal* or *degenerate*. Can you imagine it, biting your tongue like that? Silencing your knowledge and your faculty for years on end? And after? This is Poland, Gael. After, he was reduced to writing ditties for the communist regime. It eased off, eventually, the oppression, and he could work again, and then, *four decades* later, within a scythe's length of death, he composes this? *This* symphony? So brief . . . reduced . . . like something that's been boiling too long. To take on another question . . ." Sive turned to Gael and her eyes rested on the stained gown. They listened to the swelling strings rising toward the end of the first movement and aborting the climax before it arrived—meanly. In the pause, Sive continued speaking, though not where she had left off. "Love *and* lament, you think? Or"—she swallowed—"I'm wondering . . ." Her head moved but her gaze didn't. "Is *doubt* not only part of it, but the larger part. His offering." Her gaze returned to the disc and a smile came close to breaching. "I can't keep putting off the interpretation. It's my duty to see what's in front of me . . . and my privilege."

Gael's burning cheeks might have passed for a symptom of menstruation.

"After all the dreaded operas and ballets and choral works . . ." Sive went on, "might as well be pantomimes. But here . . . first *I* have to be sure. Then to convince the players. I won't just tell them: play it this way."

"Why not?" Gael was both relieved and perturbed that Sive had only been talking about the music.

"Why not?"

"That's your job." Gael gave a half shrug. "And they'll hear that it's better your way."

"You'd have me inflict the hierarchy." Sive lifted her low eyelids a fraction. The whitish shadow she'd brushed across them gave her the appearance of a mime artist. Which she was, in a way. She had only her gestures. No cheap deceits up her sleeves. No desire to escape the box, either? "They'll take direction," she said, "but if they don't understand it, resentment seeps in and rots the artwork. I don't want unfeeling technicians . . . or mulch . . . or each to his own like so many cats. The onus is on me to keep their minds and hearts open." Sive lifted the needle back, because she hadn't been paying attention, then added, puzzlingly, "There are fifty meters between one side of the orchestra and the other."

Gael sat there awhile and Sive behaved as though alone again.

Her stamina for solo labor was impressive. Still, something rankled. Why hadn't her mother asked the obvious questions? It was their first conversation in ten days. A lot could change in ten days. She'd saved her drowning brother. She'd eaten half a hash brownie. If a B-minus was anything to go by, it was fair to say she now spoke French. Right this minute, she was flushing her womb.

"Mum." Gael held the robe, blood side up. "Earth to Mum."

Sive pressed her fingers tremblingly to her temples and steadied her head. Then breathed out slowly and paused the record. "What . . . love?"

"I'm throwing this out." Gael hopped off the cardboard box she'd been perched on. "Safe to assume you've no housewifey tricks to clean it?"

Sive looked directly at the blood but her gray eyes misted over. "Do you . . . need anything?"

"If by 'anything' you mean tampons, advice, hugs, painkillers, a pep talk, a hot chocolate . . . I've got myself covered, thanks. But I will take a fifty-euro guilt payment."

Sive's eyes refocused and she said, "Will you take it in monthly installments?" Gael gave her a withering look and her mother's smile broke the surface. "And in a year or two," Sive said, "when the novelty wears off, I'll take you to Family Planning for the pill. Had it been available when I was young . . . I wouldn't have bothered with a single wretched period. You can skip them without consequence, the science says. So far. . . . Not that we're informed. Barely a sinew holds a woman's body to her will, Gael. See it doesn't snap."

Gael struggled to keep up with this information. "You'd skip *all* your periods if you could change things?"

Sive unrolled the too-short sleeves of her shirt. "Don't be dramatic."

Tetchiness spread through Gael's body like a chemical, but her mother was, in fact, being honest and this length of conversation was rare. Perhaps for good reason. In her most neutral, mellow tone, Gael said, "I *have* always wondered why you had us. You've never seemed . . ." In the silence that followed, Gael missed the music.

Then, Sive responded simply: "Your father had political ambitions."

It was as if she were speaking to Gael for the last time. Saying everything. Or perhaps it was leading by example, to help Gael tell her mother what she knew. The word *What?* must surely have been audible for how loudly Gael thought it. Sive was looking upward, as if to a projected film of her younger, more lenient self. "'A nod to convention wouldn't go amiss' was how he put it. The wording stayed with me. Poetic and pedantic at once. 'Politicians have families. If you won't *marry* me . . .'" Sive didn't do Jarleth's voice, but Gael could tell when the words were his by how they changed her. "The National Treasury Management Agency, was it, he wanted to join . . . or the Economic Advisory Council . . . At any rate, the government works for the banks these days. So . . . he's politicking away."

The period pains were catching up with Gael, and climbing down the attic ladder brought back memories of a ferry journey to Iceland. She hadn't known she was seasick until Guthrie told her that her face was green. Dubious, she'd gone down to the cabin to put on blusher and found herself hypnotized by her vomit streaming slowly from the door to the wall and back with the waves, as she'd counted how many minutes there were in three days.

Soon, she was napping, waiting for round two's painkillers to kick in. Something was kicking. No, something was knocking. Guthrie was at her bedroom door saying they were waiting in the car and it was only a fracture and they were going to the museum, *all* of them, and to hurry.

◆

The weather blew a bit and spat a bit and the sun ducked its head through the curtains but didn't stick around for coats to come off. The traffic was so bad that Jarleth flicked from station to station and waited out the whole track of t.A.T.u.'s "All the Things She Said" in order to get an explanation. They'd been held at the same junction for four light changes. The radio announced:

"Only a few thousand were expected to take to the streets for today's Iraq invasion protest, which is disturbing traffic throughout the city, but the Gardaí are at sixes and sevens at the estimated ninety to a *hundred thousand people* marching from Parnell Square to Dame Street, passing through the Department of Foreign Affairs at St. Stephen's Green presently. Babies and grannies, uncles and aunties, *gach naomh agus peacach* is picketing today. At the final destination, Labor Party politician Michael D. Higgins is scheduled to speak out against the invasion, and Christy Moore will bring a defiant tune to the platform, alongside other, lesser-known artists. With placards reading 'No War for Oil,' 'Weapons of Mass Distraction' and 'Stoppit Now,' protesters demand that the Irish government stop allowing the United States military to use Shannon Airport as a transatlantic refueling point in bringing soldiers to the Middle—"

Jarleth switched it off. "A hundred thousand Irish step out of the Church of Consumerism to wag their fingers at the sky." He dropped his hand from the wheel and landed it on Sive's thigh. "Whoever said the rebel consciousness died with Pearse?"

He looked at her. In a way, his hand on her was ludicrous. In another, it was charged. In the passenger seat, Sive huffed (a laugh or a sigh?), since no answer was required. Her questions were rarely rhetorical: "If we carry on down to Fitzwilliam Place, could we come in the back of Merrion Square?"

Jarleth said nothing.

Twisted around to scan the traffic that had backlogged, Guthrie undertook a social study. "A lot of cars only have one person in them."

Gael saw the data differently. "Is that a Bentley?"

"How you can tell," Jarleth called back, "is if the driver's wearing a hard hat."

The lights had turned but there was no room on the other side of the junction to go through. Jarleth lifted his hand from Sive's leg and indicated in the opposite direction to her suggestion. The national museums and galleries were all between Merrion Square and St. Stephen's Green. "The museum's not on."

Guthrie thudded the car seat angrily with his good hand and Jarleth told him to send his complaint to Tony Blair. He checked the rearview mirror and Gael felt a certain obligation to smirk, even though she didn't find it funny and now the day could be consumed by bickering and errands. As if it carried on from something they'd been discussing, Jarleth said, "And I don't condone your mother's system of rewarding you for every hike in our insurance premiums." The sighing competition that followed was elaborate and Jarleth finally had to offer something in the way of a conciliation. "If you have no suggestions other than sitting in traffic, then so be it. Homework."

"You didn't *ask* for suggestions," Guthrie said, somewhat heatedly.

"Well?"

Guthrie leaned his shoulder against the window, cheek to the glass, and stared at the skyline of cranes to think. Everything was in town. Everything that you could do with a fractured wrist. In a voice too faint to be heard, he proposed the cinema or bowling, but Gael stepped in with what he wanted. "Isn't there an art gallery, like . . . on the left side of town? Away from the center."

"The *left?*" Jarleth said. "My oh my."

"Go easy on her," Sive said.

"Go easy on *her* now *too?*"

"East," Gael said. "I meant east. And Mum means go easy on me because I'm on the blob, Dad. For your information. Okay? I have the woman flu. Code Red! There's a leak. My Vesuvius is erupting. Red lights at the Y junction. Okay?" Gael looked at Guthrie, who seemed to have inflated and had made an n of his mouth in order not to laugh or cry. "Quick! Give me your gauze! I'm losing blood!" She leaned across and angled for his bandaging, which made him go ballistic, and Jarleth put the radio back on, shaking his head. Sive pronounced, with the zeal of an epiphany:

"IMMA. IMMA. IMMA is on the left. The Irish Museum of Modern Art."

"Oh good," Jarleth said, "the museum at the Royal Hospital Kilmainham."

"Exactly," Sive said.

"Out by St. James's Hospital."

"Exactly."

"Out by St. Patrick's University Hospital."

"Yes."

"Van Gogh's red period!" Gael was still going strong.

"Hospitals on all sides," Jarleth said, "in case Guthrie falls left or right or sideways."

Gael was still high on ibuprofen WITH CAFFEINE, but she could sense how they were close—perhaps only one quip away—from killing however it was they hoped to be. She said: "I'm hungry, though. Is anyone hungry . . ."

"No," Guthrie said, catching his breath.

". . . or is it just the ravenous mutilated soldiers in the trenches of my—"

"It's twelve," Jarleth said.

"—cooch."

"Will we lunch first so?" Sive said.

Gael asked, "Is there a restaurant at IMMA?"

"There'd be something . . ." Sive sounded encouraging.

"I'm not hungry," Guthrie said.

"Nor am I. Not for cafeteria giblets." Jarleth lifted his jumper to get his phone from his shirt pocket (passport blue linen, nicely offset against the darker cashmere). Gael and Guthrie leaned in to look-see the new model. They'd been getting their father's cast-off phones since '98. This one would be Gael's, because thereafter she planned to be generous. Such chattels would be Guthrie's one hope, come high school in September.

Jarleth had time for technology. He consorted with people at Google, and it was one of the few things besides food, durable clothes and holidays about which he was prodigal. Dell's revenue last year equated to six percent of GDP. More to the point (he'd recently explained), depreciation comes off your tax bill. The Samsung SGH-S105 was a silver flip phone with a color screen, a camera and flash and polyphonic ringtones. It would be the most valuable castoff yet. Jarleth phoned his PA (on a Saturday) to ask was there somewhere to eat near Kilmainham. He hung up and she called back a minute later with the verdict.

"The *consultant* chef? What use are Michelin stars if it's not the Magi making the grub? No no no. No gimmicks. Give Prendergast's a call and say we'll be in shortly. Thanks, Ann." . . . *for two?* Her voice came through faintly. "Four," Jarleth said, then hung up. As he drove, he looked at Sive, regularly. Her chin rested on her fingertips and she seemed to be reading between the double yellow lines by the roadside. "Pop-up restaurants!" Jarleth said, conspiratorially, but she didn't hear. The windscreen wipers automatically came on and weather whistled through the car's clefts and cavities. He gripped the wheel as though they were gliding on black ice. He wouldn't repeat himself. After catching Gael's eye in the rearview mirror, he adjusted it so they wouldn't catch again.

◆

They were sat at the special guest table. The cloistered, white-clothed mafia table had been generally unoccupied since the Irish brotherhood—*na fir maith*—were forced to close the government tab in back in '97, when one of its very coked-up boys let the cat out of the hotel window, instigating the Moriarty Tribunal. (The coke and the pussy and the hotel room had been paid for by the public purse. Nonetheless, the trial was ongoing and most of its members had since found employment in finance. A helicopter to the races was the new working weekend.)

Guthrie only ordered a starter—a vegetarian one at that—which annoyed Jarleth considerably. It wasn't like Guthrie to be deliberately cantankerous, so Gael could only assume that something had gone on at the hospital. One of their Conversations. None of them said anything meaningful through the main course (Wicklow venison in spiced wine sauce with duck fat roast potatoes for Jarleth; seared scallops over black pudding with colcannon for Sive; and Jerusalem artichoke and pearl barley risotto, chanterelles, hazelnut and truffle pesto for Gael, which she found to be absolutely and utterly disgusting).

"Should've gone for the fermented carrot jus," she said, pushing the bowl away, but no one laughed. They seemed to be done with laughing and she was done with trying to dispel tension. Maybe what was festering was like a cold sore that would express just in time for the family portrait. The restaurant was in a historic Victorian building, all wooden cabinets and wine shelves and bacon bars hanging from the ceiling, and if they'd only been seated in the busy section, at any of the tables by the bar running down the center, their problems might have been less conspicuous. But, as it was, despite her seeming engaged, the only conversational batons that Sive caught were logistical. The thing was, this wasn't new; she got like this—or something like it—when her work was going well, when something worthwhile was coming to pass.

"I'm home very late on Monday," Jarleth said, "then I'm in London the following week."

"That's fine, love. I'm in Dusseldorf on Thursday week, but it's only two nights. To conduct *Così fan tutte* with Valery Gergiev—"

"Well, that won't do. We can't both be away on school nights. You'll have to take the kids with you."

"Not at all. There's Carla . . . or Sarah-Jane . . . would happily stay the night. It's easier for her to get to Inchicore from ours—"

"The kids haven't seen Dusseldorf, have you? Gael?"

Sive finally drew her eyes from a painting to the left of their table, just behind Gael, who kept feeling as though her mother was looking at her, but now she knew it was at something past her.

"Where's Dusseldorf?" Guthrie asked, spooning ice cubes from his water glass.

A busboy took their plates away and the head chef came to greet them and to congratulate Sive on the Beethoven concert in January. He and the wife had seen a matinee, and it was "just a relief, truth be told, to hear a classic. In the theater, what you really want is Shakespeare. In the orchestra, what you really want is Beethoven." The man had a gentle manner and an onion sheen all over.

"It's actually pronounced Bait-hoven," Gael explained, "not *thoven* because *hoven* means 'farms.' Ludwig of the beetroot farms. And it's *van* Beethoven because that's his whole surname. Like if your name's de Lacy and someone said, 'I love Lacy's cooking,' for centuries after your death, you'd be mad. It's the same." Gael knew this from Sive, who'd tried to find a diplomatic way to correct the orchestra's pronunciation.

"Well," the chef chuckled forcedly, "you're your mother's daughter."

Something flickered across Jarleth's face that wasn't straight anger. Sive's gaze traveled past Gael again.

"Did you like the cooking, at least?" the chef asked.

Gael tightened her ponytail, to buy herself time. All she could think was that his first comment had been wrong too. *In the wine shop, what you* really *want is the merlot . . .* was the equivalent she was concocting to illustrate the point.

"Excuse her insolence," Jarleth interjected. "She's . . . coming of age."

"Oh," the chef said, with surprising calm. "Iron is what you want, then. Try to get plenty of red meat this week."

Gael felt her head tuck backward, as from a badminton shuttlecock that travels far faster than might be assumed. "Thanks."

Jarleth tongued inside his lower lip to free venison from his bottom teeth. "Has Curragh dried up enough yet to take out the horses?"

"Stephen's on to it for the season," the chef said. "I'm out there less and less, truth be told—"

"It was a bowl of soup last week, according to whatshisname . . . Magnier . . ."

They blathered a bit, until it got to the stage that Jarleth was keeping the chef from the kitchen, testing the confines of a conventional job. By asking where the loo was, Guthrie gave the chef an out. Then Jarleth spotted someone in the restaurant and he, too, took leave of the table. With the plates cleared, wine spills on the tablecloth and abandoned napkins, it looked like the end of an ill-advised wedding.

"He changed the music to György Kurtág," Sive said quietly. "Isn't that lovely?"

Gael listened, picking crumbs from her lap. The music was frustratingly quiet and delicate and then, after almost *nothing*, it bellowed glaring and cautionary, as though a composer had been asked to invent the nuclear alarm. "Bit intense for a restaurant."

"That's what makes it lovely. It's only twelve minutes." They savored one of them then, until something that sounded like a twig breaking made them start. "Trust Frederick to challenge his patrons' senses."

Another of Sive's admirers, Frederick, was the owner. He must have known something about her, for her gaze now was back behind

Gael. Gael turned her chair to see what behind her was so fascinating. Almost the very moment she did so, as the image hit her retina and flipped, she said, "Mum?"

They stared at the painting together, while Gael searched for her wording. The pencil-drawn backs of two nude women. Their rippling bodies of a piece; interlinked like an edgeless jigsaw. A watercolor, with pastels and white—chalk, perhaps—shading the headless figures. A navy blue moonlit sky. The bodies pale. Their headlessness not grotesque, but necessary. Both were seated and one body was falling into the other and always would be, and Gael watched the grip she had of her lover's forearm. The hand too large. The forearm sturdy. Gael felt it. How one figure braced the other's limb like a flagstaff on the moon. There was no time for the right words. They didn't exist. "He doesn't love you like that. He's cheated and cheated." Gael sucked her teeth so they hurt. So the pain occurred to her as merely physical. Gael turned back around to her mother and saw the white shading of her eyelids as chalk. "It's like it's . . . a gap. It's . . . as if—"

"There's no gap," Sive said, her mouth loose. An open purse to help oneself to.

"Yes there *is*." Gael gripped her mother's long, slender forearm, hung by her side. "You have to go."

Guthrie had returned and was lowering into his chair one millimeter at a time. As though an infant were sleeping, he said, "Is it the music?"

Sive turned to him gratefully. "May his voice never break." She smiled and held out her arms and he didn't hesitate to interlock with her and to stay there and to admit the absence of his head.

Something was very, very wrong here.

By the bar, Jarleth was talking with Frederick. Gael lifted her hand and Frederick waved back with some reservation. Could they tell? Gael didn't look to her father's eyes, only his smooth lips. If she tilted her ear, just so, she could catch bits of their conversation. "The hammer price . . . one-ten. . . . original . . . sales record . . . labels . . .

back . . . not an investment, in this case . . ." Jarleth had taken out his checkbook ("twenty percent . . .") and whatever he showed Frederick must have been enough to settle some bet. Fred's whole body dropped an inch in the pained relief of the worst being over. Jarleth put his hand on Frederick's shoulder and squeezed it, just as he'd clutched Sive's thigh. With the same possession. Why was he marching over, then, to Gael? Why was his face so wild with erudition? Why was she standing up, in fear? Stumbling . . .

"Dad?"

And then he passed her and, with the handling you see in movies, when a man takes a woman up against a wall, Jarleth took the painting off it. He said, in a granular timbre, to Sive, "I want to take you home with me. And this is how. There is where you've been. Here's your portal. I want you in my house. I want you in our bedroom. I want you downstairs. The way you were absorbed in this, it's already gone. But when I bring it home . . . you'll be coming with it."

Guthrie was pale and Gael's fists were ready and Sive was saying, "Yes."

"We have to get out of here," Gael said.

"Gather your things."

Gael took all their coats into her arms, and her mother's bag.

Frederick called out as they left, "Sive, pet," his mustache a comic frown. He pronounced her name: Soyov. "*Figures in Moonlight,* it's called," he said. "Louis le Brocquy. 1944."

She pressed her hands to her chest and said, "I love his early ones. . . . Forty-four?"

Frederick nodded minutely. "Nothing neutral about it."

Sive shook her head. And they were gone.

III

The kitchen floor of the Foess household had been tiled with egg-shells; its walls papered with prescriptions, none of whose medicines lessened their mother's hurt.

How long had passed, since Jarleth left? The clock had been stopped and progress seemed immeasurable. But the children's bodies extended to make up for their parents' withdrawal, as cork expands to stopper the bottle and prolong its contents' life span. Guthrie was sixteen now; Gael seventeen.

Sive had known, of course, long before Gael's restaurant outburst. But she was a pillar of forbearance. She held up. The years phased on, ever more unseasonable, eroding their home. The London office suddenly couldn't do without Jarleth. He began to commute. In late 2007, he stopped commuting. He was gone. The months since had seemed endless.

As if to censor the contrast between their mood and hers, the children barely spoke. They became fluent in the language of shoulders. They learned to move light-footed in the kitchen; Guthrie revel-ing all the while in this courtesy of woe, as if other states of being were insincere. He was Melpomene—tragic mask at the ready. Gael played along, to a point. How does one expedite a coma? She held her tongue while nonstop noise played through her headphones: a hunger striker hooked up to an IV line beneath her clothes.

They were advised by relatives to make themselves scarce: To Give Yer Mother a Wide Berth. To Be Loving and Supportive and Patient but Not to Expect Much in the Way of Parenting. Sure That One Never Mollycoddled, Even When She'd a Man to Impress. That *Might* Have Had *Some*thing to Do with It. Aren't Ye Self-Sufficient Now? We Were Working Ourselves at Sixteen and Aren't You Seventeen, Gael, and the Leaving Cert Just Around the Corner, and Guthrie Only Two Years Behind. No One Would Be Surprised If Ye Grow Up Quick. Ye Might Be Wise to Do the Same.

Sive's will to live now seemed gossamer-sheer, fickle as a whim. She'd become a muted rendition of herself. It was true; she'd always been what busybody misogynists bitterly described as a "hard woman," the very oxymoron embodied. But gossips have no register for nuance. There's refusing to applaud when a Ryanair plane lands and there's neglecting to congratulate your son for coming Highly Commended in the regional watercolor championships for under-eighteens. Not all coldnesses are equivalent: a person's spirit can freeze at almost any temperature.

In the worst months—when Gael had taken up residence on friends' couches, leaving Guthrie to ensure that no razors or ropes or Sibelius records lay within reach—their mother would forget to open the curtains or to switch on the central heating or to eat or to visit her father after he'd suffered another minor stroke in the Mystery Rose Residence, as if the fact that he wouldn't know her from Eve had suddenly become relevant. She began to resemble a bass clef, arched and draped in a wide black shawl. Her fingers were willowy wands, but she'd forgotten the motions to get them to work. She changed her clothes only when her son delivered half-ironed piles of laundry to the foot of her bed. Guthrie's homeopathic method was to heap all the clothes in a tower, vaguely folded, and to press the iron down on the upper item, hoping the whiff of heat from above would flatten out the whole stack. She refused to open a score. She was on temporary leave from the orchestra. Guthrie was worried dizzy she'd be elbowed out of her job.

"What if she's not ready to go back for the summer round? What if the stand-in conductor gets to do the tour? What if he gets good reviews and the players prefer him and they make some kind of petition to the musical director and—"

"Stop it, Guth. The guy's a breathing metronome. Mum's a composers' necromancer," Gael said.

"A *what?*"

When they gently knocked on her door to see if she was alive, she would say: "Never underestimate what can be slept off. Pull the blinds and leave me be."

Gael imagined her mother's heart to be caked in kettle limescale grunge and was fairly confident that some solution would scour her right again, this year or the next. There was that bottle of red— Settlesoul—on the mantelpiece, still unopened, which Gael had bought for her, for its name. Well, she'd stolen it from Tesco but it served them right. Gael foresaw her mother succumbing to cobwebs like a dust-stuck tuning fork.

She observed Sive one day: standing at the living room bay window, one hand bracing the sill, the other pressing a Maldives travel brochure, sopping with weather, against her thigh. She had been out wandering in a downpour and hadn't bothered to towel off. It seemed to mark a new phase: a willingness to go out, to look outward, Gael had hoped. Though, the pane of glass returned a self-portrait in a crestfallen mirror. A sneeze. When Gael said, *Bless you,* Sive startled. Her hair appeared as a whitewashed black, ashed with age. She wore it in a graceful loose French twist, but most of it had fallen down behind her ears and it dripped like a convent faucet.

"You frightened me," she said. "Why aren't you at school?"

"I don't really go anymore."

"Oh." She stared blearily at Gael's chest, as though there were something written there. "Will they let you do the exams?"

Gael nodded.

"But you'll fail?"

"No."

Sive wiped her nose red with her damp shawl. One would have wanted measuring tape just then to prove she was a tall woman. "If you say so, Gael. Only, don't have me visited by social services. The mind is custody enough."

Her mother turned window-ward again and, after a long while, said that she had been trying to convince herself that the rainwater wasn't laboring down the panes. That it was the other way around: gravity working to draw everything down, angling for its loot. She could hardly bear to watch it. It's a dreadful torture to remember that nature is there, permitting us to play some trifling part, as if it mattered, she said. A second-cornet part. The third violin section droning two-four tonic. "You'd rather just be a mechanism altogether, rid of the *idea* that we perceive anything or participate in some culture. Meaning. Do you believe in anything, Gael? Any organized idea?"

"No." She felt how dry her lips were. This weather. "No idée fixe," she added, but her mother didn't hear.

"Not even in family?"

The strangest sensation pulsed through Gael's center at this rare communication. She felt that her mother was sizing her up, as a species, that she might suddenly announce a figure she had come to: See? What use is that? It's nothing personal. Gael wondered if either of them had ever heard *just* what the other had intended to say. "Not really," Gael said. "Not in the way you mean."

"Not even in markets, then?"

Gael sighed and looked down at her Taiwanese knock-off

Converse trainers. "Grafton Street looks like one giant closing-down sale." It was the bust half of 2008, after all. She picked off her stolen silver nail polish with her thumb and let it fall to the floor as sarcastic confetti. Her mother's teeth chattered and her breath was distantly visible. The exhaust pipe of an idling car. Sive hadn't updated the payment method for the gas bill.

"Gael, I can't be responsible for you."

"I know."

"You don't know. I feel that I should be. And it's exhausting me." She said this in a low and pragmatic voice, though there was barely any will behind it. "Every day the thought of it, another . . ."

Gael shifted her weight, searching for a body part that would put up with it. Her mother turned toward her, eyes dimmed with the dissociative pain of the past months, and looked at the wall to the left of Gael, at the spot where a family portrait might have hung. "You can go and live with him," Sive said, at length. "You may, I mean. You have the choice. I won't hold it against you and I won't love you . . . any less."

The last two words were grace notes. Gael saw her mother's skin goosepimple so piercingly it might have been for good, as though her thoughts were cold enough to benumb their environment. Being let down by the one person you had ever trusted, had entrusted some twenty years and the very pith of your being to, involved a pain unlike anything Gael recognized. Gael knew now it hadn't been cheating. Cheating implies a thing gotten away with. There is something very fun, very blithe, about cheating. Whatever it was though, the way to keep living through it was to move headlong, the way a shark can breathe only by conveying water through its body—all the time advancing, even if that movement is in circles.

"I'm moving to England."

"You're—what? *Are* you?" Sive turned fast, her shawl sloughed off one shoulder to reveal limbs, ribs, her structure defined as cast-iron railings. The impulse was to run one's fingers across her to hear the hollow *thrum*.

"For college. But I won't, if you need me to stay."

"No. When? I hadn't realized, you were, there already, at that stage."

"It's nearly May, Mum. It's been—" Gael stopped herself and allowed time for a response. "I'd only get in somewhere useless here, but England only counts three grades so I could—"

"Go! Of course. Go. Live your life. I'll have your brother to keep this place lit, unless he chooses Jarleth."

"Stop, Mum. He won't."

"He'd be entitled to."

"Stoppit."

"Don't tell me to stop. Your father might be better for him." She lifted the travel brochure and held it before her for a long time like a treasured photograph. Then, she slowly wrung it out on the sill. It dripped an unrealistic blue.

"You could take him away with you?" Sive said without looking up, appalled at the truth of what she wanted. It had stopped raining and everything smelled of what it had been before. The front lawn. The letter box. Electricity cables. The corridor. Dried lavender stuffed in hessian sacks as moth deterrents. Ash in the hearth.

"Mum?"

"What is it, Gael."

"Is this rock bottom, do you think?"

Sive burst into a coughing fit, which she tried to disguise as surprised laughter, but it ended up causing her to choke on the unswallowable substance that was this moment of her life. As her mother tried to catch her breath, Gael looked to the oak parquet flooring, which was buckled all over—especially by the fireside, where clarinet lessons had dribbled through the floorboards and down the drain and, soon, by the bay window, where Maldivian fluorescent heavens were seeping in wrongly. At last, Sive replied and it was with a question.

"How would I know?"

✦

Sive refused Gael's pleas to drive to the Fitzwilliam Casino & Card Club that night to gamble whatever lay in the balance of Jarleth's and her overlooked credit union account and thereby occasion rock bottom and catharsis all in one. Instead, she consigned to lying back on the easy chair, taking as a blanket the pearl-and-plain slate-gray scarf Guthrie had knitted her in home economics (adamant that if his mother was going to wear mourning clothes, they should at least be made to measure). When every whisper of resistance had been wearied out of her, finally, she resigned to helping Gael draft an obituary.

Obittery: A Loath Story

On Friday May 2nd 2008, Jarleth Moeder Falker Foess, of 24 Amersfort Way, County Dublin, failed to pass the ECG-SE exam of why he should remain plugged in. The IV league of afterlives wouldn't take him, on account of too much vain. Jarleth was a small man with a large heart attack and a malicious malignant egosarcoma. He deceived experts with his apparent good nature/health. What were initially believed to be scruples were in fact scabies. Jarleth was a families man, borne by his children, liked by his partner, prayed for by his mother, and dearly preyed on by his girlfriend. He will be sorely miffed.

For her every surge of weepy laughter, her mother sank a measure farther into the chair, as if into long-denied submission. She reclined crosswise so her legs hung over the arm. Gael lay on the warped oak flooring and blinked cracks in the ceiling plaster into view. She read the final farewell aloud seven times, each more conclusively. The words vibrated between her rib cage and the floor, and her mother said she had always been a cello being sanded by the skilled hand of time into her final form and that, before long, Gael's complex timbre would be listened to and danced for and pored over and when that day came she should refuse every follower, every accompaniment, every offer of rest most certainly—all that she was bidden—and live only to satisfy her own ear. That is what she would have to sleep on for the rest of her life. Gael didn't want to say anything contrary that might coil her mother back into herself. Surely she knew that the worst time to impart wisdom was when you'd been humiliated to the point of psychosis?

She'd been dozing, imagining closing a Velcro strap around her mother's upper arm and listening for a little hiss of pressure releasing, when clattering keys brought her to. Guthrie stood at the open front door in the hallway, a draft pursuing him. He let his satchel fall from his shoulder, worked his shoes off at the heel with the toes of each foot and took his place on the living room floor, all too readily. The span of his grin made Gael want to spit something at him, to spare her brother of an optimism that could only ever be briefly lived.

Though his eyes and heart were wide open, Guthrie couldn't see from where he lay—though Gael saw well enough for the both of them—that their mother was dreaming of the life she could have lived without Jarleth; rid of the desperation he elicited; innocent of the assertion of his body upon hers and the pain of its lifting away. Reclining like Anna, that personification of a river, confined to a pond, she dreamed a life free of his soldering. The welded join holding her in place, to the ground. Ever the child who walks toward her.

✦

A few days after a version of the obituary had been published in the only newspaper whose subeditor it had slipped past out of the dozen she'd sent it to, Gael had to stay home to field calls from Jarleth's gallingly large circle of friends and family to assure them she had no idea as to Jarleth's state of animation and couldn't give two fucks. She protected her mother from discovering it had made print, aided by her sequestration. It had been a selfish little act and a good one. Gael wasn't the sort of person to keep mementos—she clung to nothing, not savings or compliments or favorite items of clothing—but if she had been, the newspaper column would have made the scrapbook. Guthrie cried angrily. His chest swelled with all he had to, *had to,* say. How could she. He was their father and always would be. He was dead to no one. Gael was vicious and heartless and *evil* and he had *willed* her to go to England and that was why she was going, so that she would leave them and he could look after their mother properly alone and Gael could just go and leave them to be gentle to one another and kind.

Grow up, Guthrie. Watch this line you're taking. You're becoming a holy prig, she said. His face bloated and shone with a virgin's integrity. Gael left the phone askew of its cradle to silence further calls. She hauled the largest suitcase from the attic, swatting away its confusion of dust.

It would be a year and a half before she returned.

That was before Art.

Before Art arrived, dancing whatever foxtrot, backstep or pallbearers' shuffle the mood required of him.

3

A Man Walks into a House
AUGUST 2009

With corrections from her brother, Gael told Art the evincive story of the painting hanging in their kitchen, *Figures in Moonlight.*

He'll see it differently from now on, she hopes. Maybe he'll persuade Sive to sell it. "2006 was le Brocquy's big year," Gael says. "Some of his paintings went for a million euro before the crash. Which is like . . . unheard of for a living Irish painter. It's the only thing Mum has that's worth anything, besides instruments. But no one's buying art in Ireland right now. They're all, like, reading the return policies for their indoor swimming pools. Maybe you know some moneyed Brits?"

"Gael!" Guthrie says. "Don't be obnoxious."

"Oh, aye," says Art, "I frequent all the la-di-da circles in Leeds."

Gael and Guthrie laugh. Art is handsome in a very different way than Jarleth. He's thick in body, yet flabless. He has tanned skin, round green eyes and his chest hair greets the stubble of his throat as if he's almost fully colored-in (aside from the crown of his head, gleaming under the incandescent kitchen lights).

"Let me tell you two *my* art story that happens to be about the only la-di-da person I've ever known. Our Auntie Beverly."

"*Our* auntie?" Guthrie asks.

Gael shushes him. "Let him tell it."

"Beggin' your pardon. *Our* is Northerner for *my*. My Auntie. Our Bev. Anyway, Bev married into money, but it were for love. Her husband were an art dealer. Got that gig from his lot who'd left him a collection of paintings he never learned how to appreciate fully, though he did learn how to *appreciate* them, if you follow.

"Since her thirties, Beverly'd been a professional fund-raiser. Did her homework too. Only worked for charities she could stand tall behind. Didn't go in for heartstringers—balding children or adorable three-legged pugs. Eh, Guthrie? I'm not telling you two anything new when I say people's mostly bastards, and they'll not actually give money to blind people if you show them videos of blind people struggling with daily tasks, but they'll donate their livers to lovable Labrador pups. Anyway, Bev fund-raised for all the worthy stuff that weren't an easy sell. She was phenomenal at it. She only got better once she married Lucas. Could hold benefits, auction off paintings, that sort of thing, to those lucrative circles. She were so knowledgeable and likable and persuasive, she knew she were making a difference, though it tired her badly. She worked like a madwoman to make that difference. Every moment not working was a responsibility that weighed on her, sickened her to the belly. And she'd calculate all what she'd lost in funds over morning tea.

"Lucas hated that about their marriage. Her dedication to altruism was what you might expect of a nun and won't get from one neither. He couldn't see an end to it—no cushy retirement. Bev wouldn't have it. He knew she'd always secretly wanted to paint, but she wouldn't allow herself the luxury of time to learn. Nights he'd wake up and catch her standing close as a crew cut to a landscape piece in the corridor, trying to study its technique. Oils were dead hard. She might've tried watercolor but she didn't think she could draw well enough to warrant all that self-indulgence. Called her a charity case, Lucas did, but it never changed nothing. Till he died.

"He wrote a will. Asked her to leave off fund-raising and take over the family business longside their nephew. They'd never had kids. Made him use rubber johnnys right through her menopause for all the funds she'd be robbing the world of with a miracle babe. Anyhow, the will specifically asked her to retire early—she'd given fund-raising the best part of her life, Lucas said, and he as good as ordered her to take up painting. It w'n't legally binding, but it'd been his dying wish like. So, she did it. She told me once the only thing to remedy the guilt was the relief she felt at finally stopping the sales pitch. Everything's for sale, she felt, and what worked best in fund-raising was to sell ideas. It was like you were selling the portrait of the benefactor to themselves, only they got to have less baggy eyes and got to stand with a nice famine-free world in the background that had been partly their doing. Slowly but surely, Bev got a touch more comfortable holding a palette in place of a subscription form. She were working part time for the dealership, but she w'n't really needed for t' business side of things, just her connections and arranging skills. And after all them years of abstinence, at long last Beverly was doing what she'd always fancied. Though she knew she hadn't much in the way of skill, the more she did it, the more the guilt fell away.

"Still, she were shy as you like. Worked up in the attic where no one'd stumble on her handiworks. I'll happen it were serendipity she found a whole stack of blank canvases up there with lovely old frames to go with. Won't have found them had she not been so coy as to hole up up there. She'd never've been so bold as to frame her own paintings, but she didn't like to see a thing go to waste, so she thought to make use of the materials best she could. They were old used white painted-over canvases, home-primed with gesso, from what she could tell. She liked the way all the old layers of paint made her painting on it more interesting. Give it texture, helped her along to cast shadows in the sea surf like real waves. There were a kind of ghosty communication she felt going on, not that she fed on that baloney but, she liked the notion of it, bringing old things back to life, for company, seeing as Lucas couldn't be restored so easy. Esprit de corpse. Give her solace, you know. She'd've been lonely something proper had she not them canvases to lift her blues.

"It were Shrove Tuesday—stack of pancakes, caster sugar, wedge of lemon, no mucking round—when Bev's-your-Auntie phoned me up. It were late-ish and I wondered had she taken a fall or OD'd on batter. The excitement in her voice was like a child's. Did I remember that quantity surveyor from Bristol, Something-or-other Ramsley? The handsome one, she said. He'd called round to the house when there were no one else there and she'd asked him to help her carry down a box from the attic. When he got to the top of the wee ladder, his mouth hung open in a leering sort of way and Bev suddenly felt the tightness of the space, the dust in her lungs and Lucas's absence hit her something harrowing. Were Ramsley making a pass at her? Nay. He'd caught sight of her work and insisted on buying one of *her* paintings! She dint want me telling nobody, but she had to share the news and she knew I were out of sorts at the time—another story—so she thought it'd lift my spirits, knowing I worried after her. And it did. Glass of Cragganmore good as levitated to my lips. I'd seen her paintings and they were . . . abstract, to be kind. She were no Guthrie Foess, regionally Highly Commended child prodigy. But I were well pleased for her. Till she said the Ramsley bloke'd *commissioned* her to paint him another, so long as she'd use the same materials and throw in one of them old frames—he'd have it mounted. Were it anyone else, I would've cautioned them somehow but, it were as if . . . her life had just begun, the second life Lucas left her in his will. I'd not be the one to snooker that.

"Cut to t' following two long years she spent toiling for your man Ramsley. Seven days a week, she poured herself into them canvases. He'd said something to her about the 'generosity of spirit coming through in the delicate detail' and so she told me that if she didn't wring some deep mineral from herself into each work, Ramsley'd surely see through her for an amateur. I dunno what sort of manor she supposed he lived in with so many blank walls to decorate, but the commissions kept coming, till she was down to the last canvas of the attic stash. Finally, he declared his wife would leave him if he bought a single new Beverly Aldridge masterpiece. He thanked her for her work and she never heard from him again. That were that. Bev fell into an exhausted state of satisfaction she'd never known the like of. Now, she hadn't only spent her life drawing resources from others—albeit redirecting them to where they were badly needed— she'd contributed something of her own too. Something original. Something that could someday be auctioned off, p'rhaps, like a beautiful renewable energy.

"Call me cagey, but it just sat wrong. The whole story. I mean, her still-life daffodils looked like a Simpsons family picnic. 'At's putting it soft like. So I went on a bit of a snoop. And . . . you would not believe . . . what I found out. Either of you fancy mincing up that load of garlic? It's not the pong. Just garlic's bad as onions to my eyes. Reminds me too much of—"

"Wait!" Guthrie says. "What did you find out?"

The kitchen is cozy and convincingly crammed with the accoutrements of a functional family. Finicky single-purpose utensils that accumulate over the years: Nutcrackers. Preposterous salad scissors. Hanging basting spoons. A spatula smelted to a rugby player's ear. Multiple blenders. A bemagnetted fridge. The pressure cooker lying under the cake tin below the chafing dish beneath the sink; it's all still there, except for Jarleth.

The seating is a table-and-bench affair T'd up against the wall opposite the kitchen worktop, stove and oven, above which a double window would look out onto the dusky August evening were it not fogged with dinner-in-the-making, potatoes aboil, frozen fish fillets whitening, tomatoes roasting. Gael sits on one bench with her back against the wall; her right boot up on the varnished maple, the other stretched out—heel to the tiled floor—making a leisurely ten to twelve with her limbs, though it's ten past six. Guthrie's straddling the edge of the other bench, near the end so that he keeps tipping forward. He allows himself to be unconscionably vulnerable for a seventeen-year-old, as if he doesn't believe in the armor of body language or the refuge of teenage skepticism. His hair is free of product and hangs light as parchment over his Pavlova-like, shatterable features. He's wearing a shirt for their mother's big night. It's the closing of the Autumn Program, the Bruckner symphony, which she's allowing them to make an occasion of because of Art. Guthrie's shirt is bedizened with tiny violins. The sleeves don't cover his wrists. It had been a Christmas gift from Gael a few years back.

"Eh?" Art says.

"What-did-you-find-out-about-Ramsley?" Guthrie says again, letting the bench clap to the floor.

"Just the taytoe dish won't do without chopped garlic—"

"I'll chop the garlic!" Guthrie says. "*Please* finish the story."

Art's jovial accent and languid way of speaking are misleading. He's sharper than Gael had supposed when she'd first clocked him in London's Tate Modern last year. She'd taken a measure of him as a potential fling for Sive, who'd been in town to give a guest concert. (Gael knew well what her mother needed.) She'd seen him linger in the anonymity of the film screening rooms to watch films replay in their entirety. She'd seen his eyes still glistening from one showing as he chuckled at another, his feelings layering like paint. Gael had still been of the age when strangers can only be ascribed one adjective, and *passionate* had been the adjective she'd apportioned Art, which meant he couldn't, too, be bright. But now he is a stranger in their kitchen, holding the mother's-day-special dishcloth. How, if not by wiles, has he managed to nestle himself so suddenly and surely into their home?

At least he's as handsome under kitchen lighting as gallery lighting. He went bald when he was thirty—a fact he blames on a single dart he lost eight thousand pounds on in the autumn of '95, but the story doesn't stack up. He gives the impression of a person robust and immune to regret. Though, last night he alleged in passing (Gael forgets the context) that there's a world of difference between regret and remorse, which gave her pause.

Gael looks disdainfully at a calendar pinned on the wall beneath the clock. "You won't touch the garlic, but you'll let my little brother's fingers smell of your ex?"

The bowl Art is drying slips in his hands, but he catches it. "You what?"

Guthrie throws a cautioning look Gael's way, but she doesn't notice, so he throws a clove of peeled garlic. He has already given Art his wholehearted approval, but Gael doesn't believe in blessings and her confidence is less easily won.

The sound of the front door opening interrupts the conversation and bags can be heard thudding to the carpet. Guthrie jumps up to help and, after a frantic assurance of love and a hurried scaling of the stairs, he returns to the kitchen bearing groceries. Sive peers through the door frame. "Oh," she says. "Good."

"Lady of the hour." Art throws the tea towel over his shoulder and plants a kiss on her forehead.

Sive glances at Gael. It's as if someone has thumbed the basins above her cheekbones with mauve paint, to frame her Irish-landscape-gray eyes. "I keep forgetting you're here this weekend."

"'The advantage of a bad memory is that one enjoys several times the same good things for the first time,'" Gael recites, as evidence she's been attending lectures. She memorized that one, because she suspected it would be ironic to misquote it.

Sive looks blankly at her, as if there can be no change worth documenting in such a stalwart person.

"Nietzsche," Gael says.

Art knows by Sive's tone that he's the one being addressed when, with her eyes trained like shadows on her daughter, she asks: "Can you manage?"

"Oh aye," he says in a hurry, "nothing I can't handle. Is your shoulder any better?"

Sive withdraws a fraction. "It's just, I'd lie down for a minute. I'm tired today. I won't doze but, just to be horizontal for a moment." She pauses in the doorway. "Is that desperate?"

Guthrie has finished organizing the groceries in the fridge and stares.

"Don't be daft," Art says. "I'll take you up a brew in a bit. Up and have a rest." Art follows her out to the hall for a word.

"I can iron your suit," Guthrie calls. "Mum." When there's no response, he drops an inch from his tiptoes. He opens the pantry and makes space for rue on the seasoning shelf. Gael wonders if he's jealous, yet, of Art's arriving so surely. Of the whispered hallway con-sultations. He reminds her of a wild foal. No, a captured reindeer, unsteady on its legs and shorn of antlers. He could be broken in for the better, made less isolate, but there's something striking in what is inoperable about him. His morality has only intensified since Jar-leth's violation of the eleventh commandment. Jarleth, who'd been the one to convince him of the Lord's unknowable ways from before he could speak; who, in one of his many tactical efforts, warned Guthrie that his fits were the Savior's way of shaking his fallen child into realization of original sin, that they would stop when he learned to repent. He's all but an adult now, Gael has to admit. Taller than her, just. That chin is nearly always lifted so his nostrils are a pro-nounced feature of his face. Choices have been made for which he received no counsel and something at the edges of his expression speaks to that.

"Wanna play pool after the gig?" she asks, lifting her boot back onto the bench. She's wearing black skinny jeans with a rip across one thigh and a delicate auburn silk camisole with a band of lace across the straight neckline. The kitchen is warm with cooking, so her pale, toned arms are bare. She keeps the muscles in shape, but has no time for lotions. "I'm in the mood for pool."

The tendons on the back of Guthrie's neck engage, where his hairline dips into a woolly W. His voice is tight. "To see how many guys spill their beer when you lean over the table?"

Gael tilts her head to her shoulder. "Don't you think the girls'd spill their drinks too? Spilt Tia Maria and milk?" Gael watches his back, half expecting to see all the cut threads of a tapestry's under-side. So unravelable. "Come on, Guth. We all know you're popping cherries like bubble wrap."

He lifts the loaded pot and steam surrounds him. There's some bite to his enunciation. "You should go out with your old school friends. Elaine's always asking what country you're living in. She's not heard from you once since you left. None of them have."

"Yeah." Gael runs through the people who might want to see her, then wonders if there's room in her carry-on for those unworn tennis shoes. They could be useful. Double as golf shoes, should she find herself needing to play the ponce. Guthrie drains the boiling water from the still-hard potatoes and readies the skillet, butter, milk, corn flour, all the pinches of herbs. His chicken-gristle body says he con-sumes the dish all too rarely, but has often watched it made. His skinniness becomes suddenly alarming. He had once told her about the ancient Greek method of treating epilepsy by fasting. Then he'd explained that anticonvulsants only work for eight in ten people. She asks, "Have you been fasting again?" right when Art returns to the kitchen and claps Guthrie on the back for having taken over.

"So." Art peers through the oven door at the blistering fish. "I'd like best guesses from the both of you, if you please. How does that hand play out: Mr. Ramsley, pile of paintings, the attic."

"Is Mum okay?" Gael asks, glancing in the direction of the stairs.

"Ramsley's her son," Guthrie announces before Art can answer. He continues, newly assured that he knows how the story ends; knows the example it sets. "Beverly gave Ramsley up for adoption before she married Lucas, but when she saw how bad the orphanage was, rotting mattresses and everything, she started fund-raising for it on Sundays after mass, but that wasn't enough, and then she did more and more. Years on, Ramsley watched from a distance, once he'd figured she was his mum, and he took the chance of the dealership to get close to her—to get to know her, I mean. And then he started buying her paintings, as a way to spend more time with her. And to have something of hers." He looks to Art.

"Blimey. That ought be the ending. Heartbreaking, that is."

Gael swings her legs off the bench and sits upright at the table, suppressing a grin.

"Because she was an older lady," Guthrie adds, "and he didn't want to upset her by asking, but he wanted something to remember her by. Because he wouldn't have been in her will."

"Right. Nice touch," Art says. "Let's hope it's that."

Gael takes out her phone and starts typing, missing the look exchanged between the men.

"Let's hear your pitch then," Art says.

"Just a sec—"

"You can't look it up!" Guthrie exclaims.

"I'm not."

"You won't find it that way," Art adds calmly.

"I'm just looking up . . . I just can't remember if it's *providence* or *provenance*. The history of a painting. Like its pedigree. Its paperwork."

"Provenance," Art says.

Gael sets her phone down and tries not to look flummoxed at Art's knowing this.

"Off you trot," Art says. "Let's hear it."

"The fish is done," Gael says, making circles with her wrists so that they crack and pop. Her nails are painted black. A neighbor's toddler screams into action somewhere outside, which compels her audience to lean in a little. She begins. "Everyone knows twentieth-century art's as rip-offable as male strippers' trousers. Not only because Miró channeled a three-year-old, Mondrian sabotaged a French flag and Frida's monobrows are just straight lines . . . but because of the materials. The older the work, the harder the hardware is to replicate. And it sounds as if these attic frames were genuinely classy. So, scenario one: Rams was buying them for the frames, which he used to legitimize his own black market fakes. Manet Monet Money. Scenario two: he visited galleries' archives under the premise of doing research, but he was really creating fake *provenances*"—a nod toward Art—"for Beverly's paintings. There was a guy who got jailed for that. Rams saw the documentary. He was a big fat copycat. Likely, Bev's paintings fit into some dribbly school of modern art and they didn't look conspicuous in the archives. Scenario three: Beverly might be no Edward Hopper, but she's got moves. And she didn't tell her nephew the whole story."

Art laughs in halting trumpet surges. "That's three bets," he says, turning to manage the potato dish.

"Trifecta," Gael says.

"No trifecta, duck. Trifecta's getting the first, second, third winners in the exact order. Win a trifecta, you'll know about it. There's only one possible answer here, so what you've done's a place bet. Lower odds than Guthrie's straight wager, mind."

"I kind of feel bad for the cows," Gael says, squinting at the fogged window.

"You what?"

"With how much you're milking this."

"I'm starving," Guthrie says.

"Yeah. Trifeck this." Gael gets up to help her brother set the table.

"Hold your horses, the pair of you. Can one of you check on your mother, please? She might rather we start without her. But—"

"Doesn't she need to be there at, like"—Gael checks the clock—"twenty to seven?"

Guthrie disappears while Gael transfers the oily fizzing fish and split tomatoes from the oven tray to the plates and checks if tinfoil has latched onto the undersides. Foil makes her mother's ancient metal fillings screech. When she'd been in one of her lighter moods, Sive had told Gael that if she'd admitted the situation to herself earlier, she would have gotten all her dental work done preemptively. Guthrie returns and puts the fourth plate back in the cupboard.

"Not hungry, is she?" Art asks.

Guthrie shakes his head.

Gael only knows of one stretch in Sive's life when she refrained from eating: the great famine of Jarleth's making. Cromwellian cunt. Besides that emptiness, her appetite has always been reliable, if particular, much to the envy of her friends as, regardless of what she eats, her body remains honed in its proportions. Her collarbones are like carpentry showpieces. She never exercises and rarely breaks a sweat, but she might well burn a week's worth of demons every time she steps up to the podium.

When Sive finally calls for them at the front door, she seems impatient to get on the road and get it over with. Her Burlington wool tuxedo suit appears to be causing her some discomfort, so that she has forgone the silk cummerbund. Gael wonders if her gestures will be looser or more conservative as a result, like a beltless weight lifter relenting to the hernia likelihood. As Sive twists off her rings and throws them in the drawer of the hall table, she grumbles about the disconcerting weather. The humidity is sixty-three percent. She reverses out the drive without turning to check the back window. They might as well be living in the waterlogged west, she says. She'll have to send the string sections to dry off in some air-conditioned foyer. "They play the scherzo so laxly when their fingers have been plump with dampness all day." No one says a thing for how inept their solutions would be, but the image of the spruced and rosined fifty-large string section cooling off in the lobby is somehow amusing. Art mouths "dis-concert-ing" in the passenger mirror, which makes Guthrie snort. "If one person in the green room tells me, 'It's awful close' . . . " Sive doesn't articulate what she would do. Art asks what she means by "close." She says it's an Irishism for declaring muggy weather that's as overused as Dvořák's New World Symphony. "Oh. You mean maffing," Art says, as if lending sense to the eccentricer culture.

They're halfway to the National Concert Hall before Art deems the atmosphere right to finish his story, which he does while rubbing Sive's shoulder as she drives—his hand beneath the suit jacket so as not to rumple it. Her baton case balances on his lap. Gael's eyes flit between the road in front and the muscles of Art's arm bracing and relaxing through his sleeve.

"Conservators don't consider an oil painting fully dry till it's nigh eighty year old," he explains. "So imagine it's dry, it's been sandpapered, had an isolation coat and a layer or two of varnish bobbed on top, it'd be solid as you like. Good as glued. Add a layer of white gesso to that lot, you can reuse it to paint on, only the paints won't behave all that nicely. There's none of the tooth of a canvas to pull off the brush. Nothing absorbs. It's more like painting on plastic. But Beverly'd no experience to complain about surface textures— she blamed everything on her lack of skill. Ramsley took an infrared camera to confirm his suspicions the first chance he had after laying eyes on them paintings. Tough to analyze, mind, all those thin layers merging into one blob. But he needn't have bothered. It was worth the gamble and a half. Fact, if you only had one sorry pound to your name, it'd've been worth a go. And Ramsley'd pounds to pave a town with."

"What's that in euro?" Gael asks.

Guthrie groans.

"The acrylic paints Bev used were soluble in a different way to the oil layers under," Art continues. "I can just see Ramsley, in his double garage, kneeling in his workshop garb—not his best bib and tucker, mind, the grubby old Dolcheegabana—rubbing the corner of Beverly's portrait with a soft cloth and a dab of denatured alcohol. Her painting would've mopped easy as jam off a scallywag's face. Bit of liquid soap and water, the residue'd slough right off and then you're down to the gesso and glazing layers. Happy as a banker in dosh."

"There were paintings hidden underneath?" Guthrie sounds more horrified than astonished.

"Aye. Late Renaissance pieces. Ramsley knew by the frames. Worth a fortune an' a half."

"And he *dissolved* your Auntie Beverly's paintings, that she spent *years* of her life on?"

"That he did. Gladly."

"Of her *widowed* life?"

"Precisely."

"And he didn't *tell* her?" Guthrie's voice is lifting into the upper remits of his head.

Art mutters, "No," softening his enthusiasm for the story.

"Have you your meds?" Sive asks.

"And he didn't give her any of the money he made off them, that was *hers* to begin with? Or compensate her for *destroying her paintings?*"

Art's eyes flick from Sive to the road in front.

Guthrie's gone red in the face and the veins in his neck are dancing. How much money could Late Renaissance paintings raise for charity? How much more on top could her own paintings have raised? Art glances back at him and withdraws his arm from Sive's shoulder. He goes to say something, but Sive clicks her tongue, indicates left and the ticking stands in for silence.

Gael wonders how much Art knows about Guthrie, who is pressed up against his door and is chewing on the outer corner of his palm, where it meets his wrist. His elbow is jerked out in front of him, so he can get at the spot.

Gael pushes back into the seat and projects her voice over the traffic din: "How'd she take it, when you told her?" She pauses, not long enough for Art to respond. "She must have been *livid*. I guess you'd have helped her take Ramsley to court, on principle?"

The car swings left onto Leeson Street Lower and Art faces the dirty fumes of the oil-leaking Honda in front. Guthrie chews his palm more hungrily, as if dinner's lone whitebait had been a poor substitute for loaves and fishes.

"You *did* tell her?" Gael asks, knowing it could push her brother to fit, but it's vital that he be warier of guests. It's vital that Art be clear about who he is and who he is not. They've missed the green light and are waiting at the intersection to turn left one last time onto Earlsfort Terrace.

"What would be the point?" Art says, at last. "Has she really been wronged? If she don't know of it. It made her happy. What's been robbed, if she don't know what she lost?"

Guthrie grabs and pulls the plastic door handle, but the child lock is engaged. He slams the driver's headrest with his palm. "Open it!" His face is flushed and his breathing pond-shallow. He jerks at the handle again, but the lights have turned green. Sive waits until the cars in the lane over have passed before opening the child lock with a control in front. He's gone. Like that. Out. All it took was one wrong word too many for Peter to deny his God. A surly honk from the car behind. Fuck. Gael twists to the back window. She can see him intimidating the bonnet of the car that blew the horn, hanging over it with football hooligan menace. As if he would hurt a fly. What did she lose? What haven't any of us lost? The separation will happen for him every day of his life. But what can we lose, if we're not wise to it? Sive drives on and, as they swing left, Gael catches sight of him lashing out at the car's rear tire and parading his grievance to the oncoming traffic until it compels him to the path—the great side track, running parallel to the main route, but not keeping pace.

When they've slotted into their reserved parking by the concert hall's backstage entrance, Sive directs Gael to trail him awhile, then to calm him down as best she can and, if she can't, to call their father. "Get him some water and see he takes his meds. You'll need to run through the whole argument with him, or he won't let it go. You provoked him, Gael. Times I'm convinced your tongue is a catapult."

Gael will go after her brother; she will solace him. But for now, her eyes graze Art's. "He's ready to fall for any old story," she says. "However it's been jollied up."

Sive tips her head back and tries to hear a violin tuning up, contracting its four discreet strings into alliance. She lets out a long stream of air. Four is not so many. You would think it could be done. That an electric tuner might be invented. When one string goes, it's only practical to replace it. But then it behaves differently. It slips and gives more than it wants.

Some patrons have arrived early, all flair in asymmetric garments, and they inspect the ground for what they have to step on to get where they are going.

There is a snapping sound as Art lifts and closes the buckles of the baton case alternately with his thumbs, at an utter loss as to how they got here and so fast.

✦

To be a conductor and female, you have to be exceptionally good. You have to live with the fact that your players don't automatically look up to you, even for the sake of appearances. You have to claim the phallic object between your finger and your thumb. Command with it. *Obviously* women are worse, Gael knows. How can you be anything but mediocre when your brain is cluttered with the politics

and statistics of your sex? You mustn't look cute and cause the players' minds to stray, so said some Russian. Pursed lips wrinkle early,
says the Television. Classical music is inherently effeminate, says
the Critic, so the translation mustn't add softness or flower. It would
be foolhardy to program the Baroque or Romantic without the male
grasp of the scales for balance. *Con machismo* is the universal, un-
written musical instruction. Females may either mimic or refuse to
mimic—whichever one stoops to, it takes energy that would otherwise be spent on the *bellicoso* March in F U major. She cannot afford
to be gifted and to leave it at that.

Last year, Sive was visiting conductor for a choral symphony at
Cadogan Hall in London which involved a forty-two-bar rest in the
orchestration. During this, the choir sang unaccompanied and were
tasked with holding their pitch until the orchestra rejoined them.
Gael writhed in her seat as the sopranos sharpened by a semitone
a minute. They misread Sive's gnashing gestures. The moment the
orchestra reunited with the choir, more than cymbals clashed. The
flinching players tried desperately to transpose their parts, bar by
bar, clef by clef, searching Sive's unfamiliar expression for rescue—
not knowing if they or the choir should be the ones to adjust. By
the coda, the symphony was having its global premiere in a new
key signature. The stiffness in her mother's stance—back to the
auditorium—suggested that she might altogether lock, offended as
she was at how they had failed the music. Sive gave not a bow but a
nod and left the stage without pointing to the leader or choir leader
for directed applause, as is orchestral etiquette. Had Jarleth's money
been available to her still, she would have reimbursed each patron,
so that their expectations might not be lowered thereafter. That kind
of act had garnered Gael's admiration on so many occasions. Her
mother's pursuit of greatness, at all cost. There is no spectrum of
greatness. No scale to ascend. Only its attainment or not.

The main annoyance was that it soured the lunch date Gael had
been so looking forward to, given that it was her first time seeing her

mother since leaving home. "Some believe that musicians shouldn't fear mistakes," went the *Evening Standard* review, laid out on the table between their bowls of Greek salad, "that today's orchestral obsession with accuracy and precision stifles risk-taking and inter-pretation. If last night was anything to go by, Sive Riordan is in that camp of fearless conductors. To describe the performance as 'sharp' risks the very misinterpretation at the heart of Riordan's direction, or lack thereof. Never before have I wished that the notion of 'throwing caution to the wind' had been taken literally. Those horns."

The disgrace Gael saw writ across her mother's mouth in that Kensington café (her baton was all that Jarleth had deigned to leave her in his wake) was one ailment Gael had a remedy for. "Tangy little Pinot Grigio'd bring out the Greek in this salad." She raised her arm, ordered a bottle on ice, then bullied her mother into buy-ing a later Ryanair flight on her phone by threatening to faff off to Toronto or somesuch far-flung place at any given minute. If she was learning anything from the Philosophy of Science at King's it was that, Life is . . . What was it? Oh yeah. They're still doing data col-lection. That afternoon was when Gael did her own orchestration in the convoluted corridors of the Tate; an arrangement intended to be of the one-night kind, but the fetching Yorkshireman had too much of a good time breaking her mother's frown apart with his ax-nt and the way he timed introducing himself, squaring up to a Rothko and glancing back at her. "Dunno what you call that, but I'm Art."

"It's all noise," Sive told the troupes when she returned to Ireland, resisting the urge to blame the choir, which would have chimed too shrilly of the indignant female. She was repossessed of herself. Her perspective was galvanized. "It all comes down to excellence of sound. Our mistakes have to sound like most people's best playing." Though she had no obligation to defend herself, she couldn't afford to lose a single player's respect. At all times, it had to be within her power to bend a roomful of professional artists to her subtle inter-pretation of a phrase, a register, a boisterous climax, or, indeed, to a month away from their newborns. Their faith in her usefulness was finally restored when they received funding for an Australian tour circuit during the Irish winter. Ah, the right sounds.

Guthrie whispers to Gael that Art is still awake, which is more than Jarleth managed at these concerts. He could only take them in small dozes. "Why do you insist on doing these long symphonies?" he'd implore of Sive. "The human attention span is short. Would you ever just do three twenty-minute bits instead of a hundred-minute marathon? It's less risky. Diversify, love." Of course, it didn't start out like that. For years, Jarleth had been allured as anyone by the figure of his lover (considering himself the loved) standing way up there, goddesslike, begetting sublime harmonies with her body. But when he came to understand that she wasn't flailing her arms about in an ecstasy of behest, that she was instead compelled by an unappeasable desire to find symmetry and realization in collective music—a form of communication grander than anything achievable between one man and one woman—he took to napping.

Gael finds it interesting not that Art is awake, nor that he seems truly wrapped up in the performance, but that he is watching the players rather than her mother. No. He is watching the players watching her mother. She follows his gaze.

Gael sees the orchestra—the music and its players both—as a flock of starlings moving in formation around a pylon. The starlings' movements are surely patterned, but who could say where they will go; how they will hesitate or surge? The timing, the extension of bows, a key signature's leeway—now A, now tonally ambiguous B flat minor—the black flock moves by an intuition that cannot be second-guessed. Nothing familiar in the cadences, comforting and dull as the pulse goes: *so la, doh me, so fah, so so,* a progression you've heard before. The key, a tonic. No, no. This swarm of throbbing temperamental strings, the shifting direction of the wind, abstruse tubas, this sound lifts its audience—lifts—and drops them. The first movement ends.

Gael plucks the program from her brother's clasp. Anton Bruckner's Symphony No. 8 in C minor, ninety minutes. The flock has paused midair, instruments suspended. The wings seem slight now—drifting. All the white pages turn in a crackling gust like so much airborne litter. Into the hush, the strings point coyly, then almost giddily lead the way toward a brighter climate; all of their statements going up at the end as if winter can be escaped by gaining altitude. Gael is reminded that this is an endangered species, this sound. The symphony has been called the Apocalyptic, according to the program. Despite their common sightings in suburban gardens, this is a desperate gesture of survival: a testimony of self. The central motif is stated again and again, as if it's stuck, as if there is no way to state it directly enough. The species is cornered into a sudden awareness of its lot. Some say it's for fun or for communication that starlings teem in configuration. But it is more likely intended to confuse a bird of prey, who, despite their efforts, does not bewilder easy. There she swipes: Sive. A buzzard, let's say, flitting at their heart, making the starlings fly even more obtusely, jabbing south-southwest, then hard north, forcing them to sharpen their will. She becomes frantic. She will exhaust the faction to a murmur and then she will have her way, but that measure of the tale is not scored. Its consummation happens in the dusk behind a plume of resin, a contraception of mutes, when the audience has fallen away.

Gael is numb to what she has just read, until a sliver of blood appears on her index finger. A gash from the program, snatched from her hands. Seeing the blood, Guthrie reaches out again in apology and Gael has to hold her hand back to stop him from sucking it. "Don't," he mutters. *You* don't! she wants to say, but her mouth is dry, as it's been hanging open. Her teeth clack shut.

The massive statement of the main theme is given impressively, again now, in its clamorous rhythm. It's neither reassuring nor unsettling—it doesn't tell the listener what to think. The weight of a flock of starlings on electricity wires can cause minor power cuts, Gael once read. But these players have no such power; they can't cut her off. They're band members trying to follow the timpani and get the bowing right, all the while wondering when the valuation report will be submitted to the bank so that they can get on with remortgaging their houses, glad of the excuse they had this morning for refusing to reciprocate a handjob (forearm muscle fatigue), cursing their effort to convert to vegetarianism in order to keep up with their cerebral, conscientious teenagers, who are constantly freezing and famished.

What had she read?

"This concert marks the early end of Sive Riordan's tenureship as the RTÉ National Symphony Orchestra's conductor and co–musical director" is what she read. "After seven years leading the internationally celebrated ensemble, Ms. Riordan will step down from her role as chief conductor at the end of 2009. The leader of the orchestra, violinist Julie McNamara, said: 'Sive has always been able to inspire the orchestra. Thanks to her unbelievable knowledge and commitment, she is admired both by us musicians and by the audiences in Ireland and abroad. She became my personal heroine when she introduced blind auditioning to prevent sexism and she helped to evolve the orchestra in her time with us. We missed her on her leave of absence last year, and we're very sad that this one will be permanent.' Gordon Hamilton, NSO's CEO and Chair of its Board of Trustees, said: 'Ms. Riordan is parting on excellent terms with the NSO, with deep mutual respect.'" The program note cuts to Sive's biography, but it is Jarleth's obituary that suggests itself to Gael. As if he knows what she's thinking, Guthrie shakes his head. Gael snatches at the program, but he won't let go, so they wrestle the glossy pages free of their staples and Guthrie snorts nervously, drooling onto the program's center page, smack in the eye of a young man's bravado portrait. The man wears a smirk and a licked-on black T-shirt. His tanned bulbous arms are crossed and he holds a baton in one fist like the ruler he just used to measure himself. Guthrie and Gael lean in to read the blurb below this portrait.

Looking Forward: Forward Looking

The NSO is thrilled to appoint Eoin Considine as Principal Guest Conductor Designate. This exciting, new, temporary position will see Eoin taking over as conductor at the beginning of the 2010 season (until 2012), following a two-year residency with the Salt Lake City Symphony in America. Eoin is familiar to many members of the RTÉ NSO, as he is also a talented composer and sarrusophonist, and played with the NS Youth Orchestra prior to his overseas exploits. Fans are drawn to Eoin's accessible, humorous approach to conducting. Diversity, adaptability, stage presence and intensity are among the qualities Eoin brings to the rostrum. Audiences have seen him lead everything from traditional Masterworks to multimedia collaborations to show tunes and film scores. With Eoin at the helm, we hope the NSO will attract both new and traditional patrons. Eoin said: "I'm the son of two teachers. It's in my blood to communicate—everything from the lives of the great composers to the way instruments convey a personality to the code of the black dots. I'm excited to communicate with Ireland." We're looking forward to what Eoin has to say.

Art has zoned out of the music. His green eyes are marble-round. He pitches them sidelong at Guthrie, then onto Gael. "Either of you two need your hair held back?"

The image of it skims along her ear to the nape of her neck. She lets it linger.

What are the uneven panels of Art's face primed with? What

lies beneath that veneer? He might have asked Sive to retire and his story was a kind of readying, as though her conducting were a charity she had held up for long enough. Gael twists in her seat to take in the auditorium. The rear stalls are empty. The balconies' front rows are barely in use. A surface audience. So much for ending on a high note. 2009: the budget cultural vintage. But then, this crowd-pleaser Considine doesn't sound cheap. Sive has no pension. Now's not the time to stop. She's only just back on her feet, after Jarleth. Gael recalls the formal look on her father's face when she told him neither she nor her brother needed his charity. It's better to start out ropeless than to be all harnessed up to lines that may or may not be severed. Gael was unfazed at having to pay her own way, but Guthrie . . .

"Was she fired?"

Art barely shakes his head in the prickled mock-starlight cast on him from above. The orchestra has begun the final movement, which is so erratic in mood it's beginning to make Gael feel sick. Sulky droopy flute motifs. Aggressive staccato browbeating strings. Tremolo stair-bounding breakouts. Lyrical romantic slurs undershot with dread. It's all so histrionic. So abrupt. "What's she going to *do*?"

When a *shushh* showers them in spittle from the row behind, Gael spins around and yell-whispers, "God *bless* you."

She takes her brother by the wrist and tells Art they'll be home by one.

◆

"Stop power-walking." Gael holds Guthrie back by his arm, to keep them from catching up to a mob of youths up ahead. "They can smell it if you're tense, like dogs."

"I'm not going faster than before," he says, "and anyway, when you stand still, you're moving at a hundred and eight thousand kilometers an hour."

A window creaks open—to scope them out or to release toaster smoke? Plastic bags skitter and snag on car door mirrors. One misappropriated wheelie bin leaks fetid compost all about the rim of a gutter, as they move from one block to the next, into up-and-cominger neighborhoods. Cider cans make drunken gyrations around driveways. The atmosphere is thick from gorging on the country's liquid constitution. You find your way home in such conditions by groping forward from one orange streetlamp to the next, like lifebuoy stations.

Gael had tried to convince him he wouldn't be ID'd if they walked into Fibber's hand in hand—he behind her—but he pretended not to hear. When he's like this, Gael knows not to push. The pressure of his temper hasn't quite let up. Being turned away would have added one pascal too many. Then again, given his skittishness and his unreasonable scanning of shadows, it may have been better to drag him, kicking and screaming, to the guarded side of a wall.

"This was a bad idea," Guthrie says.

"If you keep repeating that, it might come true."

"You don't know how bad it's got."

"I don't need to live here to know."

"Everyone's leaving," Guthrie says. "The ones staying are despairing." Gael groans, turning left down Synge Street onto the South Circular Road. "Guess how many people the government gave methadone to last week?"

"You'll work yourself into a tizzy," she says, evenly.

"They just want everyone to fall asleep for a few years. Until it's over."

"Well, I left, Guthrie, and now I'm here. So we can't very well go home. To sleep. You mightn't see me again for . . . who knows how long, since you won't come to London." She sees that she's losing him. "Even though I told you death-by-black-snot is rare." He spins round to identify some noise; to control the darkness by knowing it.

"I'll shout the airfare if you come for Christmas. My flatmate'll be away so I wouldn't even have to listen to you grinding your teeth."

Even if he wanted to, Guthrie couldn't hear her. It's like a helmet—he had once explained—that mutes all familiar, consoling sounds and amplifies instead the anonymous: changes in direction of the wind, paws clicking asphalt, the lick of substances dissolving in fluid, sun salutations, whistling, glass cracking, hue and cry, tides retreating, fast-food wrappers, keys, leashes, cartilage, prognoses.

The moisture in the air has muscled up into drizzle. Not quite droplets, nonetheless wet. Gael takes out a small umbrella from her shoulder bag. Its flimsy metal skeleton cracks a joint when she forces it open. She pulls Guthrie under, holding on to the arm of his vintage tan leather jacket, which feels damply like skin. It's the kind of clothing that gets him pummeled. ("Very Oxfam," she'd said when she arrived home to see how her absence was making its mark on him.) Guthrie veers to the far left of the pavement, almost onto the road, pulling Gael after him. I'm not walking, he says. Gael can feel the pulse at the crook of his elbow.

"I'm turning back—"

All at once, she sees them. "Guthrie. Walk normally." She holds her brother fast, approaching the threat that's come darkly visible as a cloud of bees. "I've got you," she says, but she has to straightjacket him to keep him from fleeing.

"Let. Go."

"Stop. They're only knacker brats. Don't make eye contact."

Cheshire-cat kids choose dare over truth in their little circle of tracksuit chaos: spin the bottle, smash the bottle, bottle whatever ye bleedin' well like; bottle it up, lads; they slink round a homeless man; daunt one another into nicking the meth without waking the junkie. Crust cracks on his sleeping bag and the kids are let down by the lack of hidey-holes on the dirtied naked limbs. Not a steroid, a pipe, the eye of a needle to embed. "Dry cunt," one says, hoicks up phlegm. Someone is making a small to medium-sized enterprise of robbing the clothing bins around Ireland. Everyone is blaming the Polish. The Polish are nowhere to be seen just now. Two wrongs make no one right.

If they're spotted now, they're done for. Guthrie won't be able to move—not to soften his smack against tarmac, not to free Gael's arm, which might spare them a few teeth. They'll make a piñata of his head. She toys with getting her keys from her bag to set between her fingers. Mace wasn't allowed in her hand luggage. It takes all her strength to goad him toward and past the hissing, helium-voiced arsenals of disentitlement. "Prick!" a giddy rat-tailed boy slurs at the tramp, throwing a half-dozen kicks like eggs, so puny they remind Gael of her recurring dream: she punches a familiar stranger over and over, but each time her soft punches land, his face becomes fleshier and chewier and—though she punches until all her energy is spent—he only chuckles and swipes her fists away like ditzy blue-bottles. When she described the dream to Guthrie once, he told her it was because she didn't pray.

In a decent neighborhood, in the light of day, a passerby might call social services, with how Gael is wrestling him. He's going to shout. The guards will come, he'll say, and you'll be caught, the lot of you. What consolation it must be to believe in hell. Gael can feel the seizure start in the augmentation of his chest. Not here. She drags him from the road. Just then, he managed to say, "It's because of me." He's dazing out; setting like concrete. "Mum quit—" he sputters, thick-tongued. He is conscious for this part of it. It begins like this. "—'cause of the babies." He gasps. "Look—morning—" His arms go stiffly up before he falls, as though he might be thrown a rope. Gael reaches around his ribs from behind and takes the brunt of it on her spine; curses the pavement. His fingers go numb, he says, until they no longer belong to him—then it spreads up his arms and to his tongue. He sees brilliant cloud-break light. An aura. Most often, he remembers and describes it as butter-yellow on ice-white.

But it's a color all of its own. Teeth clamping is what hurts the most. It feels as though the roots retract from the irradiated soil that is his head. Tin for a hard palate.

In catching him, Gael dropped the umbrella—their slapstick shield. The wind picked it up and has blown it onto the road. Gael watches it move in half circles, back and forth, a pendulum, as her brother shivers and calms, shivers and calms in her arms. He makes fists to regain control of his hands. Maybe it's the fists and the mention of babies, but Gael is reminded of Monday mornings before French in school when Tamana Tiernan used to pound her stomach with her fist. The womb-pounding was the knelling of her hollow Angelus: an alternative to the morning-after pill she treated as a nutritional supplement, of which she'd exceeded her lifetime's quota.

Gael lets go of him and watches his tense, forced recovery—defying exhaustion, like a new parent bolting upright to the soundless alarm of silence in the night. When they're both standing, she sees that the kids have scattered off down a side street. "Jesus." She wipes her palms on her jeans. She bends to collect the umbrella and tries to joke. "Which came first? The sperm or the egg?" They look at one another, properly, finally. Guthrie's face is a mess of tears, rain and perspiration. He has skipped several stages of emotion. "Hey?" She pulls him back into her arms. He passes his weight to her again, knowing it will be taken automatically, as one takes the salt at a dinner table. She rubs the wet leather of his back clumsily with the umbrella handle. "It's over. They're gone. You're safe." He's heaving in her arms, weeping hoarsely into her neck from the depths of himself, his front teeth slipping against her skin. "I'm sorry I left you for so long," she says. "You're right. I didn't know how bad it's got." She pushes him away to arm's length, holds him by the shoulders and searches his face. "How bad is it, Guth? Is Jarleth having a baby? Did Mum miscarry? I thought she looked gaunt."

"It's me," he says. "I am."

The adrenaline of a moment prior is gone. There's no hormone in her body that can come to his rescue. "Oh *fuck*," she says before she can choke it back. "Whose—" She stops short. The first thing Jarleth would ask. "Forget it. It doesn't matter. Don't—" She has let go of him without intending to. "Just—" Catch up. "Tell me it was immaculate conception."

Guthrie's sobbing bursts into laughter, as if coming up for air, and surges back toward despair, with only a hiccup's worth of oxygen. Gael stands out in the road in front of an approaching cab and collapses her umbrella. "Thank fuck." She shakes it off. "Come on. You need to get to bed. You'll get sick." Do you have money, he might be thinking, unable to ask. "We'll sort it out," she says. "Remember Tamana Tiernan? With the lovely hair . . . and face and body? She had a method for dealing with these things. Very scientific." She calls in the driver's window. "Crumlin?" He nods, with a hassled look. Gael tries to move Guthrie about, but he won't be pushed.

"It's twins."

He's standing by the door Gael's holding open. The gang's bedlam still sounds in screeches and clatter—it pings around the corners of the neighborhood like ball bearings.

"Yous in or yous out?" the cabbie says, all eyebrows.

"*In*," Gael says. "Give us a sec."

"I left school." He insists on telling it now. His breathing has eased. He's calmed almost too much, too sudden. "Ára wanted to put them up for adoption. She's going to Holland to study. They're letting me . . . Because I can't . . . not. The doctors even said it wouldn't be good for me, to have had them and then to lose them. But Mum has to help. There's an agreement."

"The meter's tickin' here, lads."

"Let's get home, Guth."

"One girl, one boy." The chasmal pupils of his eyes are the only parts of him to brave movement. "Due in seven weeks. Forty-eight days." They search Gael's face, as if for proof otherwise. His lips are the pasty-purple color of an empress plum—one not yet ready to be picked. He adds, "But they don't . . . you know . . . come on the day."

He sounds to Gael like a stranger who has mistaken her for a confidant. She would offer advice, if she could have nothing to do with the consequences. She feels her own chest complain and gets into the cab to control it.

Seventeen.

"Aura?" she hears herself say to the headrest, shrinking at the sound of it, knowing somehow that it's spelled with a *fada*. It feels a luckless sort of fluke. Ára. The light he sees before his seizures. The medical term for this perceptual disturbance is an aura, he almost proudly informed the family one teatime when Jarleth still lingered.

She can see it now: weary before he's thirty, nursing a prescribed addiction, scraping by on benefits, investing his life in the children as if their loyalty is a given, as if their happiness is worth a methodical kind of loneliness. And the mother will swan in one day, in homemade culottes and a hemp blouse and long chalky hair she cleans with baking soda weekly, and she'll discover the truth of his condition, deem him unfit for parenting, and whisk the kids off to her cousin's commune, where their brains will be washed to vegetable broth so that by the time they recall they had a father, they'll know they can live without him. Though the reverse won't be true.

The radio says the unemployment rate has just broken state records. Tests carried out on four Irish people with suspected cases of swine flu have proved negative. A near miss. More details about the Bank of Ireland burglary that took place in February will be revealed tomorrow. World news to come. By the time Guthrie's sitting, there's four euro fifty on the meter and two in the corner for unspecified "Extras."

"Planning on robbing us, are you?" Gael says, leaning forward from the backseat.

"Policy," the cabbie says, in place of *Yep*. "It's the going rate."

Right. That's the stuff that will accrue, in these mired years, on these stagnant waters, Gael thinks. Slime.

"Can we go the Clougher Road way?"

"Doesn't matter which way yiz go this late in the day. Tariff's the same. It'll land yiz in the same spot."

◆

The volume on the TV is almost at a whisper. Belt and shirt draped over the ottoman, Art is down to vest and trousers. The hot air balloon tattooed on his bicep expands and hoists up whenever the muscle is put to work, though tapping the remote control doesn't quite inflate it. The pink and green ink has faded pastel. His shoulders are almost black with hair, no matter how the light from the TV washes them. Guthrie'd headed straight for the living room when they got back, sure of Art's being there. "Turned in soon as we were home," Art said, when Guthrie asked after Sive. "She were fair jiggered." Even though Gael warned him against being so high-minded, Guthrie wanted to apologize to Art for earlier. Auntie Beverly probably would have suffered if she was told the truth more than Ramsley would have been brought to justice, he'd decided. Gael had the feeling Guthrie was practicing for being a parent. If he could teach another human being one thing, it would be how to express regret. She steps out to clear the composting pile of junk mail that's shoved to the side of the hallway welcome mat. Another thing she's missed by not coming home. She should have been chucking expired medicines, tightening flickering lightbulbs, replacing fire alarm batteries, clearing out whatever belongings remained.

Junk mail is invariably depressing and the hall has accumulated a particularly sad lot. CLOSING DOWN SALE! Liquidation! All Stock Must Go. *Our economic sovereignty, going, going, go—*She takes it all to the recycling bin in the kitchen. Separating paper from plastic, she sees that a few letters addressed to Sive are mixed up in the junk. One is from the bank, but the others don't look like bills. A speeding ticket for driving at ninety-five kilometers an hour in a fifty zone. Sive owes sixty euro and has incurred three penalty points on her driving license. Gael will phone in the morning and pay the fine with Jarleth's MasterCard, which are the only details of his she cares to recall, for settlements such as these. Looking through the plastic window of the last envelope, she sees an embossed letterhead: Hurley & Co. Solicitors. She opens it.

Dear Sive,

In lieu of an eviction notice, I am writing so that you might more gently come to terms with your circumstance.

As you know very well, the title deeds for 24 Amersfort Way are in my name. For the sixteen years we spent under its roof, your income supplemented household costs, but the legal situation is that you did not make either direct contributions (toward the initial down payment or monthly mortgage installments) or indirect contributions to the property. You may look into what "indirect contributions" are, but let me save you the legal fees by passing on, verbatim, what my solicitors have said: "It is held in the courts that working in the home, looking after children and money spent on (or work done on) home improvements are not contributions that give the cohabitor any right of ownership." Your NSO income was your own, for shopping, holidays, your retreats, what have you. I am in the process of closing the mortgage and have employed a manager to arrange the property's lease, as its sale should be postponed until the market recovers. It's bad luck I didn't sell a year and a half back when I had a mind to, but I didn't want our separation to be more painful for you.

By now, the children are no longer children. Gael has already fled the nest, as we knew she would. Thanks to your

repeated rejections of marriage proposals in the early years
of our relationship, much to my mother's chagrin, I am not a
legal guardian of my own children. I don't intend to seek joint
guardianship at this late stage. If I did, you would need to sign a
statutory declaration, involving costs and headaches. I propose
we avoid all such nastiness, custody and so forth, and accept
that our offspring are now adults and should they continue to
have a relationship with either of us is a matter of their choosing
and, of course, ours.

It is both parents' legal duty to financially maintain their
children until the age of eighteen. Gael is nineteen in August.
Nonetheless, I offered to pay her college fees. She refused. Even
in these difficult times, I have no fear for Gael's financial well-
being. She is industrious, if mulish. Guthrie would be wise to
take whatever support he can get. I intend to bring the subject
up when next we meet—I assume his every waking hour is busy
with Leaving Cert preparations, and that he understands the
permanence of his score. His college plans are unclear to me,
which is a concern. Again, you'll see that no legal intervention
need be necessary. We are all adults.

You can respond to my solicitors' address with suitable times
for the property manager to show my house to prospective
tenants. Dare I suggest it, you may rent it yourself. I understand
there's been a cohabitor for some time now. With you already in
situ, it would save me the nuisance of vetoing tenants. It needn't
be impossible for us to be civil toward one another, and sensible.
Refrain from posting death notices and the like.

I intend to discontinue payments for your father's care in
Mystery Rose Residence this month. It would be odd, my
keeping on that responsibility. If you cannot manage the fees
and you won't have him moved to a public facility, we can
discuss options. After all, Guthrie would be traumatized to
think his grandfather wasn't having the burn scraped off his

toast for him, which is about the height of what I've been paying
for with that place. Unless I hear from you on this, I'll assume
you can make arrangements.

Regards,

Jarleth

The letter is several months old. If she destroys it, Guthrie might
answer the door before long, nappy in hand, to some young profes-
sionals and an estate agent arriving for the open home. Would he tell
them they have the wrong address; that this home may be open, but
it's not for sale? Then, hearing his father's name, would he stand corrected? And Ned—had he been wheeled from the nursing home to
a bus stop, unbeknownst to his daughter? A feeling comes over Gael,
as if her loved ones' passports are set to expire. She wonders if Art
came here by boat. Yes—there's something in that. He was once a
pilot and now he is decidedly not. She takes the letter and her phone
into the living room, where Art is watching darts, making pencil
markings on the back of the *Times*. The slats of Guthrie's childhood
bed complain from the room above and she shuts the door after her.
Art sits up a little. The slim cigar that's tucked behind his ear drops.
Gael places the letter on top of his newspaper and leaves the cigar to
roll under the armchair. In the rinse of television light, it becomes
clear that it will never be smoked; that Art keeps these things close
to hand—scoreboards, tobacco, spirits, solitude—to remind himself
of what he's negating.

"Should've known you'd have a comedy tat," Gael says, expres-
sionless.

Art idly searches for his cigarillo. "Comedy *tats*, I'll have you
know. Got 'Made in Bolton' on me fewt. Copilot had me branded
in the air force. Case I wound up out me tree and crashed in some
forrin land . . . I'd find my way home. Were the idea. It dint work
though, when the time came. And I needed it."

Just when Gael realizes he's telling her something and tries to put her other line of thought on hold, he closes up again: "'Sides, I never known anybody go for just the one tat. Pair is what's normal."

"Good to know you've the full set," Gael says, distracted. She paces the room, tapping her phone.

"One up on normal, me." Art pulls down the neck of his vest with a tearing motion, as if to check for a scar—to prove to himself that whatever it was had really happened. Behind the steel scouring pad of his left pec, a faded red Cupid's heart is arrowed through. It says:

<h1 style="text-align:center">Your Mother</h1>

Gael stops pacing and looks at the heart. It's concealed by the vest again, but Gael stares at where it had been, putting the right words in the right order before giving voice to them. Art angles the newspaper and letter to the light, finally catching on to its weight. "Oh. I've never shown that to anyone an' had it be . . . true." He pats his chest. "I hope it wun't, inappropriate—"

Gael shushes him. She's making a phone call, he's relieved to see, and he runs his chunky fingers over the letterhead and then along each line, as though reading Braille. His lips move as he reads.

Jarleth picks up after one ring. He must be in bed, flanking some class of twat Gael doesn't care to hear named. She's changed her mind about the student fees, she tells him. She's finally realized his generosity and that she's been ungrateful to turn down his support. (Art raises his formidable eyebrows at this and at the letter.) As she accepts her father's munificence, she wants him to redirect the fees for her education to his own account to pay for the rent he's now demanding of his children's mother.

However she tries to swipe them from her memory, there are details besides Jarleth's MasterCard number Gael knows by heart. Holidays, for example. Lents he made them go without sugar for their betterment. Evenings spent in spare meeting rooms of his office, doing a fortnight's worth of homework, swallowing fusty air and saliva for sustenance. Car journeys. Thursdays.

One Thursday in October 2001, Guthrie's fourth ever fit played out in the Accident & Emergency clinic for half a day. Sive was in Cork, so the comforting was left to Jarleth. This was six months before Gael and her father's shower conversation.

Whoever had flushed the contents of Guthrie's schoolbag down the toilet had fled when they noticed his gaunt body seizing, so it was without witness that Guthrie saw light flood the boys' toilet cubicle at St. Enda's. His cheekbone cracked against the bowl and broke the eye socket, as cleanly as an egg. The eyeball had slipped out of its recess. For weeks, the celestial glow he saw would be as real as the bite of bleach.

There's always some kind of trauma preceding it, Jarleth claimed. It was a studied kind of victimhood. He wasn't following his father's or the doctor's instructions on how to manage his condition, Jarleth edified no one in particular, as they sat on the yellow plastic chairs of Our Lady's Hospital for Sick Children; Gael pat-drying her brother's nine-year-old version of Van Gogh's sunflowers that sagged and trickled yellow watercolor piss.

That night, when Guthrie was deep in painkiller sleep, Gael heard a voice answer her father's in the living room. She stretched her eyelids open with her fingers to be sure she was awake; then, pajama-clad, tiptoed down the stairs and perched on the bottom step. Ice clicked in crystal tumblers beneath the men's low, heavy-duty voices. Work talk. Gael couldn't make sense of what they were saying, but she could understand the urgency of getting Coleman's to sign before "end of day tomorrow." Eavesdropping had never felt good, especially with such disappointments as "end of day." Why not *the* end of *the* day? Everything he said was beginning to vex her. Though still a child, she already felt that straining to hear was not a position to be in, so she got up and, with an air of grievance, proceeded into the living room. She viewed her father wordlessly. The visitor (who Gael didn't lay eyes on) laughed a foghorn laugh at her bunched expression. Who have we here then? he said. Are you the little entrepreneur, or the other one? Guthrie? Gael answered, without turning to address him: "Do I look like I just broke my eye socket?" Jarleth would punish her later for Answering Back. The man loomed almost to the ceiling, it seemed to her peripheral vision, and he rattled ice cubes in his glass like dice. Gael remembers the look that crossed her father's face as he told her to get back to bed. If anyone could embarrass him in front of a colleague, it was his pre-pubescent daughter. Your daddy told me about your little head-lice enterprise at school, the man said. You'd buy lice from the plagued kids, was it? Sell the nits on to them wanted to skip tests and go home early. That's a fine little business model. Do you want to grow up to be like Daddy?

"I want to be like my mother," Gael said.

"Is that so?"

"She directs a hundred people at a time, not including the audience."

"Power hungry, is it?" the man said. "Little tyrant like?"

"You say the word *little* a lot," Gael said. She finally looked at him and forced herself to hang tough, even though his enormous lower jaw jutted out in a highly entertained sort of way, which made Gael feel like setting fire to him. She became newly aware of her pajama set, covered in a starry night sky. (That week, an imbecilic hairdresser had cut her hair into a bob with a thick black fringe and had complimented her handiwork as "so *cute*," so Gael had bit her dirty nail off and dropped it in the hairdresser's cappuccino.) When she felt her cheeks flush, she went to the liquor cabinet, where a plastic sheet of ice lay thawing. She doled a cube into her palm and placed it on her tongue with the significance of a Eucharist. "Off to bed with you," Jarleth repeated, but the man was not done being entertained. She likes staying up with the men, he said. He ground ice cubes with his molars. She knows where the real deals get done and it's not in school, is it, little girl? Gael spat the too-large ice cube into her palm to say, "I'm not a little girl." What are you then? The man leaned down so she could see his mealy tongue. A mini woman?

Gael looked at Jarleth, who was watching her, not with amusement or interest but with disgust at her sex. It would be most despicable in its adolescence, he must have feared. The parting of his black and gray hair looked wide as a spoon so close to the ceiling light. The oval ladle, the shining line of the handle. The man continued to await her deliciously righteous retorts, but Jarleth waved her away. "Auch," he said. "She still wears pink knickers."

"Pink knickers?" the man said. "Is that right?" He was asking Gael.

Gael dropped the ice cube to the wooden floor, whose preservation was one of the major hassles of Jarleth's household. She saw his eyes go to it.

"I am *not* wearing *pink knickers*." Gael began to tremble, blood rushing to her face. Could something that sounded like a curse and felt like a curse not be one?

"Less you buy your own clothes with the head-lice fund," the man said, "then your daddy'd know what knickers you've on, wouldn't he now? Sure, your daddy foots the bill for your frilly pink knickers."

"I'm NOT wearing pink knickers," Gael said and then said it again and again, until the image of the man—failing to control his laughter—blurred with the dream she'd been having and the pain in her head. Don't worry, little woman. All sorts of business can be carried out in pink knickers. You could be a pinko president, he said. Isn't that so, Daddy?

"SEE." She was almost screaming. The pajama trousers were deposited at her ankles. "I TOLD you I SAID I'm NOT WEARING

PINK KNICKERS." She leaned toward the man to advance upon him, to make him take it back, but the trousers held her in place and there was the ice cube to contend with. She thought she heard the words *spider's legs* but she didn't know what that could have referred to and she didn't know how anything could be better proven. Half-blind, she pulled her trousers up. Jarleth had ordered her to "before I get the wooden spoon to pinken that bottom." Gael kicked the ice cube across the floor and ran out of the room and up the stairs. Guthrie would be awake. Getting in beside him would remind him of his favorite thing: that he could help. That his presence was a consolation. It would remind her of something too—something she needed to know more than how far she could get with no money or coat. And, if she slept there, he wouldn't come to get her. He'd wait till the next day, till they were out of anyone's earshot. The next day, before school, he'd turn her by the shoulders and smack her through her pinafore with his hand. Two shrill disgraces. "Now you'll have a pink rear end. And you won't have to lift your skirt to prove other-wise."

I didn't lift my skirt, Gael would think. There was no skirt.

Her father's eyelashes—pale and straight as a heifer's—cut through his gaze. He was always pulling at them, as if some dust or crud was clotted there, but then he'd determine it was only whatever nuisance fence lay before him. He would blink and get on with it.

Not one gesture could she forget. There are fifty-two Thursdays in a non–leap year.

Art doesn't drink. He doesn't drive, he doesn't drink. He has a son a bit older than Gael, but they don't see one another. He lives in Cape Town with his wife. Stuart and Matilda, married at nineteen in the Dutch Reformed Church of South Africa. Small affair. European relatives weren't asked. Anyway. "Most days I think it's best Stu in't near, ghosting me with his mum's looks. And his scars from being abandoned."

Gael looks at Art's fingers for signs of a white stripe. Too much hair. (Too much time, is what she doesn't comprehend. Enough time for moss to grow over the markings of a tombstone.) "Will you get a job?" she asks. Art doesn't know yet what will happen. "Well, if you decide not to," Gael says, "could you tell Mum? Soon? So she doesn't have to quit. You can help look after the twins. Isn't that why you came? You moved in so fast."

Art checks the score on the TV. "I daren't try coaxing your mum's choices. Them's hers to make. Besides, the film were two men and a baby. Not two men and two babies."

Gael watches a dart being knocked off bull's-eye by another that's already taken claim. It's not enough to be exceptionally good, she recalls, then cuts off that stubborn chain of thought which is in fact a manacle. If Sive hasn't completely abandoned herself, she'll find her way back to the podium. It's only a matter of when. It's that symbol in her score that looks like an eye—*fermata*—a grand pause, where the note is prolonged beyond its value, for dramatic effect. How long it's sustained is up to the conductor. How long she can hold her arms aloft, making the blood pump so far away from herself as to contradict the heart.

"If Jarleth ever comes round," Gael says on her way out, "do me a favor. Flash him your tat. And keep him the fuck away from those kids. Three men and two babies sounds dire."

4

The Gates of Horn & Ivory

APRIL 2011

I

"If I pose the salient question, I fear the answer will render all others redundant as your Irish civil service. So let me first ask this: why, after having arrived an inefficient half hour early, did you ignore the Admissions Officer's direction to mingle with the other candidates over luncheon, unapologetically and assiduously use your phone, and refuse the clerk's instruction to take a seat in the lobby alongside your peers, while the portfolio our administrative staff courteously prepared for you—which includes the biography of your interviewer; that is, me—remained unstudied in the crook of your arm?"

Being watched as she descended an august amphitheater to the echo of her own footfalls—toward the pit and its chair of judgment—had been a masterclass in diminution. It had felt like sliding down the eyepiece of a microscope onto a petri dish to be assessed for viable cell density or choicest genome sequencing. Is CEO intrinsic to your DNA? Gael hears her brother's verdict and wonders why the projector screen doesn't present some riddle or demand in spidery font: "To READ THIS is to be disqualified." *Games.* She disassembles the question that's been put to her and answers, simply:

"Risk mitigation."

Gael lets a silence follow that suggests she will elaborate upon invitation. Professor Sutton makes a hurrying gesture reminiscent of the time Sive had a guest soloist for Camille Saint-Saëns's Cello Concerto in A Minor who preferred to let his bow set the pace rather than the presiding baton. "Of the forty percent of interviewees admitted to this MBA," Gael says, "less than a quarter are female. The odds are one in ten, against me. But I figure I'm in the tail of the distribution, of candidates' abilities."

"Which tail?"

Gael checks a smile and tells herself not to get drawn into any pissing match. It's all part of the process. "I assume that the entrepreneurship taught at London Business School is reflected by the institution's practices. In which case, you'll not shy away from an atypical candidate. With respect to my arrival time: if you're half an hour early, when you're fifteen minutes late, you're fifteen minutes early. I always use that half hour for client management. It's Friday at two p.m. Moscow's three hours ahead—some emails needed to be seen to before TGIF, some after. Hence the risk mitigation. To me, strategic expertise and prioritization are one and the same. I didn't read the bio in the orientation folder because I'm already familiar with all the faculty members' profiles. At some point, I'd love the opportunity to ask about your time as consultant for Citigroup—what your thoughts are on the LIBOR manipulation's global repercussions and whether you expect to be part of the legal proceedings. If I'd gotten a sector consultant for an interviewer, then, sure, it might've slanted the questions asked and, if I'd read the bio, I'd have had an extra few minutes to prepare for that. But an interview is an opportunity to present myself and my potential. That needs no half-hour head start. Whoever the interviewer turned out to be, they'd likely decide if I'm a suitable candidate based on my conduct. As to my standing up in the lobby, my interviewer might have come to the corridor in person: I didn't want to be looked down upon, or to have had to haul myself up from those low chairs. The dynamics of the first encounter are critical."

The skin protrusions where Professor Sutton's eyebrows should be are arched. "Apposite that you mention evidence," she says, "since yours is the lightest portfolio I've been handed by the admissions committee in the history of my tenure here. No résumé. No transcripts. GMAT scores. References. Amazingly, no application form. If there weren't twenty-eight double-sided pages of single-spaced ten-point-font dissertation, I should expect you are trying to save the planet, one rejection slip at a time. Instead, I expect worse. You're the niece of a distinguished alum or a colleague's daughter-in-law who has far too much faith in nepotism. Ms. Foess: how did you get this interview?"

Gael assesses her inquisitor's hands, which rest palm-down on the huge leather-topped desk beside a cup of steamless milky tea. Her fingers are like Savoiardi biscuits. "There's a Japanese proverb," Gael says. "'Beat your wife on your wedding day and your married life will be happy.' . . . Let's just say I'm no traditionalist. I knew I'd never meet the criteria to get this interview, but I felt that if I got one, I'd have as much chance of admittance as if I'd met them, so my priority was to get into this chair. I didn't get here the traditional way."

Professor Sutton jolts with a hiccup. "There's an Irish proverb," she says, and swallows loudly. "A thing gotten badly goes badly."

That her voice sounds so large in such a bullying space impresses Gael. And yet, it is not without restraint. The demography of fiscal know-how is straight and white and narrow. Her wan skin is that of a conference pear, ensconced in coarse brown moles. No padding bolsters the wide shoulders of her suit, nor is any needed. Gael is already imagining how this interview might conclude. *However sound your justifications for standing up, Ms. Foess, I trust—for health and safety reasons—you'll consent to taking a seat in these stalls come September.* "A thing gotten badly goes badly? That sounds like postcrash revisionism," Gael says. "Pre oh-eight, anyone would've said a fifty-meter heated pool goes well in your back garden however it got there."

By Professor's Sutton's pushing back from the table, it suddenly, sickeningly occurs to Gael she's about to be shown the door.

"I said I'm familiar with faculty members' profiles," Gael says in one breath. "That's because my plan to get here involved homework. First, I scoured the staff's active research interests. I found a conference that was to be hosted by UL. I spent weeks drafting an abstract that fit the call-for-papers like a glove. Once it was accepted, I contacted the organizers to ask if any future colleagues from LBS were presenting. I was told Dr. David Fernley would be. I asked to be on his panel, as they hadn't finalized the program. Then I had to write the paper. My first. When I had a draft, I submitted it to the *European Journal of Business and Social Sciences,* not expecting it to be seriously considered, but to get the readers' reports, which I used to reshape and strengthen my presentation. I spent the last two months leading up to the conference writing material beyond the personal essays LBS asks of its applicants. At the conference last month, Dr. Fernley was impressed with my paper, but when he found out I was twenty and a liberal arts undergrad at King's College, he had questions. I used the opportunity to give him my pitch, along with my portfolio, which he mustn't have taken lightly, despite its weight."

Gael regrets wearing the outlet-store Versace skirt, which was affordable because it's a size zero. It cleaves to her hips and waist. She wants to sit forward on the chair's edge, to uncross her legs, to let her knees go where they will.

"Why London Business School?"

"It's rated second best in the world. The best's in France, but I don't have time to learn the language and, sure, they teach in English but most of the value of an MBA's in the networking. I did consider Oxford, because a brand like that lets you sail on it for the rest of your life. Even if you fail, your having gone there's enough to alter people's perceptions of you and your business. And I wouldn't sail on it. I'd build a port. But in the end, I figured they'd be less likely to read a portfolio by a twenty-year-old Irish girl with an aversion to the Oxford comma, pecking orders and tweed."

"Are you accusing Oxford of anti-Irish sentiment?"

Gael allows herself an openly confused expression. "No."

"Where else have you applied and what is the status of those applications?"

"Nowhere."

Professor Sutton lifts her right hand to her mouth, hooking her squat index finger around her philtrum and her thumb under her chin. She narrows her eyes on Gael and doesn't say anything for a moment. Gael glances at the wastepaper basket to the side of the desk, supposing it to be lined with her peers' freshly embossed business cards. At length, Professor Sutton says, "Not *one* other application. What will you do if you fail?"

"Realistically, I'd break something. Not like a jaw! A laptop. Crockery. The hourglass my father got me as a metaphor-heavy gift. And then move on. Take especially good care of my clients. Restrategize. I don't make plans for failing with my personal goals. Pursue success and deal with failure if and as you hit upon it."

"These ethereal clients you keep mentioning . . . Of which putative business are they customers? I have no résumé, you understand, or way of knowing what your work is."

"Do you have a smartphone?"

"Indeed, Ms. Foess, I am one of the few proprietors of a smartphone, but at this moment, I am conducting an interview. I don't use my phone during meetings, as a rule."

"Of course, just, I was going to show you, but it's as easy to explain—"

"Oh, I'm *relieved* to hear it." A smirk finally arrives on Professor Sutton's face, a little late.

With a conspiracy of blood in her cheeks, Gael tries to remember the rehearsed bit of the interview, to recall her recitation in the shower that morning, right before she decided to wear the immobilizing skirt instead of trousers. In the lobby, all of the female candidates had been in skirt suits that led down in neat curves to one-size-cuts-all heels; their streaky shins were lined up like a platter of raw lamb cutlets.

Gael explains that her business offers translation services from Russian to Executive English for Russian sites appearing in UK search results with senseless autotranslations. How she hired someone to develop online profiles and how she did free work for testimonials; how she went on to purchase VIP access to Russian online business networks so that she could directly target budget holders. As she'd never intended to carry out any implementation, from her first client on, she hired contractors and spent her own time refining the pitch, creating a list of targets and streamlining client management and business operations. By the end of her first year, she had eight contractors, one of whom managed the others, so that Gael only had to deal with one alias. By year two, contractors were up to thirteen; forty clients were on the books at any one time—mostly one-off contracts, but some on a monthly retainer—and her accountant deemed her sole tradership to be breaking even, given expenses (student loans and scholarships aren't taxable income). She could write off the "workforce development" fees of the MBA against future income. Gael settles into herself, now, and begins to enjoy the telling. It's a history so neat and likely as to warrant memorization. There is a force behind her story—a capricious, yet inevitable progression.

"Describe your leadership style and how you redress inadequate emotional intelligence," she had been bidden, all at once, without a moment's basking in the climax of her financial acumen.

"Leadership can be delegated," Gael says. Hearing the impatience in her voice, she thinks to relax her drawn brow. Her scalp shifts against her skull as if on unset glue. "Women are always told to develop their leadership skills, to build confidence in their people management, to get a mentor, be authoritative, assertive. I prefer to spend my time on *business* development and leave the emotional intelligence requirements and relations to my trustiest freelancer."

"Explain your exit strategy. Do you consider the business saleable and, if so, how would it be rated by Wall Street?"

Gael's jaw is beginning to ache from holding shut when she would rather say all sorts of things, steer Professor Sutton to the point. "Let's see," she says. "It has no real assets, unless you count a cutesy thousand-rupee logo and a client list of SMEs, none of which are obliged to stick around beyond seven days post-invoice. It's run by a walk-in-wardrobe-based uni student. It's scalable to the nth degree, but it'd be a bad investment to grow to twice its size in its current form because it won't appreciate in value—it's not even an LLC. It's ultimately composed of a sales pitch with no tangible, demonstrable product or assets to withstand due diligence, unless a backbone counts. In fact, you can boil it down to the one-line story behind the brand: the Russian equivalent of 'Adversity is a good teacher,' **Без муки нет науки**, autotranslates to 'Without torture no science.' That got me most of my clients. So how would Wall Street rate Translations Without Torture? Wall Street would pinch us on the cheek, say we need some fat on that backbone and slip us a quick grand for candy."

Gael faces Professor Sutton's blank expression and sees in the momentary widening of her neck something being swallowed alive—a laugh or a yawn, Gael can't tell. An African bullfrog comes to mind. The next question might as well be *ribbit*. But it isn't.

"What are your values?"

Gael had seen Professor Sutton's lips moving, but heard mostly her digestive tract aslurp. Shouldn't it be the tyros who are hungry?

"My attributes, you mean?" Gael says.

"I mean your values."

"In how I run my business?"

"Your. Values."

"I can tell you my personal net worth . . . but—" Gael watches her audience's lips more carefully this time, but they don't latch. Her eyes flit minutely, as a multitude of sentences occur to her all at once like ropes swinging and she calculates which one to take, knowing she'll have to climb it, hand over hand. "My values? That's an un-answerable question. It's only answerable with a library of disclaim-ers. I could say something inane, something innocuous like, I could say, 'I value courage, progress, advancement,' but that's so reductive and simplistic. I don't value the courage of suicide bombers or the advancement of deserts. So the statement, to mean what I want to say, would be legalese. My values? I can say I respect fearless pur-suit of one's goals, I respect vision, imagination in what those goals are, humor and resilience in attaining them, but, that question, I didn't come all this way to—" She stops herself, just. "I didn't come all this way without values, obviously." Of course, this question was designed to put her under pressure, to reveal how she deals with an intractable problem. Another rope. A big fat fibrous lie. "I value meritocracy."

"As do we," Professor Sutton says, with as much luxury as can be parceled into three monosyllables.

The word had sounded so restorative just then. So self-possessing. Meritocracy. It had sounded of a closing cadence she might well have sung. What they wanted to hear, no? Why, then, was she being motioned to the exit? Why had she not been told: we'll be in touch? She had to swivel round to understand what was meant by it. She'd never seen a door slammed open.

Blisters were forming on her arches, she could feel, as she took each deliberate stair. The arches were falling, despite the insoles she'd borrowed from someone-or-other's cabinet once upon a time for a few millimeters of advantage.

She concentrated on the pain of each step—on not lessening it by altering her gait—as she clacked along the tiled corridor, all along the puerile speculation of the claimants, the conservatives, the semiconscious acronyms, the unvaccinated neoliberal multinational monominded corruption of cunts.

✦

The building is on the outer ring of Regent's Park. Four times Gael paces back and forth along its railing. In spite of the cream Corinthian columns, the pointed cupolas, halfway between turrets and mosque domes, this grand establishment is made of lime, sand and water. Mere clay. Its stately gardens are deciduous. The keenest of each generation has to step in to releaf the weeping willows with their parents' monies, swap out the old muck for a new grade of soil, consolidate the pillars where expedient. Corinth, it should be remembered, succumbed to a quake.

No amount of brisk walking will hurry this spring into summer. Gael wraps her coat around her. She carries on through the park's inner circle by a boating lake that was once deep enough for boats, until an ice cover collapsed a century and a half ago and forty people drowned and then, as might be expected, the lake was drained. Like most things, once sucked dry, it never returned to its former wealth. Its depth was lowered to the height of a cot before it was reopened to the public.

Gael continues walking the three kilometers to King's Cross Station so she can take the direct line to her Finsbury Park layover home and not have to get on and off and on again. These stoppages. She doesn't look left or right at crossings, or see where the skin of her heels has come off.

Her lower body is numb by the time she gets home and all sensations seem to have collected in her neck. They aren't good sensations and they won't redistribute of their own accord. She'll strap her feet in bindings and go for a very very long run, all afternoon, she's thinking—she recently found a route along the canals that's not too rapey—and she'll listen to Thomas Adès, or Sofia Gubaidulina (she's been searching for new composers to tempt Sive out of her ridiculous retirement). Perhaps she'll take her CameBak and Oyster card and run as far as Gravesend. Make a marathon of it, if not a morality tale. You can learn a lot about a subject in four hours running. The subprime mortgage cockup, say. Beginner's Japanese. Card counting. Genghis Khan. The meaning of *quality spread differential,* which sounds like margarine, but it isn't. There's the danger she'll not get as far as she'd like, given her blisters. She's decided it's thirty kilometers or nothing by the time she reaches her gate. But there, by the hedged driveway, she comes to a halt.

Some guy is crouched at her front door, peering through the glass panels. He squats down low as a break-dancer, lifts the letterbox flap and pokes his finger through the bristle. Gael can almost hear how the metal would creak in the hallway; can almost see the way it would look from inside. An envelope of eyes.

"Hey, perv?" She approaches fast, key-fisted, ready to cut. "I can make it so that you fit."

He springs up. "Whassat, luv?" Squinty. High, patchy eyebrows. He's too calm. Gael glances down the drive and spots a van parked opposite. "You Miss Aar-pah . . . Schiarda?" he says. "Got a delifree for Miss Aar-pah. Was abaat ta leave. No one answerin. Fought you forgot. Got a few fings ow-ur aye keeya."

"Ow-ur aye keeya?" Gael echoes him, dropping the keys from between her knuckles to select the gold front door one. She gives him a stumped look and employs her Japanese: "*Nihon go ha na shi ma sen,* sorry." She turns her back.

There's a brief pause. "You kiddin?"

Gael opens the front door.

"EYE-KEE-YA," he says, "EYE-KEE-YA," leaning forward like he's singing the chorus. "DELI-FREE." A thin silver chain slips from the collar of his vest and reveals the word "WORD." Gael can hear the sales pitch: "Meh-a, innit?"

Gael says, "Oh, Ikea," and bumps the door back open with her hip. She kicks vehemently at a cat who's trying to slip in. "Yeah, fine. Harper never said. I'll leave the door off the latch. But if you let that motherfucking cat in, it's caterole supper and I don't give an SPCA who squeals."

"Right, miss." He shakes his head. "Yor scary."

There's a whole flat full of furniture in the boxes they haul up the three flights of stairs. A cupboard, dining table, chairs, bedside cabinets, an office desk, a chest of drawers, rugs. All sorts of kitchen tackle. Before they leave, Gael doesn't disguise her taking in of his unexpectedly fresh white musk while she signs his sheets. His skin is buffed as young leather. He's wearing a ribbed gray vest and jeans. He's a foot taller than her, while she's still in heels. She looks up at him, with a stern expression, then down again. She mutters over the third and final signature, "I bet all the girls let you make the bed."

They're both breathing hard. Gael had insisted on lifting boxes. The other bloke's back in the van already. She feels this one take stock of her. Her photo-free, plant-free, relic-free flat. He slides the pen from her grip and goes to the kitchen counter. He rips a sheet from a roll of paper towels and writes his number. He struts back. Passes it into her hand, by her thigh and, like an actor delivering his only line, says:

"Case tha pussy-cah sneak in lay-ah."

He puts the pen between his teeth, walks backward to the door, squinting, and smacks the top of the door frame with both peach-clean hands.

When Gael hears the front door shut, she strips off her rigid, clammy clothes, kicks her shoes so hard across the living room that one heel lances the wall plaster like a dud dart, then she tears open every piece of packaging in sight. Tying her hair back with an elastic band that had held two desk legs together, she spreads a manual on the floor with her knee and stuffs the plastic sachet of nails into her bra as a slipshod implant. She builds the furniture into being. Its stability is tenuous, but one can only work with what's been given. Each nail gets hammered irremovably in. She doesn't pause to put on music or to draw curtains or to drink a glass of wine or water or to piss. Not for five hours does she remember that she has a body. Not until Harper, who obsessively controls her disorder with medication, gets home at nine to find all her furniture fully assembled and loses her actual shit.

Harper had introduced herself as a Las Vegan, riding on the cashmere coattails of her folks, who didn't know she'd switched from architecture to comparative lit (and her dad's idea of a good book was the Book of Mormon), "but London's a long-haul flight from Rack City, so they'll just have to do like the locals and deal."

She'd said all this to the sixteen-strong class during icebreaker intros to a course called Descent to the Underworld, which the tutor hadn't shown up for and which Gael had decided to teach.

Gael was trying out a literature course, partly because she wanted to know what Readers—that boredom-resistant species—had over everyone else evolutionarily (she suspected there was something), partly because it was an assignment-only course (no exams) and because she'd found a contractor online from Sri Lanka called Sangeeta who was halfway through a PhD in late medieval writings about the body and was willing to work on single-use essays for a nominal hourly rate. (Having an escrow account made the whole thing fair trade.)

Gael had passed the tutorial room an hour before class to find a memo taped up, declaring the afternoon's 6AACTL65 Descent to the Underworld seminar canceled, "due to personal circumstances, with apologies for the short notice." It was the first day of the semester, the first day of year three and a crying shame to let a class go untaught—an underworld un–descended into. Gael pocketed the memo and returned when the students were seated. She found Harper loitering by the door, yell-whispering into her BlackBerry: "*Get a friggin autopsy already.* I'm coming home when he punches through the coffin lid, Mom. So you can take your airline tickets—" If one could print one's inner turmoil on a T-shirt, Harper would have it in six shades of purple. She lent instant color to the circle of gray-skinned lethargics. Gael gave her a discreet nod and ushered her in. Closing the door behind them, Gael took a seat at the head of the table.

"I've just received a message from Dr. Wilkins asking me to sub in for today's seminar. She sends her apologies. Personal circumstances. As her PhD supervisee, she's asked me to lead our opening seminar on Greek folk laments translated by David Ricks, which I trust you've all read carefully, ultimately to understand how ancient generations of poets considered the afterlife. But first, put your laptops and phones away and we'll do a round of intros. Your name, birthplace, major, favorite opening line and what you'd say to Ovid if you met him in a pub. Let's go counterclockwise, like the shadow of a north-facing obelisk."

Inertia is most people's default state of motion. Their only mode of progress, if you can call it that. They are startled—grateful, even—to encounter a force that might change their assumed trajectory. What is this sudden expectation up to which one must live? Steadily, they inflate. They'd do the work for the rest of the class. Gael could have sat back, prospecting, if it weren't for Harper. She was her own force pair; at once the action and the equal and opposite reaction. The human experience was a conundrum for the elucidation of which she sure as heck wouldn't look to other people. To books, perhaps, or to the medicine cabinet. When asked to introduce herself, Harper had said: "I'd prefer not to," then stared expectantly at Gael, who knit her brow and gestured to the next student along. "Like Bartleby? The scrivener?" Harper looked around the circle of scalps disbelievingly. *"Melville?"*

"Very good," Gael said, deaf to the joke as the rest of the under-read class.

"England's such a letdown if you grew up on Dickens," Harper said.

No one even took offense, for how genuinely she meant it. Harper was to Gael what Gael was to everyone else.

(The next day, in the most well-meaning voice she could muster, Gael told Dr. Wilkins she'd led the class as a favor. Mortified, Dr. Wilkins warned Gael she could be charged with impersonation and be expelled and how could she possibly. But what are a group of fee-paying students to *do* when a tutor cancels class at the last moment, when they've already paid for their train tickets and textbooks? Gael passed for attendance without joining a single other seminar and graded well above average on her coursework. Sangeeta was a dab hand at Dante.)

When they bumped into each other in a café a few weeks later, Harper took off her headphones. "The underworld's been dull with-out you. It's like we're tryna get to Hades but the ferryman went AWOL." She was listening to a *Café Sounds* soundtrack, in a café, which Baudrillard would be proud of, she said. Gael said no one should be proud of that. Harper said she didn't come to a café to hear public mastication (glowering at the guy next to her who was slop-pily fellating a sausage roll). "That's super antisocial." Harper turned back to Gael. "Meat eaters. Someone's gotta give em beef." A half hour later, Harper had invited Gael to move into a one-bedroom flat she was in the process of buying on behalf of her property tycoon dad. "It's got a walk-in wardrobe that'd make for super cheap rent, if you're chill with having a roommate who could trump Freud's Dora with an ace of spades and bury her with it."

"If you're saying you're nuts, I've a brother with a delusional disorder. He thinks he's got epilepsy. Takes placebo drugs in careful doses and won't step foot in a nightclub."

Harper cast her unmade-up hazel eyes over Gael. "If he looks like you, is he single?"

"If you don't count his two kids."

"Are you single?"

"And I plan to stay that way. Does this walk-in wardrobe have a lock?"

Harper knocked back her coffee and pulled a tequila-shot face. "Come on." She swung round on the stool, her feet dangling above its footrest. "I'll show you."

"Now?" Gael asked.

"It's now or now. Stein time, baby. If you hate it, make like Nancy Reagan and Just Say No. I still win cuz I get to tell my therapist I took someone home with me. That'd be a *big* step for me. Like . . . lunar."

Gael was running through all the ventures she could put the saved rent funds toward; as if her decision would come down to expediency and not that she found it difficult to (want to) tune out of Harper's singular frequency.

"I hope you ride sidesaddle," Harper said, accusingly.

Gael followed her out of the café to her rust-caked, basket-case bike. "I most certainly don't." Still, she hopped on the pannier rack. Boycotted the zeroes of her code. Observed the marzipan-hued tan of Harper's nape as they rode; held the tender of her midriff. Harper was oblivious to the coup that had been getting Gael to ride sidesaddle.

Over the months that followed, Gael was clear that they'd be flatmates only; that she wasn't in the market for friends; that she didn't want to get to know Harper because she found people disappointing and would rather be spared the daily tally of Harper's shortcomings. But Harper vetoed that scenario, saying part of her OCD was the compulsion to speak her mind frankly and indelicately, regardless of consequence—she found it practically impossible to bend her behavior gently around others and that was why her life has been how it's been. "How's that? you ask." Gael hadn't, but was given the information nonetheless. Harper managed her behavioral issues by burying her head in books. Through her first undergraduate degree in literature and creative writing (at twenty, her thesis had been a memoir called *Chronicles from My Porn-Flyer School Route*), she'd gotten a clerk job at a Las Vegas library. Alphabetizing was eighth-of-an-orgasm-satisfying and there were no patrons to brashly shush. "Vegas isn't famous for its libraries." In books—particularly history-drenched European fiction—she found the perfect antidote to her only-childhood of sprinkler weather, window glare and donut glazing. Her commune-nostalgic mom and low-double-digit-IQ dad feared that the only career for bookworms was teaching and, knowing Harper's way with people, they tried to encourage her in other directions. She took them up on it. London for a degree in architecture. She was halfway through a scholarship-funded master of arts at the time, but they agreed. And so she came.

Though they've lived together for seven months now, the apartment has been basically unfurnished. Harper drops her backpack and her jaw upon arrival and gusts around the newly Ikea'd living room, opening and closing all the doors and drawers, which takes quite a while and serves to calm her down from raging to merely riled.

"It's like giving someone a sheet of bubble wrap that's popped already."

Gael wipes her brow with her slippery forearm and says that some people would consider it a favor and why wasn't she home to collect the delivery anyway.

"No one was supposed to be home. They were supposed to think it was their bad and come back in the morning. I got the *Gravity's Rainbow* audiobook so I could spend the weekend building this stuff . . . *I* wanted to build it, Gael. None of the NHS shrinks know how to friggin medicate. Wait, why is there a hole in the wall? Put some clothes on so I can think straight. Good *Lord,* why can't you keep the apartment neat as your bikini line? What *is* that, a Venezuelan? That is the flag of one patriotic country." She clocks Gael's interview outfit on the carpet and hears the familiar silence following a roulette spin. "*Shit,* I'm *sorry.* How'd it go?"

Gael pulls the plastic sachets from her bra and drops them to the carpet. "I got a woman."

Harper raises her hands in the air and plonks them onto her head. "That *blows.*"

"Played by the rules."

"Sure she did."

"Roadblocker fuck."

"Forget it, Gael. Get dressed. Take a shower first though. Something stinks. Whatta ya bet the cat dumped a bunch of rat guts in our drainpipes? Wait. Did she not go for the Russian business thing? I swear-to-god, if it weren't for Kipling, I'd never believe this country was ever an empire. Don't even tell me. Let's take a walk around the block. Those goddamn wind chimes kept me up all night. I'm gonna find em, cut em down, make em into earrings, gift-wrap em and mail em to the owner so they know how friggin ding-a-ling my world's been."

Gael holds her hand out to stymie Harper's talk. She runs through several scenarios in silence, as if angled in a game of snooker, figuring a way to get at the object ball by cueing the black. There's no reason not to take her time, except for patience.

"What?" Harper says, wary of Gael's design.

"Put on something posh," Gael says.

They've never gone out at night together. Harper's stunned. "Posh like, equestrian?"

"Put on the classiest clothes that you own." Gael heads for the shower and revises the demand over running water. "Nothing on the color spectrum, unless it's mulberry silk or vicuña wool or obviously designer. Think, if Eton let in girls."

Harper shimmies in pleasure and bother, as if one or the other can be shaken off. Dressing up and leaving the house on a Friday night is something that friends do. Gael had warned her against hoping to become anything more than one another's convenience. She'd been warned against placing her hope anywhere in Gael's vicinity. The only bond between them would be the five hundred pounds for the closet room, but even that Harper had deemed unnecessary— her dad would use five hundred pounds for a hankie.

"I got a Roberto Cavalli blouse with huge pearl buttons?" Harper offers. "In London, pearls are posh, right? In Nevada they're . . . unsanitary." As if to suppress a hernia, she places her hand over her gut as Gael emerges from behind the shower curtain, saying, "I'll dress you."

Harper's skin is tanned, but her eyes have the deeper mauve-brown color of an old bruise, which offsets her healthy countenance. She has a creased neck, like linen that's been worn all day, which Gael constantly finds herself wanting to stretch out. Her toffee-colored hair is shoulder-blade-length, layered and tied in a ponytail so high it fountains down on her face, and a grown-out fringe falls all around her temples. Though she's short, she likes to rest her elbow on Gael's shoulder when they're waiting for the kettle to boil in the morning. She knows not to talk pre-coffee. They have their own, separate cafetières. Gael's always up early and Harper eventually emerges to find Gael with her arms crossed before the kettle, staring at the clouds out the window, envious of their pace and impulse.

"You're an anomaly," Harper says, assessing Gael's appearance. "Most Irish people are radishes. Pink on the outside, white underneath. Speck of mud on their cheeks. Kinda oval. Adorably bucolic. If you're Irish-American, you're a conch. Same pink-white thing going on, only with more rolls, and shiny, like you been glossed. But you, you're just white. Whiter than a French flag—"

"We have to switch to the Jubilee line," Gael interrupts. She hasn't heard a word. She is busy reconfiguring her immediate future; since the moment she'd finished weaving a magic carpet, the higher-ups had brandished a staple gun. Her finances feel newly like her feet—cinched. The government's Student Loans Company covers her tuition but, instead of taking their fixed-rate five-thousand-pound-a-year "maintenance loan" (and supplementing it with bar work), Gael had found a private provider of a larger "prodigy loan" that didn't require university sign-off but for which she'd had to pay an "origination fee" and whose variable interest rate was tied to the London Inter-bank Offered Rate. Had she consulted Jarleth in 2009, he might have directed her otherwise. Then again, statistics attest that one is generally richer in the future. After rent and utilities, Gael has seventy-eight pounds a week in spending money. What she earns through project-based online enterprises, she reinvests into her education (Sangeeta and suchlike; prodigious robes like the one she wears now).

Harper groans and fishes two weighted poker chips from her bag. A black and a blue. She flips them over and back between her fingers. It sounds like the start of a hail shower. She doesn't play poker because—although it's largely a skills game (the house wins all luck games in the end)—it requires careful control of one's opinions and tells; a mastery of interaction unavailable to Harper. Chess, by contrast, is an *all*-skills game. No conduct control required. Harper *can* play chess (though she was kicked out of the college club for not having the basic requisite Cold War subtlety) but Gael won't compete with her because she can't stand being locked into an inevitable sequence of losses. Why play a game in which you only have a few precious moves at the start to determine your fate? There's no improvising, after a point. Just death by inches.

It seems as if everyone on the Underground is entitled to stare at Gael, from the black thrust of her hair to the shadow cast by her tapered chin, down. As if it's their right to engulf a person, as if the person has waived the privacy of their skirt, yielded their direction to a greater body—the public—by coming out Dressed Like That. She thinks of Guthrie. How people leer as they like at his seizures. The only windfall of his life is that he wasn't born female. A man sitting opposite gapes into the cleavage of Gael's toes in her stilettoes. She's wearing the interview shoes. No bandages. No stockings. No ointment or relief. When she put the shoes back on, the pain reminded her of a wasp sting: the sharp difference in positions of attack and defense. Gael slips her feet out of the shoes and watches the man's reaction to her sores. He remains po-faced, sluglike, but she can hear a newly heavy breathing through his nose. Finally, he looks up. Gael leans forward a fraction and, very slowly, very quietly—so that even Harper, who's standing beside where Gael is seated on the busy tube, doesn't hear—says, "*Disgusting.* Isn't it." Something at the other end of the carriage urgently requires the man's attention.

Harper, however, isn't so used to the stares. She's standing and gripping a pole, which means ogling is solicited. Especially under artificial light. It would be a waste to miss out on those detectable, delectable seams; the soft bulges surrounding them. Harper is much curvier than Gael, so the body-hugging, long-sleeved mottled gray dress makes a louder-than-intended statement. A chiffon scarf is built into the neckline and hangs as a loosely tied bow over her bust. To shake off some of the eyes, she wrestles on a Vera Wang charcoal coat. She's used to wearing designer clothes, but of the harem pants and boxy polka-dotted shirt variety. It's not her looks that usually get her noticed. It's the other thing.

"Everybody stay calm. Uh-huh, I'm a train wreck, but you don't need to freak out unless you're *inside of me.* The damage is contained to the dress." A few people do the socially responsible thing and avert their gaze. Others snicker. She turns to Gael. "I feel like my mom's Pilates coach Sandy from Palm Beach. Only, Sandy gets gratuities. In the States, people say what they want and they're not shy about it. They own it. Here, they just, like, squint at it sourly. It's lame. Anyway, I judge you for owning this dress. And for not wearing stockings. It's sub-sixty. Your nipples are like candy corn. Are we getting off here? I sure as hell know that guy is."

Yeah, Gael absently affirms. But then she thinks to caution Harper. After all, she doesn't know the thickness of this wise-guy armor; which arms it can resist. Prepare for more of it, she says. The slavering. Prowling. The pant of expectation. Only worse. Animals are allowed into these casinos. They are the ungelded defenders of Finance. This is the Isle of Dogs.

II

"'You seem all here so hideously rich.'" Harper cranes her neck at the glass skyscrapers. "Henry James. *The Ivory Tower.*" The gloom across her eyes might be homesickness or, just as easily, pity. "Difference is," she says, "in Vegas, the shiny buildings invite you in. They're welcoming."

Gael looks up at One Canada Square, clad in stainless steel and paned in glass dense enough to bear an abnormal loading of wind—to insulate its people from rainy days and thermal expansion both. The pyramid roof flashes to let aircraft know it's there, lest anyone forget. Its ranking as the tallest building in England will soon be bested by The Shard, being erected to the west, but that's half owned by the state of Qatar, so who's counting. Citigroup. HSBC. Bank of America. Barclays. Clifford Chance. Fitch Ratings. J. P. Morgan. Moody's. Skadden. State Street. Thomson Reuters. All the menfolk, none of them gents.

"Wall Street would be a fairer comparison than the Strip," Gael says, "but I get what you're saying. You guys own all of this anyway. Canary Wharf. For now. One of Morgan Stanley's groupies. But the US lost its wallet and is resorting to selling its body. So it's only a matter of picking the sultan with the deepest wellbore."

"Touché!" Harper says. "Can we leave now?"

"Not yet."

"I want so bad to be out with you." Harper looks in dismay at the demographic. She's never been to this part of London and there's a reason for that. Gael has only ever run past and she has always picked up her pace to a veritable sprint. Shaped by a loop in the Thames and a loophole in the public consciousness, the wharf makes for a turning point. Running always seemed an apt mode of movement through the region. She'd often imagined coming here on purpose and not in running shoes, as she would have for the MBA's internship, and she'd have said, "There's been some mix-up. I'm interviewing for the Business Line Specialist position," once she was in the chair, and there was a whole script that would have followed. It would have been like using one's queen early—right at the outset—and skipping over the laborious middle, the tedious pawn movements which are only a means to an end. She looks around, as if for a lever.

For an age, this was one of the world's busiest docks. Sugar, coffee, bananas, elephants, huge hogsheads of commercial cargo would arrive from the Canary Islands, heralding Britain's prosperity—in an age when worth wasn't yet wed to perception.

"It used to be all warehouses," Gael tells Harper. "The workers wore pocketless clothes to stop them hiding fistfuls of sugar. There were heists in the night. So they built warehouses to store everything, half a mile wide." She sweeps her arm out in front of them. "It must have seemed so solid, half a mile's worth of brick. So secure and permanent. Till it was poleaxed in the Blitz. Sugar bricks and mortars make ash, evidently. And look what rose from it. A phoenix on steroids."

"If you said all this to the MBA lady, it explains why you didn't make the cut."

Someone drops a champagne flute into the water from a yacht that's moored at the quay and all the guests on the deck make a fuss until some bright spark shouts, "It was plonk!" and every Thomas, Richard and Harrie repeats it in hysteric concentric circles and someone thinks to write it down for posterity. "Priceless."

"Uncle Avery had a catamaran," Harper says. "Before he went

under. Now Dad's got a catamaran. And a new condo in Malibu, cuz you can't set sail on a mirage. He wants to do a big Schiada spree this summer but he's gotta learn to drive the thing. You should come."

"Yes," Gael says with energy, remembering. "Just keep talking like that. Perfect." Steering Harper toward a swanky bar on the ground floor of the Bank of America building, she adds, "You're perfect."

A bloom of color appears on Harper's neck, which makes the creases stand out, and she says, "Thanks," with no attitude whatsoever. Gael can almost hear the click of the drawer Harper has opened in her mind to store that in—*You're perfect*—a drawer she will open and shut and open and shut and open. "It's all I ever wanted to be," she says, recovering.

Gael wonders if she has spoiled her prop at the last moment. She halts. Toughen him up, went Jarleth's instruction. No one's going to shake his hand if they think they'll break it. "Go straight up to the counter and open a tab on your dad's card. I'll have a Mayfair martini, extra olives. I haven't eaten since breakfast. Get yourself a bourbon. Do not pay. Meet you at the bar."

"Wait—you're not coming with me?"

"In a minute." Gael audits the buildings up ahead. "I'll come in the private entrance."

"Are you tryna get another interview?"

Gael starts walking off. "No. I don't want that anymore."

Harper cracks all the knuckles of all of her fingers in a leftward and upward motion. She calls out: "You're always saying how women change their minds."

Gael turns back. "And you're here with me. Don't change yours. Just . . . use acronyms."

Harper nurses her knuckles now by pressing them against her ribs. "Like OCD?"

"Like CDO."

"What's that?"

"You don't need to know."

"But I wanna."

"Don't forget the olives," Gael says, and grimaces, the pain in her feet catching up with her each time she comes to a standstill.

"Well, that's rude." Harper uses her loud voice. "Dress me up like a doll. Duct-tape my mouth. Wanna punch me in the intellect while you're at it?"

Gael is facing the ticker tape alighting and bending around the corner of the Thomson Reuters building, with its cryptic script of letters, arrows and numbers that Jarleth had once taught her to regard like a grown-up alphabet. All alphas. The fluctuating price of securities. The ticker tape spells out: "The right information in the right hands leads to amazing things."

"I'm the one that picked you for a fake tutor," Harper says. "What's CDO? Teach me to speak BS, Irish."

Gael takes a sharp, shallow breath and comes right up to Harper, as if to deliver a slap. "Take a type of debt, like a mortgage. Investment banks look at debt and see products. Once upon a time, they decided to buy mortgages in bulk from lenders and to group that debt with other loans into little tradable clusterfucks. Then, they sold those collateralized debt obligations—bunches of mortgages—to investors who couldn't be fucked to look beyond the sexy interest rates. They sold *so* many CDOs they ran out of debt to chuck in the silo. So to continue their spree, they gave mortgages to people who *really* shouldn't have them. 'With all this demand, you'll make free money when your house price leaps by twenty percent against the teaser interest rates, which aren't fixed but don't concern yourselves with that.' Meanwhile, the investor's licking his lips at the loopholes the investment banks are designing with rating agencies, whose job it is to say: Well done, Morgan. You got a triple A in accounting.

But there's not enough As to go round. So when they start running out of safe triple A–rated CDOs, they figure out how to wave their dick wands and turn BBBs into eighty percent AAAs. AKA: shitty mortgages went through a rigged calculator and became safe ones. Abracadaver. Traders were making more G than they could stuff down their hookers' thongs in commissions while, on the side, they took out insurance against it all, for good measure. You could get insurance on CDOs called credit default swaps, because there's always a Congress-sucking insurer willing to make money off Armageddon. AIG took the flipside of the bet. The quarterly premiums from the credit default swaps gave them shedloads of cash to pay themselves bonuses, because Armageddon almost never happens. Speculators could buy credit default swaps too and did, by the billions. Deep down they knew you could take money both ways and, if it was fucked, so was the economy and no one needed to lose sleep over it because bankers aren't friends with the plebs who'd get kicked out of their homes, and their AIG friends would survive with their hands in the government's pockets because there's more than lint in those chinos. What are you going to do? Let the planes fall out of the sky? Besides, all the newly homeless people who'd been robbed of everything they owned probably needed to learn how to live within their means."

Harper's gaze has been going from Gael's mouth to her eyes and back again, as if trying to catch the subtitles without missing the action. Gael adjusts the scarf on Harper's dress the way old movie wives adjusts their husbands' ties in the morning before they go breadwinning. She points to the Bank of America sign nested high in the building before them. "Your dad's on the board."

"Oh great. I'm a son of a cunt."

Gael nods slowly. "Aren't you?"

"Oh sure." Harper takes her time. "Pop's got a big old stake in this place. And we were brought up vegan, so I'm not talking sirloin."

"Sterling," Gael says, smiling finally.

"You bet your ass."

They can take their liquor. They've been practicing by keeping up drink for drink with the characters of *Mad Men* while sitting cross-legged on the living room floor, watching Gael's laptop blearily like sunrise after an all-nighter. These glasses are heavier than the tahini jars they're used to drinking from. The spirits are smoother. The granite bartop doesn't need wiping, though Harper unconsciously does so every time she rests her elbow on it. She's listening to Gael listening to the trio of suits next to them the way a cub listens to the movement of the mother lion's body for signs of a prize. The bar is quieter now than it would have been earlier. It's a postwork sterilizer kind of place: Copper pendant lights on dimmers. Reflective surfaces. Synthetic music whispering sweet-'n'-sour nothings.

Gael, Harper and the three suits are the only ones at the bar. All the round tables are occupied. Gael doesn't have to say much to be heard. She's speaking a language Harper isn't versed in, but Harper leans in and involves herself like a customer. "It's risky post-crash, now they know the tranch engineering's titanic," Gael says. "It comes down to how quickly they'll act. Student fees are set to double next year, if not triple." She goes on like this. "Right," Harper says, then indicates (by pointing longingly at her groin) that she has to pee. "But Gael," she adds, in what she thinks is a whisper, "I'm sitting here like an extra, in it for the snack bar. When I get back, my part's gotta get interesting. For a start, you could call me Ginzel?"

Gael waves her off. This day has to arrive somewhere, in the end; grant her some access. Perhaps bringing Harper was a mistake. She won't be made a wingwoman. She's too inflexibly, unreservedly herself.

One of the men is Australian, on a jolly. He has skin the color and grain of mature cheddar, light-brown hair and a goatee in the shape of a beer-can pull-tab. The can's open. He watches Harper dismount her bar stool as if she's a waitress managing a tray, impressively for that sort of thing. His stance is impractically wide. But it's the guy closest to Gael who's been listening to them. He's turned to the barman to settle the tab. As he takes his credit card back, Gael can see it doesn't belong to him. It's not platinum. Lowly gold. A company card probably. His jazz-hands splay of straw-textured, straw-colored hair signals a kind of disarray that would never have been tolerated in the financial district a few years back. Now, reckless abandon is a good look. He has an accidental time-traveler air, in a tucked-in navy polo shirt, a Hilfiger cardigan with navy piping, checkered trousers and tidy leather sports shoes that so perfectly match his belt they might have come in a set.

"I'll bet you our bar tab that's a golf glove in your pocket," Gael says, without glancing again at the bulge.

He only flashes his veneers for a brief moment, in place of eye contact. Then he lines the bottom row of his big-ticket teeth with the top and makes a small whistle, directed at the barman, holding the credit card out between his index and middle fingers, like a cigarette. The barman feigns confusion, buying himself time to control his anger before deigning to pluck the card from the golfer's neatly cuticled fingers that show no sign of a tip. The golfer jolts his head to his right and says, "The ladies' beverages." (Pronounced "behfridges.")

Gael resists giving the barman a sympathetic look. The whole part, nothing but.

"I have a client who loves to knock one off on Saturdays at dawn. Then he likes to play golf." He shakes his left wrist so that his watch hangs loose as a bracelet. He checks it. "Plenty of time to drink enough to make his defeat a near miss and not the total fucking disgrace it would be were I to play sober."

"What's your handicap?" Gael asks.

"Single malt. Ten or so."

She smiles, a little.

"Let's just say I catch the occasional birdie." He smiles, a lot. "No. In all seriousness, I'm decidedly average. But my client's diabolical, so it's a picnic. Are you here on business?"

"Are you asking if I'm an escort?"

"Should I be?" He puts his hand in his pocket and takes out what was, in fact, a handkerchief.

Gael considers it. Who carries a handkerchief? She draws her hair from her right temple and across, so that it's after-hours hair, which trickles back into place.

"Allergies," he says, in an accent so posh Gael takes a moment to translate it and is reminded of her interview.

"I was giving a presentation," she says.

"A pre-sentation? That's vague. What symptoms were you presenting with?"

Gael takes a deep breath. "Oh, ennui mostly."

The golfer makes a disgusted face. "Sounds ghastly. By the way, your American friend, she's loud. Are you doing her a favor?"

Gael lets out something like a pant. "If you think she's loud, you shouldn't compete. Not in here. Her dad's the chief." Gael sticks her thumb up to the ceiling.

The golfer curls his lip. "The chief what? The chief philistine? The Almighty Chief?"

Gael shakes her head, dismounts the chair.

Returning to the bar, Harper veers a little, eyeing up the white baby grand in the corner. She delivers her purse to Gael (as if to fix up), looks right through the golfer and addresses the barman: "Is this one of those bars with no license to play music?"

"Excuse me, ma'am?"

"Like, what's it, Weatherfork? Can't play tunes."

The barman sucks his lower lip and raises his brows. It's not his night. "There's music playing, ma'am."

"Not that *I* hear," Harper says.

"Is it too quiet? I'd turn it up . . ."

"Turning it up won't make it music."

Harper walks over to the piano and lands on the chair. Now the golfer, the Aussie and the other sharp-suited one are, all at once, her audience. *De-du-de-du-de-du-deh-deh-deh.* "Für Elise," right hand index finger only. The barman shifts his weight and dries his brow with the towel he's been polishing glasses with. *De-deh-deh, de-deh-deh.* Harper moves her feet onto the pedals and adds the left hand, remembering how it goes. With each second, she picks up pace and fluency until the music is recognizable, until its rendition is adequate, then more so. *De-du-de-du-de-du . . . De-de-de-de dedl-dedl-deh-deh, de-de-de-de dedl-dedl-deh.* Mozart's "Turkish March" for a few bars, then she moves back to "Für Elise," as if she's forgotten what she was playing. But no, she's alternating between them. A "Für Elise"–"Turkish March" mash-up, then something by Chopin, expertly woven in. She plays with precision in place of musicality. She doesn't sway forward or close her eyes. She sits up perfectly straight and watches whichever hand has the hardest part. Sive would never hire her, but Gael would. All the conversations in the bar have stopped and a few people get up from their seats to move closer, mouths agape in delight. Then Harper halts in the middle of a phrase and stands. She looks at the barman. "This thing needs tuning. It's flat as Uncle Avery's EKG." She closes the lid.

The golfer takes out his phone and car keys. He talks to the receiver: "Siri, call the club." The automaton responds: "Phoning the club." He puts the phone to his ear. "Charlie. We've picked up a couple of strays. Jules plus four. . . . Just so." He hangs up and tells Gael, "You and Ludwig come with us."

"She's called Ginzel," Gael says.

Harper arrives in time to hear this and beams at Gael, taking back her purse.

Jules says, "She's Gin, you're Tonic, I'm parched."

His car is parked around the corner. A silver convertible Alfa Romeo 8C Spider. 2010. Harper and Gael sit in the back with the Australian. Miller, they call him. Jules drives, moving the group through its gears. The most serious of them is in the passenger seat, with a set of golf clubs between his legs. His wet soil hair is hoed backward in a Germanic style, circa 1940. His suit is postcoital slick. His name's Aaron, based on what's coming out of Jules's mouth, which doesn't once address Gael or Harper for the fifteen-minute ride across town. Miller helps himself to a little stash of coke from his shirt pocket. Gael considers asking for some to rub into the sores of her feet. It would burn like an electric eel and make the skin numb, she imagines. It seems an appropriate request. But Miller passes the sachet to Aaron, who sniffs straight from the plastic, grunts, closes the zip lock and pockets it. Miller opens the window. He bites his nails and spits the slivers out. Gael clenches her pelvic muscles at the jagged bitten remains.

"Miller," Jules warns.

Miller closes the window. His right leg jigs. He stares now at Harper's knee, the contours of which are sheathed by the gray dress and a stocking beneath. She's sitting in the middle, with her seat belt on. As if it's a square of chocolate he might break off and eat, he reaches out and traces the outline of her patella. He takes it in his pincers and squeezes.

Barely keeping it together, Harper asks Gael: "What's the acronym for this situation?"

Miller lets go and says in an accent that makes his tongue sound half-swallowed, "You've got large kneecaps. Laaage."

Harper lifts her purse to her lap as a shield. "All the better to knee you with."

Miller tightens his lips, which makes the pull-tab goatee warp. He bucks forward and grabs the driver's seat by its headrest. "Will those fuckwits from Lloyds be in Zurich?"

The women are dismissed. Harper makes an *Are you kidding me* face. Then: *I can't even.* She hates herself for being in this car. It must bring back high school traumas, where the boys could break your spirit with half a sentence. Gael's grateful for her half-arsed single-sex schooling. She takes Harper's hand, knitting her fingers through. "They can be so kneedy."

Harper watches Gael's hand in hers, feels the weight of it on her lap. Two hands are disproportionately weightier than one. "I always wanted to do a car-door jump and roll," Harper says. She glances at the door handle, then at Gael, who is meeting Aaron's challenge in the mirror of the lowered passenger sun visor. He suspects her.

"*Doku kuwaba sara made,*" Gael responds, and holds firm, staring ahead. "Japanese proverb. If you're going to eat poison, include the plate."

◆

At first, Harper was aroused by the three layers of plum velvet curtains in the ladies' club entrance, which had the façade of a multistory early-to-bed Victorian town house and no sign outside to let the public know it was there. And what a quirk that behind the third curtain, a tuxedo-clad lady waited to take not only their coats but their bags—this was a place where people had all they needed in their pocket or on their tongue—and gave them merely a nod in place of a ticket. Harper made a scene of fishing out her poker chips before she would hand over her purse. This behavior was treated as admirably demanding. So far so good. But then she caught sight of the clientele. Sherry-suckling Tory champions. Mute blond globe-boobed beings who survived on liquids and preferred pin-striped laps over seats, as if they were kitty-cats. Bartenders who had been to finishing school, had had their certificates framed, who weren't even "really actors."

"Good luck getting that back in the bottle," Harper told the cocktail waiter when she was charged ninety-two pounds for a shot of bourbon (which she had selected by pointing at the shapeliest bottle). "Just cuz I got cash don't mean I'm gonna suck it."

Miller cocked his eye at the server in a *tosh* sort of way and took the bourbon from the bartop. He sniffed it luxuriantly, dipped his pinky finger into the glass, then wiped the finger behind Harper's ear. She flinched. He leaned in and sniffed her. Then withdrew from slapping range. "Nah," he said. "Still cheap." He knocked the shot back, slid the tumbler across the counter and absconded to the cigar room, where the others sat in padded, high-backed chairs under hundred-thousand-pound paintings hanging casually as mistletoe. The place was lair after lair of opulence—private cocktail corridors that opened onto a dark disco basement with talcum powder pluming all around, a soundproofed Victorian drawing room, a library lounge, a billiards room with decorated leather walls. In the washrooms were alcoves with stools before floor-to-ceiling mirrors where daddy-long-legged women were struggling to find fault with their pores. There were heated towels and little perfume vials to slot within one's cleavage. It wasn't long before Gael realized that Harper would never ever serve as a prop.

The only reason she hadn't left was that she was enjoying cracking Gael up by practicing the comebacks she could have used on Miller, had he been worth it. This place was nothing new to Harper. She had seen some equivalent of it before and, anyway, like most Americans, she said, she was happy to glean from movies that places and people like this exist. "We're big old believers. Don't have to peel back the bandage to know what's infected." But Gael hadn't been to a place like this before. And it was better to step into a world, however unwelcoming, than only to see it through a window.

"There's a taxi rank around the corner," Gael told Harper.

"The lady's seen the headlight! Halalooyah. Let's get the heck out of here. Falafel kebabs on the way home? You're reminding me of Kafka's 'Hunger Artist.'"

Gael looked down the corridor. She could see Jules's golf shoes, crossed at the ankles. She'd lost the feeling in her feet, but didn't budge. It finally dawned on Harper that she was being sent away, alone, and she stood there, stunned. She let her belly hang, the moderate swell that was in it. "I don't get it. What are you planning—"

"Please don't make a scene," Gael said, finding it hard to meet Harper's eye. "Just—"

"Right. Sure. No. I'll just hit up Craigslist or whatever. For a new roommate."

Gael took a deep breath. This was a reminder. "Honestly, this isn't about you."

"Oh sure. That's obvious." Harper shook her head and shoulders. "C U L." Harper made the letters with her fingers, then stuck her middle finger up and flushed. "Or not." She left. A minute later, she hustled back up the stairs—her chest and neck blooming like strawberries dropped in a flute of champagne—with the message: "If you let that drunk-driving golfer drive you anywhere, I'm never speaking to you again."

It would be some kind of relief to have told Harper. But she had already gone. He won't be driving anywhere. Gael had left the passenger door open. Soon, she'd insist on their taxiing to his apartment. Her dad died in a drink-driving accident, she'd say, when he got pushy. If the car hadn't been stolen by morning for the clubs alone, its battery might well be flat as that baby grand. But no. She couldn't have said that much. If she had, Harper would have needed to know why. She would have wanted to grasp the untouchable ins and outs of Gael's devotions, as if, like the whole train carriage, she had a right to watch every contour of her intention—each and every girl give herself away.

✦

In the billiards room, Miller had been harassing Aaron about his ranking on April's scoreboard for their little VP team game of clocking up the most expenses per month on their company cards. They get receipts from escort companies for laundry services ("she'll never get the stain out, gents"), they buy new suits as protective clothing ("for rainy days, bankers need insolvent bibs") and return flights to Fiji whenever their air points for any given airline are set to drop from Heroin to Platinum membership. The night reached peak backslapping when Jules used Gael as an excuse to recall the time they employed Citigroup's teamwork ethos to book out the whole business cabin for a flight to JFK, which they knew had been the flight decided upon for an international Deutsche Bank conference. "Way to put the *douchebag* in Deutsche Bank," Gael muttered, filling in what Harper would have said and looking around for her reaction. Jules pulled a disappointed expression. "The lady's getting grouchy. Had we best get you to bed?" The image of all three of them surrounding her, gaffing about compounding interest rates, made her gag on her cognac.

The transformation was almost immediate, when they stepped into his apartment (heat blasting, windows open wide, lights left on—including the spotlights above his paintings, the floor lighting below the kitchen cabinets and the film studio standing lamps—all incandescents). "Sorry about all that. Trying company, I'm sure. It's all showmanship, really. Our way of alleviating the nefarious pressure of our jobs. When we're sober, we're sober. We treat our work like bloody brain surgery. And not remote-control-robot-up-the-nostril twaddle. I mean lifting skulls off like . . . yarmulkes! I'm dreadfully conscious of how many lives are on my desktop, Tonic."

"My flatmate just lent me *The God Delusion*. If you like, when I'm done—"

"It's no delusion, Tonic. No matter how much money you make for others, it's the failures that stand out in one's memory. The individuals on their knees. You do what you can to make them cognizant of how complex our products have become—how they can't possibly . . . That they often—we often, even—don't fully understand what it is we're dealing with. I forget what you do, but I know you know what I'm talking about. If I make an error . . . a misjudgment . . . it's consequential beyond . . . so many lives and careers . . . It's dreadfully . . . demanding. It's . . ."

Gael couldn't believe her eyes when Jules's chin dimpled with cellulite. "*Fucking* exhausting." He threw himself on the green leather Chesterfield and limply wept. Gael was more amused than she'd been all evening, since being with Harper. She poured herself a bourbon at his antique globe bar and considered the situation. Nothing here was from Ikea. It was the weird mixture of aesthetics afforded by someone with the means, but without the modesty, to hire a designer. He had warned her in the taxi that she might have to wait until dawn before the Prime Minister's tranquilizer wore off— he'd consumed *a stallion's dose* of the stuff—but that her removing her frock and languishing on his carpet might prove just the antidote. When he realized she had no intention of doing housework in the nude for him or of swallowing his tears, he flicked on his sixty-five-inch curved-screen TV and began defensively explaining to Gael (who sat behind the couch at the enormous dining table, messing around on his laptop) how much one could learn about markets from StarCraft, which was on the TV. He was watching people play a computer game? Gael asked. "Electronic sports. It isn't gaming. This is witnessing the nimblest, sharpest minds of our generation challenging the bounds of pattern recognition and prescience. Titter all you like, Tonic, but there are ten million followers in South Korea alone. Since my MBA, I've learned more about strategy and tenacity from watching StarCraft than I have from any roundtable or mentorship. The truth is, I have eSports to thank for salvaging my relationship with my father . . ."

Gael tuned out his hero's journey, took his credit card from his wallet on the hall table and carried it back to his laptop. Jules twisted around, his arm across the top of the couch. "What are you up to?"

"Buying lingerie," Gael said. "How do you feel about latex?" She gave a little smile. "You can write it off as protective clothing."

She could see the briefest of considerations challenging his torpor. Then he waved his hand, which sent him slipping down the leather. He drew a blanket to his chest and breathed the greedy wet breath of a drinker.

Gael opened her calendar to do a little planning. In a few months, she would have been three years in London. Far too long. She never wanted to spend another underwhelming year such as this. This was not the heart of things. Here, there was too much protocol and not enough staking. The city was sprawling and uninspiring and flat. It took too long to get across it. She needed a hill to consider her prospects. She wanted a sore neck from looking up. She searched the weather. New York's snowplows bank meters of the stuff along the sidewalks until as late as March. That means it will still be cold and the wrong side of the work year. Wait a few months. Go in August. September, maybe. After summer's dormancy, when the sharper air of expectation blows in. In the meantime, check in on Mum. Spend a long good-bye with Guthrie. Make sure his kids have an image of their auntie while she's young. It would be a while before they'd see her again.

Round-trip business-class flights, Dublin–JFK. Pay Now. She listened to Jules's snores, which sounded glad of their lot. No timbre of a life more vitally lived.

Proceed to Checkout.

No, she caught herself just in time. She'd only be met with more of the same. More Jarleths. She changed the selection to first class. Unticked the return box. One-way. That's what she wants. She clicked: Enter. Only those who will have to click Return.

✦

To sober up on the tube, she texted "unsatisfied customer" to a contact made earlier and worked down the backs of her shoes to stand on them walking home from the station so she wouldn't have to suffer a shred more than she deemed fit. A shred? She looked up the unit of measurement for suffering but found only *dols* from the Latin *dolor,* which brought to mind Jules's wad of dollars and false idols, specifically the scarecrows in cucumber fields from the Book of Jeremiah Jarleth loved to bring up, because the name began and ended as it did.

Thus He said, "Learn not the way of the nations, nor be dismayed at the signs of the heavens because the nations are dismayed at them, for the customs of the peoples are vanity. A tree from the forest is cut down and worked with an ax by the hands of a craftsman. They decorate it with silver and gold; they fasten it with hammer and nails so that it cannot move. Their idols are like scarecrows in a cucumber field, and they cannot speak; they have to be carried, for they cannot walk. Do not be afraid of them, for they cannot do evil, neither is it in them to do good."

✦

Arms crossed against the cold, shoulders lifted to the rain, her delivery waits in the doorway. He'd gotten the message. He pulls down his hood when he sees her. "Had me dow-in was you comin."

Gael drops her bag beside the pink panache plant on the doorstep. It's not the worst neighborhood in London, but she's amazed every day when the plant's not been stolen.

"What do I call you?" he asks.

"Names *can* hurt, Ikea. They're wrong to say that they can't."

The orange streetlight skims his cheekbones. "If I'm Eye-keeya, you're Buy-ah."

Gael takes out the fifty-pound note from Jules's hall table and pushes it into Ikea's trousers—not into the pocket, but inside the belt, inside the boxers, drives it past the warm tight knit of his pubic hair. "A tip." She feels the blood rushing into him. "My gosh," he says. His teeth sing in the dark. "Thass problema-ick, love. You can take that back when I done wiv you. Miss Aar-pah paid already. This just checking in like. Make sure you serviced propah." He picks her up as if she's a strongbox to carry into the house.

No. They're not going in, she says.

"Wha? You don lif wi your movah. I seen your flah."

He complies, coolly, when she says to put her down. He smoothens his clothes with his hands, trying to figure where he misunderstood. Gael doesn't spot the offense in his expression because he's squinting in the rain, which is spilling like an argument that will leave everyone cross and sick. His thin rain jacket can't be waterproof but his white musk scent must be. Without holding hands, he follows Gael around the side of the town house, where there's a strip of pavement, a narrow column of grass and a six-foot hedge for privacy. "Vat's ha' a body get pneumonia," he says, eyeballing the pavement. Gael draws him up to the textured wall by his belt and opens his jeans buttons. He lifts her face by the chin and stalls until she looks at him. Her makeup runs. "Beau-y. Like Lois Lane, comic sty-el." When he tries to kiss her, she turns her head. He turns it back to him, looks confounded. "Can't ki-shew neevah?"

She takes his hand from her chin, brings it to her mouth and spits. The saliva is half rain. He's tries to pull away from her, deciding she's a nutter. "Nah," he sings, "vis ain't worf it," but she keeps a firm hold of his hand and draws it down between her legs. She pulls her knickers to the side, keeping them on. He falters only for a moment, then wrestles with the obstacles, presses her against the wall, one arm above and tries to interlock his fingers with hers. The scabrous wall exfoliates their knuckles. She wonders why Harper's dad didn't buy a solid British redbrick, like the old warehouses of the dock. He must not be an idiot-romantic. When he moves, Ikea's jacket hisses and cracks like firewood. His muscles and ligaments inside the nylon slicker feel like bagged butcher's cuts. Skirt steaks, maybe. His penis is so thick Gael feels a tiny tear on one side of her on first entry—a soft-tissue slit that keeps being worked, as if by a thumb—and the mild pain trumps whatever pleasure could have been achieved. She draws him down onto the pavement to have all his weight on her, which is not enough. His brow is furrowed but it's too late now to change anything. Her tailbone digs into the coarse cement. He tries to protect her back and her head with his hands, cradling, but she pushes all the nonessential parts of him away. She turns from the convex meniscus of his lips, like a child from a spoon of medicine. "Do you wan this?" he's asking, gently, over and over. "You wan it like this? Out hee-ya? Say what you wan." He's asking. He's forced to take consent from her fingernails tearing his buttocks, the back of his neck, his skin that fits so tightly to his muscle that fits so tightly to his bones, it's astonishing there's any give. She's feeling for it. The margin of error. "Shit, can't you relax?" he says. "I can't keep goin you tight like tha, girl. Juss relax."

But she couldn't. She can't. She couldn't let go of him. If you press your fucking lips against my face again, she says, you better fucking draw blood. "Aw-right, I won't ki-shew." Bite me instead. "Nah. White skin mark easy," he says. "Bruise like when you squeeze a flower peh-al. I won't bite you. Won't ki-shew neevah."

Good.

"Won't warm you wi my hands. Won't hold you. Won't ask your

name. Won't come inside. Won't come back." His groin goes and
goes. Uncircumcised. And there it is. There's the give. His eyes startle like hazard lights. "Come on now, girl. You geh-in weh."

◆

The hallway lights flicker on when Gael finally goes in. Her trodden
shoes lie on the grass somewhere. London can have them. Three
flights of stairs thaw her just enough so that she can turn the key
in the lock. She's functioning in the way a phone with no credit still
lets you call emergency services. In the dark, she soundlessly goes
to the front window, looks down the street. Ikea is gone. The living
room is equipped with his wares, as if it always has been. His cum
is like sleet on her stomach. She wipes her dress against its glacial
slip. The only movement out there is weather and animal. A large
rat, or a small fox, worrying a flooded gutter. Gael reminds herself
of a shop owner, just now, standing inside her shop window, looking
out, burdened by what's going unread, unpurchased, stale. Then, the
tableau of her own mother looking out the rained window occurs to
her like a gas. She starts. Harper is there at her room door, lifting her
eye covers (cucumber slices on white cotton) to her forehead. Her
hair is a thorn-halo. She goes to say something, but breaks off at the
sound of Gael's teeth chattering. She turns on the light and forgets
sarcasm. "Where's your coat?"

Gael shakes, or shrugs, half turned.

Harper steps toward her. "Are you hurt?"

"Outside, maybe. Switch off the light."

Harper approaches Gael warily, peers out the window down to
their gate, then draws the blinds. She gets her dressing gown and
drags her duvet—still warm with sleep—from her bed to the couch.
"Get under."

"I think . . . I'll shower."

"Later." Harper sees that Gael is dripping wet and holds out the dressing gown. "Take that thing off," she says, eyeing the dress.

Gael didn't realize how drunk she must have got, but her head is hot and thick as if filled with an untried substance. There's no spinning, but her sinuses throb and all down her throat, it aches. She's on the couch when she starts to tremble. Or it could be the kettle boiling. Harper reaches around Gael's hips and behind her bottom to lift her. She peels the dress upward and Gael puts her hands routinely "up to heaven" as Guthrie had done by the pond. Just as matter-of-fact, Harper peels off the wet underthings. The shivering is its own force. She feeds Gael's hands through the gown's fleece arms and the dampness of her skin makes the fabric clump and stick. Soon she is covered by the duvet and Harper is kneeling on the carpet, cupping one of her soiled and blister-ruined feet. When the towel lands on her skin, Gael cries out, but the heat is a greater relief from the stinging cold than the sting of the sores is painful. Harper has a whole stack of face towels beside her, with one empty basin and a basin full of boiling water. She throws the first towel into the empty bowl and takes a fresh one, dips it into the boiling water and scalds herself trying to wring it out.

"I was reading Nabokov. To remember what it's like to have a friend. An' a intact ego," Harper says. "Vicodin sucks. An' I broke my vibrator. Anyway, in his novel, which is mostly a poem, there's this bit that reminded me of your brother. How you said he's barely having fits now, even though they got way worse when the kids were due. At the start. The way he talks about them like they're a gift, when they happen? The auras. Nabokov went:

> There was a sunburst in my head.
> And then black night.
> That blackness was sublime.
> I felt distributed
> through space and time.

After a moment, Harper takes another face towel from the stack and soaks it. She squeezes the excess water out. It steams around her, as if—with the cucumber eye covers on her forehead—she's performing some lavish spa therapy. She runs the hot towel up Gael's shin, then along the inside of her knee. And doesn't stop. She doesn't look up and Gael doesn't make a sound. Only, she thinks, *Of course*, and aches with all that hasn't been achieved. Harper must be able to see her, finally, how she has always wanted to see her. So she could relieve her doubt: the biggest distress of Harper's life. "It's beautiful, I thought," Harper says. "When I read that poem. Even though . . . it's meant to be a farce." She pushes the duvet aside and kisses Gael's thigh just once. She wipes Gael's white belly and hip with the towel, where someone had left their mark. She will leave no such mark. No one will ever make of Gael territory. Harper knows this. She draws the towel across Gael's sex and then meets it with her lips. The soft tissues stick, because the hot towel made the pink delicate skin dry and tight, so Harper traces her tongue around her lips and it's hard to believe anything could feel so excessive and essential at once. No textile could approximate it. No precipitation. No thing could be sunk into like the organs of speech, belonging to no one, just as Gael had wanted. Belonging only to the moment. The glug of water is the basin spilling its contents into the carpet. Tomorrow's mess. But Gael had already decided to have left, by then. She had stayed in one place too long. Foolishly lingered long. A little longer, there . . . here . . . No—it can't. It's all too formal. Foreseeable. What quality of person would push a boulder along an even field? She needs to lift herself up to be lifted. Her hips rise with her pulse and the cucumber slivers are staring at her like an idol. This is less . . . routine. This is not at all—take it or, left—hips above her head and, leave it, how did they get? there or that, dizzy. She is so like a sunflower turning, up, in spite of, its long tough stem needing, take its, light, its synthesis and she is she's, uproot risen, symbiotic—barely as much as needs bloodleft in wherever her head—the blood reversed course, must it have—it was; she tries though, tried then, to tell her, self to say nerve ending, it's, fuck, nerve only—all nerve us less— just—fuck—no function to it less, least of all, least of everything, meaning—she can't

felt

only

she could have

swallow the sound it makes
the bliss
too like a

whimper

Over.   all   too   much
                              much

now

all   too

Off.

Over.

She pushes Harper away.
She pushes her away, lovingly.
Forces her away.

5

How to Price an Option
AUGUST 2011

Home was no longer where she'd left it by the time Gael returned to its doorstep. In the year and a half since she'd been home, Guthrie had moved into a one-bedroom flat with the twins. Croftwood Drive, Cherry Orchard, Ballyfermot. The address didn't seem so bad. The Cherry Orchard part sounded romantic, even. (Granted, Harper had once dragged Gael to Chekhov's play by that name. Their seats were restricted-view dress circle perches, so it was all a bit of a blur, but Gael recalls the sound of the cherry orchard being cut down at the closing curtain.) But the reality of Guthrie's place is more marble orchard than cherry. At least Sive and Art's new address isn't misleading: Ashbrook, Pelletstown.

Standing at the window of her mother's study, Gael surveys the ashes and pellets. The urban-sprawl territory of half-dreamt, half-cement department stores, FOR SALE luxury apartments still-not-sold by the furlong, construction-site car parks without arrows to tell cars which way to carry on because no one really knows what's up ahead or if we're better off circling back or staying put. Sure, all sorts of things are put on the back burner. Wasn't the Tower of Babel left up in the air when they ran out of funds? A load of foreign workers left in the lurch. Couldn't understand a word of their eviction notices.

She kneels down on the window-side rug, with her arms on the sill, her head on her arms, and feels the radiator ribs against her chest and belly. The heating's off because it's August. She's heard about how radiators hiss and spit steam nonstop in Manhattan; how people have their ceiling fans on and windows wide open during brutal blizzards; how rats get in and you can't tell what's screaming.

Only a week to go now before the flight and new horizons. Only a week left in the cramped study of her mother's single-glazed apartment with no spare rooms for her kids. Gael feels bad for having taken over Sive's workspace since May, when she left London and Harper and finished up her degree from a distance, but she would make up for it. She would more than make up for the advantage that had been taken.

The study is furnished in a we-just-downsized manner. There's the futon Gael's been sleeping on, a rug concealing glossy laminate flooring, a kitchen rack drilled into the wall from which small wind instruments hang for easy access (a piccolo is of more use to Sive than a wok), an electric piano in place of a desk (Gael's laptop rests on its closed lid) and a floor-to-ceiling shelving unit stacked with Sive's belongings: Penguin Classics she's had since her days at UCD's School of Music, sheet music categorized by group type (from Concert Bands to Wind Quintets), an ancient DVD collection (all the Fellinis and Viscontis in a nostalgic gesture to her minor in Italian, evidenced only by her pronunciation of *bruschetta*), Dictaphones and a thousand-strong set of vinyls bookended by the knurly bowls that her kids had pottered and painted at a craft class once. Another mother might have filled the bowls with potpourri. Sive had filled them with pencil shavings, leaded rubber shreds, snapped elastic bands, hangnails, scuffed bifocals.

Removed from the provision of Jarleth's roof, Sive's belongings seem a kind of fort. On the floor by the piano desk, an empty cafetière balances on a stack of original handwritten scores. The stack goes from the floor to hip height. From what Gael has gleaned by asking Art, Sive barely coped with having two newborns living with them in the old house for the first year. "The noise drove her doolally," Art said. More than the noise, Gael knew, she would have been fraught by the implication. For every common sound that can't be quieted, an uncommon one goes unheard. Sive would stay up half the night working on compositions, wearing noise-canceling headphones. Gael thought it mad she hadn't been trying to get her work programmed. "You don't understand how it works," Sive told Gael when she pushed. Sive felt no obligation to make herself understood.

"So enlighten me?"

"It's writing to discover. Not to be discovered. At this stage."

Over the past fortnight, Gael has taken a selection of the scores to a seedy Internet café in Ashtown to copy. The problem was that she didn't know quite what she was betting on. How one might price these options. It's impossible to tell how a symphony sounds by tutting, or to spot a masterpiece just by skimming, but Gael could tell which ones had the best titles and the value of titles is obvious. An oboe concerto called "You Don't Want What I've Got" was what she decided upon as her mother's tender to the music patriciate. She wrote personalized cover letters for each recipient. Dozens of propositions to musical directors and artistic directors around the world. The New York Philharmonic, Philadelphia Orchestra, Chicago Symphony, Los Angeles Philharmonic, San Francisco Symphony, Berlin Philharmonic, Vienna Philharmonic, London Symphony, Dutch Concertgebouw, Boston Symphony, London Sinfonietta, the Chamber Orchestra of Europe, Orchestre Révolutionnaire et Romantique. Each addressee she researched for tastes, suitability of the music, specific praises to bestow, names to drop, the statistics of their programming ("It's been fourteen years since you've done an oboe concerto and not once have you featured an Irish composer. But I don't blame you. There's been nothing worthwhile, until now").

But unless they have an existing relationship with the composer or its recommender, world-class orchestras won't consider unsolicited scores, she's learned. Without the backing of serious connections, they simply don't care. Besides, musical directors, artistic directors, CEOs and principal conductors are all senior enough to have mail-sifting assistants who, in almost all cases, jettison unsolicited scores. Gael has to make a *very* compelling case if the music is to be looked at. Maybe "rare terminal illness" puts "You Don't Want What I've Got" into sufficiently dramatic light?

Much as Gael is a fan of the long shot, the more she's read, the clearer it's become that egos, over heartstrings, needed to be played to gain access to the classical music scene. She recalled Sive lauding her principal oboist from the NSO as their best musician and lamenting the fact that she'd "never been able to explode his talent into sound, because the oboe concerto repertoire is so thin. There's the Mozart and the Strauss—the two concertos every oboist worth his reed has done to death." But if Gael plays her audience right and if the music's good, this would be the most viable way of having a score considered.

For a soloist on any instrument other than piano, violin or cello, a new work will at least prompt pussyfoot interest. Yes, the oboist would then have to fight for its inclusion on a program, but when you've got an ipso facto novelty concerto, orchestras might just double down on the outlander by playing an unfamiliar work. Shoehorn it between an overture by a composer everybody knows and a major popular symphony. *Dear Revered Oboist . . .* The next challenge is in making it sound like a "proven work." Taking snippets of reviews out of context is one thing, but if the orchestra's management can't hear it or watch it, if they can't read a review, then there's zero chance with the heavy lifters. She's already received emails saying as much and requesting the recording.

Blinking at the screen doesn't clear the fog. Twelve fifteen p.m. She coughs. Better not be getting fucking sick.

She'd submit composer-in-residency applications too if there were time, but Sive's probably too old to be eligible and Gael has her own applications to get back to. If Sive's conducting career has been brought rudely to an end, her composer's career is just about to start. No one need know about her stint behind the Palmerstown Cash Converters' till.

These are the moves Sive would be making herself had she been born somewhere other than this don't-get-ahead-of-yourself island. The recession made it worse: the false-humility epidemic. But it's not enough for your relatives to know your worth. For your gifts to be put in a cabinet like ornamental photo frames, destined to tarnish. For your name to be printed on bills in the archive of your youth. As if success should be rationed and no one—excepting a certain sum of men—can go one better than their quota.

Forget it. Compose.

To Whom It May Concern.

Cut. Paste. Alter. Send.

Her email pings. She looks around. Coughs. What's that smell?

The fire alarm blares into action. The room is out of focus with smoke. Or she's been looking at a screen for too long. No, it's smoke. She leans in. Breathes through her sweater sleeve. On occasion, it pays to reply at once.

> As for the genius composer bit. Maybe we'd be losing some-
> thing. Maybe not. Being a composer's partly about coming
> up with ideas to give performers, but the bigger element
> is communicating those ideas. That takes in what's on the
> page, but even more knowing how to use rehearsal time,
> how to clarify interpretation, manage personalities (you piss

players off, you won't get works played again, that's a fact).

I'll look at your score, but if you can't—

She smacks the laptop shut and tucks it under her arm. Some fucker's lecture. She slides along the varnished hallway floor on her socks all the way to the kitchen, where Art, clad in a loosely tied dressing gown, is directing the handle of a broom at the ceiling, poking all around the too-small alarm button like a maddening fairground game, trying to protect his ears from the wail.

"Happy birthday, duck! Made you brekkie."

The whole stovetop is blackened and draped in charred tea towels. "What the hell?" Gael wafts smoke from her face with her laptop, which she sets on the table and goes to open the balcony door, past the open-plan living space. She darts back to the kitchen for a towel to direct the smoke outside. The alarm stops and starts again. Curses fling like divorcées.

"No use being lippy," Art calls. "Just needs"—he grunts and tugs—"t' battery taken out." Having given up with the broom handle, he's now up on a chair.

"*You* need the battery taken out."

"I were making you crumpets"—he pulls the alarm off the ceiling entirely so it's hanging by wires and still going—"but what happened . . . I dozed off . . . partway through. But don't fret. It's easy fettled." He presses the button and the alarm stops, finally. He dismounts the stool with all the sound effects. Sizes up the embers in the pan. "We'll scrape the burn off and bob a few candles in. Right as rain." He claps his hands.

Silence. Gael turns on the extractor fan.

"Good thinking," says Art.

Gael takes a nectarine from the fruit bowl, looking witheringly at Art as she wipes it on her jeans.

"Happy birthday, anyway!"

"Cheers."

"Just in time for a legal pint in America . . . and a concealed weapons permit. I don't doubt that were planned."

There's a little packet of birthday candles on the countertop. Gael tips one out and sticks it into the nectarine.

Art starts folding the burnt tea towels into a neat pile. "I'll make up a new batch, if you leave off glowering at me!"

"I ate breakfast five hours ago."

"On a Saturday? Aw"—Art shakes his head—"*disappointing*, that is. Nothing worse than having already ate breakfast on a Saturday."

"Hey, did the phone ring earlier? Like, half an hour ago?"

Art tightens the belt of his green-and-navy striped robe. "Aye. Ta for reminding me. Some chancer from Microsoft." He does air quotes. "Swears my computer's been hacked. Needs to talk me through resetting all the security." He goes over to the phone, which is off its cradle, mouthpiece to the table.

"You there?" he asks the receiver. "Ta for waiting. My comput-er's switched on now, just like you said . . . Yerrit's an ancient com-puter . . . Takes an age to boot up . . . My password? Oh, aye . . . 'od on, what's your name, so I know what to call you. . . . Peter, is it? . . . Peter. Jolly good. Tell me, Peter: does your mum know you're a thief? . . . Microsoft don't phone people. Get an honest job. Tarra." He hangs up.

Some nectarine spills down Gael's chin. She tries to swallow it in between laughs so it doesn't go up her nose, but it's one of those unexpected laughs you snort your food for and Art's registering the success with raised brows.

"Peter from Microsoft's Bangladeshi headquarters. I'd have done the hoovering had I thought he'd hang on for me. Had a shave. Mopped the floor. That's half why I fell asleep cooking. Dream-ing how long he'd hang on for his mark. He were so sure he had me. Oooo aye. I'd sounded just the type they like, them scammers. Crumbly. Lonely. Vulnerable."

Her laughter having turned into a cough, Gael goes to the balcony for fresh air. It's a fine if blustery August day and gulls gracelessly pirouette on wind buffets. There's blue sky behind the fast-moving clouds. The view is the same as from Sive's study, but here, beyond all the cement, you can see more of what the suburb once was. Horse paddocks. Fallows. Hawthorn hedges for local kids to do covert body-barter behind ("Giyiz fifty cent for a look"). Gorse for the finches to nest in. There's a few acres of it yet—thistled green fields—and that's where they look to now. Art runs his palms along the balcony rail like he's dewrinkling a bedsheet. A mannerism for when he wants to say something. He does it on tables and counters and desks—all level surfaces: rubs his hands from the center to as far as he can reach and back in again, as if his hands are wet cloths to wipe away all manner of spills. "Good to see you out the cave."

As a fresh graduate, Gael can't hear the word *cave* without thinking of Plato. "I was forced to turn around and see the fire."

"All this time holed up working and you'll soon be off. You've hardly spoke with your brother?"

"I saw him on Thursday! I took the twins out so he could nap."

"But you've not stayed round at his?"

"It wouldn't matter if I had. It's like hanging out with a specter." Gael's cheeks flush a little. It's not until she says it aloud that she's articulating it so plainly to herself. "He's so preoccupied, he can barely get to the end of a sentence."

"He's got better."

"I can't see how that's possible."

"Trust me, duck. He has. This time last year . . ."

Gael sighs and looks to the far left, to where the road curves out of sight.

"But that's why you ought to stay with him," Art says, "so you've time in the evening, while the kids are kipping."

"His gaff is pretty damn grim."

"It's precious time, this."

"And Ronan's a creepy little wraith when the sun goes down."

"A toffee poppet, that child."

"Poppet my ass! I had to barricade the living room door when I slept on Guth's couch 'cause I woke to Ronan stood in front of me in the middle of the night, *staring. This* far from my face." Gael holds her hand a few inches from Art's nose. "Just kind of . . . swaying in the moonlight, mouth breathing. The smell of his nappy brought me to. Kids should be kept in cages at night. Not their dad's double bed. I'm amazed he hasn't rolled over one of them. Done himself a favor."

"The size of Guthrie, he wouldn't harm a cricket by rolling over it." Art gives her a sidelong glare and says, "You best watch that wise-cracking in America. They can be ever so credulous."

Gael looks at Art in wonder. "Am I getting fatherly advice for the first time in my life?"

Art does an inward whistle through the gap in his front teeth where his gums have receded. "Not half."

"Avuncular advice then?"

"I funk you what?"

"And anyway, how would you know?" she asks.

"Know what?"

"About American humor?"

"Oh, I only lived there fourteen years."

"No. Way."

"Way!" Art says.

"When? Where? Which state?" For months, Gael's been probing Art about his story and he never lets anything slip more than he wants to, but this has the feel of an unplanned admission. "What were you doing there? Gambling? Eloping?"

"Listen here—"

Gael gasps. "Evading your debt?"

"Before I say no more of it—"

"Come on!"

"I'll not go on an' on about it on your birthday—"

"Don't change the subject!"

"But it's important enough to warrant my being pushy."

"Forgodssake."

"Have a proper chat with Guthrie fore you go." Art's hands, which have been grooming the railing, making the sound of jazz drum brushes, come to a rest. "He's been having some ideas . . . he ought to run past you. He holds your opinion very highly."

"Yeah right," Gael says, genuinely incredulous.

"I'd've no cause to say such a thing w'n't it true."

Gael pauses for a moment. "What kind of ideas?"

"Summit to do with healing. You'll av to ask him."

Gael looks down at her socks. She's wearing washed-out jeans rolled at the ankles and a dark-brown fine wool sweater. Some of her hair is held up by a teaspoon she stirred her coffee with. It's grown out a bit now and nearly reaches her shoulder blades. "I think he's past the point of no return. The way he's doing things." She shakes her head. "It's—"

"Not how you'd do things?" Art says, a bit gruff.

"Well—"

"Not how you'd raise two babbies on your lonesome, at, what's he now, nineteen?"

"I got my degree, Art. If I wanted more lectures, there's an MIT series online." Gael hurls her nectarine stone out over the road and into the wayside hedges. The sound of it landing doesn't reach them in the second-floor apartment. Not one to torture himself, Art heads in, but Gael apologizes and that stops him. "I'm cranky," she says. "Waiting to hear back from a shitload of things I've applied for. I feel fucking edgy."

Art leans against the white plastic frame of the sliding door. "Right?" He's got his knee cocked out so the robe is flapping in the weather. He doesn't think of things like that. Some of the cars driving by are getting an eyeful. Only when he spots Gael sizing up his hulking calves and the bald patch on his inner knee does he reposition himself, sharpish. He'll do something daffy in a minute, let out a trumpet fart or a drumroll burp or sing "The 59th Street Bridge Song (Feelin' Groovy)" in order to quash any tension that could be thought to have built up. Like a professor who gets accidentally kinky with an undergrad on the topic of thermodynamics and has to figure out how to put the heat back in the Bunsen burner, asap. It's one of the reasons Gael likes Art: the ludicrous ways he finds to defuse a situation. But the energy he normally gives to that is moderated now, as if the bridge is a little too large between his experience and hers. "I thought you 'ad it all worked out?"

"What? The interview stuff?"

"It were Gael, with the revolver, in the lobby!"

She laughs. "Yeah . . . I'm just . . ." She watches her wording. "I'm allowing for the revolving door."

"Eh?"

"Working on backup options."

He considers this. "Hedging."

"Yeah."

Art nods. "Canny."

Does he know, Gael wonders, that it will fall to him or me?

He adds: "You make your own luck, then? That's good."

"I don't bank on luck," Gael says. "I don't bank on skill either. Neither gets you a fair return."

She expects the obvious question—What then?—but Art's gaze has moved to the field across the way, behind where Gael's stood with her back to the railing. She swivels around to see what's caught his eye: a brace of teenagers scuttling along the stone wall of the field, trying to go unseen. They might as well be brandishing a picket sign: "Up with No Good."

"The Irish Rapscallion Army!" Art announces. "What your mum called them."

"Ha."

"Thought that were dead good."

"Doing a bit of fund-raising," Gael observes, "of a Saturday afternoon."

"Auntie Bev never knew how easy she could've had it, fund-raising, had she waved a bit of fence pronged with a rusty nail at a cashier."

Scampering forward with their knees bent to keep out of sight of the main road, three teenage boys and one girl (differentiable by dint of gold hoop earrings the size of showerheads) are on their way to rob the local newsagents for the second time this month. All four of them are styling bum-fluff mustaches, puffer jackets and giddy smirks, making their advances cross-country from one estate to another. Nylon stockings—swag of an earlier robbery—trail from their fists through the mud and the grass like the true flags of New Ireland.

Gael slides her phone from the back pocket of her jeans and finds a number under recent calls. "Close to smooth criminals as the Irish get," she remarks, while dialing. Someone finally picks up. "Hi, is this Spar?" Gael says. "Hiya. Just to let you know the ganglet's on its way to empty your tills for you. . . . Yeah. I'd say they're . . . ninety seconds off. Will I call the guards? . . . You're sure? Okay, grand. . . . No worries. Good luck." When she slips the phone into her pocket, she feels something else being slipped in alongside it and jumps. Sive's fragrance of vitamin E face cream gives her away, even over the lingering aroma of burnt egg and flour. Gael's heart trips a little at her mother's warm cheek grazing her own cold one.

"Happy birthday," Sive says.

There's the sound effect of a kiss, but no such contact. Sive moves straight back in off the balcony to check on the sooty kitchen. Gael finds a wad of US ten-dollar bills secured by an elastic filed into her pocket. Twenty-one notes.

"Now then!" says Art, winking at Gael. "Forrin dosh." He whispers: "A dime's what they call a hundred-dollar bet. A nickel's five hundred."

"Mum," Gael steps inside, "you shouldn't have—"

"None of that, please," Sive says. "It won't cover a night's accommodation in Manhattan. But I can't dictate where you go. Twenty-one going on forty. Only I couldn't manage forty notes, so. Just as well I have your birth cert for evidence." She'd done half a shift at work. At the Palmerstown Cash Converters. She'd brought a few pieces of furniture in there when they were moving house many months back and, eyeing up a beautiful antique violin that sat behind the counter, she commented on the music that was playing through for-sale speakers. The boss cottoned onto the connoisseur before him and asked would she mind giving some valuations of the musical instruments. Then he asked her to value a quiet, comfortable easygoing workplace to which she would lend priceless class. "I don't know quite how to explain it," she'd told Gael on the phone. "There's something . . . so . . . down to earth about it, but at the same time, comical. It's almost a relief, the mundanity of it. The simplicity of the exchange. I'll only do it for a short while, but I must say I'm not half as loath to go in there as I sometimes was to go into the NSO."

In acknowledgment of why she was hired, she dresses tastefully for work. An old but well-kept plaid green blazer with navy corduroy elbow patches, tailored navy trousers, a white cami and a beige silk scarf tied at the bosom. She hasn't dressed with such harmony in years.

She bins all the tea towels that Art uselessly folded, and floods the charbroiled pan with water and liquid soap to soak. "Sorry to do this to you now," Sive says to Art, "and you still in your robe, but my father's down in the car."

"Right-o," Art says, locking the balcony door. "The bomb's ticking then."

"I couldn't face getting him into the chair and into the lift to bring him up here just for a quarter of an hour. If you could keep an eye on him while I throw a few things together."

"I'll bob some shorts on," Art says.

"It's cooler out than it looks," Sive tells him.

"Oh. Fore I forget." Art trots to their bedroom and groans with the effort of rummaging under the bed. He returns a moment later carrying their old picnic basket. He must have salvaged it from the attic of Amersfort Way. It looks full. He lands it on the kitchen table, then goes to the fridge for two bottles of Lambrusco Bianco, a carton of apple juice, two blocks of cheese and a jar of fig jam that's been chilling. He loads them into the basket. "From me, to you," he says, poking his thumb at his own chest and then at Gael's before disappearing down the hall into the bedroom.

Sive is working off her good brogues to change into low-key shoes. "A picnic in Phoenix Park," she says to Gael, cautiously. "We thought we'd do the zoo after. It's free entry for the twins until they turn two, so Guthrie wants to get you your ticket as a gift. I hope you don't mind the lack of style"—she stands up and takes a breath—"with Dad beleaguering us besides." In trying to work off her scarf with one hand, she causes a knot. She flops her long arms by her sides with defeat or release, it's hard to know, and addresses Gael squarely. "But it's one way to celebrate a birthday anyway, isn't it?"

Gael wafts smoke that's no longer there from her face and frowns up at the fire alarm, hanging by its wires: a lampoon chandelier. It's so ridiculous, what's happened. Maybe laughing would clear it, but what's funny? No smoke without fire and all that. "It's fine," Gael says. What's fine? What's funny? "A *fine* idea," she says in Audrey Hepburn elocution, at which Sive knits her brow. Gael steadies her voice. "I'll just fetch my white kid gloves."

✦

The sycamores are beginning to dry and discolor at the edges like fresh food left out. Grape, pear, cheddar, Brie, torn baguette. Lime trees, horse chestnuts, oaks. So much grass, the rug is hardly needed and the deer grazing near the towering Papal Cross in the backdrop tire their jaws feasting on it. The twins pick up everything that's fallen within their reach. They could stand and take what they want—they've been steady on their feet for months and can manage a lurching run, which they practiced earlier, trying to catch a mallard by trapping it with their body weight ("really gently," Guthrie directed)—but they're aware that this array of food is not normal. It's not porridge. It's not steaming spud, carrot and broccoli mash that needs to be blown on by Dad before it can be airplaned into them.

Soraca takes whatever she likes the texture of and directs it at her face in small wet slaps. Food is clotted in her hair, making it strawberry-blond. She likes banana most of all and squeezes one so that it pops up out of her two-handed grip like a fish. What she *doesn't* like—chopped-up chorizo, for example—she passes to Ronan, who is sitting upright in the nook of Guthrie's lotus pose. Ronan: light and shallow-breathed and unreadable as his stuffed animals. As he's mildly allergic to grass, Guthrie holds him by the waist and wipes the slather from his chin. (He always wipes their faces with his hands, then wipes his hands on something else.) Like his twin, Ronan is white as unrecycled paper and he wears the same featherlike hair tickling his shoulders. He blinks pink-eyed indifference at Soraca's tackles and declarative gobbledegook. He does have bouts of animation, during which he points at everything that is a thing and has a shape, but he spends much of his time staring at people's chests as at an aquarium.

A gust of wind shoves the family vehicle onto its side in a *clatter-smash* and Ronan's whole body hiccups. Cue tearless bawling from both children. "T minus five, four, three," Gael says, getting up to resurrect their trusty method of transport: a granny bike with a wooden box out front, an inverse trailer, which the twins rattle around in like the last two Smarties in a packet. It's the plastic cover of the trailer that's trapping the wind. Gael zips it shut.

Guthrie's sniffling all the while. He's had a cold for as long as Gael's been home—months, now. A combination of his moldy house, cycling in all weather, staccatoed sleep, being around children non-stop (playdates with neighbors' kids included) and poor nutrition. His cheekbones are like mussel shells: tough and arched. The only difference is the color. His cheeks are the silvery blue of the mussel shell's interior. The curve of them angles down as he turns toward the fastest-growing loves of his life. His hair, more mouse brown now than beige, is tied back in a bulb Gael says he can just about pull off if he's going for the Finnish transsexual high-fashion look. "I'm going for the don't-call-social-services look," he'd told her. More than once, strangers have approached him to casually-not-casually inquire after his relationship to these two babies. This might have to do with his youth. Or the fact that, when they were tiny, he would swaddle them in a blanket, top and tail, and go for walks just holding them in his arms. No sling or backpack or pram. No one ever told him That's Not What One Does. Sometimes, it seemed as if he needed a permit for them. The long hair does make him look older and more likely to have had kids early as a lifestyle choice, the way one might keep chickens or tend a marijuana plant. He's struggling to cut grapes in half with his one free hand, so Gael takes over. "Thanks. They can choke on them."

Gael hums in dismissive acknowledgment.

"Did your mum tell you lot about t' fella come into the shop yesterday?" Art says. "And what he tried to fob off on them?"

"No?" Guthrie says.

Art turns to Sive. "Go on! Give em the yarn."

"You tell it," she says. "You've more energy."

He pats her on the back, goadingly. "Go on. Av some pop." He uncaps the bubbles and refills their plastic cups.

"I won't listen to her," Sive's father declares from where he's perched in his wheelchair, having heard the word *pop*, which he is vaguely aware has to do with himself, or at least these people keep telling him so.

It takes them aback whenever he says something coherent like that and Gael has to bite her cheeks not to laugh. "Good man, Ned," Art says. "You're with us."

"Am I?"

"By the looks of it."

"What are you looking at?" Ned says. "Who are you?"

"Your personal chef." Art hands him a filled baguette he's been putting together, which Ned cagily accepts and holds like a prop. Ninety-one years of life and mild obesity restrict him to the chair, where he looks the permanent fixture in his cap, coat and mantle as if it were January, shoulders coated in dandruff. Through their milky film, his gray eyes are wild and searching: Sive's eyes when she's conducting. The wrinkles that are deepening on his daughter are in full form on his own cheeks—black lines dropping directly from the bags beneath his eyes all the way to his jowls like windscreen wipers at rest. A smile would set them in motion.

"You're a good man," Ned tells Art, as fact.

"I *am* a good man," Art agrees. "Always thought that."

"*She's* not," he says, eyes darkening on Sive.

"She's not a good man, no," Art concedes.

"What she's after?" Ned says, a little slurry from sedatives and minor strokes. "Disgrace of a woman. No . . . qualifications. Don't let me alone with that bitch."

Sive has her head knocked back and is smiling up at the clouds, eyes flooding. Gael considers crawling across the rug to hug her, but there's too much stuff in the way. Sour cream crisps, a banana skin having found its moment, the knife Soraca eyes up for a toy. Gael puts it away in the basket, reaches for her niece instead of her mother and shows her how to push the curds of fat out of the chorizo slices: a game that will beguile for at least thirty seconds.

The Saturday in May when Gael had arrived back from London, Sive had answered the door. After a moment's shock at seeing her daughter stood there with a suitcase, Sive took her by the elbow into the study and shut the door. "Dad's in the living room," she said. Gael hadn't visited her grandfather in years and didn't even know he'd been moved to a new facility. "I don't know if I ever explained to you," Sive said. "According to the nurse, this often happens that people get locked into one mode . . . related to how they were, or what their profession was, but tangentially. If someone was a social butterfly, they might get stuck in that loop, where you can't get them off the subject of arrival and departure and what's to eat and drink and where are the napkins, or others, maybe their thought-rut will be dirtier, darker. And it's a horrible shock for people who knew them. It makes sense, an actuary's default state would be one of suspicion. And we're lucky Dad's mistrust hasn't extended to food and medication. Because if that happens, then, that's that. . . . Just to warn you. The things he says to me . . . It's a sad loop. He's confused and fearful."

He's on better behavior in front of the twins, now, as if he knows he could frighten the wits out of them by showing his panic. Whenever he moves, they watch him, the way a dog's tail goes stiff when it sees another dog coming its way. Ned is a shorthand he could never abide while he still knew his name was Eamonn. Sive called him Ned once to hurt him after he'd struck her and he didn't seem to notice the name change, so Art said she should keep calling him that as a reminder that he's changed. Ned opens the sandwich, withdraws the slice of cheddar like a note from a wallet and puts it in his mouth. The side-to-side working of his jaw suggests its slow, toothless disintegration. Ronan moves to the grass and hunkers down to dig a hole. Soraca brings over her small pile of pig fat to plant in the soil, a moment of supreme generosity for which Ronan is cooingly grateful. Pat pat pat.

"So this customer . . ." Sive smiles widely and looks radiant, resisting her sadness. "We saw him coming a mile off. Jazzlin was outside the shop having a smoke and she rushed in to say there was an '06 Audi indicating our way that bore the innards of a dead marriage."

Art leans in and kisses her shoulder.

"Jazzlin with the quiff the size of a top hat?" Gael says, one eyebrow cocked. "Put it like that, did she?" (Guthrie swats his pear core at her.) "Jazzlin with the diploma in motorbike backseat ridin."

Guthrie cracks a laugh. "Don't!"

"I wouldn't underestimate Jazzlin's way with words," Sive says.

"I won't underestimate you having your way with her words," Gael says, "but go on."

"Only if I have your permission." Sive drains her cup. "So the Audi reverses to within an inch of our door, making a hostage scene of the shop. And in this fellow arrives."

"Hang on," Gael says, but Guthrie shushes her. Sive continues:

"Were either of us golfers, because he could return another time when the boss was in. He wouldn't see his clubs undervalued. They were a collectors' affair, once owned by Sr. Christy O'Connor. Jazzlin asks him: 'Is that Sinéad's da?' Bless her timing. 'Google him,' your man said. No, there was no proof of ownership, but any serious golfer would know, the drivers alone were worth a fortnight's pay. He didn't specify *whose* pay. He'd have to pick up a new set in Dubai, where he was headed for a job opportunity because there's different sorts of clubs there. To suit to sandier courses and all the rest."

"Did you buy them?" Guthrie asks.

"He suggested we hold off and make an offer on the whole lot."

"Did he, now?"

"He was the actor, stage manager, director and front-of-house all at once," Sive explains. "We were the set."

"Natroly," Art says.

Sive feeds Ronan a bit of bread because his mouth is hanging open and any excuse to fatten him up. "The next offering was a his-and-hers watch set. He opened the cases, tapped the side of his nose and said, 'Personal fitness monitors. It tells you how many steps you've done in a day and how many hours of deep sleep you got.' Jazzlin was swayed by that and inquired, very seriously, 'Does this thing make ye skinny?' He wouldn't dignify that with a response and went out to the boot to get the next thing. A cinema projector. You begin to picture the household that had broken up?"

"Not half!" Art says.

"Jarleth might go for the clubs though," Gael says.

"The home cinema on all day," Sive says, "projecting a Caribbean beach on the living-room wall."

"The moody Cliffs of Moher!" Gael corrects her. "Patriotism, Mum!"

"To be sure," Sive says, ham-sandwiching it. "The magnificent cliffs cast onto a big swathe of wall. Oh the *lumens*, he was telling us. The *definition* of definition. The *quality* of it was undeniable and fifteen hundred he'd bought it for on the Continent and a steal at that. Hardly used. Would we consider the fact that it was in the box? We might appraise the surround sound separately, he said." Sive's gestures conduct this small concert in the park, her arms lifting as she describes the columns of aluminum he needed help to carry in. "Like a syndicate of skyscrapers, he erected them on the countertop."

"Crikey," Art says, as if he's not heard it already.

"Ostentatious as Austen," she adds.

"Love it," Gael says, thrilled to see her mum raconteuring like this and thinks, because of Austen, of Harper.

"Nothing!" Ned arrives at the punchline of his internal narrative and showers the party in bread roll confetti. "Zilch!" The twins scream in approval and Soraca is nudged toward the realization that gardening is unrewarding in the short term. Bury things in the ground, they disappear. Throw things in the air, they hit somebody on the head. She bullies Art's flip-flops from his feet, flings them away, runs to where they land, steps into them (keeping her own shoes on for practicality's sake), test-runs them around the grass, trips over and over before deciding they're defective and kicks them lakeward for the ducklings to use as floaties.

"She wants my money," Ned informs the vicinity. "But!" (If a bite were a weapon.) "I spent it! I've nothing left. So you're welcome . . . to my nothing." When Sive won't meet his gaze, he glances from stranger to stranger. Who'll listen? They're connivers on all of this. He looks at the scenery. The liver spots on the hands. Don't know that that's good. Skin like wrapping paper, scrunched and discarded. Bones protruding like . . . like, what's it? Tents. Poles. Sticks. These people have no clipboards. What do they want—

"What'd'ya blow your money on, Ned?" Art tries to dissolve the panic that rises reliably as tides in him when he's been away too long from the administers of meds—those clerics, so good at taming their congregants. Ned groans. Ignoring him can make it worse. "Was it ladies?" Art says. "You spent your money on?" Art's wiping grass from the soles of his feet to reveal the "Made in Bolton" tat, like wiping snow from a headstone to reveal a history.

"What?" Ned buys himself time to squint at the palimpsest of his memory, to see if he can't make out the shapes of what was there when there was something . . . "What?"

"I'll tell you what I spent *my* money on, shall I?"

Ned looks guardedly relieved.

"On a zoo," Art says. "I bought Dublin zoo."

"You did not!"

"Oh aye."

"How much?"

"Cost an arm and a leg. To a cheetah. But prosthetics are dead good nowadays, don't you think?" Art's camo-print cargo shorts allow him to make a show of himself. He models his calf muscles. Ned looks vaguely appalled but amenable to this one, to whatever's going on. A smile threatens to set the windscreen wipers going.

"It were a rainy day in Ireland," Art begins, "round the time of the great recession and no one could pay for t' animals' feed. Me, I'm good with animals. Bit of a rhino whisperer. An' I'd sacks of cash from making smart investments in York. So when I come and seen all the poor giraffes, shrinking to straws, I thought: I can't av that. No, I can't av that. Thing was, I'd said it out loud, and someone had heard me and *she'd* said: Actually, you can have it. It's for sale. The whole hog. We've run out of dosh. So we shook hands and that's how I come to be the owner of a zoo. Not bad, having a stake in a zoo. Get a load of these two monkeys, for a start." Art takes Soraca by the arms and swings her from side to side, then up into the air before landing her on the ground, where she squeals and stamps her feet and nurses her wrists and giggles. "Not the most attractive specimens. But it could've been worse. You should've seen their dad."

Soraca claps for everyone's attention. "Da da da da da da da da da da da da da da da? Da!"

Ronan laughs because he knows a good line when he hears one.

Soraca's temper turns because her arms feel weird now from the swinging.

Guthrie packs away the kids' things and the picnic, which means it's time for meerkats.

Gael doesn't help because one of the downsides of having Art around is that Sive has relaxed into her role of hearer. She's never been a natural talker. So it had really been something to get her to tell a story, before she was rudely cut off by her father. What is it with this family and its fathers? Maybe Guthrie will break the pattern. She's forced to stand, as the rug is literally being pulled from under her, but she asks what happened with the customer. Brushing the crumbs from her lap, Sive dismisses the comedic value of the rest of the tale. "Come on, Mum. Don't be such a woman."

"For goodness' sake, Gael. He brought in a safe and asked us to make an offer on it without showing what was inside. It was clear the wife had changed the code on him. That's the height of it."

Gael's jaw drops. "Did you buy it?"

Sive ignores this—her obligation isn't to entertain—and takes the picnic rug a few feet away to shake it clean, but the wind blows the scraps back at them and, before long, a riffraff of magpies rallies nearby.

Ned is mincing his jaw: his telltale sign of muddled delirium that spirals into aggression like a raver on rock. Mildly narked, Gael helps settle the twins into the bike box, among the cushions. She awaits the inevitable: "You lot go ahead to the zoo while Art and I take Dad back."

Gael studies the magpies bouncing around the grass. Their tails make up half their length, so they seem much bigger than they are. They're not migratory. It's rare for one to fly ten kilometers from where it was hatched. She concentrates on this so that all the sounds of logistics and see-yous are muted and missed and Guthrie has to repeat himself.

"Gael? You don't *have* to come. I've got something else for your birthday, but the ticket was meant to be the *main* thing."

"What? No, I'm coming."

"Oh," Guthrie says, with some relief. "Good." Perhaps there's something lonely in fathering twins. To come so close to that togetherness. "You might've had work to do."

"And miss seeing chimpanzees with alopecia?" Gael says. "From a binocular-worthy distance? Are you mad?"

Art and Sive are already en route to the car park, with Ned in tow.

Guthrie hunkers down and tucks the twins in for an excuse to look at them. If his love were bath suds, they'd be up to their necks in it, clapping their hands through it to hear it fizzle, bursting its bubbles for merriment, knowing there's enough of it that they can afford to let some go down the drain—enough, even, that some can be urinated in. In the half-song, half-whisper voice that's just for them, he tells them to tip their hats to the magpies, so that their lives will be lucky ones. Ronan points obediently. Guthrie asks his rhetorical questions. "Will we try it?" The twins sit forward in the box and grip its wooden rim with their sticky mitts, unused to riding with the plastic coverlet open. What's this? What have you got for us? Guthrie tips their hats for them. "Can you say, Good day, Mister Magpie? Huh?" He kisses the back of Ronan's hand, which is prickled red from playing in the grass. "Good afternoon, Missus Magpie." Guthrie's eyes are reflective enough to appear green below and blue on top.

"Pood!" Soraca says. This is the word she uses for food and for defecation, so she may well be suggesting they take a magpie home to roast.

"Wise move, Sorsh." Gael kicks the bike stand back out for the nappy change. "A load of shite indeed."

"Don't listen to Auntie Gael," Guthrie says. "She doesn't know her own luck." He lifts Ronan up for the smell test. Puts him back. At twelve kilos each, lifting the twins hundreds of times a day is having its effect on Guthrie's arms. Thin as they are, they're newly strappy.

"*Do* listen to Auntie Gael because she knows that luck boils down to Right-Place-Right-Time, and fowl have fuck-all to do with it."

"Lel el el," Soraca attempts the name.

Guthrie grins, despite himself, lifting Soraca back out of the box and laying her down on the grass for his magic-trick blink-of-an-eye nappy change. "Trust my sister to spend three years in college and to come home with a four-word philosophy."

"PS," Gael leans in to whisper, her hands making a furtive delta around her mouth. "Vaginas count as a Place in the Wrong-Place-Wrong-Time scenario."

Guthrie's expression darkens.

She's thinking of asking him if he remembers that deluxe magic set he got for his seventh birthday. She's thinking of asking if he recalls not being able to make any of the tricks work. If he recalls, in a moment of rebellion, taking the small white plastic ball from the cups-and-ball trick and directing Gael to wait outside while he practiced. How, when she was let back in, tears veined Guthrie's face so that he could barely get it together to wave the wand in the direction of his penis. How he dropped his pajama pants and popped the ball from his foreskin like a strip-club ping-pong show, saying, "Ta-aa-aa . . ." How he couldn't stop hyperventilating to pronounce the "da!"

The new nappy is on; all the wipes are secured within the dirty one and the plastic bag is double-knotted. Meanwhile, Ronan has climbed out of the box and, led by his finger, tottered toward a large bridled dog, mid-dump. *Zoo!* he must think. Gael has clocked this and wonders how Ronan can tell it's an animal, seeing as its ears and tail are cut. What makes something an animal, at first glance? Incisors? Haunches? The stink. It's a pitbull-somethingbigger-somethingmangier-cross. The owner is a hard-as-flint hard-done-by with his hood up. The no-way-out sort you fear more than fear for, because nothing to live for is the same as nothing to lose. His track-suit looks empty, but for the spurs of knees, elbows, shoulders. He is hooked forward in a C shape; back to Ronan, who comes to a stand-still a meter from the dog's fresh turd.

"Don't look now," Gael says, "but what's the likelihood Ronan would eat—"

Don't say "Don't look" to a parent whose toddler is out of eyeshot.

Guthrie practically pounces on his son, who is indeed reaching for a handful of shit, sure to startle the dog. Gael rushes over too because something feels familiarly wrong and, without looking at her, Guthrie passes Ronan to her for safekeeping. She has to take him back to the other one, the girl twin, so that she has them both because their dad is not quite . . . posture stiffened. Is he about to? At least grass makes for a soft—

"Excuse me? . . . Sir?"

Man and dog are moving on. But the dog pulls back. He whines, sensing unrest.

"Hey!" Guthrie calls loudly, ignoring Gael's frantic gesturing. No one can hear each other clearly, purely. It's as if the whole park has tinnitus. The owner turns. High and twisted on the comedown as a shoddy kite. There's an unlit fag in his mouth and he pulls back his lips so it's held by his gray teeth.

"Can you clean up after your dog please?" Guthrie says. "There's children in this park."

The owner shifts from foot to foot like a wrestler; eyes flit from the kids to Gael to this one. . . . He pockets the fag. "Do you think I done that?"

"Your dog did."

He leans in. "I *seen* who took a *shite*."

"You need to clean up after your dog."

The dog stops and starts like a bus trying to merge with traffic. The owner pulls back his hood and his grease-flat hair looks like it's permanent-markered onto his scalp. "—smack the head off yeh."

"My son was about to pick it up."

"Leave it," Gael says.

"It could have killed him."

The dog's tail stump twitches and he whines. Ronan is scream-ing. Gael's searching with one hand for his meds, or keys, her phone, but it all happens in the time it takes to unzip Pandora's daypack.

It makes a prison percussion sound. The heavy-duty chain that serves as a leash. When he whips it up to lash Guthrie's face, chin to cheekbone. The dog doesn't bark so much as howl at being tugged and jerked away before the blood comes. Fled fast. And Gael has to dump both kids into the bike box—Soraca with her pants down—to get to Guthrie, painting the grass sloppily red as those Queen of Hearts cards he so pitied. His hand's out in front of him for balance, as if he's trying to get up. But he never fell down. He's pushing his other sleeve to his lip so Gael chases back for a towel. Curses are the only words that come and Guthrie groans at her to stop in front of the babies. Some time must pass before either manages to say more.

"No. Don't phone. No. No ambulance. No police. No hospital.

Don't frighten them. You're S C A R I N G them." He can talk, with a spoof lisp, without using his bottom lip. It's split deeply but he says lips can't be stitched anyway.

"Don't you have health insurance?" Gael asks.

"I do. Yeah, I do."

"Then let's get it glued. Disinfected. Come on. I'll call a cab."

"I've got first aid at home. We'll just go home and put the kids in the pen in front of YouTube and wait to see if it stops bleeding."

"That's insane, Guthrie! You've got insurance. Let's go."

"No, Gael. No. It's a cut. It's a bruise. There's an excess."

"What?" Gael scans his injuries for some literal meaning. "How much?"

"If I'd broken a bone . . ."

There's another reason he's not articulating. But Gael can't think, not with the mauve tinge broaching on his cheek alongside his nose, like when you press a tea towel onto a red wine spill and it just begins to soak through. But way down in the fibers still. The twins are bawling and Gael goes to them to pull on Soraca's trousers. The temperature seems to have dropped.

Then, because it's very hard to do things like button buttons and lace laces when you're thinking of all the things you should have done, shouted—*he has fucking epilepsy, you scabbydickedtwat*—she has to slow down and concentrate to fasten Soraca's booties. "Shushushush, it's okay." One task at a time. One boot. One boot. These booties. She holds them. A yellow embroidered logo on fawn leather. Blue-and-white striped cushioned interior. Ralph Lauren. Knockoffs, she thinks for a moment, but it's obvious. Ronan has on a matching pair. A few hundred quid's worth of footwear. Jarleth. His way of "providing" because, of course, Guthrie wouldn't take money.

"Gael," Guthrie says.

Did he see her cop on to that just now?

"Will you come and stay the night?"

Gael finally quiets the twins and zips the plastic cover shut. "We need to get ice on that." She takes the bike off its stand. "Tell me you have an ice tray." She waits. "Tell me you have a freezer."

Guthrie hands her his keys. "Could you take them home?"

"What'll you do?"

He looks around vainly. "Walk."

"Don't be an idiot."

"A bus. I can't cycle them home like this. With one hand."

"I'm phoning Mum."

"Don't. Please don't."

"What if you—"

"I won't."

"But what if—?"

But she didn't need to ask it and he didn't need to answer.

"Don't worry, Gael. I'm fine. I'm better."

Gael goes over it on each of the seven kilometers home. Why had she been so slow? She should've photographed the fucker. Taken a video. Damages might've been worth it, to have that dickwad declared officially bankrupt. There was even a bike. She could've chased him down. Áras an Uachtaráin, the President of Ireland's residence, was right there in the middle of the park. Within egging distance. Did his people not look out the window for fear of what they'd have to report? She should've known the zoo would come to them. The road would rise up to meet them on the chin. Slow-motion punches never land.

How had Guthrie's voice sounded, though? How had he made it sound so . . . calm, authoritative? At the corner of the estate, a woman in a Hubba-Bubba-pink velour tracksuit is pushing her mother home in a SuperValu shopping trolley. The nearest SuperValu is an hour's walk. Sisyphus, eat your heart out.

The twins sleep the whole way home. Gael missed the turnoff

some blocks back going over it all again, thinking. Thinking: there's no way this is it.

✦

It was evening by the time things were back under control. Or at least under its semblance. Gael had bathed the twins and dried their unbearably soft, warm bodies until they glowed as if firelit. Getting them into new nappies and jammies while keeping both of them alive was something she considered an accomplishment, but had no interest in repeating on a daily basis for years on end, however lovely it was to be the recipient of their pure spontaneous smiles or to feel their awe at adult coordination.

With a sock full of frozen peas duct-taped to his cheek and a temporary dressing on his chin, Guthrie had taken up his usual sleeping post between the twins on a double mattress on the floor (so that they wouldn't fall far if they rolled off) and he closed his eyes to set an example, to listen to Gael's rendition of *Where the Wild Things Are*. "If I read it to them, like this, they'll have nightmares," Guthrie had said. Gael gave in. She was curious to remember the feeling of reading to her six-year-old brother when no one else would. It had been a sort of homework for both of them. Gael would point at the long words for Guthrie to pronounce, developing her ad-libbing skills when faced with his courage of questions: *Are pancakes alive? Is Pooh a real name? Is oldness contagious? Do we have a stepmother? But where will they sleep if they run away? Why can't he have more if he's still hungry?* When he developed a taste for didactic Victorian literature, Gael had quit. "Read yourself to sleep. If you're stuck on a word, ask the Internet. Or Mum, if she's around. *Don't* ask Dad because his answers aren't reliable."

The twins' breathing slowed and deepened and their eyelids fluttered like filament bulbs burning out. Guthrie stayed with them until the slow lapping of their breath assured him they were asleep.

❖

On the couch, Gael's watching *The Daily Show* buffer on Guthrie's shonky laptop, soaking up the sitcom that is US politics. To be fair, only a couple of weeks back, Ireland elected a seventy-year-old poet for a president. So if poetry can be called entertainment . . . "It can't," Gael says, in the form of a grumble, to cancel out the image of Harper reciting her way across Gael's delineations. In any case, the Irish had learned the meaning of "no laughing matter" and "not amusing" these past few years and were taking all five-foot-three-and-a-half of the poet-president to heart. He would reacquaint politics with philosophy.

"Huh?" Guthrie shifts his head on her lap.

"Kicked in yet?" she asks.

"Huh?"

"The Nurofen?"

"Oh."

Guthrie makes an effort to sit up.

"Whoa-whoa-whoa easy there. Watch the scissors."

Gael had redone his dressing even though the twins would only pull it off in the morning. She said she'd gaffer-tape mittens to their hands if he didn't rest his head on her lap pronto so she could see what could be salvaged of his face. He'd submitted, a little more reluctantly than she was used to. Had he pulled his head to the ends of her knees? Had he tilted his split mouth, his nose, away a fraction? Had he flushed when she loosed his bun? All the more reason to draw him toward her: if you forgo that sort of intimacy too long, it can't be recovered. She disinfected the cuts and used Steri-Strips to close the slit in his lower lip, which would take the longest to heal for how often the twins would break him open. "Keep a tub of Vaseline handy," she said. Again, the flinch. Did something else hurt? Beneath the dressing, his chin had looked like a beadlet sea anemone: the bloodred rock-suckers that retract when the tide goes out and become slimy blobs. If you press them, they squirt maroon liquid in defense, like a teenage girl calling "period" when she doesn't like her dare and wants out. When they went to Dún Laoghaire on summer days as kids, Gael would scour rock pools for those creatures and poke them dry. Guthrie would try anything to stop her from doing it. It pained him. "I found a ring!" he'd shout, knowing full well it was a bottle cap. "Let's collect periwinkles for pets!" Then he'd try, "You could sell them?" until finally being forced to play his last card: the thing that would make her drop anything, up to and including a future. Freeze, throe, flash.

"Delete that," he says.

She had taken a photo of his unbandaged face. "Just in case you decide to press charges."

Guthrie sits up on the tan pleather couch and picks from a bag of unsalted peanuts, one nut at a time, like a garden finch. His hair is down still and messy from Gael's toying with it. *The Daily Show* clip ends on a low note: a *Freakonomics* contributor is interviewed about his research on the economic disadvantages of being ugly. He demonstrates his data collection method by stalking a university campus, grading women's attractiveness on a scale of 1 to 5. *She'll be lacking financially as she is aesthetically,* his glib 2 portends. When it's over, Gael says, "We're both 5s. And fuck that guy."

Guthrie points to the cornflakes Gael spilled on the floor from her cereal supper, but she can't see them because they're camouflaged on the florid brown, orange and mustard carpet (the sicked-up design might well explain Ronan's perpetual space-out). Guthrie leans down to collect the flakes and put them in the bowl. The absence of a coffee table is for childproofing purposes. The absence of a TV, speaker system, shelving unit and any ornaments whatsoever, ditto. Though, the room is small enough to feel cramped with just the sofa, the twins' playpen, a beach shelter tent, a box of toys and books and a beanbag. It's a three-bedroom terraced house that's been subdivided into two apartments of fifty square meters. Someone's galumphing around upstairs.

"Can I cut your hair?" Gael snips the air with first-aid-kit scissors. Guthrie stands. "Where're you going?"

He pulls a ratty tissue from his sleeve—the first magic trick he ever mastered, a prelude to his nappy-changing skills—and dabs his nostrils. Though ice curbed the swelling, all along one side of his nose is lavender-colored and the skin is glossy and taut.

Gael says, "That cardi's a real lint magnet."

"Come here for a sec, will you?"

Gael frowns. "O . . . kay?" She puts the scissors and the laptop on the floor. "What's up?" Trying to recall Art's forewarning, she follows her brother to the hallway door (the main entrance to his flat) and watches him put his slipper at its base to keep it from locking. They step out to the corridor. It seems as if the cupboard under the stairs is their destination. Guthrie disappears into it and, a moment later, a light comes on. The yellow, fuzzy light of self-delusion. "Hurry up," he calls. Gael takes a deep breath. She prepares herself for a flower-strewn shrine with tea lights, plastic disciples and a framed Sacred Heart. Or a guilty dynasty of moon-charged crystal skulls that he knows deep down are incompatible with Christianity and/or realism. "Is this where you keep Jarleth?" she asks, hopefully, crouching through the doorway. "I figured the stench was just nappies."

As soon as she's standing upright inside, she sees what he wants to show her. She throws her arm out to push Guthrie back by his chest, holds her other palm to her belly.

"Easy on the theatrics," he says.

She doesn't speak for what feels like a mistaken length of time. Like the five minutes of crackling silence before the hidden track on

Sive's Nina Simone LP they discovered one Christmas Eve, when they let that vinyl silence play out—too full-bellied to lift the needle, Jarleth too boozed to give out. How they had jumped when the extra track started, out of nowhere. Out of the white, noise. Jarleth insisted on a manufacturer's error, but Guthrie believed it to be a once-in-a-lifetime cue from Samuel himself: a lack of patience causes missed blessings.

"It's for your birthday," he says. She can feel him study her profile.

"Guth—"

"I know you don't have a home for it, but," he says, "sorry. A house—"

"Guthrie." Her right hand is still pressed against him and she can feel his heart-hit: the most resolute thing she knows. "This is insane." Dust swells and shifts like starlings.

They look at the gift.

Guthrie looks at what it is; Gael at what it could be seen to be.

And what she can turn it into.

This parenthesis of a space reminds her of the confession preceding the sacrament of Confirmation, when her inventory of sins, mouthwatering and perverse, had the priest stirring in his robes and breaking in early with his absolution before she'd even had the chance to flex her imagination.

"It's for me?" she says.

He nods, trying not to smile, she can tell.

"How many are there?"

Guthrie shrugs, stiff-shouldered. "One for each fit since . . . the twins."

Gael shakes her head. "I can't believe it. I'd kiss your poxy face off if it wouldn't make you bleed." She drops her hand from his chest and reaches into her back pocket for the $210 Sive had put there earlier. She hands it to him, but he steps back, as if from a flyer for Speed Dating Saturdays at Chapelizod Community Center.

"No, Gael. I'm not taking money. It's your birthday gift and so is that money."

"Yeah. And it buys me a venture capitalist license."

She lets him absorb this. Now, she has a viable plan. Better than the others she'd come up with. It sounds as if the upstairs neighbors are doing Zumba.

"First the license, then the capital," Gael says. Clearly, the neighbors haven't yet done enough Zumba to be light. "Come on. I know exactly what to do."

◆

An "A-line long bob" YouTube tutorial plays on silent and Gael kneels on a towel in front of the couch, in front of Guthrie. There's a pair of scissors between them.

"Above the mole or below?"

"What mole?"

"You know the mole," Guthrie says. "On your neck. There . . . on the bumpy spine bit. In the middle." He prods it with his finger.

"Ow."

"The on/off button," he says.

Gael lifts her arms so that Guthrie's knees are beneath her armpits. "I'm not *that* easy to turn on."

"No. Like a droid, I meant—"

"*I* know what you meant," Gael says, with I-know-what-you-meant intonation.

"Stay still." There's a strange new baseline to the tone he takes with her—a tone newly solemn and off.

"Above the mole," she says. "But *just*. I want it long enough so I can pin it up but short enough at the back so the angle down to the front is steep. Artsy."

The snipping sounds and the dissolve of clippings falling to the carpet are restful. The black cut hair makes a sodden manuscript of the towel she's kneeling on. Guthrie can't afford the blood-loss of a yawn. Gael resists the urge to ask him, "What's this healing hooey Art mentioned," because he's exhausted and she knows the way to make him talk is not by asking. Also, she doesn't want this to end. "The twins' hair is so blond," she says eventually. Guthrie hums. "Not like yours was when you were small," she adds. "Theirs is almost white."

He's done the back and is on to the sides now, which should slope downward so that the hair is longest at the front and brushes her collarbones. The lady on the video demonstrates how to level the comb at the shoulder and then keep it horizontal as you pull the hair around the back, to make for the perfect diagonal angle in one fell snip. The pregnancy-test ads popping up at the bottom of the video reckon Guthrie for a thirty-something female.

"What color's Ára's hair?"

Guthrie stops cutting. He puts his thumb into his mouth, as if to pick peanuts from the back of his teeth. Then, after a pause, he gathers the last thick section of Gael's hair and shears it in a single slice. He lets the locks drop down across her face like a veil. "There." He stuffs the scissors into the first-aid kit and zips it shut. "I need to sleep." He presses Gael forward so he can get up.

"No," Gael tries, "not yet. I'm sorry. For asking. That was dumb. You mustn't want to think about her—"

Guthrie makes a noise for her to stop talking. The same noise he makes when he needs to listen for the twins' cries. He's up now and rooting in between his bottom teeth dangerously. "What time is it?"

She checks the computer. "Nearly ten. Don't put your fingers near the wound."

"I'll get the sleeping bag." He goes to the bedroom and returns after too long an interval, pulling the mummy-bag from its stuff sack.

Gael gets up and helps him drape it along the couch.

"Do you need a pillow?" he asks.

"A cushion's fine. But come here, Guth. Come here to me—" She goes to embrace him, but he's wincing, pressing the bandage to his chin like a surgical mask. "Are you headachy? It's been a few hours. Take more drugs."

Guthrie ties up his hair and glances at her. "Don't make a big deal of it."

"What?"

He's working his gums with his tongue now, frowning in concentration.

"Sorry?" Gael bends for his cautious eye contact.

One of the twins starts sobbing on and off, at a sliding pitch, as if tuning up and Guthrie goes to the door right away.

"Wait, make a big deal of what? When I see my hair in the mirror? Is it fucked?"

"Just . . . Sleep in in the morning. Don't answer the door."

"Guthrie?"

"Soraca'll wake Ronan—"

"What the hell?"

"—and they'll start knocking on the floorboards upstairs. They've peeled back the carpet just so they can knock."

"If it's the healing thing," Gael says, hoping to take him off guard, "Art already told me. I wanted to ask you about it. Burp the kid and let's talk. If it's some kind of business, I can help. I'm good at getting people to pay for shit that . . . Let's just say, I'm good at—"

"You're good at lots of things, Gael. All the things." Guthrie holds the door frame as a shield. "And that's great for you. It's a blessing." For a moment, he looks valiant. The sobbing sounds redouble for their Doppler effect of an approaching father. "Whenever Dad's in Ireland, he takes us to mass. Tomorrow's Sunday."

Gael crosses her arms and rests her lips on the knuckles of one hand, or rather, presses her knuckles as hard as she can against her mouth. Her jaw is clamped. Who the fuck is Dad. *You're* Dad. The whimpering from the next room loudens. He comes to *this house* in his *family man car* and he puts his *wank rag cash* in the fucking *Collection* the *waste paper bin* in the *wicked basket waster fucking wicker-dicked provider Himself the philanthropher philandering—*

"Night, Gael. Happy birthday."

She stays up for hours and hours watching the news and sending emails. A couple of bites from oboists, but dammit more nibbles than bites. She can see this had been a weak approach. It presented itself too much as an offering, requiring assessment. Wanting approval. Look, world, at these pages: they speak for themselves. But they can't. She knows better than to think that skills are securities. She must overstep the process of evaluation, take the worth as a given, conceal her signature's sex. Researching a thousand things, she doesn't feel the slightest bit tired. Because she skipped her evening run.

Why, though, had mentioning the mother had the same effect as that dog leash to the face? Surely he sees her every time he looks at the twins and slides his thumb along their upturned noses. Remembers the lovemaking of which small humans had been the upshot. Is it that the Bible rebukes their unwedlocked existence? Hadn't he been pardoned? That's the kind of thing Jarleth could see to. Make a large enough donation to heaven.

When she gets up to piss and wash her face in the fugue of night, she throws a cotton pad in the wastebasket and sees it. The long, elegant incisor. Its single root slick with bloodstained saliva. Its enamel pure and intact as a principle—no sign of a crack. It is not a baby tooth.

6

The Art of Integration

SEPTEMBER 2011

If London Business School had taught Gael one thing, it was that if you don't *really* want something and you try to get it just to prove you can have it, if it's a coveted thing, you won't get it. Even though all you needed to do to get it was *not* to have needed it.

Coveted things include: capital, confidence, access, assumed status, say-so, no invitation, no introduction, nothing needing, no regrets, physical prowess, risks for a lark, bets coming off, undreamed-of options.

"The Dom Pérignon or the Krug, Ms. Foess?" The steward presents both sweating bottles, which might as well be her breasts. "The '04 Pérignon has a rich taste of toasted almonds," she adds, "and the Krug is an aged champagne with a nose of croissants and frangipane. Or perhaps you'd prefer a mandarin mimosa?" Her lipstick is mimosa-colored and absolutely matte, as is her skin and beehive hair, as though she's been blotted so as not to outshine the clientele. She's not much older than Gael, whose skin is dewy from the facial she agreed to endure "to prehydrate the skin" in the First Class Lounge Spa and in so doing had left off observing her mark: a buffet-loitering elderly man in a baseball cap. As the mud had dried and tightened on Gael's face, she felt, for a moment, what Anna Livia's cast-bronze life might be like—or her mother's, if she doesn't play this right.

"I'll go with the Dom." In contrast to the crew's Received Pronunciation, she can hear the twangy Dublin diphthong that a few months at home has drawn out. She'll have to straighten her vowels.

"Lovely. We'll begin the lunch service once we're airborne. You're welcome to browse the menus in the cabinet." The bubbles sound of rain on pavement as she pours. "Just for takeoff, Ms. Foess, I'll move this item to a secure location, if I may." She nods toward the package. The respect for privacy in the choice of words—*this item*—isn't lost on Gael. Getting *this item* through security had entailed thorough hand-searching and screening of her preapproval for oversize carry-on luggage. Restricted articles—Gael had had to remind the security personnel—included guide dogs, mobility aids, musical instruments and sports equipment. There should be no surprises. She had paid her dues.

"Please don't rest anything against it."

"Of course," the steward says. "I'll return it the moment we're in the air."

"That's fine."

Another crew member, a man with eyebrows like correct-answer ticks in a child's copybook, comes to assist in carrying the package toward the cockpit. The *item* is the size of a fifteenth-century door. They carry it as if it's just that. Of course, the only other passenger in the cozy eight-seater first-class cabin notes this odd carry-on. He's sizing Gael up for an envoi. It's the elderly man Gael picked in the lounge for a first-class passenger by his worn-to-bits baseball cap, unironed slacks and the pin worn proudly on his breast, which she hasn't quite been able to make out but can imagine him pinching free each night, setting it on his bedstand and pinning it into a fresh sweater each morning. The business-class passengers had all worn fine suits, heavy watches and targets on their foreheads.

He has the window seat to the left. Gael had the window seat to the right, the row behind, but she asked to move forward with the excuse that she wanted to rest her luggage against the partition. Just the two of them today, so they could do as they pleased. Still, two lamps, more than a meter and one dedicated crew member all threaten to keep them divided. She doesn't have long to set things in motion. He could turn on his entertainment system at any moment (flat-screen TVs and a touch-screen tablet in a docking station on the sill); he could disappear into the distraction of Wi-Fi; he could avail himself of the noise-canceling headphones, or draw the curtains, closing off his private sanctuary for the duration of the seven-hour flight and then Gael's six-thousand-euro ticket would boil down to bubbles (a toast to Jules and Citibank), some very fine dining, a facial, chauffeur service and the general comfort of travel, which is all very well and good and utterly do-without-able.

As soon as the seat belt sign switches off, Gael gets up to remove her dark green blazer, rolled at the wrists to reveal cream silk lining with minuscule black polka dots. Underneath, she's wearing a crisp cream bodycon dress with a belt of plaited black and cream leather strands, gold buckled, to match the gold buttons of the blazer. She's bolstered her five-six stature to five-nine with nude pumps. Her luggage contains a handful of suchlike costumes, which fit her like crossed fingers to the underside of a tablecloth. They weren't clothes she *liked* so much as the investment required. She hangs the blazer in the jacket closet, where the steward has already hung her coat, and she makes a show of considering the pajamas and slippers inside. They're tied together with a ribbon.

Pulling on the ribbon to undo the bow, Gael says, "I will if you will?" to the man, who she can feel observing her. She turns to catch his eye. He gives her a startled look.

"Tell you what," he says, "I heard of worse ideas."

Gael laughs, slips out of her shoes and into the slippers.

"Alexi?" the man says to the steward who has arrived to take his lunch order. "Pamela?" he calls. "Get over here, will you?" The stewardess comes with the champagne bucket that was removed for take-off. Holding Alexi's hand, the man addresses Pamela. "If I were to get into my PJs, I'm talking before lunch and everything, would you consider it an act of terror?" No, sir, says Alexi. Certainly not, says Pamela. "And if this young lady were to join me, you wouldn't spread rumors down through the plane, would you, that anything"—he purses his lips and whispers—"untoward . . . is going on up the ranks." Nothing of the sort, sir. We'll keep mum. Now he slips something into Alexi's hand and mutters, "But if a few of those momma's boys in business hear word, I won't press charges." He winks at Gael, who says:

"The pensioner and the princess is an original fairy tale."

"Ha! The gall!" he says. "The pensioner and the princess. Last time I sat in this cabin, the princess of Saudi Arabia sat where you are, sweetheart. Do you think she knows who I am, Pamela?" Pamela places his slippers on the floor and opens the Velcro of his leather sneakers. "The cat's pajamas is who. Now, everyone knows cats eat fish. So I'll take the caviar, the whitebait, the wild salmon and, for supper, close as you got to cardiac arrest, you hear me, Alexi?" Would he like wine matching? "I certainly oughta suit up for wine matching." He hoists himself up using the upholstery and wheezily addresses Gael. "I'd say ladies first, but, what can I tell you? I'm incontinent."

He returns before long, sighing. "Who knew happiness came in extra large." He places his clothes on the ottoman. "She's all yours." Flapping a hand toward the bathroom.

"Oh thanks, but I'm fine. I changed my mind." Legs crossed, Gael flips through a lifestyle magazine from the demographic-specific medley.

The man stands in the aisle, staring down at his pajamas in wonderment. He's swimming in them. Still wearing the baseball cap.

"That's a cute trick," he says to himself, in his slightly nasal, gravelly voice, whistling his T's and S's.

Gael looks up, straight-faced.

"That's some stunt she pulled on me."

Gael mimics the wink he gave her earlier.

"I see how it is. I been duped. But are you really gonna let a senior citizen have a pajama party all alone?" He tilts his puppy-dog head. "My wife died. My kids hate my guts. I never met my grandkids. I'm an orphan . . ."

"Fine!" Gael gets up. "Alright. Annie. Daddy Warbucks. Whichever it is."

"It's Wally, as a matter of fact."

"Just know, Wally, that adorable only works once on me. Next time you won't get off so easily."

He shrugs. "That's what my wife said." His shoulders in the gray cotton are like the knobs of two walking sticks.

Gael gasps. "TMI, Wally."

"What's TMI. I know FML? My granddaughter sends me that every week via text message. My phone beeps. FML. I make a deposit. She's good till Tuesday." Gael throws her head back in a nonvocal laugh. She passes Alexi in the aisle, returning her package to the wall in front of and in between Gael and Wally. "Tilt that down a notch, will you?" Wally says. "So's me and the lady can talk."

In the jacks, Gael notes the sprinkling of freckles the Irish summer goaded out of her pale skin, only visible since the facialist cleaned off her makeup. Her eyes, the whitish-bluish-gray color of meltwater, are sleepy-looking, pupils dilated from the early-afternoon alcohol. She'd look too young free of makeup had Guthrie not cut her hair so decisively and had she not dyed silver a pinchful of strands from her window's peak and temples. Subtle enough that it looks like threaded early graying. Three flutes of fizz have compromised the hold she has on herself and the hold she'll need to have on her cards for the all-in moment. She folds her clothes, splashes cold water on her face and considers switching to coffee for the next few thousand miles.

"I took the liberty of ordering you a glass. It's delicious!" Wally brandishes his wine for a clink. "Slanty. Oh wait, that's Chinese, not Irish."

Gael takes a big gulp of the honeyish wine, despite preferring brisker whites. It treacles down her throat, helping to forestall what she would say. Nothing would be gained by calling him out on this. Nothing profitable. A cloth-covered table has appeared meanwhile, set with heavy cutlery, glasses made of glass, napkins folded into airplanes, one china plate atop another, mini salt and pepper grinders and a basket of fresh granary bread with coils of butter in a little dish. "*Sláinte*," she says, clinking his glass. "What is it?"

"No clue. Called something like chameleon. Don't like it, spit it out. Life's short."

In the nick of time, Gael stops herself from saying, "That's what your wife said."

"Sémillon," Pamela corrects him, delivering Gael her starter. "It's somewhat of a sweet New World wine." The way she says this, it clearly wasn't her recommendation. It's only dawning on Gael that the courses won't come together. Of course they won't! But she has only ever had all her courses come together on flights, on a sad overloaded plastic tray. Gelatinous potato side salads packed in finicky containers. Pamela describes Gael's starter—Gressingham duck breast, shiitake mushroom, ginger consommé—and quietly conveys that the wine was matched for Wally's foie gras (he changed his mind about the caviar), so if she'd like something better suited to duck, just nod.

"What's the conference topic, ladies?"

"It's fine." Gael smiles.

"I don't like to know brands is all," Wally says. "I don't eat food that's been advertised. Anything on a billboard, I don't eat. Period. They make a commercial for the granola I been buying all my life, I switch granola. I'm eighty-two. I don't give a damn. I'm switching granola."

"Wally," Gael says, "you don't look a day over eighty-one. Don't switch granola."

They banter their way through bread and butter, starters and entrées. Salmon with fennel and Pernod sauce for the gentleman. For the lady, seared sea bass with samphire, red pepper pearls and bouillabaisse sauce. Napa Valley Sauvignon Blanc to wash it all down. Though Gael sadly knows she'll have to chuck it all up in a half bottle's time if she's to have any wits left about her when they're needed. That in mind, she takes the opportunity of a lull in conversation to change its direction: "'Boot and rally.'" She sips her wine. "Is that what it stands for?" Wally looks a bit confounded for a moment. He squints, as if not seeing what she means is a physical condition. Then it comes into focus. The gold pin glinting at them from his sweater on the ottoman. Gael had only just made it out for a delicately crafted boot. "It doesn't look like an army boot," she says.

"My pin." The tide goes out on his expression.

The crew arrive to clear their dinner plates and Wally loses the thread of his thought, or the energy of it. Gael sees this and makes it clear they'd like some space, not to fuss over wine and water. "We need half an hour before dessert." She waits until it's quiet again and their glasses are full and says, "Your pin?"

"I had it made special," Wally says, distantly. "I got the right boot. My brother got the left. But I just visited and he wasn't wearing it. Says men don't wear jewelry in Ireland. I guess it's a long story." He takes a few wheezy breaths.

"Give me the gist of it," Gael says.

"The gist?"

Gael shrugs softly.

He takes some wine into his mouth and swills it through his teeth as if to clean them. He holds it in his cheeks, then swallows noisily. "Put it this way. Wherever you get to . . . on this rock in orbit . . . you gotta remember where you come from. I don't wanna forget how I started, you understand? Heck no, course you don't! You're a kid flying first-class. We had different paths, you and me."

"Don't assume I didn't earn my way here," Gael says.

"Well, if you did, I'm certainly interested. But I bet you ten thousand bucks right now, I'll write a check, shake my hand on it kid if you're for real, I *bet* you didn't have to take turns going to school with your brother 'cause you only had the one pair of boots between you. I bet you had more than half an education to work your way up from."

Gael watches the tilt of his mouth, like a picture hung with neither love nor leveler.

"It's smart to be cautious," he says. "Caution keeps you in the black. Not very far into it, it oughta be said, but in the black all the same. Our pop had a heart attack on a boat out fishing for mackerel. He was alone so he drowned. Fell into the water, got caught on his own line, so his heart kicked it, he drowned and he hung for a bargain. Tell that to your kids at bedtime. Don't feel bad about it 'cause I barely knew the guy, just knew he drank like a fish and beat on Mom. She had me and Seymour and she was pregnant with Bernice. For me, she parked cars, for Seymour, she tended tables, for Bernice, she baked breakfast muffins. We'd wake up to the smell of her determination. Bernice was easy to look after most of the time. She wasn't *right,* see." He taps his middle finger to his head. It thuds against the fabric of his cap. "She was gentle and still like a lake with no fish in it. Far away. You could sit her in front of a toy car and she'd be pushing it forward and back an hour later. She never got diagnosed 'cause she wasn't registered or anything. No birth certificate. Born in the tub with the help of a coworker and a fillet knife. Mom was in her early forties. Clocked up so many miscarriages it got to the point she never expected a live one, and it was premature, and we was all mourning, so that's how Bernice turned up. With death on her tail. One day I'm at school, sixth grade, Seymour's kidsitting, this is Providence, where we grew up, and he was working real hard. He was ahead of me, on paper at least. Something Pop had said to him stuck, but I never got told it. We shared everything, except that. Like it was meant for his ears only. To give him a leg up. He changed, one day to the next. I slept on a hammock on top of his mattress on the floor. 'The bunk.' Whatever that thing was, it got between us like . . . moisture in cement. Swole up. Started growing mildew. He got studious, I got good with girls. It was an instinct for me. Knowing where the value was. In people. With *people* a' course. We fought for Mom's love. And so it happened like that. Seymour's chewing on the end of his pencil, Bernice is in her playpen, choking on a coloring crayon. You'll never guess. Sky blue. She was dead a half hour fore Seymour knew about it. You couldn't even tell what's wrong . . . just a blue stain. Anyways I wasn't there."

The side of his mouth that's tilted down is closest to Gael. It's as if he's trying to lift it with a very weak muscle. It quivers and tightens, quivers and tightens. His eyes are black and the peak of the cap casts an inverse shadow of pallor around them.

"I'm sorry," Gael says.

"Yeah." He stretches his chin upward, so the sinews of his neck become harp strings. "Bunch of legal hoo-ha like you wouldn't believe. Reporters loitering, photo-ing me and Seymour. The government people put us into foster care. We threatened to wring each other's necks till they split us into separate houses. Nearly got sent to juvie for that. That's a fast way to go, after Bernice. Our mother was *not a fit parent*, they said. She was distraught. She aged like fruit in direct sunlight. Certainly didn't look fit after all that. Which alone was a tragedy. This beautiful woman." Wally holds his palm out and dips it a few times, as if weighing bullion. "Then, outta nowhere—

get this: something crawls from the woodwork of our father's coffin. His old boss had been watching from the sideline. He'd always had a soft spot for Mom. Transpires, this guy'd taken life insurance out on Pop. Smart fella, *way* ahead of the game. It had took its time, but it paid out at long last. Eighteen grand." Wally coughs. "He didn't know it *would* for sure, pay out. This is 1935. The goddamned Depression. I'm not a historian. I'm no economist. But that was a *lot* of money. Don't ask me how, don't ask me why. All's I know is he kept a couple grand for himself and cut the rest into three parts, for Mom, me and my brother when we turned legal. Alright, sunshine. You tell me what you'd'a done with a small fortune, no schooling, short pants and shorter teeth? World War Two bucking up. Franklin Roosevelt in office telling us: far better is it to dare mighty things, to win glorious triumphs, even checkered by failure, than to rank with those poor spirits who neither enjoy nor suffer much, because they live in a gray twilight that knows not victory nor defeat." He catches his breath. "See? Victory, defeat. Triumphs, failures. Grand stuff. Defeat gets to be more powerful than survival. Having *gone after* something. There was FDR telling us, the most important single ingredient in the formula of success is knowing how to get along with people. Oh boy. I heard that. That, I heard. But Seymour, he heard other things. It's only through labor and painful effort, by grim energy and resolute courage, that we move on to better things. Seymour heard, 'A man who's never gone to school can steal from a freight car, but if he has a university education, he can steal the whole railroad.' He wanted to be among the six percent of men with a college degree, so he finished high school, enrolled in medical school in '39. Blew half his brass on the degree and upkeep, the other half on a deposit for a two-bedroom near campus. A medical degree sure as hell looked like bootstraps to us back then. All he'd need was a wife for the house and, wouldya look at that: upward mobility. But not so fast, not so fast, cupcake. In the interest of protecting his new home from being powdered like Jean Harlow's nose, Seymour signed up. As a combat medic. Served in the navy. Late '43. Way to go for timing, buddy. Top marks for survival. When the boys come back, little over a year later—well, the ones that *did* come back—there's no jobs. The government's scratching its head what to do with them all. So what did they decide, those yahoos in Congress? To pay for education! Any GI Joe who wanted to be Joe MD could be." Wally shakes his head and lets out a big crackling sigh. "He earned plenty in the way of stripes, Seymour. But he never got to owning no railroad." He lets that comment sit in the air-conditioning, neither cold nor warm. Not new. Not right, necessarily.

Gael takes the bottle from the bucket, refills Wally's glass and empties the remainder into her own, directing herself to have patience. She's getting there. "I hated this wine at the start of the bottle."

"Oh." Wally looks at her. "Has it grown on you?"

"I've grown on it. That's how it goes. Tell me, Wally, were you among the six percent, with a degree?"

"No, I never was. I never went to Harvard or Yale. I got that check, came of age and you know where I headed?"

"For the drafting station?"

"For the one percent. The zero point six percent. Don't need no algebra to know how that works out."

"Didn't you have to enlist?"

"This was only after Pearl Harbor. Look, none of us knew our president couldn't walk. You couldn't hear that sort of thing on the radio." Wally stops talking for a minute and makes some private connection. He chuckles. "I became quite intent alright."

"Intent on what?" Gael says.

"What?" He cups his ear and leans into her, suddenly almost shouting. "What's that? Problem?" He turns and smacks his ear like he's swatting a fly. "Problem solved." Delighted with his own schtick, he wheezes and rubs the side of his head. "Stand in what line? Sign where? Can't hear you, kid. I bust my eardrum."

Alexi and Pamela arrive to reset their tables for dessert. They refrain from irritating nicety chatter. Just do their jobs, removing the signs of what's been consumed and what's been wasted, letting Wally run the Wally Show, letting the girl heed his story, as she seems to want to do. The afternoon has worn on, but the sky outside lingers over lunch as they coast into an earlier time zone. (Pamela tried to catch Gael's eye to see if she needed saving, but no. You've read it all wrong, Pamela.) Who wouldn't want to live like this, evading nightfall? A thrill runs along Gael's chest when she thinks how unlikely it is to be pajamaed, thirty-five thousand feet above homelessness. She hasn't anywhere to sleep and there's only seven hundred pounds on her credit card. She has cash, too, but she won't count it up, nor is she wont to count it down. There's so much daylight still for options to open up like thighs. She tries to imagine Wally's house, but she only knows the Manhattan homes of the screen and he hasn't even said if he lives in the city. If he has a guest room. Some gesticulations are going on and the crew serve desserts of fresh fruit salad with cappuccino and Scottish shortbread for Gael and a treacle and lemon tart with vanilla crème anglaise for Wally, who asks if they ran out of Doritos. "So." Gael prongs a cube of pip-free watermelon. "You got by?"

"Good God this pie is appetizing. Gimme your fork." He lops off a chunk of the lemon-treacle tart and passes the loaded fork back to her. "Get that in you." Crumbs in the corners of his mouth fall down to his lap as he talks. "So. Here's me. Biding my time. Had to wait the war out. I just knew it. The only use for those years was finding unassuming, farsighted men to get in your corner, on your books. My pop's boss was a man like that. It was hard to stay patient, but was I right to wait? Yessiree. Yes I was. Oh me oh my. The 1950s consumer! What a business. It's not even impressive, really, to have skipped a few rungs during all that. Anyway, my philosophy's simple. First, find out what needs to be done, however long it takes, then go at it with everything you have. Whatever you got in you."

How very American. Gael licks the cappuccino foam from her upper lip and reaches into the storage area in the sill where she spotted a writing set earlier. She takes it out and immortalizes Wally's wisdom, which makes him chuckle. It makes him sit up a little, even though he's clearly getting dozy. "What was the question?" he says, realizing that he's spent an hour going off on one. He swallows a yawn, resting his eyes, hung-lidded, on her luggage. "Sorry for the sermon, kid. It's not often I get to converse with such a . . ." Gael smiles politely as Pamela clears the plates and tables (". . . tolerant . . ."). More beverages are offered (". . . young lady")—they might like to switch to red—and Wally looks to Gael for her inclination. No. She wants him alert and keen and he, unlike her, refrained from coffee, so she asks Pamela for blankets and suggests to Wally—reaching across the aisle to rest her hand on his forearm—that they put their eye covers on and recline their chairs for an hour or two. Try out the massage function. The noise-canceling headphones. Because of the time difference, the day will be five hours longer. So the farsighted thing to do is log some sleep now so they'll feel like dancing their dinner off later.

"Kid, if you were any uglier, I'd swear you were my daughter."

Even though she went for a run this morning, before finding room in her cabin baggage for her trainers, she isn't in the least bit tired. But she puts on the eye covers and waits until Wally is snuffling and slack-mouthed before sneaking off to turn the lavatory into a purge-tory. Then, she brushes her teeth, arranges her belongings and takes out her laptop.

"It's a rare condition." Gael spoke Wally softly to wakefulness, his jowl bathed in milky afternoon light that poured around him and kept him half-drowned in stupor, susceptible as a child in a blankie. A mug of fresh mint tea steamed on Gael's sill. Vapor snaked through the space between them. The snack baskets had been replenished. At long intervals, Wally pushed single Reese's into his mouth and let them melt like lozenges. Gael had opened the pack and offered them to him. She didn't like them, no, she'd said. The fact was she loved them to the point of mewling, but they were food for the listener and the listener only. Peanut butter glues the tongue to the hard palate. Instead, she'd taken a pistachio macaron and twirled it between her fingers the way Harper did poker chips.

The particular condition is extremely rare, she explained. The first time it happened was the Sunday following his Holy Communion. He had just received the Eucharist in earnest—not for show, nor as a means to an end—and was kneeling in the pews beside their father. She hadn't been there to see it. She'd refused to sit up front with them. She'd snuck outside and climbed the wire mesh netting of the basketball court as an alternate route to the heavens. So she didn't see it happen, but later she could piece it together: Guthrie's body had shivered, stiffened and convulsed, eyes roaming the skull-cathedral. Jarleth would have shushed the nearby parishioners—warned them not to overreact, the boy has just fainted—and carried him out for fresh air. Though it might have been a blessing to choke on the body of Christ, it was with utter conviction that Jarleth Heimliched the sacrament out of his son, fracturing two ribs in the process. He was *angry* when nothing came flying from Guthrie's windpipe. He was *furious* at the flock that had scuttled out for a gawk, the biddies who cried *cursed*, who cried *ambulance*, who, fumbling through their purses, cried: Is it *911 or 999 or 666 or what*. He was *livid* when nothing came of the allergy checks that followed, the MRIs, x-rays, ultrasounds, EEGs, blood tests. Through the months of not knowing, the sharp but delicate bones of Guthrie's face took more knocks than a list of bad jokes.

Her only brother. She'd imagined lesions on the soft tissues of his personality. But he himself imagined something else, he confessed to her once, holding his bruised ribs. He imagined a mark somewhere deep within him the size of God's thumbprint, both small and larger than anything we know of. He would crawl into her bed, having understood early that the way to fall asleep is to stop listening and he couldn't stop listening to God. He could only stop listening to a sinner, like his sister. He would clutch her spare pillow and gaze at the pages of her grown-up magazines taped to the walls until his eyes glossed over and he was carry-outable. Then began the process of elimination. All we can do, said the doctor, is test each reasonable hypothesis. Later, much later, a neurologist proffered a verdict. A word that makes us think of a spectrum: on one side, fantasy, on the other, falsity. Untruth. Unreality. And Guthrie was no liar, though Jarleth promised him he could lie and still be God's beloved child. "Where would the church be if Saint Peter didn't lie?" he said, all negotiation. The way of His world is complex, he argued. Guthrie cried and cried and clapped his ears. The way you did, Wally. Only, when he did it, what burst wasn't an eardrum.

Somatic delusional disorder. A recurring nonbizarre delusion. A syndrome. When there's no synonym, how do you explain it to the sufferer? Wally worked the peanut butter with his tongue. *Why not tell the kid?* he was thinking. This was clear. *Could you not just say: You're completely sane, brother. You're a hundred percent sane except for one itsy-bitsy madness. You think you're sick and you're not. Here it is in writing.*

This is where the delusion comes in. Any attempt to disprove the epilepsy would wind up reinforcing the delusion—the brain's hijacking—as Guthrie's evidence was his own *experience* which no one else would *want* and no one *could have* excepting fellow sufferers. One in twenty-six people develop epilepsy at some point in their lives and the thousands of descriptions of seizures he'd read described his own. Although his aura was unusual, he could admit. Very few patients experience auras like his.

"Auras?"

Wally had been listening.

Gael ordered a bottle of red from Pamela when she came to re-fill their water glasses. Pigheaded. Old World. With a bouquet of cobwebs. Pamela strained to smile at Gael's command. These pas-sengers were in another world—the kind of place you only get to pass through once, like the shadow of a total solar eclipse. The flight map glowed on Wally's screen. Two hours forty to destination and dinner had yet to be served. This place couldn't be returned to. Cha-teau Destieux 2008, Saint-Emilion Grand Cru Classé. No need for tastings, no. Gael ordered the Devon crab, apple dill and avocado with smoked salmon and osetra caviar. The grilled Aberdeen Angus beef, oxtail *croustillant,* braised root vegetables, red wine, horserad-ish and port sauce. The chocolate hazelnut cake and scotch sorbet. Absorbed by her every word, Wally couldn't pronounce his own. He held a peace sign up to Pamela: times two. But give us forty minutes to find our appetites, Gael said, and looked at Wally, who halted the peanut butter cup's journey to his mouth and put it back onto its paper, gently as a string of pearls onto a neck.

An aura is the first symptom. It's a kind of warning. A blessing, according to Guthrie. Not all people with epilepsy have them and they differ depending on where in the brain the neural malfunction takes place—where the electrical storm strikes its lightning. You might smell or taste something off, lose sensation on one side of your tongue, have déjà vu, lose sensation on one side of your tongue, have déjà vu, see zigzag patterns or hallucinations, hear something shrill or grating, feel fingers raking your insides, queasy-making, lose con-trol of your bowels. Overpowering sensations. Seldom pleasurable. The aura can be the seizure itself, if it's a partial. With Guthrie, it only marks the first phase of a full grand mal: the foreplay to violent convulsions, loss of awareness, clinching blackout. He breaks into a prickly sweat and becomes unresponsive to sound. Catch him quick, before his eyes roll. The light follows.

This is the rarest type of aura. Tears stream. The light, he re-ports, is euphoric. A white dome growing into the blackness that constitutes the whole world for as many milliseconds as there are between Achilles and the tortoise. No people, no landscapes, just the color—no color and all colors at once—in a conception of space based on a different understanding of how the body exists in its environment. Geodesic, he once said, wherever he got that word from. Not from his dropout education. He didn't have the words to begin with to describe it. He still doesn't, but he seeks them out. He called the color zinc once. Now, he knows it's a color there's no paint for. It's not comparable to anything, because it's beyond the known spectrum and he can only see it when he fits. After, it's a sense memory and the shade is all wrong. He aches for its warmth and sobering clarity, deathwish. He turns bluish and thrashes after it—the light. Thumps his head. The blackouts last only a moment, but when he comes to, he doesn't speak for minutes, hours sometimes. He trembles until he finds a place to fall asleep. Later, there's a new crack somewhere, outside or in. And we weren't brought up in Japan, where cracks are patched with gold epoxy. In Ireland, cracks are borne brazenly or privately and are damnwell unadorned.

"Your brother sees a color we don't see?" Wally asks, stumped.

Gael looks into his eyes. "And if you're an artist," she says, "that's either the purest form of torture or—"

"He's an artist?"

Gael lifts her chin, like an umpire.

"Your brother?"

"Didn't I say?"

Wally clocks the luggage encumbering the cabin. He sits up and cradles his glass in both palms. The wine and the baseball cap and the airline pajamas add up to one thing: patron. "Are you, uhm . . ." His mouth clacks with residue peanut butter. ". . . his manager?"

Gael shakes her head in a don't-be-daft sort of way. "I don't like to think of myself as his agent. I'm meeting with gallerists on his behalf. He's my brother. He won't fly. There's a lot of things he can't do for himself."

"That figures."

"His condition's . . ." Gael looks a long way ahead and takes a mouthful of wine. She does her best to summon a surge of emotion; restrained below hardened layers of herself like a hundred-mile-deep low-magnitude earthquake. Some people sleep straight through that sort of thing, Wally. Fools miss it completely, unprepared for the tsunami that can follow. The daylight outside has eased and pinkened. Two hours twenty to destination. Green encroaches on their flight maps. The scent of dinner preparations carries down the aisle but she waits and waits, holding off while Wally's lips do this dance of pursing, relaxing, pursing in the corner of her eye. He has to be the one to ask for it. Just as he'd had to don the pajamas.

At long last, it comes in an effort to sound offhand. "What's he do, landscapes? Portraits?"

"No."

Wally's lips try out all sorts of responses, none of which he's satisfied with. "What else is there? Still life? Nudes? Whatdotheycallit, life drawing?"

Gael inhales deeply and doesn't let the breath out, as if she's been putting up with this man because of his wealth and gender and elderliness and rightly so, young lady. She stands up and begins to maneuver the luggage. "It's easier just to show you. But I don't know how they've packaged this inside. Let me see." Wally makes no objection. He sits on the edge of his seat and pushes up the rim of his cap. This is his privilege. A private show. The case is a steel-reinforced leather portfolio like a giant briefcase. When she carries it by its shoulder strap, the case reaches her ankles. It weighs fifty pounds, filled. And the three hundred euro it set her back. Spending so much on the case made her feel better for having taken all five paintings, rather than just the one he had gifted her. With any luck, he won't notice their absence. And better to have them out in the world than growing mold in that dank cupboard.

Inside are sheets of foam padding. With her back to him, she pulls some out for effect. "Close your eyes, Wally." She checks his obedience. Then she carries the best three along the aisle and tries to arrange them to fit. They're not canvases. Guthrie had retrieved a bunch of school desks from a skip—too viciously vandalized to be sanded down or painted over. He'd dismantled the desks for their lids and pried off decades of Wrigley's with a butter knife. Each painting takes up two desk lids nailed roughly together, with thin strips of wood running along the back so they don't bend. The rust from the nails has bled into the edges of the white paint. The way they're laid out, the hinged vertical rectangles make them look like shutters. Only, they do the opposite of shutting light out. They're darkness's negatives. More dramatic vertically, she decides. Height trumps breadth. Besides, there's no space for them all lengthwise. She transforms them into vertical diptychs, just like that.

Alexi is assembling the dinner trolley at the end of the aisle and Gael holds her hand up to him: five minutes. He bows. Then, she points at the lights and makes a twisting motion. It's a touch too dark. Alexi turns on overhead lighting selectively through the cabin, biting his lip as he comes back and forth to check the effect on the works of art. Finally, he points to the paintings and then from Gael's head to her toes and he mouths: Wow. *Mourns* is too strong a word, but Gael pities the fact that this exchange would never have happened with Pamela. No matter how much you pay them, women never want the best for one another.

Wally's breathing loudly, as if having his eyes closed is effortful. "Can I look yet?"

"Just a sec." She shifts them around, so the brightest one is in the center and the one with the dark stripe is to the left. The wheezing loudens as everything else falls silent.

"If you're robbing me, no attorney on God's greenbacks can help you."

Is that a hint of discomfort she hears? She laughs lightly. She doesn't tell him to open his eyes. They might still be shut for another minute for how quiet he is, how heavy is the labor of his lungs. He seems to be waiting for the paintings to come into focus. Blinking doesn't make them less abstract. But then it happens. They *do* come into focus. Wally's black eyes mirror the panels of categorical white. Not clouds, but stratosphere?

"Oh boy," he says solemnly, almost resigned. He sticks his head out and tucks it back, like a chicken walking, only he's rooted to the spot.

They are more beautiful than Gael remembers. Their limit of color; the leftmost bold stripe of black-brown, where the blackout creeps in; the thin-as-floss shapes hinted at beneath the huge white-wash layers in the middle; on the rightmost, the injury of scraped-off moments, like the ones he loses, every time, revealing brilliant yellow prints beneath—the marks that look in some places like angry scratches and in others like structured appeals; the distressing texture all over, given by the graffiti base layer, silts and filaments. The whiff of white spirits.

"Are these . . ." Wally starts to say. "I mean, it's the aura. Right? I know that." He breathes heavily. "Is there a title?"

"Just numbers. A catalogue of fits," Gael says. "These are 8, 13 and 21." She watches this sink in, then adds: "Acrylic on desk."

Wally gets up and inspects the pieces individually, asking if they're a set or separate. Separate, Gael replies. She's bringing over a sample of his work before making a shipment. It's important to see the materials up close. He does classic representational work and all that, but everyone wants the auras, she says with an air of nuisance. And since he's constantly trying new "medication" and he strictly does *one painting per fit,* sooner or later a placebo pill—Dilantin, Epilim, Trileptal, Zonegran (she does air quotes)—will bring an end to these ecstatic paintings. He'll move on to something else, beyond the expression of catharsis, and maybe these will become collectors' items, like Van Gogh's briefly lived white period. Gael gives her most frivolous laugh at what she's suggested, which could only be a joke.

Still standing, Wally has his back pressed against the window, trying to see the artworks from a distance. His hat is pushed high. "There's a guy called Twimbly paints something similar," he says. "Twombly. He's huge. I seen him in the Frick. Very modern. He's good." Wally glances away from the paintings for a split second only. "But his stuff's not as . . . Not like this. With the story and all."

"Yeah," Gael says simply.

A pause. There's something a little frantic in his tone when he says, "And he can draw, too?"

"Draw? Since he could hold a pencil. I have pictures on my phone, I think . . ." She lets her voice trail off, staring at the paintings dreamily. Who needs proof he can draw? is the unspoken challenge. Surely you're not a man who second-guesses his own instinct. The blood of the beef reaches them, despite the air-conditioning. Their appetites are back, larger than before. Gael takes a deep breath as if gathering the courage and energy to put them away again, which must be done. Wally coughs nervously, then goes to his closet to rummage through his waxed-canvas duffel bag. For an inhaler? He turns to her, tosses open his checkbook.

"Okay, kid. What's the hammer price?"

Gael does her best to blush, about to lift number 8 back to its home. "Sorry?"

"It's dollars to donuts I'm having one."

Struggling to be polite, Gael says, "I'm glad you're a fan, Wally. Really. But I can't jeopardize my meetings—"

"Take em wherever you gotta take em," he says. "Just put a red sticker on that one. Mail it to me after."

Gael smiles again, sliding number 8 carefully back into the portfolio, between sheets of foam.

"I'm not kidding," Wally says, ever so slightly aggro.

Gael considers him. He reminds her of a younger version of herself. "I appreciate that," she says.

Wally starts scribbling so forcefully his hat falls to the table and knocks over his wineglass. Pamela comes rushing down the aisle with tissues she must have been blotting herself with. "Not now, Laura," he tells her without looking up and she halts, stunned. Gael ignores the apology Pamela is hovering around for. The woman's got tissues to hand, after all, and there's only one sort of white flag in America. Wally tears off the check and holds it out to Gael, who lets her hand hesitate as one does before swatting a giant hornet. Four zeros led by a five, she sees, folding the check.

"*I* appreciate it," Wally says.

Gael gives him a chastising look. "I'll need your address."

◆

US Customs is the great democratizer. Isn't that how the saying goes? It counts for nothing that she'd come through the priority lane and that a chauffeur service awaited her in the arrivals hall. The customs official didn't like the look of her luggage, which was only one up from not liking the look of her surname, one up from not liking the look of her headwear. Of course, Gael hadn't declared her newly acquired goods over the value of ten thousand dollars burning against her left breast where she'd slipped it into her bra for safekeeping. The paintings, she argues, were only worth the hundred bucks of paint that went into them. The wood had been free. She's not a professional artist or anything. She's taking them over to a friend, Harper Schiada, who she used to live with in London. They're a gift for her—a good enough friend that she'd like anything made by Gael.

"Is Miz Schiada an American citizen?"

"She's from Las Vegas."

"I'mma ask you that again: is Miz Schiada an American citizen?"

Gael can feel how wide her eyes are. She tries to relax. "Yes, she is. Sir."

"I'mma need Miz Schiada to verify what you're telling me is true."

"But it's a gift!" Gael says, faux-heartbroken. "Telling her what I'm bringing would ruin the surprise."

"United States Customs has no interest in surprises. Matter of fact, we hate surprises."

Gael sighs. Nods.

"This right here looks like commercial goods to me."

"No, sir, it's not."

"Ma'am, I'mma need you to call Miz Schiada to confirm your story. You can either do it right here right now, seeing as you're a first-class passenger and there's no one standing in line, or you'll be taken to a private room where you can make the call at your leisure." He pronounces "leisure" so that it rhymes with "seizure."

"I'll phone now," Gael says. She takes out her phone and finds it extremely difficult to locate the right contact with her heart racing and the customs officer's face contorting as he uncaps a red marker and circles her arrival card.

Without looking up, he says: "The address you put down here. This is the address of the elderly gentleman I let through right before you. Have you got a explanation for that?"

Gael covers the mouthpiece of her phone, waiting for Harper to pick up and save her. "I didn't write down Harper's address yet, because she's coming to meet me in New York. So Wally just told me to put that down—we got to know each other on the plane. I'll probably visit him." *Why didn't I just write down the fucking Ritz forfuckssake.*

"Ma'am." This was a whole sentence, Gael could hear. It had a beginning, a middle and an end. "The address you write on your arrival documentation needs to be a bona fide address. Not a false accommodation. It's the address you're staying at tonight. We put it in the system, where you're staying at. That's our procedure. I do not like one part of this. I'mma need to see your return itinerary, ma'am."

Gael holds up a finger and looks attentive and serious, to show that she knows he's in power and he can send her home on a whim and she can't very well tell him she doesn't have a return flight. This situation might just require tears: the next best thing to getting on her knees. But Gael's more worried than anything at the heat behind her eyes that she hadn't yet solicited and the break in her voice when she says, "Harper?"

Most of the seven hundred pounds on her credit card disappears with the forced purchase of a return ticket, on the spot, via airport Wi-Fi, so that the customs official is satisfied she can afford to leave the country. (She picks the farthest-off date her ninety-day visa will allow. Mid-December.)

Up fifty. Down one.

Not terrible, she tells herself, as a bead of sweat travels from her underarm, beneath the portfolio strap, all the way down her side. She has to make the portfolio look light, so that her carrying it herself, along with a rolly bag, seems like a choice. As she passes through the automatic gates into the arrival hall—not all that auto-matic, after all—she wonders: if she takes the chauffeur service, will she have to pay?

7

Opportunity, Cost

I

The American Dream is best dreamed on one of the seven pillow options at the Plaza Hotel. Goose down; the valerian-infused aromatic
pillow; the cloud pillow filled with ten million synthetic microbeads
to cry one's Rosary into; buckwheat, should one countenance neither the animal nor the synthetic; the sound pillow with soothing
rain forest noises to drown out the city's cacophony of road works,
hydraulics, air-conditioning relics, sirens, anachronistic horse-and-
carriage clatter and, above it all, ricocheting between the tallest,
glassiest of skyscrapers: talk. Gael, though, doesn't sleep on a pillow.
She sleeps belly-down with her arm for a headrest. Wakes with Ro-
dinesque knuckle imprints on her chin.

It's been a week. She's no longer dreaming, but assessing the cost
of her mistakes.

When the airport chauffeur had asked *Where to?* she'd envisioned
a lobby full of Wallys and replied: the Plaza. No harm multiplying my
options, she'd thought, with the city glittering at her in the Lincoln
Town Car, making goldilocks of her profile, committing her to dine
with bears. As the hotel concierge made an imprint of her credit card

and photocopied her passport, he quietly declared it six-ninety-two-per-night excluding tax and city charges. There wouldn't be funds on her card for one night. She wouldn't be able to check out. Seeing her flush, the concierge asked if she was averse to heights. "No," she'd said. "No no. The seventeenth floor is fine." The concierge looked relieved—as if it would have been his embarrassment—and assured her it was the very best room in that price range.

She took the check to its issuing branch the next morning and the cashier looked at her passport the way a midlife-crisis-stricken woman looks at a pregnancy test shelved beside menopausal bone density supplements in a pharmacy. Vacantly, she recited: Due to the size of the sum (won't fit your pencil sharpener vagina), without a second form of ID (a passport where you're older and uglier) and a letter addressed to you (the kid inside the blanket fort, Mom's house), we can't cash this check at this institution (lodge it elsewhere). Gael stuck out the staring contest. Or you could wait for it to clear, which takes five to ten working days minimum. We'd need a phone number to let you know if and when it's processed.

"You can reach me at the Plaza. Shall I give you their number?"

That silly little chest-jut had double-locked her into her new abode. She made the requisite moves to lift the limit on her card and applied for new ones, but she couldn't afford to dwell on cash flow. Moving the paintings from the hotel-room floor onto gallery walls would require all of her focus and industry.

But here too she had erred, thinking portfolio meetings would be the way to get the work seen. She'd been sending out requests for appointments since the night Guthrie'd cut her hair, but, as with Sive's scores, this was looking more and more like a dead end. She began phoning galleries, wringing information from the interns manning the front desks. Credentials are everything, they told her. Artists eventually shown in galleries are often first discovered in an academic context. Others explained that if a curator spots an artist's work at a fair or another gallery and is impressed, they might arrange a studio visit to see the artist's body of work. To get a show in Manhattan, an artist already needs to be on the Ladder of Divine Ascent, was the message.

Gael had lost whole days researching how best to present her brother as an artist with credentials (degrees are purchasable; posters of past exhibitions are fudgible; fake reviews are publishable) before it dawned on her that many interns in Manhattan sleep on goose down pillows and would dream accordingly. Broke and overworked, yes, but choosing to go practically unpaid in the city because the alternatives make less sense, because of the dream's promise and because they can. She had to get back on the phone and find the insomniac among them, falling short of rent and belief.

"What would it take?" she'd asked. "For an outlier? No sugarcoating *please*. I'm diabetic. I just want to know. Under *what* circumstance would a gallerist give a walk-in artist a shot, if she came in holding the most astounding, thrilling, undeniable art you'd ever seen? What would it take? How good would it have to be? Who'd have to see it?"

The guy hesitated, perhaps to imagine such a cheapening of the establishment. "Ye-ah," he drawled, "none. No circumstances. I mean, it's never happened. A nobody walking in with incredible work . . . but it wouldn't. Happen. That's not how we find artists. It wouldn't matter how good the work is. That's just not how it goes in this city. In any reputable gallery. At least since the '80s. Maybe it's different where you're from. Or in like, Arkansas. Do you go to school here, or—?"

So unlikely, so unexpected that she might just pull it off. But this city has a keen radar for chancers and she doesn't feel like being taken for one. There is another, narrower route to take—tricky terrain but much more immediate. Who is it that described a net as a series of holes connected by a string?

❖

The gold-trimmed hotel-room curtains are open, showing fast September cloudshift like an 8mm film. Spitty rain: vintage scratches on the reel. Playing journalist with *ArtNexus* magazine, Gael is interviewing Dr. Raina Menendez, whose exhibition (Gael saw in SoHo) involved a series of hyperintricate paintings of alternate-history scenes, hooked up to canvas-length dispensers of paint stripper. Solvent began pouring over the paintings at erratic intervals, sending audience members scurrying from one piece to the next to take them in before the images were liquefied. Beneath each, long transparent boxes caught the paint drippings. These were the artworks for sale in the gallery: plastic buckets of paint smoothie. That anyone would pay six figures for a painting's residue was the challenge the gallery had taken on and perhaps they only did so because of Raina's reputation. Or they knew that buyers would want to prove their appreciation that one form was not a reduction of the other, but a translation. This was the sort of pandering palaver found in reviews online. By Gael's measure, Raina wants to be put to task intellectually and to be spared personal questions. "You're satirizing value attribution, not only between states of composition and in capitalism's mechanism, but in the subject matter: politically charged photorealist townscapes, rather than, say, fauvist still lives or color field works. The loss is more tragic. The obscene generosity of *time* weighs on the viewer, rushing from canvas to canvas, unable to commit to one narrative disintegration."

"Is this a question?" Raina asks.

"You're exposing art's potential for radical responses in the moment, followed by political inaction once the narratives stop being reported on." Gael continues, undeterred, needing her vexed. "But above all that . . . is the *begging* . . . for acknowledgment that art and the artist—the body and the body of work—won't remain in a state of aesthetic acceptability; that the sacred terrain of beauty and orderliness be trespassed; that *time* and *output* and *bloom*—which we treat reverentially and with such effort of conservation—be humiliated. No?"

She had to go through this whole rigmarole and several tea refills before she had Raina where she needed her to be. Subsided. Convinced. Conversant to the point of spilling her tea. Retrieving a towel for Raina's lap, Gael finally draws her gaze along the array of paintings, which are out of their portfolio and draped in packing mesh.

Raina stands. "I'm tired of my voice. Send me the magazine when it's out. 128 Central Park South. It will find me." The photosensitive lenses of her glasses tint a little darker as she takes a step toward Guthrie's paintings. "Did you find something good at the fair?"

"Oh. No," Gael says. "Well, *yes*, but I didn't buy anything for myself. I brought those with me. My sister's an artist with a disability and she can't travel. I thought I'd squeeze in an appointment or two to help get her work shown in the city. But it turns out gallerists demand studio visits and they don't rate Irish art degrees and it's all a bit of a boys' club. No offense. I mean, for outsiders. I don't usually see things from the artist's side. I studied art history and I have a master's in journalism. So, I forget what it can be like. Should've known. Even though my sister's the most talented person I know, I wouldn't trade places." Gael raises her brows and goes to the bed. "Don't forget your coat."

When she holds it up for Raina's arms, Raina has uncovered two of the paintings. "What are they called?"

Gael clears her throat. "One, two, three, four, five."

Raina glances back at Gael with a frown and sees the coat held up. "Her titling needs work." She feeds her arm into the sleeve.

"Those are the subtitles," Gael says. "The series is called 'Miscarriage.'"

Raina, facing the paintings, doesn't move. After a moment she tugs the coat away with her. When she turns back to Gael, her glasses are clear and imperiling. It was too direct. She had found it buried way back in the documentation of Raina's past shows—an early exhibition, twenty years ago, involved a bloody, grisly painting with extracted cancerous uterine mass. Her interviews around that show had been the most radical and raw. Gael feels her own uterus lurch.

"It's not a boys' club," Raina says. "It's difficult. But it's not like that. Not yet."

"No," Gael says, "that wasn't fair."

Raina closes the buttons of her coat. A man's coat, so the buttonholes are on the wrong side. "M.F.N.," she says.

Gael says nothing.

"M.F.N. Gallery. . . . Call them. Say I'm sending you over."

As if a bill had been squeezed into her hand, Gael demurs. "That's very kind, Raina, but . . ." *I have a wage.* "I'm not in town for long—"

"So go there now." A current of anger charges Raina's mouth and Gael isn't quite sure how to conduct it. She stands at attention. Lets her arms hang defenselessly by her sides.

"And I've changed my mind," Raina says, pointing to the tea service. "I don't want to read this. Don't send it to me. I explain too much."

✦

Chelsea has a very different vibe to the ironed-clothing know-where-you're-going keep-right district of Midtown. It's quieter, in an industrial way, with wide roads and freshish air coming in off the brown Hudson River to counteract the trudge of cars stopped at rusty yellow traffic lights dangling from steel poles like bellworts. Besides the large residential complexes, the buildings are stocky and low-rise. Two-story offices, kooky boutique shops, cheap corner delis, grim-looking tenements and tree-shaded brownstone row houses contribute to the '80s milieu, in among newer apartment blocks and big-box retailers. The odd person in overalls not strictly for fashion. As with everywhere in Manhattan, construction scaffolding brackets most corners.

Set between the whipped-cream-shaped glass tower of InterActiveCorp's headquarters and the riveted steel High Line viaduct, the gallery isn't even at street level. Gael doubts that the people who come here to visit it would have money. She checks her phone for a missed call from the bank. Probably closed on weekends. It *has* to clear on Monday. She calculates how much she'll have left in cash if she gets a taxi home. The brick exterior wall is painted black; their sign graffiti'd in white stencil:

M.F.N. Gallery

Before pressing the buzzer, she pauses to collect herself, to control the factors of perception. The hidey-hole gallery puts on one-week, one-artist exhibitions with absolutely no advertising other than word of mouth and an email invite to their mailing list. Their website is a static page with a list of what's currently showing, contact details and opening hours. Gael only had time to do the most cursory research, because they'd said on the phone, "At three, Ploennies's large-scale metalwork installation arrives. So we'll be buried. If you can come in the next sixty to ninety minutes, we'll see you. Otherwise, it'll be a couple weeks."

She buzzes #3 and looks up. The industrial grid window with an air-conditioning unit hanging out looks to be covered from the inside with plywood. For some reason she tastes the familiar annoyance that precedes a waste of time, like a fling offering to hang around for breakfast. A voice cracks through the speaker—"Yup"—and cuts out before she can utter a response. The elevator doors ping open inside. Maneuvering the portfolio in, she doesn't know what button to press as the doors shut. There's movement, snail-like in comparison to the acceleration of the Plaza's express elevator. She's trying to figure out how they got the lift doors to open downstairs when they open on the third floor. A black brick wall greets her, with the same white-stencil M.F.N. logo writ large above a wide pop-art-style painting of five identical women sitting on a couch, each holding a different Technicolored muffin on her lap. The women look solemn. Gael relaxes her expression and her aching shoulder.

To the left, a cluttered reception desk and bench are tucked into a nook by a divider wall, forming a little foyer of this section, presumably so the gallery space is disconnected from the comings and goings and admin. Rising from his chair (a leather-cushioned swing, hanging on thick industrial chains from the high ceiling), a smiling, thirty-something, lilac-afro'd man juts out his hand and follows it to where Gael's standing. "Welcome! I'm Enn."

"Gael. Nice to meet you. Are you the guy I spoke with on the phone?"

"No." He hesitates for a moment. "You spoke with M." The press of his lips suggests she's already said something wrong.

"Nice scarf," she tries.

"Oh," he looks down. "Thank you! That's sweet of you to say. My niece crocheted it for me. She's like, three."

Gael smiles, glancing at the skinny fuchsia-pink scarf that's so long the ends hang down past the knees of his gray leather trousers. Then she frowns. "Three?"

"Oh, three or five or twelve. Who cares. She lives in Maui. Her making me a scarf was basically an *up yours, frigid.* So let's take this into the space and give it some context." Enn lifts the portfolio from Gael's shoulder, a little unexpectedly. Not to plan. She follows him into the gallery, where two other people stand conversing.

Gael looks around as the discussion finishes up. She's assessing the space as much as they're assessing her goods. She knows that this isn't about them deeming the paintings worthy. Now that she's here, the only thing that will ensure wall space is her cogency; her taking that space as a given. The audition goes both ways, is the point of her body language.

It's one large rectangle room—wide rather than deep—with a silvery-gray lacquer on the cement floors, white walls and a ceiling that's pitched asymmetrically so that the spotlights can be directed just so. In the middle of the room, there's a freestanding panel of wall like the inverse of a stone arch. It's designed to have one painting hung on either side. It also helps to dampen light on the main back wall, which faces the street. It's not plywood covering the windows but some kind of gritty fabric.

"Do you need a water or a tea or anything?" Enn asks.

"Still water, please."

She has a feeling that Enn is the tone-setter and she'd rather be left to pitch her own introduction. F could be Sive's age. She's wearing a high-necked, long-sleeved, floor-length, dark vintage dress with a stonework of dark-gray hair bridging her skull to the small of her back and is holding a long-lensed camera in one hand, as if it's not worth months of someone's salary. Her right hand is scrunched up in a crab claw, so when she goes to shake Gael's hand, she tucks the camera under her right arm and proffers her left hand. Perhaps whatever condition she has made a curator of her. Her expression is attentive. "Raina is a very special artist. One of our favorites. We had her Patagonian collage show last year." She glances to the portfolio resting against the arch in the center of the room. "How do you know her?"

"Raina must be a lot of people's favorite artist," Gael says. "She's one of a kind."

"She *is* one of a kind," F says.

"Though our connection's professional—"

"Business" is the man's first word. M. "I thought you looked cor-porate."

Gael laughs. He doesn't.

"You're on the donut hunt." He's well over six foot, stocky, bald, with a walnut woodchip beard. Gael guesses late thirties. His plain white T-shirt is rolled at the sleeves. Classic blue jeans tucked into distressed brown leather boots that come up to the tops of his shins.

Enn arrives back with a glass of water that's basically a fishbowl.

"It's true I'm not an artist," Gael says. This halts Enn en route to the portfolio to lay out the work. Gael needs to keep them listening, not looking, yet. Without bending her knees, she places the glass of water on the floor. Then, she removes her coat, folds it and places it on the floor beside the glass of water. You can't win people over in a coat. It's where all the politicians go wrong. Enn, F and M all watch her, with their heads tilted like the various hands of a clock. As long as it seems like performance art, which they can't interrupt, she'll hold court.

"It's a very rare condition," she begins.

Later, without anyone having so much as cleared their throat, she concludes in the tenor of a late-night radio host: "But if he won't travel, we just have to accept that that is his reality. It's self-preservation, not self-harm. To try to make him understand, again . . . would be dangerous and selfish. And traumatic. So I'm here. Bringing an ex-traordinary mind and talent to light." It seems as if the sun has, against all forecasts, broken through the clouds. Enn points to the portfolio as the fabric blinds behind him glow.

"Are these . . . of the auras?"

Time to pass on the power baton. Gael will be the one to bend her knees. She will unpack the paintings and space each one along the wall, without anyone's help. Flee their eye line as soon as she can. F extracts a pair of glasses from the pocket of her dress and cleans them for a very long time, taking in the paintings blurrily.

M paces back and forth along the lineup, as if they aren't autono-
mous, but Enn has homed in on just one. Wally's. *Put a red sticker
on that one* had been his order. Enn has one end of the fuschia scarf
bunched in his fist and is holding it against his mouth as if to catch
the scent from a lover's fast-cooling pillow. Gael drains the water
bowl and swears she can feel something go slimily down her throat
while this silent jurying takes place. They're getting very close to
the paintings now. These people assess art for a living. Guthrie's
secondary-school arts-and-crafts supplies must be glaring. They step
in. Her story must not have allayed their need to look closely. From
the lobby, a delivery person yells: We're downstairs. After M's hand
lands on F's shoulder with a *thud*, she yells back: Give us a minute.

A minute.

Is a minute good or bad?

Then something has happened, because F and M are approaching Gael, and Enn is carefully returning the paintings to their case.
They're sending them home with her. Apparently, the packaging isn't
satisfactory, so Enn dashes off for more mesh. This is going on in
the background. In the foreground, Gael is being read her rights.
No. Her Terms and Conditions. F's teeth are short and stained as
peanuts. "We take fifty-five percent of sales. That's standard. Some
galleries take sixty. I set the prices and run those by you. If you want
to do advertising, flyers, magazine ads, helicopters, that nonsense,
you foot the bill. We don't press artists to advertise. We get traffic
here on rep. You'll be billed for painting the walls and for the opening night refreshments. Twenty bottles of wine; twenty still, twenty
carbonated waters. As a rule, artists pay for framing up front, but I
don't see why we'd frame these pieces. My partners agree they work
as they are. The desks are great. Superb."

"Those big hooked nails on the sides?" M says. "The red rust pol-
luting the white? It's . . . evocative."

"So if you'd like to work with us," F cuts in, "we're offering the week of October fourteenth through twentieth. One of our sculptors has had a minor catastrophe with a piece and she'll need her show pushed back. Otherwise, we'd be talking mid–next year."

Gael feels her head go up and down. It's just one step of the dance she's doing inside.

"I'll have a contract drawn up." F must read something in Gael's expression she doesn't like. "I hope you realize a solo show by an unknown vacationer in a space like this just doesn't happen."

The older woman puts the younger woman in her place: check. And the beat goes on. To break the so obliged/so grateful pattern, Gael says: "A nineteen-year-old unknown vacationer at that!"

F narrows her brown eyes and twitches restrainedly as a stabled horse. "Of course, we can't do anything with five pieces. We'll need at least twelve." She looks around the room. "Fifteen," she says. "You have fifteen? In the same vein?"

Enn returns, rapturous. "Did you say the artist was *a teenager?*"

Gael nods discreetly and slips her coat back on. She lifts the portfolio onto her shoulder and now feels how much heavier it needs to be. She feels sign language going on around her. At last, F holds out her left hand to shake. Gael looks at her crippled right hand pointedly and says, "Left hand . . . closer to the heart."

F drops the handshake, fast, and looks directly at Gael with her jaw set together, as if it has reverted to its statue form. But after a moment, it unlocks just enough to say, "I've never heard that."

Gael kneads the muscle of her aching shoulder. It was something she'd heard Sive say to her soloist during a rehearsal of Ravel's Piano Concerto for the left hand. It had struck Gael as typically urbane.

"One other thing," M says. "We need a headshot."

"Of the artist?"

"If we like the photo, we'll print it."

"I'll have a look," Gael says.

M rubs his knuckles roughly into his reddish beard. "Look. I don't mean to come off as . . . exploitative . . ."

F snaps her gaze so abruptly, her gray hair makes motion lines. What's this? What's he after without consensus?

". . . but if you've got a photo of him . . ." M pauses, looking restive. "Gah. Forget it." His eyes are trained on the tailored hem of Gael's skirt.

"What?" Gael asks. "Of him having a fit?"

"Forget it. I didn't think that through."

"Well . . ." Gael says lingeringly, taking her phone from her coat pocket and scanning her photo library. "You guys are the experts. I'm the middleman. Were you thinking . . . something . . . like this?" She holds out the phone and all three of her marks close in on the electronic image as if its pixels are a *mise en abyme*. The slashed canvas of Guthrie's face. The photo she took the night he lost his tooth, just before he drew his head from her lap.

A dusting of salt glistens on M's bald head from whatever he sweated over earlier. The grooves in his forehead look as though they've been scored. He's crouched down, resting his hands on his knees to see the photograph, so that his head is at Gael's chest height. He looks to her with a grimace. Yeah. Yup. Yes. He'd let her beat him like that right now, to a Schnabel. Pollock the lip. Torsion the frame. Twist the rust, not one bit biblically. Hard pulse *thuds*. Brunting her shoulder ligaments with the luggage is all she can do to restrain it. She lurches to the lift, averting her gaze from the swing that hangs, daring as a rope.

"Kudos," he calls after her, but she won't twirl, no matter how easy it would be. "You just made business beautiful. Raina's got an eagle's eye . . . for what's worth chasing. This kid is gonna be huge."

◆

At the corner of 10th Avenue, she hails a cab and tips recklessly. By the time the porter knocks on her room with the portfolio, she is bathrobe-clad and has no dry hand with which to pass him a banknote. "*So sorry,* just in the middle of something." Barely holding herself back from straddling the door, she shuts it and leaps onto the bed to writhe seven heavens into a pillow.

After, her phone reads 15:45. *Fifteen.* Shit, yes. Next order of business. She uses the Wi-Fi to phone Guthrie. He sounds groggy. He's five hours ahead. Was he sleeping? He was hanging out clothes, he says. The image of this has a sobering effect on Gael, cashing out the tab on her thoughts. She must pause for too long, because he starts asking questions one after another, as if to relieve her. He wants to know all about the city. They'd been to California as a family once, but hadn't been anywhere else in America. Has she seen the Statue of Liberty? Is the Ground Zero memorial open? The Obamas were there on the tenth anniversary. It was on the news. Where's she staying? When's her interview—what's it for again? Has she met anyone yet? When will she start saying "dude," "awesome" and "super"? Have taxicab drivers been telling her they're Irish? And why taxi *and* cab?

"Yeah," Gael says, lying on the bed, looking at the French chandelier.

"It's so redundant."

"You're redundant."

"Cop on! I'm a stay-at-home dad."

Gael envisions him balancing tiny tiny socks on the clothes horse. Blankies. Little leggings with threadbare knees and bottoms. Maybe jumpers Jarleth bought them in pink and blue, to better establish what's what, this time round. "My first time on the subway," Gael says, "which smells of pee by the way, everything smells putrid here, like you get home from summer holidays and realize you left a bowl of cereal out and the sour milk has condensed to cheese . . ."

"That's a very specific smell."

"Anyway, someone started break-dancing around the subway pole."

"Cool."

"Then I switched lines and three black dudes broke into Gregorian chant. Your favorite!"

"African Americans," Guthrie says primly. "Did you give them a dollar?"

"I didn't give the black dudes a dollar. You'd spend a thousand dollars a day if you gave a buck every time you're asked for one, or every time you're impressed by someone."

"That's sad," Guthrie says, sounding tired.

"It is. It feels too arbitrary to reward talent when there's so many people just . . . struggling. That should be enough of a reason. But, I dunno. People don't seem *that* bleak."

"No?"

"Well, some really do. Like the ones who apologize. Drag their kids down the carriage asking for help to feed them. The kids look you straight in the eye."

"Gael—"

"But mostly, they're characters. Like, there was this ancient Asian lady riding her Rollerblades down the middle of the road like she was a vehicle. In hot pants and kneepads in autumn. All the cars honking, threatening to run her over, out their windows going, 'What the fuck?' I'm shaking my fist here. And she's like, '*Do* it, sons of bitches! Obamacare!' She was amazing."

"It sounds . . . alive. I hope you're taking pictures."

Gael gets up from the bed and goes to the iPad by the door to turn on the air-con. "Speaking of taking pictures—"

"Oh, before I forget, Mum says someone's been calling for you."

"Oh. I can guess who it is. I'll phone Mum later."

"She doesn't pick up at work, but you can text."

"At work, as in at Cash Converters?"

"Mmm."

"She hasn't quit yet?"

"I think she's working something out. Something important."

"She's losing it."

"She's happy."

"*Ish*," Gael says. "Mum's never been more than happyish. And that's pushing it."

"That was the menopause," Guthrie says.

"You're the menopause."

"You give me such a hard time when I make that joke and you've made it twice in—"

"Sorry," Gael says. "'Merica's making my jokes mac 'n cheesy."

Guthrie laughs. Gael plonks onto the low gold-velvet chair in the recessed reading area by the window. She puts her bare feet on the footstool and pushes back one half of the gauze curtain. The calm circle of the Pulitzer Fountain is down below, people going here and there, ambling around the flowerbeds—faceless from this far up.

"So you know the painting you gave me?" Gael says. Guthrie yawns on the other end of the line. "I sold it."

"Jeez!" Guthrie says, doing his best American accent. He *has* softened around the edges since the kids. "Get this gal with her sentimentality!" he says, goofily.

"That's actually pretty good! That's convincing! Guthrie the Godfather. But, seriously though. I did sell it. For serious money. To a rich guy on the plane. He fell in *love* with it, Guth, of course he did because it's gorgeous and he wrote me a check, well, *you* a check. It's for you. And I'm waiting for it to clear but basically, as of tomorrow, you've officially got bank."

There's a pushing sound on the end of the line and Gael imagines her Edvard Munch painting of a brother getting up to check on the twins to help him process this utter surprise. She wonders how his face looks. Has it healed? The tooth would be missing still. An implant would have to be measured and made and so on.

"You sold the painting I gave you?" He sounds confused.

"With ease. You're an incredible fucking talent, Guth. I hope you know that. The world should know it. So I want you to be able to paint, properly. We only get one life. I want you to do something for yourself. Not to have to worry about money or health insurance or what school you'll be able to afford for the kids or what welfare you're eligible—"

"Gael." Guthrie's voice sounds off. She heard the sound of one door closing and another opening. Then another creaky door and a light switch.

"The fact of the matter is, you owe it to yourself to at least try to make a living as an artist. Not as a—" She would've stopped shy of saying "dole bandit" had he not stopped her first.

"What did you do?" He must be holding his breath. In the cupboard under the stairs, if you breathe, dust catches in your throat and you cough.

"Okay." Do the merciful thing. Quickly. "I'll tell you."

"What. Gael. Did you do."

She realizes that she too is holding her breath, sitting upright on the chair, feet flat on the carpet. "I took the four others with me and they're going to be in an exhibition in Chelsea." She waits. Then adds hurriedly, in case he didn't understand, "In New York."

He's breathing in through his nose and out through his mouth, in little whistles.

"A bunch of gallerists think you're insanely gifted, Guthrie. They wanted me to—"

"Cancel it."

Somehow, the silence on the line renders the city hushed, too. Her "What?" is tacit.

"Cancel it."

His voice reminds her of the last night she saw him, when he'd made her shadow manifest in black cuttings all around her on the floor—a shadow she hadn't cast so acutely until then. Of his warning not to make a scene when Jarleth showed up for mass. Of his ordering that dodgy fuck in the park to clean up his dog feces. It was unwavering. Gael knew he meant it. And meaning, for him, isn't pliant. But this is a fixed, short-term loss. It will matter less and less over time. Whereas money accrues interest. Money can give him choices he has forgotten exist.

"I can't," she finds herself saying, instead. "I've already signed a contract. But I swear you'll feel different when you get a—"

"The twins," Guthrie says, "they're crying . . . Ronan wouldn't eat. I have to go."

"Guth?" Gael takes the phone from her ear and sees that the call has been dropped.

◆

The weekend inline skaters, skateboarders, elbow-swingers and off-the-saddle-riders are out in full force in Central Park, which aggravates Gael, as if she has some right, already, to space. But for the few to have a wealth of space, the many must have a scruple. She runs quickly through the busy paved part of East Drive until Jacqueline Onassis Kennedy Reservoir: her favorite section of the park. The soft cinder path hemming the water. The simulacrum forest. The incongruous skyline of the Upper West Side, seeming much farther away than it is. The space in between: a half-trillion-dollar real estate prospect, forfeited through the kind of obliged philanthropy that leaves more than teeth marks in fists.

It's one of those dreary skies where the sun is a torch beneath a blanket fort: small as the star we forget it is and not at all wishworthy. Even so, the trees are vivid with memories of summer sun and are only beginning to dwindle from frog green to lizard.

It's that proud poor thing, she thinks. It's a fucking religious thing. Don't fear poverty; don't fear death. But he's subjecting his kids to his values: deprivation in the short term for the payoff of infinite abundance in everlasting life. Which, anyway, sounds like a consumerist ideal to Gael. And what if the kids don't believe in his short term; what if, for them, life on Earth is all the term there is. Yes, it's short, so it should be celebrated and lived abundantly as means allow, until it's spent.

She drinks from a water fountain and realizes how hungry she is. She's not running as fast as her heart rate suggests. She'll speed up. Catch the body up to the mind, rather than trying to calm herself. She was doing something good for his family. It's not as if she took the talent itself, took his unique sensibility and inclination and experience and sold it. It's not a commodity. He should know that. She knows it. She's just managed to convince other people—powerful people—that the paintings are goods. Really, they're just a pretty snapshot-insight into Guthrie's faculty, which cannot be sold.

He can make more paintings.

Yeah, yeah, she hears his counterargument. The reverence he has for the fits, as if they're hallowed and each aura is an absolution—a benison—and not just a synaptic blip. It's egregious, to give them this status in his life when all they've done is persecute him. They're a gift's opposite. That's the truth of it: they're something he gives himself. He couldn't possibly treasure the five auras his sister is selling if he knew he could experience them again at the click of a finger, like orgasms; have as many fits as he wants, as many as he chooses to endure, because they're *self-fucking-induced* and even if they weren't, even if he really were physically sick, isn't it self-pitying to hold fast to one's damage? It's all so exasperating and loss-making and always has been. She picks up her pace to kill all concentration. Like a kitchen spray that kills "all known bacteria." The unknown will just have to wrangle with the gut.

Onto the dirt trail that runs along the far side of the park, parallel to West Drive, she's turned back to the city. Her stomach grumbles, contending with what might just be the germ of an idea. The kind that does well without the mind for scrutiny. Passing fast under a long bridge and then another, the cold hits her like a core memory. The buildings are there now, impending behind the trees to her right—tall enough that she would have to crane her neck to see a patch of sky and recall that they're not the backdrop to everything. Trade coruscates all year round. Is it not the one-season system we live by?

From it, the idea stems.

✦

Caricaturists are reliable, is Gael's feeling when she stops by one on 59th near Columbus Circle and asks for information. But she phrases it badly.

"Where would you go in this town to find an artist?"

"Fuck you too."

She breaks into laughter, which she often does uncontrollably when she's tired and hungry.

"The fuck off my porch."

Once she's apologized every way she knows how, he still seems sure that this Irish pot of gold is drunk on her own lucked life and spitting up judgment on every corner. She says she can explain but he's welcome to hurl insults at her for a while if it would help. "Tell me how you'd draw me." She points to his cartoons, whose clean, Picassoesque lines are pitiless. "What bad features you'd exaggerate."

"I'd have your nasty-ass tongue hanging out like a bitch's, covered in boils."

"Seriously. The truth."

"Oh, for real, you want abusing? That's your kink?"

"Listen, I'm sorry for the accidental insult. I was genuinely asking you—as an artist—if you happen to know . . . but never mind. I'll figure it out." She starts to run off again and he watches her for a few ass-bouncing steps before calling, "What sort?" She jogs back. "You looking for what, a graffiti artist?"

"An oil painter. A good one."

The guy shakes his head. "Don't know no oil painter. But you know painting-decorating pays more than that shit."

"I'm not looking for a job or a date."

"You sure about that?" The guy kisses his teeth.

"I'm sure. It's for a project."

Now, he's checking out a lady parade passing by, all soft lines and shading. "Now you mention it," he says, "I heard something. Yeah. Tha's right. I do know where you find that sorta artist right now. Yeah, they hit up one spot. I know where they at. But it's too far to run."

"Where is it?"

"Financial district. You go all all all the way downtown."

"Yeah?" Gael gets the sharp feeling she's being mocked. "Do you have an address?"

"Called Zuccotti Park."

✦

The chanting carries from blocks away, before Gael stops running or notices the NYPD officers in front of barricades and motorbikes, with crossed arms and wide stances—PlastiCuffs hanging from their belts by the dozen. "Whose street? OUR STREET." "Wall Street, shut it down." Random tourists and pedestrians gravitate toward the crowd, unsure of what's going on but intent on documenting it with smartphones. "Human need, not corporate greed." "No justice; no peace. OCCUPY WALL STREET." Approaching from Greenwich

Street, Gael takes a left past the 9/11 Tribute Center and onto Liberty Street and that's where she can see the edges of the demonstration and things get so busy she can no longer jog. It had taken her an hour to run here from the park. "Banks got bailed out, we got sold out." "People, not profits."

"Too lazy to march the whole way to Wall Street," one passerby says with delicious scorn.

It's hard to judge how many people are protesting and how many are just passing through or prying, but everyone is looking around, for what to run away from or toward. It's a little close to the 9/11 memorial for ease of atmosphere, with the new World Trade Center under construction on one corner of the square. Zuccotti Park itself, which is grassless and small and shadowed by the black grate of One Liberty Plaza on the north side, the statelier Trinity Place to the south, the Bank of America building, the Marine Midland Building, the Equitable Building . . . all this and change roaring into the sky in capital hurrah.

Once Gael gets close to the barricades preventing people from spilling out and blocking traffic, she sees the scale of it. At least a thousand protesters are assembled in the granite park, in little scrums of discussion and performance. Placards bob above the crowd like cormorants on a chockful sea. "We. Are. The 99%." Other messages are scrawled on cardboard signs laid out on sidewalks and against the honey locust trees, which provide a softer roof than a glass ceiling. There are blue tarpaulins and sleeping bags near a confrontation going on with the police.

There are block tables and stools made from granite and lights built into the ground, which are on, though it's not quite evening. These areas are being used as podiums for group leaders who have come together and brought with them their online audiences. Gael must have moved inside the encampment's confines, because she's in the middle of the park now, exploiting body heat, looking up to three young people stood on the seating area behind a flowerbed.

One wears a Guy Fawkes mask. The young woman, wearing an army surplus jacket, a backpack, black-rimmed glasses and jeans with the number 9 spray-painted onto each leg in luminous orange, speaks out:

"Protesters are being arrested for using sound equipment without permits. Mics, amps, megaphones. Occupy *needs* to be lawful, so we can remain here. Friends: we plan to stay. We plan to set up tents and kitchens, stage general assemblies and peaceably occupy Wall Street for the months it takes until President Obama forms a commission to address our concerns and *commits* to financial reforms. We will demonstrate that the ninety-nine percent won't tolerate the greed and corruption of the one percent. So, our first issue is our biggest issue: how to be heard. We'll have to demonstrate our ability to respect one another. One another's right to speak and to be heard. We have to organize if we want to have the conversations the one percent doesn't want us having. So. If you hear the words 'mic check,' this means someone has a message they need to share with you. If you hear those words, repeat them. This will be our people-powered sound system. Let's give it a go. MIC CHECK."

"Mic check," Gael finds herself saying, along with everyone. The drums have stopped and more people gather round this ad hoc lectern. The demographic is predominantly young. Lots of kaffiyehs and rucksacks and hoodies and iPhones and layered clothing and a kind of edgy look of expectation. The sides of the speaker's head are shaved and the dark brown hair in the middle is flicked backward. In small chunks of speech, repeated by the crowd, she explains that police are prohibiting tents, citing loitering laws. Occupy plans to work with the police. The police are the ninety-nine percent. They're looking for workarounds. For now, don't erect tents. There are loose tarps for shelter for those who'll stay the night. People are donating blankets. This park is private property. "The police led us here. They fenced off our first two locations. But they let us come here. That's because"—the crowd echoes "that's because"—"they can't legally force protesters to leave . . . without being requested to do so . . . by the property owner. . . . And Zuccotti Park . . . which we rename Liberty Plaza . . . its original name . . . is not subject to city curfews. . . . Meaning no one has to leave." She smiles cautiously. "We welcome you. Thank you for being here."

"THANK YOU FOR BEING HERE," echoes the crowd.

Some people peel away into smaller rinds of conversation. Others cheer and jump with arms thrust into the air. A pain stabs the base of Gael's skull so suddenly, she clasps the back of her head to feel for a knife. She gropes whoever's in front for something to hold on to, but it's canvas and there are so many people her hand can't make lasting contact with anything. *Sit . . . till it passes.* The only seat she knows is where the speaker stood so she pushes toward it on legs now cramped and stiff. She must be holding her head in her hands, doubled over, because the mohawked speaker hunkers before her, trying to get Gael's attention without touching her. "Where did you run from?"

Gael squints and holds up a finger to indicate it's a little too painful to talk just yet.

"I'm Nina. I'm going to get you water. Stay here."

Sweat has formed a grit between her skin and her clothes. It's not water she needs. It's salt. She bashes her quads to ease the lactic acid burn. There's so much talk going on with a tenor of vital import that she's not quite able to tune in. It's all loose ends and unvoiced counterarguments and so much jaw; facts thrown around like ugly heirlooms among siblings. Hey Fed: here's the end of free-market capitalism. Catch. Here's the blame for fifteen million jobless people. Here's the inevitable reinstatement of labor camps.

Here's a pretzel.

Gael drains the water and the fog in her vision begins to clear. Her headache subsides from blinding stab to general throb. She stands, wincingly. Though the warm pretzel held out to her in a napkin, with its giant white salt crystals atop the glossy dough, makes her salivate so that she has to pretend to wipe her nose, she doesn't take it. That's exactly the kind of debt a new credit card won't cover. "Thanks, I just needed water." She'd taken the bike path all along the Hudson River, to incessant heckling, because she wanted to avoid traffic lights on every block. Otherwise, she'd be freezing before reaching downtown. But she'll take the direct route back, all along Broadway and onto Park Avenue. It's another eight kilometers, enough time to come up with a plan. The only artists here are the ones sitting around paint cans, improving the placards' accessibility. Not exactly the disposition needed for the job. Gael balances on one leg, pulling her other foot to her bum to stretch.

"Do me a favor. Eat half this pretzel. I'm on a mostly protein diet to build my abs." Nina flashes Gael her belly, which is indeed muscular. Before the crowd, Nina had been playing up her intellectualism. Now she's playing up her street. The smile crookeder. The syllables sloppier.

Gael switches the leg she's balancing on. "Are you hitting on me?"

"Listen. This pretzel was straight too before I touched it."

"Ha!" Gael takes the piece held out. "I owe you, but don't expect interest." She stuffs the whole portion into her mouth and is rendered beatifically silent for the next minute. During which Nina urges her to stay. They'll find her a sweater. She looks cold. Has she heard of Adbusters? There's a talk about to start she *has* to hear. And there'll be pizza. To have been here from day one . . . it'll be something to tell grandkids. "Or nieces and nephews. Whatever." In the background, Gael can smell burned falafel. Harper's favorite. She looks around and regards this less, now, as a mecca for discontent and more as a carnival.

She catches her breath and sees Nina's spectacle-shrunk eyes awaiting the verdict. That's the thing about nearsightedness. It makes the future seem further away than it is, so you can see it how it should be; when, in fact, it's already upon you.

"Honestly, Nina?" She thinks about saying it: I'm an aspiring one-percenter. It's only sane to be appalled at the country's dysfunction but, come on, kid. Calling it out gets you nowhere. Enormous calamities cause change. Civil wars. Natural disasters. Not street marches. Once customs are established and prejudices rooted, reform is a dangerous and fruitless enterprise, said Rousseau. The truth brings no man a fortune; and it's not the people who hand out embassies, professorships and pensions. The people give out pretzels, used clothes and coping mechanisms. Gael wipes the crumbs from her chest and admits, instead, "I wouldn't have your best interests at heart."

The run back doesn't feel good, but she'll manage it. The muscles will tear and repair as is their bent. Tomorrow will do for interviewing job candidates. She'll comb the classifieds on Craigslist for gay men whose profiles imply fine art degrees, consumerist aspirations and studio living. America will have one more job provider. One more tax-evading entrepreneur making a magic hankie out of red tape.

II

A picture is worth a thousand words or fifty thousand banknotes. That Monday morning marked the beginning of a busy two-week period. Gael had made for the bank bright and early, unable to check out of the Plaza until the check cleared. She'd begun to think of the hotel as a costly gaffe, even if its plutocratic crowd had been available to her as a place bet. The credit extension on her card wouldn't have come close to covering the bill. The check not clearing could be, she'd thought, the trivial logistical failure that scuppers the whole enterprise. "We charge a six-dollar transaction fee," the teller had announced. Gael must have stared blankly at him while she tried to work out his meaning. "What demonination?" he'd said, then, "Sorry. Bleugh. Mondays. *Denom*ination." Fighting the urge to sing "Hail Wally," Gael had said calmly: Hundreds. The teller didn't put her through the awkwardness of counting out five hundred notes one by one. An electronic gadget measured ten wads of five thousand. Each was parceled into a separate envelope, placed inside a larger envelope, on Gael's request, so that when she went to pay for the hotel, they wouldn't surmise she'd been operating a drug cartel from the seventeenth floor.

When she'd returned to pack up and settle the bill, she regretted not having at least *considered* her drug cartel options. Laundry, rare room services, daily Palm Court coffees, along with taxes and city charges brought the eight-night stay to $7,083.22. No time to mourn the fourteen percent burned—she had to get to work.

Though already checked out, she'd spent most of that Monday interviewing candidates in the Palm Court beneath the diffused light of the stained glass ceiling. Seated at a green velvet-cushioned seat with her back to a palm tree encircled by orchids, Gael reassured herself that she had only to find the right bearer to carry this thing off. Everyone having high tea had high-tea posture, reviewing the epicurean contents of their brass birdcages. Gael was hunched over her laptop, which the wait staff overlooked, now that she'd been established as a pays-cash person-about-the-Plaza.

She'd thought it a savvy move to target classified ads on Craigslist for several reasons, but out of the three artists who turned up, none were too pleased to have been misled, nor were they interested in becoming intern to any artist, differently abled or otherwise. The fourth, however, had had a long day. "At least you're manlier than my last date." He'd ordered a glass of Nero d'Avola and told Gael he knew the direction to point her in, if she bought him lunch. She'd relaxed her posture and said, "The squid ink spaghetti's delicious." Slate-toothed and loose-tongued from Sicilian wine and squid escape mechanism, this stranger let her in on a black market called Silk Road. Hidden in the deep web, the site is uncrawlable by search engine algorithms, and cryptographic software is required to access it. The interface is anonymous. Payments are traceless. Transactions are made with the cryptocurrency Bitcoin. It's a libertarian business model, he'd explained. The founder, or founders—no one knows— based the whole idea on an Austrian economist's philosophy; Ludwig von Mises, who said that citizens need economic freedom to be politically and morally free. Silk Road's founder interpreted this as citizens' rights to buy and sell whatever-the-fuck, without monitoring or regulation. From black tar heroin to firearms; social security cards to hit men. Everything shy of human hearts. "And you're saying I can find an artist on this underground eBay thing, to copy paintings?"

The guy had gotten her to scoot over on the velvet cushion. He'd turned her laptop a fraction, dimmed the screen lighting and spoke furtively. "First thing is to install a Tor browser, so your IP can't be sniffed."

"I'll do it myself."

He'd sighed. "Fine, just drag that folder over there and right-click to open the browser."

"If you fuck with me," Gael had said, seeing what could be going on with a drunk's clarity, "I'll pay the hit man extra to . . ." She swept her hair from one side to the other. "You know . . . make it sting-y."

The guy let his wide slopey eyebrows slug toward the cabbage leaves of his ears. Gael took a bill from her blazer's breast pocket and tapped his glass with it. "Now. Let's hire a fraud with Monopoly money."

That evening, when she'd sobered up and brushed her teeth, she did as Xavier (said fraud) had directed in their encrypted instant message conversation. She went to the Mall section of Central Park, opened the portfolio and exposed one painting at length, the way a flapper-era hooker might expose a juicy thigh. She didn't know if he'd arrived and left, or had even walked by, but when she returned to the hotel's Wi-Fi, a TorChat message awaited her: "Yes can do. Will neg $ in person. Meet at 8pm at 116th and Manhattan Ave." Only when Gael looked up the address did she note it was practically in Harlem. Plenty of time to think that over while she shopped for a robust backpack and less restrictive clothing. It was *Pretty Woman* on the flipside. She made no move to hit rewind.

The subway stop was within holdup distance of his place: a

crammed 220-square-foot artist's alcove studio with a microwave for a kitchen and a mezzanine that hadn't gone through building inspection. Once she'd sized it up and decided the guy seemed decent, if cagey (much as anyone might be who wears a fanny pack), she'd asked how long it would take to create ten iterations of the samples she'd brought. He'd inspected the paintings with a pout made unreadable by his harelip. "They're color studies." Flipping through them like records in the discount section, he said, "If I'm given the materials—the desks, nails, the right paints, which don't look like oil paints all through by the way, there's some household stuff in there, mixed with a thickener . . . K-Y Jelly or something—call it a full day's work per painting. Eight, ten hours apiece?"

"Fifty bucks an hour. Five hundred per painting. Half in advance. Cash."

He had barely widened his eyes to say "Deal" when Gael began adding fine print: "Obviously, I'll have to oversee the project. There's a timeline and I'm here on behalf of the artist, who has a very serious physical condition, very sensitive, so the whole job is confidential. Strictly. I'll have you sign an NDA. IP stays with the artist. It's sensible for me to stay here for the ten days or so it takes you to get it done. I'm fine with the sofa. You won't know I'm here. Unless it turns out you can't paint. Then you'll know." Gael removed her backpack and put it in a corner, where it would stay. Xavier looked tentatively appalled. He was one of those people who thought before he spoke. When his lips moved it was to do the multiplication. Five K for, at most, a fortnight's work. Gael counted out the first installment of bills as loudly as the bank teller hadn't. "Oh, and do you have a van?"

It had taken over two weeks to get down to the last painting. The copy of #8, Wally's order. She can't very well tell M.F.N., The one you all crowded round worshipfully was already sold, sorry, but here's a bunch of others. The copy will have to go to Wally. Octogenarian eyesight blurs nicely. To make up for the fact that he's getting a painting worth one percent of what he paid, she'll hand-deliver it to him, wearing something that could be mistaken for a negligée. Not today, though. The copy won't be finished until tonight and it won't be dry for several days.

Busy Sharpieing the last pair of desks, Gael considers the fact that she'll have to leave all the paintings here until they're fully dry, if she doesn't want to be hung out to do the same by M.F.N. With blue biro, she grooves *WTF* into the wood. The desks had been the cause of the scheduling setback. She'd had to ransack every thrift store in Harlem for them. Old-school, graffiti-free desks—a rare commodity—which she had spent the rest of her time defiling. American slang would've been a giveaway.

It's too much effort to read #8's graffiti through all the paint, so they're making some up. It's the only direct copy she's asked Xavier to do and he's holding his tongue on questions. But she can hear the slip of tongue against hard palate. "Tyler hearts Pedro 4eva"? He holds the craft knife like a scalpel. Prepping the desks has been Gael's job, for good reason.

"There's literally no one called Pedro or Tyler in Ireland," Gael says. The blue biro is tucked behind one ear, a red one prongs her ponytail and now she uses a technical compass to incise a scrotum.

"Do you have smiley faces?"

Gael looks at him unsmilingly. "Think: school kids who haven't gone through a metal detector to get to Civics."

Xavier wears a long-sleeved T-shirt and drawstring trousers, both weighted with dried paint. Gael still doesn't know if he's straight or what. In over two weeks, they've barely asked each other anything of consequence. Gael's wanted to ask lots, but he has a way of making her feel (without stating it) that conversation isn't part of the service.

And she respects that. She has to. He's done most of the painting work at night, after day shifts as a lift maintenance technician. She did ask him once if he'd gone to art school. Columbia University takes up a huge section of the neighborhood and they'd shared a moment student-watching from the window while he smoked. His parents had lived a block away. They died young, in '82, in a brewery explosion where they worked. Xavier was one when he went into the foster system, but he'd always planned to come back to where he should have spent his childhood. This was the only answer he gave to Gael's question on what art school he went to.

"That's how the kids had the knives to carve with," Gael adds. "No metal detectors."

"I'll just do a leprechaun and a pot of gold."

"Swap the leprechaun for a Celtic tiger."

"Celtic? You mean a green tiger?"

"Why not. Coated in banknotes. Pissing in its pot of gold."

"Jesus."

Gael shakes her head. "*Jay*sus," she says. "Here, I'll make you a list." She writes: "Niamh needs to take a bath. Mr. Monaghan's bad at wanking. Eat your carrots so you can read this. Postman Pat Rulz. Pray for your sins and they'll come to you. Go home Tommaso ya foren prick. Gerry Adams. What a tweedledick. Today I did this many poohs ‖‖‖"

Xavier starts gridding out Sudoku puzzles.

"If in doubt, draw tits."

Tight-mouthed in concentration, they work to the calming sounds of blade on school desk and drill on sidewalk. They sit *seiza* on tatami chairs: cushions on wooden frames coming just high enough off the ground for them to tuck their legs under the cushion part. It looks as though they're sitting on their heels. This is one of Xavier's space-saving tactics. Gael admires his organization. Collapsible furniture. Paints in shoeboxes. Palette knives for cutlery. Rags and sponges on a line strung up by the window, which looks out onto a fire escape. His own cityscape etchings balanced on clear thumbtacks on the walls, the smaller boards stacked in DVD racks. Shallow shelves circumnavigating the walls. Beside a set of nunchucks, a vintage Japanese military gas mask hangs, buying him a few hours to catch up on prayers in the event of chemical warfare. His easel and all the drying paintings take up the main space beneath the mezzanine, so the gas mask is occasionally required to get to sleep. The reek of white spirits is so pervasive that Gael can't smell it anymore.

One thing he had told her was that Silk Road had been, for him, a one-off experiment. People paid well for good forgeries. (Gael could imagine: Look at this Hirst we inherited from Auntie Ivy; no one spots the difference.) But then, those clients were too freaked to use a site like Silk Road and didn't know how, so Xavier would've ended up working for some art pimp. Gael's was the only job that had transpired from his listing. His income as a lift mechanic wasn't quite enough for White Harlem. "It's the Upper Upper West Side," he told Gael. "You won't be the only yuppie on the block."

"I'm still telling people back home I stayed in Harlem. And I'm not a yuppie, thank you very much."

"If you get off on poverty tourism, yes you are."

They had glanced at each other in recognition of a point well made. A warranted insult.

It's October 4. Nearly a fortnight till the show. A week till the work's fully, fully dry and ready to cart downtown. A week's a long time to leave your figurative checkbook on a stranger's bed-stand. Gael untucks her legs gracelessly from the chair and gets up. "I'm definitely not turning Japanese. Where's the nearest cemetery so I can drop my knees off?" She goes to her bag and starts changing into her running gear, profile to Xavier. "I won't get the chance to work up a sweat for a while. You're welcome to join." She looks at him squarely, in just a sports bra and leggings. "Clear your head of white spirits?"

Suddenly channeling his inner vandal, Xavier graffitis with new-found vigor. "I need to get this done today."

"Great," Gael says, still the employer. She pulls on her black compression top and lifts a foot onto the steel mezzanine ladder to tie her laces. "I don't feel the need to oversee the last one. You've got it." She smiles and takes her phone and earplugs, purposely leaving her backpack slightly unzipped. "I have the spare key. When I get back, I'll pack up and get out of your coif."

Xavier stops. "But the work won't be dry." He puts down the craft knife and looks worriedly at his studio, seized by fifteen burdensome auras.

"I'll take the five originals, to clear up some space. But what say you to an extra two hundi to keep the rest for the few days till they're dry? Then you can send me a message and I'll have them picked up. I have to hand it to you, buddy, you've done a great job. Just what I had in mind." She surveys the paintings, able to differentiate the originals mostly by where they're set. "I'd hire you again."

"Thank you. It's been good working for you—" He hesitates before adding, "Ms. Koons." Gael frowns at this. "But," he continues before she can ask, "Ms. Who?" "Honestly, I'm not that social. I'm grateful and all, don't get me wrong. I'd be open to doing this again, but it won't include digs, next time. I need my space."

Gael zips her key into the pocket of her waistband. "That wouldn't be an issue, Xavier; now that I trust you. Your skills. I wouldn't need to stay here and supervise. Anyway. Have productive alone time. I'll make it a long run."

It wasn't, of course, that she trusted him. It was that she understood the perils of risk aversion. The larger risk of two months' opportunity cost in New York (if the paintings disappear or are even so much as documented while she leaves them with him over the coming days) is offset by doing this test run: temporarily leaving a forty-thousand-dollar envelope with a guy who fixes lifts and dabbles in black market trades.

✦

It's bugging her that she missed Xavier's reference, so she stops running to look it up on her phone. "Ms. Koons Artist," she types. "Jeff Koons: Shiny on the Outside; Hollow on the Inside." No, that doesn't seem right. But after opening a few more results, she sees that it had been. Shit. Had she missed a warning just then? *Bitch, I'm gonna clean you out.* She reads as fast as she can.

With a portfolio valued at more than one billion dollars, Jeff Koons, whose wife works with him in the studio, acts as a kind of art foreman. Seldom physically involved in the process of making his artworks, he has 150 people on his payroll. He provides them with the concepts and paint-by-numbers instructions, he himself never wielding a brush. "I enjoy readymades," one *Guardian* article quotes Koons. "It's a way that I can communicate a form of acceptance, that everything is perfect. It's about accepting ourselves and accepting others." He talks about his art as an extension of the democratic principle—the moral dividends to be gained from "participation." Who knows how his apprentices "participate" in the (upward of) twenty million dollars individual sculptures fetch at auction. Once a commodities broker on Wall Street, Koons now works from a studio-factory in Manhattan's Chelsea district.

"No way!" she says. "Chelsea!" Then looks around for a notary, getting completely sidetracked from her thoughts about art and commodities and whether Xavier felt demeaned to be somewhat of a Koonsesque line worker. She'd sprinted through the rather sketchy Morningside Park and now finds herself at the spectacular, gothic Cathedral of Saint John the Divine. Before her stands a bizarre, grandiose bronze sculpture of a slayer-angel in a dry fountain. Given its setting, Gael takes a guess that the sculpture's narrative is one of good and evil. A plaque reads: PEACE FOUNTAIN CELEBRATES THE TRIUMPH OF GOOD OVER EVIL. Ah, she'd missed the capitalization.

The Archangel Saint Michael beheading Satan. A big smiling sun, a sleeping moon. Many peaceful, playful giraffes. A crab trying to pince Satan's decapitated head. A lion and a lamb chillaxing in God's kingdom, where lions don't eat lambs if they're posing for art. Subtle as a Koons. One thing going for it, though, is that it's honest in its delusion. There's no way the artist believes this story of virtue's triumph, the way Guthrie believes in the hallowed auras. This is a sculpture about narrativization; proclaiming our nostalgia for a simpler time and ethic. Sizing up Satan's knuckle of a penis, Gael starts to laugh at the whole absurd congruence of things. But the laughter isn't freeing or irreverent. It doesn't feel cheerful or deliberate. No. She's nervous.

❖

"Xavier?"

It's a stupid thing to do. Calling out. Were he there, she'd see him. And he her. She counts the paintings. All still there. On the easel, the #8 duplicate is under way. He's done a good job on the nails, soaked in saltwater to make fresh, bloody rust. The bag. It's there still . . . but askew. . . . Hadn't she faced it the other way? Opened it an inch less? She cracks her neck and takes a long controlled breath as if through a straw. Then clears the room in one stride.

Pulling out the cash, she sheds the envelopes like ice cream wrappers. She'll have to count. Too easy to miss a thousand. A thousand here, a thousand there. If he's taken any amount at all, then the paintings won't be safe here. An unknown number lights up on her phone on the kitchen counter but she doesn't hear it because the earplugs are still in and she's on her knees on the floor, building a cash castle. It had been a mistake to test him. It had been too risky. In truth, it had been unfair. Sirens scream past the window to what sounds like a frat party a block west, spilling its wide-necked intimidation and bad music onto the stoop. Twenty-one thousand two hundred . . . Gael loses count when she hears the unmistakable sound of a key in a lock. *Oh. My. God.* She has time only to gather a hug's worth of cash and drop it into her bag before the door opens and Xavier freezes in the entrance. One arm holds a brown paper bag to his chest. An egg carton peeps from the top. For breakfast, he microwaves eggs and eats them from a mug. With a spoon.

Gael pretends to barely register he's there, after glancing back. "Hi, can't talk," she says and makes as if to continue counting. "Twenty-one th . . . hundred and . . . Fuck. Where was I . . . We said five, right?" Now she looks up. Xavier is stood in the doorway, his harelip the next best disguise to a gas mask. Still, aspersion leaks through the filter like asbestos. Not only is this bitch devious, paying piss-all now that her wealth is laid out on the floor, she also suspects him for a thief—the laboring artist whose roof she's been under for weeks.

At this stage, it's probably safer to leave the paintings with the ass-slapping frat boys. To fling them out the window like divorce papers. She can't suddenly "change her mind" and take them away this minute, still wet; can she?

"Buddy," Gael says, all aggro. Act sure. "Earth to Xavier!" She is shaking like a junkie, but she can see only one way to play this and there's no time to weigh pros and cons.

He says, throatily, "What?" His eyes are going from Gael's bag to her hands, red with cash. "Midas," he says, and Gael guesses this is Cuban for stinky-cunt-about-to-get-rinsed.

"Five minus half up front is twenty-five hundred. Here. *Take* it. When I come to collect the paintings, I'll throw a tip at you, if not my fucking body. You talented bastard." Gael shoves all her belongings into the bag frantically and rapidly packs up the portfolio. Xavier puts the groceries on the kitchen counter. He doesn't say anything, but that's his way. "I am so fucking late," Gael says. "Can you check the bathroom for me? My toothbrush . . ."

He doesn't oblige. Gael pretends not to notice. She packs in the last of the Styrofoam and zips the portfolio shut.

"Your phone's ringing," Xavier says, his back to the counter, looking sideways at the caller ID.

"Don't answer it," Gael says. "I haven't come up with an excuse yet. Okay kay kay kay kay kay." She grabs her phone from the counter, then runs to the bathroom for her toiletries. Shoves the last bits into the pocket of her coat, which she criminally puts on over her sweaty sportswear.

That she doesn't have time to shower is meant to be the convincing part. That she hadn't been checking if he'd robbed her. That she actually has somewhere to go—somewhere with showers and bottled water and dry cleaning for fine wool coats.

"If you're that late," Xavier says, "I'll take you." His keys are still in his hand.

Gael watches the key of his VW work van swinging from his middle finger like windscreen wipers when you wanted the indicator. A penknife key ring.

She tells something like the truth. That she can't afford favors. But thanks.

No cab could come quickly enough, so she found herself descending the subway stairs at 116th with the portfolio like a double pram, Manhattan momentarily empty of people to assist. Lucky, then, that the C train serviced that station and would take her all the way to 14th: to Chelsea, four blocks from the gallery, where, evidently, she was headed, with some urgency. Flushed. Luggaged. Her bright blue Nikes dancing a kind of tap so that she might be thrown a dollar if she wasn't careful. Looking like a true artist. Or a bag lady. Or a tightrope walker, without the balance pole.

◆

Only F had been there in the foyer, standing at the desk, dictating an email. There was commotion in the main room, but Gael wasn't led in and she didn't go of her own volition because it had been an odd day and her plan to fuck M like a mouthguard-sporting, hunkering rugby player would already not be as good as she'd imagined and the hallway would do for this transaction. F was friendly, if to-the-point, explaining that they don't normally take in work until a week before a show. That's why there are only twenty-six shows a year and not fifty-two. There's no space to take in one artist's work with another's in situ, or while they're altering the space. That, and there aren't fifty-two artists worth showing in a year. But Gael insisted that it was only these five—that the rest would arrive by shipment the following week, when she'd be in touch again. Moving swiftly on to the topic of money, so as not to let F make a big favor out of a simple issue of storage, Gael said she'd like to fix up now, in cash. The more of it she could get off her person, the better. As F navigated the computer slowly with one hand to write up and print out the invoice, she told Gael there'd been a discussion and the auras could simply not be shown against white walls—they don't want to invite comparisons to Robert Ryman's white on white on white by white or harkback Ab-Ex—and that paint stripping would be the best alternative. "So you'll see on the invoice"—F squinted at the monitor: a different set of glasses, this time, tucked into the cleavage of her starched-bedsheet dress—"that's not cheap, but it's not expensive." Six thousand. When Gael fell silent, F said that the gallery is a twenty-two-hundred-square-foot space and paint stripping can cost up to fifteen dollars per square foot. So they had the artist's finances in mind when they'd decided only to strip the main back wall. "Remind me how many we're showing?" Fourteen, Gael said, and asked could they not just paint it gray, like the floor. F threw her long plait from the front of her shoulder back like a tie tossed out of grub's way. "A rough unpainted plaster wall will enhance the paintings' raw, arresting, bleached effect. You have to understand that if a work looks five percent better, it's ten times more likely to sell. If it looks ten percent better, it's the difference between selling two paintings and selling all of them. But that's only my professional opinion, on which this whole business rests."

So there it was. Paint stripping and opening night refreshments plus tax. $7,213.56.

Later, in the safety of a toilet cubicle, she'll put the remaining $30,221 back in the *matryoshka* envelopes and arrive at another percentage.

✦

"Mum?" Gael answers her phone in the café she'd come to to recover and take stock and check for damage. She hadn't drunk any water since her run and the loose cash was rammed into her bag like stolen jewelry into a bin liner. She'd sort that out shortly. And her slovenly outfit. But she'd sit here first and get her mind in order, unrushed. The missed calls were up to seven, but she had answered this one before it even rang.

"Are you alright?" Sive asks.

"Yeah." Gael wipes her nose with one of the stiff napkins from the dispenser on the table. "It's just . . . good to hear you."

"You're crying," Sive says.

"Am I?" Gael feels a smile on her cheeks, but she looks at the pile of bunched-up napkins before her like a stash of melting snowballs. She has no one to throw them at. "Oh yeah."

Sive laughs a little, warmly, and that recognition sets Gael off. She sobs and sobs the wobbly, achy outburst of gleaning, from one moment to the next, that you're lonely.

"I'm sorry for not phoning earlier, love. If I'd known—"

"No," Gael says, "I'm fine, really—"

"I suppose I think of you and I just, I think, you know. I think of the mast of a ship."

Gael inhales in intervals and hears her mother's words and voice apart and then together. She tilts the dregs in her mug to gauge if they're worth drinking. Sive doesn't rush through the silence. Some people can't bear to talk to Sive on the phone because she treats the receiver like an empty auditorium. She doesn't condense the conversation or make it efficient or audience-ready. Sometimes, she says barely anything. Just calls to spend time in that receptive place. Hums, maybe, a refrain, after a while, absolutely to herself. Gael is sure she stays with the phone to her ear, silencing away long after the other line has disconnected. Perhaps it's the static she likes. The acoustics. But mobile phones are no good for static. No doubt there's an app to add background static to phone calls like the false shutter click on digital cameras. How romantic the species can be. And foolish. "Will you talk to me," Gael says, "now that you've made me all soppy?"

Sive sighs. "If I remember correctly, I was phoning to scold you. It was my Motherly Duty. But I don't think I'll bother. If it's all the same."

Gael thanks the waiter who refills her mug for the third time and clears her plate. She had some satirically overpriced eggs, so she's bought herself another half hour of sanctuary. There's the sound of listening.

"Are you in a café?"

Gael sniffs. "No, they serve coffee in the brothel."

The clack of a tongue. "What's it like?" Sive asks.

"The coffee shop?"

"Mmm."

Gael blinks her eyes into focus and looks around. At the huge blackboard menus with chalk font listing thirty kinds of coffee up high behind the bar. The counter displaying monster pastries to take away in brown paper bags—icing a fist thick on the cupcakes. A six-strong wait staff. The chunky wooden tables and colorfully cushioned chairs. Redbrick pillars. The layout, lighting and décor designed to make a roomy chain café feel cozy and local. She's at one of those long communal tables where people come with their laptops and eke out hot drinks for hours. But there's no one else at it now. "It's quiet," Gael says, noticing that the din isn't as bad here, "in comparison. The *noise* here . . . I've been using the airline earplugs. They fall out. But at least they turn down the soundtrack for an hour or two, if they don't quite turn it off." She pauses. "It's like . . . there's no silent register. All the registers are taken. Even the ones humans can't hear. Those are taken too. With . . . unoiled handbrakes or . . . silent alarms . . . or infrastructure disintegrating because the Saudis own it and it's cheaper to let a bridge cave in than to raze it."

Sive makes a wincing sound. "You'd think we'd come on from ancient Rome."

"Sorry?"

"So many died because of the noise. Chariot wheels clattering on paving stones. The construction and carousing that went on night and day. Thousands died to it."

"Death by noise isn't a thing, Mum."

"If sheer exhaustion doesn't get you, because you can't sleep, you can have a stroke or heart attack. The body has a 'fight or flight' reaction to noise. The nerves and hormones and cardiovascular functions are all affected."

Gael's jaw is dropped. Here she is worrying about being robbed by her contractor and the damn background jazz could be killing her softly.

Sive asks, "Where are you staying?"

"Oh, you know. With a dude in a place."

"I see," Sive says. "Very reassuring."

"With a Cuban guy in Harlem."

Sive won't step into Gael's traps. "So long as you're being sensible."

"How's Art?"

"He said you've been emailing. That your interview went well and you're waiting to hear?"

Gael sometimes forgets to whom she's told which lies. "Tell him I'll get a job when he does."

"I'll do no such thing."

"Writes a good email, does Art."

"Oh?"

"But I suppose that figures," Gael says. "Since the only relationship he has with his son is by email."

Sive lets a few moments pass. And then something in the would-be static changes. "You've been pressuring Guthrie to do more paintings?"

Gael groans. "*What* is he *like*? Telling Mammy on me."

"I'm glad you admire his talent."

"Yeah yeah."

"And that you're encouraging. But you don't really know how to just encourage, Gael, do you? Only to goad."

"Whatever you're having yourself."

"Don't be facetious with me. The thing I have to say to you I hoped not to have to say, but this . . . Well. It is what it is." Sive pauses.

"What?"

"Your brother's doing phenomenally well, Gael."

"I know that."

"But you don't know why."

"It's because of the kids, obviously. He's completely high on them. He's found his drug of choice."

"It's because," Sive says steadily, "of antipsychotics."

When it comes to the truth, it can never be presented in isolation. To tell one truth, you have to tell others. Sive uses a lenient voice, which Gael knows is effortful for her to sustain and she prefaces the account by telling Gael that she needn't interject or comment. Sive will know she's there, sitting down in a café in Manhattan, doing her best to listen through all the bedlam and blare and confusion. "I'll tell you the facts first, or I know you won't hear anything else. But please know that what I say after is just as important."

Gael covers her other ear with her hand. "Mum? You're scaring me."

"You never directly asked how your brother got custody of the children. If you had, I might have told you. Or maybe I wouldn't have. It's his private life and I hoped he'd open up to you himself, when he was ready. But that hasn't happened. And now it seems you need to know. The fact is, as a culture, we don't think it's possible for young men to be assaulted by young women. Boys are physically stronger. More often than not, boys consent to having sex with girls, whatever their belief system. And anatomically . . . well, the fact is that erections are not always accompanied by arousal and certainly not by willingness to break one's pledge to one's God. One's whole belief system. I won't stay on this topic, Gael, because it's difficult. I am his mother." Sive clears her throat very harshly. "Ára coerced him. There was bruising and all that was documented at the hospital. I took him in on the day it happened, not only because I suspected, but because his fits were so frequent, he was barely recovering be- tween them. At the hospital, there was a social worker, and I wasn't privy to those conversations but Guthrie had some difficult decisions to make, and our priority was to get him into a stable condition. Whether or not to press charges came later. Your father and I had to deal with that together. Jarleth was barely recognizable. It seemed as though he was another patient, *sick* with all of it—sick with the pain this . . . girl, only a minor, too, we forget. If I hadn't met Art by then . . . I don't know. He was still living in England, but he ferried over. I feared Jarleth would set a torch to the girl's house. It was a dark, dark time, Gael, and I won't say we did things the right way, but we did them how we did them. We three turned up at Ára's family home and told her parents that the hospital had photographic evidence and DNA swabs—which was your father's idea—and that this was undoubtedly a forced encounter. Just like that, her parents knew it to be the truth. How did they know? Because she was pregnant. The timing matched. And there was a private history of violence we only learned of later. Expulsions. 'Antisocial behavior,' one school put it. We left them, that first time, with the knowledge of it. And the threat—at that stage, it wasn't blackmail—but we had to go back. Because—we don't know how, was it a text message or some sinister communication—Guthrie found out about the pregnancy and you've never seen a young man flood with such certainty and purpose. She wouldn't do this to him *and* erase the results of it. The results would never be erased from his soul and he wouldn't let another sin be pinned to him for eternity, he said. He'd raise the children. The social worker told us that, with his condition and age, he was an unfit parent, even in the hugely unlikely event that the girl's parents would cancel the trip to Manchester and in the even *less* likely event that Ára would give birth to twins she wouldn't get to keep, which was *so* unlikely, the conversation wasn't worth having, the social worker said. But Jarleth was involved by then and you know how your father reacts to being told a thing is impossible. Much like you do. And I admire you both for it. It was one of the things—" Sive halts the march of her sentence, then continues:

"Guthrie's doctor reminded us that he'd never tried antipsychotics—often effective for his disorder—of course because Guthrie wouldn't acknowledge the condition. And you can give someone a placebo, but you can't give them a drug they don't know they're taking. But now he had good reason to cooperate. The doctor told him the drug had been known to help in cases of epilepsy, too; reducing inflammation in the brain, or some such thing, he said. And Guthrie held out his hand out for the pills. They monitored him for a day or two in hospital, then as an outpatient, and he didn't have another fit. I know you're still there, Gael, and that you're listening. This is a lot for you to take in and the only reason I'm telling you is so that you know why his fits have stopped and what it means for you to ask him to do more of those paintings. He painted those to remember what the fits were like, before they left his life for good—he did one for each he's had in the two years since the twins' birth. Only a handful. The last one was in March. He won't paint another unless he relapses and I know you wouldn't wish that upon him."

A long queue has formed at the pastry counter and Gael can't understand how six staff members aren't enough to keep on top of it. It seems as if the fault lies with the girl on the till, clicking its touch screen as if playing online Texas Hold'em for all the money in the tray. Her lower lip hangs loosely. People in the queue talk into Bluetooth headsets. One reads the nutritional information on a takeaway chia seed and coconut pudding. Gael had seen those puddings on the way in and thought they looked nice. There was something else in them. What was it? Oh yeah. Raspberry coulis. But $6.95 worth? If they'd been $5.95. $5.95 is just over $5. $5 and change. Whereas $6.95 is $10 with some change back. Maybe they could have made it $6.25 and then you'd still feel it was just over five rather than under ten.

"Thanks for letting me know, Mum, okay? I have to go. I've got a thing."

"If you need to talk to someone," Sive says, "your father's on secondment in New York. Just so you know. I'll send you his number. It's not likely you'd want to, but he's there. He's been very civil. And with this—"

"Really gotta go, Mum. Say hi to Art."

Gael closes her laptop and her backpack and takes it to the rest-room to tally the cash and change clothes. The Plaza's luggage stor-age has her rolly bag, containing all of her good clothes, bar one set. But she doesn't change into that outfit. She changes into her bargain-bin boyfriend jeans and gray hoodie, all biro-marked from graffiti'ing the blackest and bluest of things. Guthrie & Ára Up a Tree. K-I-S-S-I-N-G. She washes her face and her genitals at the sink.

Forty percent is gone, she determines, when she counts up what's left of the check. She whacks the wall a dozen times. Hand over fist, options forfeited. She splashes her face again. Ties up her hair, messily. Glad not to be clean and glamorous. Glad to be dressed boyishly. A boy, destined for manhood, physical dominance, priori-ties straight. She won't spend another hundred. The change, only. She'll take thirty thousand back to Guthrie for Christmas. On top of whatever comes of the show. No less. She should never have involved him. She'd had a dozen alternative plans, before the paintings, any one of which she could have made work. This had been an error. A big one. High time to cut losses.

On the way out, she forgoes the chia-coconut pudding, but ap-proaches the loose-lipped barista to ask if there's somewhere she can pick up a sleeping bag.

The girl gives her a hundred-mile stare, showcasing her lower gums, the color of sealing wax. "You mean like, for camping?"

"For protesting," Gael says.

Make that a ninety-nine-mile stare. "Um. Lemme get the man-ager."

8

Non Zero Sum

I

The night sky is that marauding kind of dark that comes of storm clouds and too much hanging in the morning's balance. It's hard to see if her mopping is making the granite cleaner or just pushing the dirt around. As far as she knows her physics, filth can't really be got rid of. Only moved from one place to a less patronized place.

Streetlamps cast insipid orange like dawn diffused through broken bottle shards on a beach. Dawn, though, is a way off. It's five a.m. on Friday, October 14. Gael's tenth day of protest posturing. The Stanislavsky method is showing under her eyes and is expressing in the form of a constant dull headache. She hasn't taken her backpack off once since arriving at Zuccotti Park, even while sleeping. It acts, now, as a Victorian bustle beneath her see-through poncho.

"Church ain't out till we quit singing."

Gael glances across to see if that comment had been directed at anyone. On all fours, Erin is lit from below as she scrubs grime from the underground lighting; rain spitting off her poncho; bleached dreads dripping out the front of her hood like stalactites. It's a headfuck to tune into all the misdirected talk here—the interrupted points and itching, half-articulated arguments. All of it urgent. Gael had missed the camp's transformation into the tiny town it now is: library, town hall–type assemblies, food outlets, sanitation committees, permanent residents and all. She'd missed the bond-forming march across the Brooklyn Bridge a fortnight back, when police threw a net over seven hundred people and arrested them. But she'd been here for the mayor's visit to inform protesters they would have to vacate by seven a.m. Friday so that the park can be cleaned. They'd be allowed to return afterward if they abide by Brookfield Properties' rules, including no lying down in the park. That the cleanup was a pretext to dissolve the camp was obvious. Similar tactics had been used to evict M15 demonstrators in Spain. So Occupy had put out an emergency call for supporters to rally at the park at six a.m. this morning to defend the occupation. Those who'd been camping felt the crescendo as clear as the day that had to come and no one slept. Gael closed her eyes for an hour before midnight, but the clattering of tidying and trash collection kept her from resting and a heavy downpour at one a.m. had the effect of a cold morning shower. The less die-hard of the crowd fled, leaving only a few hundred sweepers and pavement-scourers. More rain took at least a hundred stalwarts—Gael among them—into the local McDonald's, which suddenly reneged on its twenty-four-hour policy and shut its doors. McFuckinChickens all round.

As six a.m. nears, the crowd thickens around her, as though she has swum far out to sea on a notion and now land is out of sight. Isn't this one of the consequences we accept when we step into an idea? That it will pull us into its riptide? Yes, the idea had begun as opportunism, but something else had held her here. People brush against her, taking her for one of them. And why wouldn't they? Erin tugs Gael's elbow. "Where're all the cops?"

Gael scans the park's perimeter. She has no intention of being netted. Some guy whose name she forgets says: "They got a load of Occupy Sesame Street and went back to bed." He nods at a kid piggybacking his dad, holding an umbrella over both of them. The skies break out anew in hammering percussive climax and a roar erupts from the crowd: a roar of some two thousand voices. A far cry from Occupy's first day when the Wall Streeters had come onto their balconies with champagne buckets to pour down scorn on the city's troops below: the piddling group of sweaty-crotched anarchists parading their puny dreams; being escorted by the NYPD to their third-choice destination.

A call-and-response begins: "We will position ourselves with our brooms and mops in a human chain around the park, linked at the arms. If the NYPD enters, we will peacefully, nonviolently stand our ground and those who are willing will be arrested."

Fingers wiggle in the air in silent approval. The Orientation Working Group are teaching the hand signals to a bunch of out-of-towners who've just flown in for this showdown and for tomorrow's global day of solidarity. Washington Square Park and Times Square are on Occupy's hit list.

A murder of black town cars approaches the Trinity Place entrance to the park. Some hurry toward them, but Gael hangs back. The crowd is denser now. It could be three thousand strong. The cars have pulled in and someone is being escorted through the mobs. Camera flashes light up a white collar and silk tie, polished as new money. Nina, who has returned from her visit to the LA occupation (as reported at last night's general assembly), is handing out bananas. Gael takes two. Nina doesn't recognize her in the dark. The rain has stopped, so she takes off the poncho and rolls it into a cylinder.

Judging by the heckling, it's the mayor taking a walk through the park to get a read on things. One grouser shouts, "Billionaire Bloomberg, go to hell!" while others vie for his handshake. "We love you, Mayor Bloomberg!" He comes just a few meters into the throng, surrounded by bodyguards. Organizers thank him for his cooperation and offer him extra security. Bloomberg says he has plenty. Whatever else he says is unclear. The visit has lasted the duration of a teenage lay. It's still pitch-black, but city business has already commenced.

Soon after, the human mic system restarts with the speakers standing on tables. "We have a proposal from Brookfield Properties . . ." Because of where Gael stands, she gets the news a few seconds late, but the speakers' faces are brightening with the sky—now navy-gray infused with yellow. The cleanup has been canceled. The call-and-response doesn't get past the first few phrases before cheers of jubilation erupt and arms fling around bodies. Someone squeezes Gael's forearm and she can feel a smile cross her own cheeks, full of banana. "The People. United. Will Never Be Defeated," chants the crowd, again and again, laughing and clapping and punching the air with every stressed syllable, leaping on the spot. "We WON!" Gael searches for anyone she knows, but all she can see are hands and cameras and hoods. She muscles through the crowd until she spots Erin's white dreads going up and down as she leaps. She's preaching Gandhi:

"First they ignore you. Then they laugh at you. Then they fight you. Then you win."

Unable to echo this, Gael is reminded of being a kid at mass, before she took the first step out the church door by telling Jarleth she didn't believe that Mary was a virgin; when she'd stopped saying the parts of the catechism she didn't believe in. Each week, she'd say less and less, only uttering the parts that were demonstrably true until there was nothing left for her to say. For the kingdom, the power and the glory are yours, now and forever? No. That's moronic. It wasn't that she gave two shits about honesty—Jesus, if ever such a generous lover had lived, wouldn't be so petty as to monitor lip-syncing during his hymns; it was that she knew that this small movement of the lips, disconnected from the brain, going going going along with things, was a gateway drug. Not to heaven, but to fools' paradise. So her closed lips were a renunciation until she was ready to tell her mother she would never go again. "If you're staying here, you can help me organize this sheet music into sections," Sive had said, as if her daughter had confessed to something so trivial as wanting to skip swimming lessons. That was when she knew that logistics had nothing to do with Sive's "duties" on Sundays.

However heartening the rhetoric, she can't sing: "We, the ninety-nine percent, are too big to fail." What planet are they on not to be able to look at the distribution of the world's wealth, historically and now, to know this isn't true? To look, even, at the one-percenters who've turned up here to speak: the commercially successful actors and celebrities. "I'll write a check when everyone else does," one had said, standing north of Kanye West, standing south of their flock of gold-toothed guardians. To have wealth distribution, the one percent would have to believe it would be better off if the ninety-nine per-cent were better off too. The rich would have to believe in mutual-ism. Commensalism. That their wealth wouldn't diminish by sharing it. That if they press the button, their peers would too. And the one percent didn't get to where they are by staking on relationships.

"Earth to Libor," the guy says, tugging Gael's sleeve as she wan-ders past in pursuit of coffee. "You coming?"

"Dean?" She finally remembers his name. Some New Jersey stu-dent of . . . bioengineering? An elastic string bifurcates his forehead from the Anonymous mask on the back of his head, loaning him a thinker's wrinkle. His spectacles are all rained-on. How he can see her is a mystery. Though she's been up all night, it's still too early not to shield her eyes from his orange raincoat. He shakes her by the shoulders. "Wake up and smell the opening."

Gael cringes. She beats him back with her rolled-up poncho. He smells not of Brie, but of Camembert. On oven-warm sourdough bread. "What a creepy line."

"Are you coming or not?"

"Where?"

"Wall Street. Where your beef's at."

"For food?" Gael looks confused and checks to see if the spare banana in her coat pocket is smushed from people freeloading on her personal space.

"Where-Your-Beef's-At, Libor. We're marching on Wall Street. Now."

He leads her through the crowd to the park's perimeter, where an unplanned celebratory march has already circuited and is coursing south on Broadway. They're able to weave their way to the front, as it's only a couple of hundred people and they see that the whole front line is wielding mops and brooms like a makeshift-weaponed mob.

The people who happened to be within earshot one drunken night last week nicknamed Gael "Libor" because of her rant about the colossal financial scandal being exposed in the UK. She'd given a tutorial on how collusion to manipulate the London Interbank Of-fered Rate had affected them all. "*No.* It's not 'the same old shit-show.' It's only got to do with the housing market collapse so much as it's got to do with *all money.* Who here has a mortgage?" No one spoke for a second, then someone said, "Nina, but she skipped town," and everyone laughed. It was days before Gael learned the No Income No Assets acronym for subprime mortgage holders. Nina was NINA. "Dumb question. You're obviously all homeless." Some-one flicked scrambled tofu in Gael's direction. "Student loans then. Which idiot has one?" A bunch of groans indicated nearly everyone and she poked the shoulder of a handsome Dutchwoman—tall, fair, limp-haired, cheeky-faced, rides-a-bike-posture—and said, "You got shafted." Then, the wind picked up and blew the Dutchie's scarf to the side and Gael openly took in the outline of her breast. "My fa-ther . . ." she'd started. Truth was, she didn't know exactly what role he had played—but that he'd headed up the relevant sector of the leading implicated bank and yet wasn't undergoing trial. Since she'd found a topic that vaguely fit within the movement's grievances (the way a parallelogram fits into a square if the latter's large enough), she was finally able to let her mouth run and she got caught up in the relief of it. Also, she could openly seethe at everyone's ignorance. What shut her up eventually was the Dutchwoman, Lotte, cutting her nails with foldaway scissors while making eyes at Gael. Later, on an air mattress, beneath a tarp (cops stationed around them like the bulbs of a vanity mirror), they unzipped their sleeping bags and Gael drew Lotte's bicycling leg back across her hip like a wheelbarrow handle. "Dark horse," Lotte said under her quaking breath and they tried to make their shuddering seem like the cold front besting their feeble female constitutions.

A few police on foot head in their direction now as the group marches past the graveyard of Trinity Church, where Gael has whiled away hours listening to podcasts and concerts to escape the vapid Panglossian hypotheses and to clear up the confused belief systems she'd been preached at about—Liberalism, Libertarian Socialism, Neo-Marxism, Voluntaryism, Mutualism, Anarcho-capitalism, Insurrectionary Anarchism, I-should-be-better-off-than-my-folks-just-cuz-ism—arriving at the conclusion that there is no modern unifying theory the left is trying to ratify and *that* is its lemon. Cold days she's spent inside the church, listening to world-class classical string quartets and charging her phone, returning to Occupy only when peckish. Though Sive is the true artist of the two, the quality of music in the church on any given lunchtime has reassured Gael that pushing Guthrie's paintings had been the right decision.

"Get back on the sidewalk, ma'am," an officer shouts, one hand to his radio.

Aided by skyscrapers' acoustics, whoops get lifted up into the sky that still has a touch of the witching hour about it. The group isn't marching so much as scurrying and no one's chanting volubly, as if trying to slip by unnoticed. They dart out onto the road whenever scaffolding threatens to slow them; each time eliciting "Stay on the sidewalk" yells from the NYPD—undeniably taken by surprise. "Do NOT obstruct traffic."

"How far behind are they?" Dean's on his phone to someone back at camp. "Broadway's barred. We're turning onto Exchange Place . . ."

Police have pulled out all the stops to block previous marches from reaching Wall Street proper, as if the movement's two-finger salute to the system (albeit a peace sign) will be deflected as long as Wall Street itself remains—as it always has been—protected from the plebs. When the huge George Washington statue beneath the flags and white marble columns of the New York Stock Exchange come within torch-throwing distance and the police can be seen up ahead hastening to form a barricade, someone yells GO GO GO and they all break into a sprint.

"Stay back!" a policewoman calls from her post, shuffling behind the cordon at the Wall Street junction. Behind her, German shepherds sniffing vehicles for explosives burst into rabid barking at the two hundred sleep-deprived bodies closing in on them, smelling of salted tenderized meat.

A lone voice from the back of the group yells: "Tell me what democracy looks like!" Anyone who can catch a breath answers, "This is what democracy looks like!" Feet rushing on the slippery red cobblestones sound of a river in flood. Someone's pushing Gael's backpack to hurry her.

The front rows clatter to a halt against the blockade. Truncheons poke at them as though stoking a fire. The marchers get stacked up together, everyone panting and pivoting and readying their phones to take footage in case anyone's heroic enough to flare forth. Despite whatever bruises form to suggest otherwise, Gael feels like a spectator still, reminded of the cat-and-mouse strategy game Jules the rueful banker had watched people play like flagitious porn. Though, Jules wasn't watching just for entertainment's sake, but to observe strategy. He had tremendous respect for the players. Gael hasn't. Perhaps that's what she's been trying to discover.

Erin yells: "Who are you protecting?"

"Take a step back, ma'am."

"The corporatocracy's the felon!"

"Stay back."

"If corporates run our government, what happens when the CEO's a fascist?" Erin leans into the barrier. "We surrender our democracy!"

"You're about to surrender your freedom."

"Exactly! This is yours, your children's freedom we're fighting for. Their rights."

"Do *not* push the barricade."

"These jerks used *your* taxes for bonuses. They're the reason your retirement's cut in half. Why are you protecting them?"

"Forty percent," the policewoman says. "Not half. Last warning."

"You don't deserve that. Honest, hardworking people. You should march with us. Swap your baton for a broom. We've got spares. Help us clean this pigsty. Here—"

The cop Erin's addressing withdraws for orders, then returns to carry the barriers backward so as to funnel the protesters toward the park. Horse hooves clatter up from behind and they have little choice now but to be shepherded. If need be, Gael will put her hands behind her head and retreat to the sidewalk asylum. Tonight is the exhibition opening and bruises won't flatter the outfit she has in mind. She should get back to business. This has been worthwhile to behold—she is now clearer on cynic statistics.

But no. That isn't it still. It isn't purely mercenary or for entertainment or out of cold curiosity that she's stayed until now. She'd wanted to hear them out. Her principled peers. To know if they have knowledge of the movement's ineffectuality and are here anyway, or if they have real hope for reform; which, in its implications of bounded rationality, would depress Gael deeply. Erin had been the only one to call Gael out on her cynicism:

"It's because you're not American," she'd said. "You can't see how *rare* this is. Us coming together like this. Ireland's tiny, right? So you can't snub your neighbor without it getting awkward. Here, you absolutely can. We're all atomized. We live in boxes. Work cubicles, huge cars, microclimates, TVs. We're divided. Race, religion, class—any way you cut it. That's by design. And those divides don't go down the center! So yeah, Occupy won't change policy. But it's got us *talking*. Face-to-face."

Then Lotte had joined them, hooking her arm in Gael's. "This is nice," she'd said, wearing her permanent gummy grin. "To hear so many voices. And to make quite some friends. But Erin, there is one divide that *is* going neat down the middle. Blue-red. This is why America becomes worse and worse. And also Britain, he has this system. Two parties is not enough of parties! Libor and me know it, heh? Little countries, a lot of parties." She then reached out to stroke Erin's blond dreadlocks. "It is not appropriate?"

Standing on tiptoes to see what's going on, Gael now sees the group obeying the police and walking on, without griping further or losing anyone to cuffs. Some feign gratefulness for being funneled out rather than kettled. But something's happening out of sight. The more acquiescent they become, the more riotous the city around them. Car horns and incantations carry on the air all the way from the park. Gael looks around to see who's chanting near her, but a horse exhales steamy reproval within smelling distance. Maybe they've cleared out the park after all. She wrestles to the front where the whispers get their rightful translation: caught out by the spontaneity of the action, most of the police force has been dispatched to a separate march on City Hall. Now there really is an opening that even the cops can smell.

When Gael turns onto Broadway, the noise reveals its source. The WHOSE STREET? rallying cry of another march farther south on Broadway coming toward Wall Street from the opposite direction. A merging of regiments would more than double their sum:

too many for so few cops to coax back onto the sidewalks and to the park, meaning they might actually make it, if they run.

A whistle blows and Gael finds herself barging with the pack like a delinquency of thieves through shop windows. Seagulls and pigeons batter their wings at the crest of this dubious wave moving too far into Lower Manhattan for it to cleanly tide out again. By the time they pass Bowling Green's charging bull, they've nearly merged groups and no one looks back to see the glint of the bull's fondled brass balls or the wink of riot shields. One-way traffic is headed straight for them, but it comes to a halt as protesters wag brooms at car bonnets. Just in front, a guy punches a placard into the air like the red hand of Ulster. The fortune on its palm reads:

> Minimum Wage = $16,000 per year.
> CEO of Goldman Sachs = $16,000 per hour.

Drivers squint at the horde and their watches and some toot and one rolls down all its windows and blasts a Billy Bragg anthem from the radio. Gael barely hears it beneath the concussion of heckling, hooting white noise. She may well be concussed. Truly, she might just be ... because no matter how she squints at it, the back of a sign up ahead reads "GAEL!" She pulls her ponytail down and feels her skull for a lump through her greasy hair. It's been five days since she's showered, when she called in on Xavier to collect the remaining paintings, though she regularly makes a bath of public washroom sinks. Maybe someone wants her for a photograph? Every other person is filming. The media team always wants her. Over the week, she's found so many lenses converging on her like flies, it's all she can do to flick them from her skin. This morning, even pedestrians are filming. They see it's not business-as-usual. The streetlamps are still lit like knobs of butter, though day has been cracked open and the white of the sky is congealing. Police call from bullhorns to keep to the curb, but this street's a narrow canyon. The road tapers to one lane—too tight for them and the parked cars—and Gael ducks around the green scaffolding like an obstacle course whose finish line is that sign that says, GAEL! bobbing in and out of view. She doesn't believe in signs and symbols like in the Nabokov story Harper described, about everything connecting back to her (Harper's way of calling out Gael's narcissism or solipsism or whatever), but she does trust her senses, against the philosophers' advice, so it's probably one of those fools who call her Friend, wrongly thinking she's an arrestable. Scooters sound close behind her and she hurries down William Street, her bag thumping painfully on her back.

By the time she covers the two blocks to Wall Street, the sign is lost to chaos again. It had just been a piece of cardboard, scrawled with black marker, and she can't be sure it hadn't read GRAIL, for example, with HOLY on the flipside—she wouldn't put it past her father to have bequeathed to her astigmatism. Police cars line the sidewalks and the mob slips around one of the bronze bollards that look like sculptures but are there to prevent car bombs from getting onto the street. Everyone's climbing over the ramps raised to stop traffic, though there's space on either side to scoot round them. It feels better to scale them and slide down the metal grilles. It's fun! And they're *here*. On Wall Street. Coffee-cart owners look on in dismay. Police scooters are lining up ahead, as if for a drag race, forcing protesters to move around them. They're stationary, but the engines are on. There isn't even the semblance of control. Who's going to give an order to tear-gas Wall Street?

Some people sit down on the road but most form a human chain, standing off with the scooters. Gael makes her way to the front. She won't link elbows but she wants to see the line between nonviolence and resilience.

"Get it out of my face," a cop tells a newscaster, shoving his camera back by the lens. "You're interrupting police operations, sir. You got that?" Those on scooters wear helmets with face shields. Those on foot cross their arms in a bouncerly manner, chewing gum so that you can count their fillings. The pessimists hold their batons. Gael scans the officers in view and decides she'll volunteer for an all-body pat-down if it doesn't come about naturally.

A kid kneeling before a scooter in an aspect of prayer is cuffed and carried off by his armpits. The righteous calls start:

"Shame on you!"

"He's not resisting!"

"What's your name, brother?"

"We love you. You're a hero!"

"Police brutality! Police brutality!"

Just then, looking back at the group from the right-side fringes, Gael catches sight of a pane of dented cardboard in the front row: held not as a shield against the forces, but as a mirror turned toward her.

> "Now that my ladder's gone,
> I must lie down where all my ladders start,
> In the foul rag-and-bone shop of the heart."
>
> —Yeats, bitches

Harper. Blood must be rushing into Gael's head because there's a thumping, slaughterous sensation. Basked in the headlights of scooters is Harper. It's Harper, *here*, shouting something Gael can't make out. Clinging to the shoulder straps of her bag as if to a seat belt, Gael tries to move through the crowd without losing sight of her, but the horns blare in unison and the scooters are now driving directly at people in an attempt to split them up. "MOVE! MOVE!" they shout, and drive into the front line in short bursts. Some try to walk backward and filter round the sides. Someone's foot will be run over. Back up Back up Back up. Screams as they shove and swipe at anyone in their way, but the crowd clusters in response around the scooters on all sides—over them, almost, like ants around sugar lumps. When reinforcement arrives, the drivers resort to dismounting their bikes and battering people back. "On the sidewalk. Let's go."

"The whole world is watching!" the crowd calls, as people are dragged off and kneeled on by cops. Camera flashes make an unlikely disco of the Friday morning business district and everyone still standing holds up peace signs for lighters. "Anyone obstructing traffic *will* be *arrested!*" Gael hears from a voice closer to hand than she'd like.

"Harper?" she cries, having lost her in the crowd, slipping and bubbling like lava. She had deleted so many unread emails, subject lines ALL IN CAPS. So many calls and voice mails, hindrance to the fore and thus unwelcome. But those distant petitions were easy to ignore and to be firm in that; the body, not.

"Don't push!"

"Everyone relax."

It wasn't just the body's lure—it was the body's being here. Its insistence. The mind in tow, with Harper. The rationality unbounded and unbending. That was the core of her oddness: her way of being in the world was internally consistent.

"GAEL."

She pivots round. Where is she?

Pressure meets the side of her head, then her mouth. The milky coffee taste of her lips; hot wet in the middle where they part; the rubbed feel of their flesh; rapt concentration like finding where you stand on a topographical map and not wanting to lose the spot for anything—pressure so sure and square that their noses bunch and the high of their smiling cheeks skim. Harper pulls back to take Gael in, holding her by the sides of her head. They're both laughing and jumping stupidly now and Harper draws Gael close enough to break her ribs and then makes up for her roughhousing by kissing her eyelids and chin and cheekbones and forehead and shoulder and the crown of her head. Not her neck. Not her sternum. Not here.

Not again. The endorphin-flooded feeling has all the weakness of addiction and Gael hasn't trained all her life to deny this vice for no good reason. She hasn't. The sudden conformist twitch in herself; the want to bond to someone, which is the same as to be bound. But no. No. There is no such need to admit.

"Tell me you love America enough to wanna marry me" is the first thing Harper says.

Gael runs her palm across Harper's breast-compressing dungarees, which are probably designer, which would make her the entire world market for designer dungarees. "Depends," Gael shouts over the ruckus and points to Harper's crotch. "Can the cameltoe have babies?"

"Hey!" Harper yells. "I'm just happy to see you."

Gael takes the smushed banana from her pocket. "Well, I just had a banana in my pocket."

They gawp for a second at the slimy mangled mess in Gael's hand, like a teenage boy's sock, and the laughter that follows is the tear-streaming kind reserved for jet lag and sugar lows and being dangerously relaxed for one's circumstances. They collapse into each other in hysterics as they're turned and heaved hither-thither by the riotous masses. A fast waltz is what they're dancing and Harper calls too loud into Gael's ear as they whirl, "I swear-to-god wet my pants when I saw you on Occupy livestream. I mean, I knew you were in the city. You called me from friggin customs. But I—" They get jerked backward as the scooters are at it again, cleaving the group like a blunt knife.

"Sorry I never replied to your emails," Gael says. "Or called back. It's just—"

"*No!* Don't *sorry* me!" Harper says. "You fried my sunny-side-up heart for breakfast and then ate a Pop-Tart instead. You don't get to say *sorry.*"

"I knew you'd be mad, but sometimes it's better just to—"

"Irish!" Harper says. "Cut it out! You're *here.*" She holds Gael by her hands and the pupils in her hazel eyes dilate. "Of all the gin joints."

◆

How they got from this moment to cuffed in the back of a police van—Gael with an aching vulva from where Harper cuntpunched her; Harper with a swelling to match the natural bruise of her eye socket from Gael's headbutt—is a bit of a blur. Gael had perhaps made it too clear that she was only at this joint because the gin was free. "Don't let the cleanup fool you," she had said. "They're all still basting in their own stupidity."

The van is on the move, finally. They're sharing it with two women who were actually arrested for protesting: one public high school science teacher from Brooklyn called Brandi and another un-responsive white lady of middle age with a bandana on her head and closed eyes. She seems to be doing breathing exercises, judging by the long, steady wafts of broccoli.

"Nice tan," Gael tells Harper, after they've both recovered from being stunned and hurt.

"Mom's boob cancer's back." Harper looks out the metal grid window.

"What?"

"So I spent the summer in Vegas." Handcuffed, Harper twists around on herself to move the strap of her plastic SpongeBob SquarePants watch to reveal her tan line. The plaid mustard and gray shirt she wears beneath the black denim dungarees is rolled to the elbows and she has a blue denim jacket tied around her waist. Gael watches her profile: her swollen eye, level with her brow and upper cheek, partly curtained by her outgrown fringe; her nose flat-tish and buttony with mathematically circular nostrils and a pepper-kernel-sized scar where she must have taken a nose ring in and out and in and out so neurotically it got infected. No jewelry or makeup or balm on her downturned mouth.

"Shit," Gael says. "That's awful."

"She'll live. She won't let me off that easy."

"I'll pray for your moms," Brandi offers suddenly—the cuffs effecting semiautomatic prayer.

Harper glances over and says thanks. She keeps her eyes trained away from Gael, but not her words. "She wants to meet you."

"Your mum?" Gael asks, shocked.

"She got duplicate bills from my therapist and pharmacist. Wants to give em to you in person along with a piece of her mind."

Gael asks, "What's her name again?"

"Kendra."

"That's it. Kendra. Did the gemstones not protect her, then?" Gael remembers Harper slagging off her mother's New Age ways, back in London.

"'I let the rose quartz go totally flat,' she told me. Literally, that's her explanation for stage three lymphoma. She forgot to recharge her crystals."

Gael frowns. "I didn't know gemstones had batteries."

"No, you gotta put em out under a full moon. Like on your roof. Higher up the better."

"Jesus."

"Not Jesus. Hekate. Zeus. Taco Bell. Anyhow," Harper sighs, "at least she doesn't talk crap all day long anymore. It's been good for us, her being sick. I mean, it's not like we're debating the great American novel or anything, but she's talking to me for real. Like: 'Harper, what did I do so wrong?'" She's doing an impression of an even louder voice than her own. "Like: 'Most of everyone I know's not in love. They're just accustomed to their spouse. They like em and that's all there is. In that way I'm glad I never liked your father. We still got a shot at love, if he's ever home again while I'm conscious. So get in the car, will you, and pick me up a wig. A nice red one with layers and a loose wave.'"

To get the impression right, Harper's had to direct it at Gael and now they're looking at one another again. It's her best aspect: straight-on. Gael wants badly to clear out the van and see what they can do while cuffed, but instead she winces in pain as they come to a sudden halt. Harper had thrown the first punch to the pelvis. Gael headbutted her back, but not forcefully, as she'd found it hard to get her footing. They had only managed to get one blow in each before they were on their stomachs on the ground with a ridiculous quantity of police hands on their bodies, feeling around for their rights. By the sound of it, they've arrived at whatever station is having them and bandana lady's breathing is now accompanied by tears silently dripping from her jowls to her jersey.

"Art's with Mom on this one. That you should pay my deductible," Harper adds, just as the van doors are being unlocked.

"Art?" Gael says.

"Yeah."

"*Art* as in . . . my mum's partner, Art?"

"Art as in my BFF," Harper says. "I don't understand half of what he says, with that accent, but he's a damn good listener. Usually he has me call the landline. But even still it's the cheapest therapy I ever had."

The van doors open and a small army of cops have come to escort the four slight women inside. They seem intent on separating Gael and Harper, so they have to be on best behavior to be put in the same cell. Calmly, Gael asks why the hell she thinks it's cool to have started up a friendship with her dad-in-law thing, to which Harper explains that she was calling for Gael every other day and Art just eventually let her talk at him.

"I've got OCD, Gael. You know this about me. I've reminded you once an hour since I've known you."

"Right. So surely obsessing over me isn't healthy. And I wasn't exactly encouraging you."

"It's a compulsion. O-*SEE*-DEE. If I try to *not* compulsively do something, it gets worse. It's better for me to work through an obsession rather than tryna act like it doesn't exist. That does *not* work. Trust me. House pets taught me the hard way. I killed Cleopatra the Chihuahua, Terry the arrogant ferret and at least three rats before my shrink changed tactics."

"Ladies," a cop says, puckering her brow at that last snippet of conversation. "This way."

Gael keeps her voice down, but she's riled at the thought of it. "You call me nine million times and clog my inbox and *contact* my *family* and—"

"I'm sorry I got a condition!" Harper says. "You can get a restraining order while we're locked up, Gael, as just another way to say you love me and that'll solve everything. Then you won't have one single sad friend on the planet. Well done. Ku-friggin-dos, amigo."

✦

Their belongings are taken from them, but they don't have to change into jumpsuits, as Gael had imagined. They're put in a cell with Brandi. A small holding cell, with an unflushable metal toilet smelling as if it's been retched in besides everything else. Though she begged, the guard wouldn't let Harper open and close and open and close the cell door, but he said that he would look into retrieving her medication from her bag. The bench is not quite big enough for the three of them and Brandi suggests they sit down in rotation, but Harper says she'll stand because of tetanus. Her mom believed that if she avoided vaccines, Harper's social skills might balance out with all the other kids'. Brandi shakes her head, as if she knows all about it.

"So we're clear," Harper speaks to Brandi, "when I said *amigo* earlier, I'm aware it shoulda been *amiga,* but I was making a point about my friend's dumb philosophies about gender."

"*¿Oh? Dime todo acerca de sus filosofías.*"

The next several minutes are a telenovela. Gael had no idea Harper spoke Spanish (though she sounds the same in both languages) or that Brandi's folks were from the Dominican Republic or that either fact would matter. She gets up and rests against the iron, looking out at the cement-wall view. There's some relief from the stench in the centimeter her nose protrudes through the bars. Surely if one person hits another person in public and neither of those people press charges, there can't be any indictments—they'd just be let out? If the arrest actually counts, coming back to America will be difficult from here on out and, to Gael, the world would feel a whole lot smaller without the land that puts tuna in opportunities.

"*Es porque sería una carga para ella . . .*"

"*Qué egoísta! ¿Quién no tiene equipaje?*"

"Trust me *enamorarme de un sociópata misógino.*"

Gael can feel fingers wagging at her back. But she tunes the pair of them out. Something's going on down the corridor. There's a voice Gael recognizes. Two, if she's not mistaken. Footsteps louden. "Lotte?" Gael calls out. But it's Nina whose bespectacled mug appears through the bars. She's being led into the adjacent cell. She resists the officer's tug so as to take Gael in for a moment. She frowns, trying to recall that face. "*Git* to your cell!" The officer yanks Nina's arm and she disappears from Gael's view.

"Is dat Libor?" Lotte says.

"Yeah," Gael calls. "Hey!"

"I don't believe that you are captured," she says. "It's a crime to put those hands in cuffs!" A squeak escapes her throat, as must follow all jokes in a second language.

"Who's that?" Harper's now clinging to the bars, caution to the wind vis-à-vis tetanus.

"Lotte," Lotte declares, like the opposite of a safe word.

"Lotta?" Harper looks sideways at Gael. "Seriously?"

Gael shrugs and says beneath her breath, "The ninety-nine percent are too easy to fuck."

Brandi gasps behind them. *"¿De verdad dijo eso?"*

"I doubt it," Harper says. "Did we just hear you right? *Gael?*"

Gael glances back at Brandi, who is stroking the phantom groomed beard on her chin. She's short. Takeable. Facing out again, Gael tries to think. She's missing something obvious here: there's some fucking iteration of events she's missed. She's meant to call in on the gallery to approve the placements this morning. Even if she's kept here for twelve hours, she should still have time to shower before the opening. She'll phone them, when she gets her stuff back. It will hardly come down to the make-one-call thing. There's mutterings in the next cell. The word *pretzel* suggests Nina has remembered the face.

"What they pick you up for?" It's Nina who asks. She sounds hostile.

Harper answers before Gael can say, "The usual."

"With Brandi, it was for noble fortitude and the country thanks her for it." Harper slaps Brandi on the shoulder and the other cell applauds. "With me and Irish, it was for cuntpunching. But it shoulda been for . . . duplicity. Whatever it's called. Get this. Irish *glared* at the Yeats poem I wrote out in calligraphy for her as if it said IOU. And I said I thought it had its own resonance with Occupy; granted, Yeats isn't the best choice cuz of his whole 'the best lack all conviction and the worst are full of passionate intensity' bit. But *Irish* said that sounded about right! And that the camp *was* full of the worst sort of ardent idiots—her words—who were so naïve, she said, they believed that one-percenters *actually pay* forty-five percent income tax and—"

A very large police officer casts a shadow now over Gael and Harper. He is holding up two backpacks. Both unzipped. He looks at Harper as if her puffy features are an anagram. "Which one of these bags is yours?"

She points at the denim one, like a kid pointing at an underwhelming fairground teddy.

"Spot the goon who'd wear triple denim," Gael mutters.

The policeman doesn't take his eyes off Harper. "Who does this bag belong to?" He lifts Gael's bag a fraction. Harper goes to look at Gael but the cop gives a tiny whistle through his bottom teeth. "Eyes here. Use your words."

"Gael," Harper says, very quietly for her. She can see the torn envelope full of cash inside the backpack.

"Gael who?" the cop says.

"Fffff . . . ucked if I know?" Harper says, come over all ditsy.

The cop fills his lungs luxuriously, which serves to make him roughly the size of that sculpture of the Archangel beheading Satan.

Can the heart lift up in the body? It sounds very very close, now, to her ears. The cop slings both bags across his forearm and unlocks the cell. He calls out a word Gael wasn't concentrating enough to register. Another cop appears to assist. The Archangel-cop hands Harper her bag and says, "Akhil here will give you a glass of water along with your court date. You can take your meds. Follow him, and the law, Ms. Schiada."

Some light gets eclipsed as he turns his head. "Ms. Foess? . . . Come with me."

He does not hand her her bag.

She does not pass go.

She does not collect thirty thousand dollars.

II

When Gael was nine and Guthrie was seven, Jarleth arrived home on Christmas Eve with two piggy banks. He landed the unwrapped boxes on the kitchen table and said: Open. They needn't have done, because a picture on the side of the boxes showed what lay inside, but he insisted on the ceremony. The price stickers read €9.95. Opening a gift before Baby Jesus's birthday seemed an odd directive to Guthrie, who looked at his mother, then followed her gaze to the clock. Nine forty-five p.m. Midnight mass began at eleven. "Before mass?" There was an unnerving feeling at Jarleth's arriving so late and that he was making this fuss. He would hurl a camera under the tree as a clump of wood to a fire. Things were things. They didn't warrant one's attention. That wasn't to say that Jarleth didn't have things and very fine things; but nearly all he deemed disposable.

When Guthrie pulled the pig out of the box, his expression fought against itself. Anyone could see that he would have preferred a pottery set with which to mold his own piggy bank, but that would have meant Jarleth's indulging his notion that it's worth spending hours making and decorating something that can be knocked together in a factory in seconds for fractions of pennies. Still, Guthrie gamely got up from the table to retrieve his net of gold chocolate coins from the living room and returned to slot them into the piggy bank, one by one, explaining that chocolate doesn't go off. He might not have any chocolate when he needs some later, he said. "What if it's in here for ages and we run out of chocolate and this is the *very last*?" He looked at Sive with eyes as wide as they would go. Sive ran her fingers through the owl's wing of his hair, but her thoughts were not in the kitchen and a piggy bank of pennies couldn't afford them.

"And what would you do with it," Jarleth said, "were it the very last chocolate?" Guthrie lifted his shoulders to his ears and held them there. Jarleth never gave him enough time. "Would you *sell* the world's last chocolate?" Guthrie's shoulders were still by his ears and soon the muscles would tire and they'd still be there even if it looked as though he'd dropped them. He shook his head. Beware of leading questions. No. "What then?"

Gregorian chant came through the radio. A low, slow, unaccompanied sentence—songless—with no beginning and no end. It had the hollow sound of a great medieval cathedral. The chant breathed in and out. One phrase. A pause. Another phrase of a different length entirely, as if the chant were attaching one truth to another and the miracle was its multiplicity of voice; that the truth could be agreed upon and enlarged among a union of men. Guthrie tuned into it. Gael writhed on the bench, wanting him to answer their father. Didn't Guthrie know that the generosity had been in posing this challenge and not in the present itself? She nudged him: "Would you let a scientist take a sample of it to his lab to study and grow more chocolate?" She wanted badly to see her father's face to know if that had been a good idea, but if she looked at Guthrie instead, then if it was a bad idea, at least it would look like she'd said it just for his sake and not for Jarleth's approval.

"I'd"—Guthrie squinted at the dust-clogged radio speaker—"get all the people who really . . . really . . . really really really love chocolate . . . more than anything ever . . . and let them all have a lick." His eyes refocused and he looked at Gael, who pressed her palms to her face. Guthrie cackled, realizing all the caveats too late.

Sive had moved to the sink and stood looking out at the dark back garden. To herself, she said, "It's frosting over."

When they returned from church that midnight, Sive and Guthrie went straight to bed. But Gael halted halfway up the stairs, spotting her father in the kitchen doorway. When she met his eyes, he directed her into the kitchen with a short curved knife. There, he tapped her unopened piggy bank with it, as if tapping a shameful grade sheet. "What to do?" He began peeling the skin off a red apple and Gael wondered if he would try to keep the peel in one piece to throw over his shoulder for luck. Of course, she had spent all of mass thinking the problem through. She had a very good answer. Smart for her years, by anyone's count. But Jarleth spoke again before she had a chance to impress him.

"Matthew's Gospel tells a story you'd do well to know. Called the Parable of the Talents."

"Talons?"

"*Talents*. An ancient coin worth a fortune. Worth years of a laborer's wage. The master has to go on a trip, so he decides to entrust his wealth to three servants till he returns. How much he gives them depends on their ability. So. He gives the first servant five." Jarleth held up five fingers. "Five talents. To the second fellow, he gives two. The third man gets one. Master mustn't think much of the third man's abilities. How do they get on? you wonder. Well, the servant given five goes straight out to trade with them. By the time the master gets home, he's made *five more* from the five he'd been given. The fellow given two makes two more. But the servant given only one talent thinks about his master's dealings, how he normally does things—he's fearful of the master too, you see. So he goes and digs a deep hole in the soil and buries the solitary talent. When the master returns, the first servant approaches and says: Lo and behold, Master, I've turned your five talents into ten. Well done, goes the master. You're invited into my joy and you'll know true wealth. Then the second approaches, says how he got on, and he too is congratulated, thanked, invited in. The third fellow goes up with his head hung and says he knew his master to be a hard man, reaping where he didn't sow and gathering where he scattered no seed. He was cautious, he explained, so he'd buried the talent and awaited his master's return.

He holds the muddy coin up then and says, Here you have what is yours." After a pause, Jarleth redirected his gaze. "Tell me now. What does the master think of this?"

Gael spoke quickly: "He might say that he's glad the man kept his money safe and didn't risk losing it, but I doubt he said that. But hang on: the second guy did just as well as the first, because he doubled his money?"

"He doubled what he could manage to double. The first doubled a greater amount."

"But that's not fair. If the second guy'd been given—"

"'You wicked and slothful servant!'" Jarleth said, stabbing the knife into the apple peel, strewn on the kitchen table. "'You knew that I reap where I have not sown and gather where I scattered no seed? Then you ought to have invested my money with the bankers and I should have received what was my own with interest. So take the talent from him and give it to him who has the ten talents. For to everyone who has will more be given and he will have an abundance. But from the one who has not, even what he has will be taken away. And cast the worthless servant into the outer darkness. In that place there will be weeping and gnashing of teeth.'" Jarleth considered the white flesh of the nude apple before retrieving the knife and scoring a bruise out of it, which he let drop to the floor.

The night reflected only Jarleth in the kitchen window. To anyone standing outside, it would look as if he were raving to himself—as if Gael weren't even there. She tried to stretch her spine to see at least the suggestion of a person becoming equal and to get rid of the tickling feeling in her neck. "I thought the Bible was all, be nice to people," she said, "and help poor people because they've got God's souls just the same as rich people." She was trying to relate this back to the piggy bank. The right answer must be *not* to put money in it because that was the same as burying it in mud. The money put there wouldn't grow by virtue of being hidden. It needed something like photosynthesis to swell. Holding her shoulders back, she said firmly: "If you have the receipt, I want to return it." Perhaps he'll ask what she'll get in its place or what she'll do with the refund, she thought, but he had taken just one bite of the apple before it thudded to the bottom of the bin.

"If you do nothing with what you have, you might as well never have had it," he said. "Your abilities will diminish and waste. But if you make something of them, you'll gain more and you'll be rich." Jarleth flicked the kitchen light off on his way out. His mood had turned. She followed close on his heels and, when he stopped at the threshold, she ran into his back, as if afraid to step out of his shadow. She flushed. Perhaps, because of this, what he had been about to say was averted like a lawn bowl butting up too hard to the jack:

"Tomorrow, tell your brother to look at the second commandment. Show him the Coca-Cola Company's invention of Santa Claus. Very magical altogether." He was gone and this time Gael didn't follow. From the top of the stairs, what tumbled down to her was an after-thought, but she took it as principal:

To get her money back without a receipt.

The cop doesn't use the phrase *piggy bank,* for obvious reasons. He calls it her "collection." But the association presents itself in Gael's mind as an out and she doesn't have time to step cautiously. The viable explanations are gone. She can't say she brought the cash into the country as holiday funds because she checked some box on her immigration card that said goods or monetary instruments exceeding ten thousand dollars must be declared. She can't mention the check, as that could lead the police down a path of discovery toward Wally and Xavier and Guthrie. The most *likely* story—that she's part of Occupy's Finance Working Group and that the cash constitutes donations—would be risky, in case Nina and Lotte are still in their cell. They can't be relied upon, now that Harper's poured paprika on the chicken in the fox den. There is only one person who would lie for her out of sheer curiosity and the chance to offer liberation on lay-by—only one person quick and plastic enough to adapt to whatever truth needs to be upheld.

"*Last* time. Before we start testing the notes for dirt. Who's your supplier?" The cop is called Derek. He is so tall, it's hard to believe he's sitting down. The sclera of his eyes is cream rather than white and his graying eyebrows pitch up in the middle so it looks like he's always fighting disappointment.

"If I tell you," Gael says, "you have to promise you won't call him." She affects to look anxiously at the door.

Derek leans on his forearms. A vein protrudes down the front of his rutabaga bicep. "We would not jeopardize your safety, Ms. Foess." The brows transition readily to concern.

Recalling Art's habit, Gael wipes the table between them with her palms. Then changes tack: "I wasn't brought in for having cash on me. I was brought in for being at Occupy. Fine, for headbutting my friend. But neither of us is injured. We were mucking around. Harper's not pressing charges. I'm not pressing charges. So the most you can keep me for is, what, forty-eight hours? Twenty-four? And I don't have to say another word."

Derek tips his head back as if to inspect a lightbulb, but his eyes stay fixed on Gael. "What country you think you in right now?"

Gael conjures her best droll voice. "The United States of America?"

"Spell it out for me," Derek says. "I'm not kidding."

"I'll play my Fifth Amendment, Derek. Neither of us likes to be disrespected."

"Constitutional rights are privileges you ain't got, tourist."

"I highly doubt that's—"

"Shut the fuck up and listen." His voice is very steady. "You had a dozen police eyes on that assault. I don't know what they call it in Ireland, but in the USA, it's called battery. When police are present, we don't need no citizen's arrest to take you in. Your friend don't need to press charges. A gross misdemeanor, is what you get. Guess the maximum sentence for assault in the fourth degree."

"Guess my cup size."

Derek looks confounded at this; the vagaries of this one. "Three hundred sixty-four days. Occupying the other side of Wall Street. Followed by two-year probation. Fine of five thousand dollars. Now that's for a first-time offender. We don't know your record in Ireland, but we working on it. But maybe we don't need to go there. Maybe we can forget all about it. Give you a 800 number for anger management classes. Maybe you play soldier in the war on drugs and we let you march on outta here with a DAT fore supper. What about it?"

Gael sighs through her nostrils. "Fine, Derek. But you're going to be disappointed."

"Try me."

"My father, the one-percenter. He pulled his great big house, his cheater's crash pad from under us in oh-seven, my little brother sick, Mum forced to quit her job, and now he's here spreading his financier fuckery to the westmost point. So I came over to Occupy to stick a fucking picket up his cul-de-sac. And this is him reciprocating."

Derek's fingers are pressed together against his lips. One eyebrow reaches slightly higher than the other.

"So he finds out I'm at Occupy," Gael continues. "However he finds out. The news, Mum, on one of his drive-bys. And he turns up with an envelope of cash, the engine on his town car jizzing, and tells me it's my start in life because I seem to have lost the one he already gave me. To book a hotel room, take a shower, get an education." She shivers, goes to say more, but Derek undercuts her performance.

"What's his name?"

"Jarleth."

"What's his number?"

Gael looks annoyed. "Do I sound like I'd know it by heart?"

Derek leaves the room. Only then does Gael notice that she's still shivering, though it's not cold. He returns with her phone. They go through the your-move, my-move shuffle until Derek gets hold of Jarleth and informs him that someone claiming to be his daughter is being held in the 34th Precinct on a charge of . . . disorderly conduct . . . and that she's in possession of contraband. He hesitated to name the charge. Bluffery. The claim Gael knows best. What is a magician, said Houdini, but an actor playing the part of a magician? She doesn't doubt she'll walk out of here with a headache, but whether a pretzel and a cup of water will treat it has yet to be determined.

"I need you to corroborate a story your daughter told us." Derek holds the phone an inch from his ear, as if it's contaminated. "If you can't get in here, Mr. Foess, I'm willing to talk it through right now. While I got you on the line. Lemme ask you—"

Gael can hear the familiar clipped voice informing Derek of Gael's rights. "My daughter was under no obligation to give you my number. She did not consent to this. I'm sending over a lawyer. Don't say a word, Gael. Don't consent to a plea bargain. If you can hear me, Gael—"

Derek hangs up. "See . . ." He sways his head from side to side. "There's a shame. There's a real shame. He coulda verified your story an' I coulda sent you on your way. Real simple." He takes Gael by the upper arm to lead her back to her cell. "Don't go slipping on me. Sound like slippery runs in the family."

Feeling distinctly nauseous, Gael averts her gaze from the detainee in the corridor who's making the officers at his sides carry him, toes dragging behind him like a wedding trail.

"Where's my phone call?" Gael asks, remembering how this goes. "That was *your* call. Now I get one."

"So you can phone Daddy," Derek says. "Feed him your story."

"So I can phone Occupy's legal aid. The number's on my arm, look." She's not cuffed anymore, but Derek's grip abjures sudden movements. "You didn't think I'd actually use my father's lawyer?

Make all his Christmases come together?" Gael glares at Derek as if he's the ghost of Christmas yet to come.

She runs through who she's touched and what she's eaten in the past twenty-four hours to identify the churn in her intestines. To which squalor she's touristed too close. "I'd like to make that call."

Derek leads her past the reception desk into a room with avocado green walls and at least a dozen cops bureaucrating behind computers, radio mics on their shoulders like inert parrots. He seats her at a mahogany desk with a landline and says he'll get water. He leaves the room. Given that there's a water cooler within reach, she takes this as an indication he's stepping back from the case, no longer worth his time or the fine it will result in. On his desk, a pentaptych of photo frames present a cubist portrait of a divorcé. All five photos show Derek with his kids in weekend clothes, doing weekend activities; no spouse in sight; the careless compositions of strangers asked, Could you take our picture? One is a selfie of Derek and his son at a baseball stadium wearing matching Go Bulldogs shirts. The clock on his monitor reads 12:53.

She asks a cop passing by, What's the number for the operator? Never in her life has she phoned an operator and she's not actually sure that's what it's called anymore or if that's from the Second World War when real human beings sat in rooms flicking switches and dialing dials, their legs firmly together, but she can't ask an officer to Google M.F.N. Gallery and risk leaving a trail. She gets through to M.

"We're *not* comfortable that the artist hasn't approved the placements," he says. "I've emailed you photos. This isn't part of the service. If you don't have time to come by, at least look at those."

"M." Gael presses her mouth close to the handset, so he can hear the smack of her lips. "Some parts of the service I'm interested in. Some, I'm not. I trust you with the hangings. You're the exhibitionist. You handle it. If your eye is anything on your arms, you'll manage just fine. Now, are you there, M?"

M grunts.

"There *is* one placement I'd like to appraise." Gael looks around the room at the uniforms. All the law and order. "In case duty calls with a patron and I have to fuck off to some cocktail bar after the show, I'd like your address." There's a scratching sound which, at first, she can't place. Hardly a bad line. But then she remembers his thick ruddy beard. He's worrying it. "Unless, of course, you're on lockup at the gallery." She pauses. "That swing, M . . . If I slip off it, I won't sue. But it'll be your fault."

"65 Steinway Street. Queens."

Gael sighs and presses her pelvis to check for bruising. "Get a pen and paper," she says.

M coughs, perhaps to bring himself to. She can hear he's walking. "Is this about the prices? I emailed you about it," he says gruffly. "You're supposed to sign off on them."

"Have you a pen?"

M mms.

"Raise all the prices by twenty-five percent. Round upward to something tidy." M begins to speak but Gael cuts him off. "This is important, so write it down. This is the message, verbatim: 'I said you turned up to the Occupy protest with a bunch of cash and insults. That's all. Don't get ideas. I don't need anything from you.' Send that message to jay-eff-oh-ee-ess-ess at gmail as soon as possible. Right now would be good. Don't send it from an M.F.N. address. I have to go, M. Thanks for doing that. I look forward to seeing how everything's hung later." She slams the phone on the receiver, a little shocked by the cop standing at her side.

"I been doin too much overtime, or was that a booty call?" she asks.

"Basically," Gael says, looking around for Derek. "Yeah."

The cop scans her body rudely. "That wardrobe work good for hookin? Like a dirty-student kinda costume?"

"Excuse me?" Gael asks. It's been a long time since she looked in a mirror. But she may have misheard—it feels as if hands are pressing against her ears and everything's muffled.

"Or cuz you got the face, you don't gotta make a effort?"

Swallow your tongue, Gael. Swallow it. The cop fizzes in and out of focus. This is how you forfeit your choices. Swallow. When she gulps, her body decides not to play along and she has a fraction of a moment to seek out a wastepaper basket. The policewoman grabs her elbow, as if she'd been about to flee, and vomit splatters her boot and the carpet in a muddy Irish rainbow.

"God *dammit*! A goddamn junkie."

✦

The cop that leads her back to the cell tells its sole remaining occupant—Nina—to have no fear. Gael's bad belly shouldn't be contagious. They see cases like this all the time. Noxious conscience. Nina pushes her eyeglass frames higher on her nose and says she's not afraid of catching a stomach bug. She's afraid of not being free to fight the pharmaceutical companies spraying stomach bugs across the nation's delis so it can price-fix the treatment. Sensing no one at the other end of her sentence, like a kid whose friend abandons the other end of the yogurt cup radio, Nina yells that standing in the wrong place at the wrong time is not a crime. It's coincidence. Everything she says sounds like performance poetry. Footsteps echo from the corridor. A voice: So's my jock itch. A coincidence. Gael expels stomach acid into the toilet like an ironic rimshot, releasing a heinous pungent odor. Pinching her nose, she staggers around half-blinded.

"You do *not* look how I remember," Nina says, turning her mohawked profile. The sides of her head that had been shaved now boast an inch of hair. The long center section is held on the crown by a bulldog paper clip. "Except for the swooning part."

Gael rests her palms against the wall and lets her aching head drop between her aching shoulders. She mumbles that the whole trajectory of our lives comes down to *where we are, when,* so Nina's mistake was to let those coordinates be coincidental. If you can't afford to control them, take out a loan, or rob someone. But all that's audible is "the whole . . . comes down . . . ordinates . . . alone." Her body must weigh three hundred pounds. She can't stay upright much longer. This is what happens when she loses discipline. Fatigue sets in and claws at her like a starving child. What she needs is red meat, a hilly half marathon and a solid week's work. That, or crack. She feels her way around the cell walls until she reaches the plank of wood serving as a bed and, the moment she's horizontal, falls promptly unconscious.

The ugly, inebriating need for water wakes her two hours on. "Nina?" Her throat is sandpaper. "If that's your . . ." She draws her elbow from under her head mournfully as if from a mistakenly intimate embrace and waits for feeling to return. "Nina?" After a while, she manages to prop herself up, though it takes enormous will. The cell is empty. No one is there. It's quiet. Cold. Her hands are translucent white. She doesn't have the energy to do jumping jacks or squats or lunges, which she always imagined she'd do lots of if she ever wound up imprisoned. "What time is it?" she calls out. It doesn't surprise her that Jarleth would have told his lawyer to give it a few hours. Give her something against which to contrast her privilege. Let the contrast settle, like a Guinness.

She can't stop her body from shivering. She's wearing her hoodie, coat and jeans, but her jeans are looser than they were a week ago and she has no socks on inside her trainers. She'd been intending to be gone already. Occupy had served its purpose. It had confirmed her suspicions. Today was for making final maneuvers to ensure tonight's success and for planning her next move, should the exhibition be a washout.

The calm is broken into by glass-shattering screams as a pair of new catches are rammed through the corridor. Gael swings her legs off the bed and hastily reties her hair, trying to smooth it with what spittle comes. Readying herself for Jarleth's face between the bars, she tries to steady her heart rate. She feels somewhat better; muscles like fraying ropes, stomach punctured by a large-gauge needle, but fully awake, at least. She picks a point on the wall to squint at, then dislikes how that would look from outside—like she's meditating on her actions—so she gets up and crosses her arms. Rests her back and the sole of her foot against the cold brick wall. Then, quiet returns and her adrenal gland stops pumping. It's not him. No one's come. Breathing is a slow, steady whistle. That phone call had been her last dollar and she had buried it. But maybe they'll be reasonable. Not an adjective she has come to associate with American bureaucracy, but maybe . . . She needs to be out by five, at the very latest. "What *time* is it?" She holds the bars numbly. "Excuse. Me." Only then does the plastic tray on the floor come into view, bearing a cheese sandwich on white bread and a peelback-lid fruit punch. A school-of-hard-knocks meal. Her mouth is full when Derek appears before her.

"Three fifteen."

Gael gulps down the toothaching juice. "This is wrong. I have somewhere to be."

Derek looks left. "Same way turkeys feel come Thanksgiving."

It surprises even Gael to hear a chirp emit from the next cell over. Or is it weeping?

"Could I get some toilet paper?" Gael asks. "And soap? And can I make another call? It's urgent. I need my own lawyer. The Occupy one's taking forever. I don't have—"

"You can make up to three calls." Derek looks tired.

Gael stares at his yellow eyes. "And you tell me this *now*?"

"We arranging a medical screening for you," he says, as an explanation. "Your daddy's attorney's one smooth son of a bitch." Still looking left, Gael can't see who he's assessing.

"I don't want a medical screening."

"Don't want your daddy's attorney. Don't want—"

"I do," Gael says. "I don't have time not to."

Derek freezes in a look of accusation and eventually unhooks the key ring from his belt and unlocks the cell. As he does this, he mutters that they let the attorney clock up some wait time. He glances narrowly at Gael. "Brought in a statement from your daddy that explains a whole lot." He's leading Gael down the corridor without holding her arm. The lawyer is bent over the reception desk, filling in forms. Leaning across the counter, her skirt is snug against her round buttocks and her hair—worn in a neat chignon—is auburn glitter. Her lip gloss winks as she looks up, after Gael has been standing there for several seconds.

"The spitting image," she says, saccharine-smiled.

Gael exchanges glances with Derek.

"Before I forget," he calls from the threshold of the room she spewed up in. "Your frenemy came back. Bout an hour ago. Lady Schiada. We keeping her note on file. Statement of sorts. But she said to tell you that Art says the house has the edge. Not to bet against the house." Derek's brows are an umbrella over his expression, keeping it dry. "Since you're a tourist, maybe you don't know. But less you're touring a Indian reservation, gambling's illegal in New York State."

"Tell that to Wall Street," Gael says.

The lawyer holds out a slim rose-gold pen.

"Initial every page and sign wherever there's an asterisk."

The attorney never introduces herself. Only advises Gael to count her cash when her belongings are returned and, as they leave the building, informs her that there have been no consequences. The citation's been dismissed. No fine? Gael asks. No violation. No record whatsoever. "Hang on." The front door swings shut behind them. "Hang on."

The lawyer stops walking and squints at Gael as if to say, How long till you catch up?

"Are you my father's personal lawyer, or do you work for Barclays?"

The lawyer checks her watch. "Personal."

Gael massages her forehead. "Are you on a salary or retainer or is it a by-the-hour gig?"

"I bill in six-minute intervals."

Gael digests this, as slowly as possible, and goes to sit on the curb by the station's parking lot. "I appreciate the efficacy of your six minutes in hell with me there, but I feel very weak all of a sudden. Very weak. So if you have a spare eighteen, twenty-four, thirty-six minutes, I think Jarleth would want you to see me through to the other side—"

"He wants me to drop you off at his office. He couldn't leave early."

"Well, that sounds like such cozy family time . . . but as I say, I'm not feeling strong. I'm actually not able to stand up. It might be shock. It might be low blood sugar. Might be my period. So what I'd ask you to do is to get me a drink."

The lawyer heaves a sigh and goes to step inside for water.

"No," Gael says. "I asked already. They don't have what I need."

"I've got a flask of scotch in my car." She points to a low-slung rose-gold Lexus.

"Sometimes there's nothing for it but electrolytes," Gael says. "You know? I simply can't get up till my tongue is blue with isotonic pick-me-up." She goes on like this, insisting that the lawyer walk around the block to find a 7-Eleven, until she does, finally, walk to the end of the parking lot to call Jarleth in private.

It's a twelve-to-eighteen-second phone conversation, presumably rounded up. Gael imagines that long auburn hair tumbling down the shoulders of her cream suit and something about her neatness makes Gael feel she should go the opposite way, so she pulls a strand of hair from her own head and begins to floss her teeth with it. The lawyer keeps a straight face, lowers herself into her sports car and calls from the open door: "He made a dinner reservation for eight. You'll get a text with the address. He suggests you follow the advice he supposedly gave you already. To take a shower." She smiles and shuts the door.

Gael goes to shrug but finds she can't manage with her pack on. "Only if he wears his shining armor," she says. The lawyer puts her seat belt on. Growls the engine. Gael smacks her forehead and shouts: "Shit, I forgot I have way more important plans."

The lawyer reaches into her glove compartment and takes a long pull on an e-cigarette. She blows the simulated smoke out the window. Just as she's about to take off, for reasons she can't quite grasp, Gael calls: "Five o'clock. At the Plaza."

The car lingers. The lawyer's lips move but her words don't reach Gael. Her earpiece must be built into her hairdo.

"Seven," the lawyer eventually responds.

"Five thirty or never," Gael says.

Blue smoke plumes from the car's rear tires as a rather stagey way of saying Check.

◆

Her phone is dead, so she has to go back inside to ask a cop for directions to the closest cheap hotel. The cop who took her for a sex worker earlier suggests she try an expensive hotel. "Might be able to afford a cuter costume. Then again, New York Encounters do rooms by the hour and it's only a block north." Her tone is sardonic. Oblivious the suggestion might actually be taken.

That a hotel room could be dirtier than a holding cell Gael had not thought possible. She drapes her coat on the bed before lying down on its multicolored hides-all-sins quilt. The red carpet looks new, as if the cheapest thing was to swap it out every month rather than prize off the condoms like chewing gum. One could only presume they were all under the furniture, along with the after-fuck fag butts responsible for the frowst. A framed image of Michelangelo's *David* hangs above the bed—its low pixel count acting as censorship. It must've been printed off at the reception, where Gael negotiated forty-five dollars for an hour and a half. She can barely afford to take a forty-five-minute nap, nor can she afford not to. After what feels like five minutes, the phone blares and Gael shoots up like a born-again from a baptismal lake.

"This is your courtesy call," the voice drones.

Charming. Her guts ringlet as she tries to straighten up. There's no door to the bathroom. Just an arc cut out of the wall. Sink in front. Toilet left. Shower right. All of which she does her best not to touch. It's discomforting to see herself in the mirror. She knew she'd been losing weight but she'd lost muscle tone too, leaving her bony and shadowy and drawn. The resemblance with Guthrie would be keener, at least, if M.F.N. uses his portrait. A lilac bruise accompanies a bump on the uppermost corner of her forehead from the headbutt. She'd have to change her parting. Just as well she had makeup with her. And the outfit. Astonishingly, a tiny fire-starting hair dryer is stashed in the drawer. As she gets ready, unproductive thoughts keep tobogganing in on the mental grooming that needs to be taking place. That Harper must have dropped out of her master's program to look after Kendra and where was the husband and, if she dies, would Harper's grief be tinged with resentment? That walking to the subway stop would be dangerous and the criminal would be pardoned because of his victim's insalubrious outfit. That Guthrie's outfit wouldn't have featured in such a story, even though his outfit would have been a vestment.

She hurries out as fast as one can on decorative stilts while carrying a hitchhiker's pack.

There's time on the subway to get what she wanted to say to him straight in her mind—she had to take the C line downtown to 50th and then switch to the E to cross town to 51st and then take the 4 uptown to 59th—but she wastes that time thinking about logistics and how, given that her MetroCard had been empty, it probably would have been wiser to take a cab.

"Can you *not* shake your leg like that, right by my leg?" a passenger asks her. "You're making me nervous."

She looks up, thumbnail between her teeth.

"Some *bad* vibrations," the passenger says to herself, and proceeds to mutter for the rest of the journey.

Under the fluorescent lights, the brown lipstick on her thumbnail looks like dried blood.

◆

The Plaza's luggage handler is new to Gael, but he accepts her ticket and fetches her rolly bag with a smile that tersens when she says she's not yet ready to collect it; she just needs something from it. Oh and also, can he take this bag too? The filthy backpack might as well be a sack of coal and the handler looks baffled that someone so chic would be its owner. But his reproach is no price to pay at all. She swaps her coat for a black blazer and pashmina and transfers her laptop and essentials to a handbag. To be willing to let these belongings go is her goal. The total lack of attachments. The feeling she gets from this notion prompts her to discard the luggage ticket in the first bin she passes. Howsoever she can spike her endorphins.

It's five forty-five p.m. Jarleth would have had to figure out which area to go to. The Palm Court. The Champagne Bar. The Rose Club. The Oak Room. She's switched off her phone. He'll assume she wanted the iconic setting. He'll assume she's his daughter, still. She slips a note to a concierge and gives him Jarleth's description. Says to approach him in the Palm Court in a moment and to inform him that Ms. Foess is in the Rose Club. Twenty is too much, but never underestimate the edge lent to the unstinting.

At Occupy, she had spent some of her time volunteering at the People's Library. Lending and organizing the five thousand books donated to the movement. She'd soon been relegated to nonfiction, once her derision of nonrealities made the scene. But she did take one work of fiction away with her. Albert Camus's *The Stranger*. It's more likely that she took it in the unacknowledged hope of some-day impressing Harper than in the expectation that she would find philosophical solidarity in its foxed pages. Every vertebra of the spine is cracked. That it's held together is a testament to its glue. Nothing more. The way to manage this night is to stick to one drink. A gin and tonic with basil sits on the little black-and-gold octagon table before her. She's chosen the gold and maroon velvet chairs by the railing, so they could look down on the Champagne Bar below and not at each other. Chandeliers to dwarf cathedral bells hang at her eye line. She opens *The Stranger* sixty pages in. Tries to make the words come together to have a meaning greater than the meaning they have one after the other. The passage has to do with teaching some woman a lesson and hitting the policeman who intervenes. The character tells his friend how a woman ought to be punished and how to handle the police: to return their blows. The girl had let him down, you see. The narrator claims to enjoy this man's company very much. Gael does not. It brings on a headache.

"I'd say you haven't aged a day, but I think you're still young enough for that to be an insult."

Gael doesn't uncross her legs or stand to greet her father; just closes her book, puts it facedown on the edge of the table and places her phone on top. "Four years," she replies, "or thereabouts." She looks up at him as if at some ancient vase in a museum after too many hours in the museum.

Jarleth scans the surroundings, shirking his coat in time for it to fall into a hostess's anticipatory arms. He asks, "Are we eating?"

"I don't have long," Gael says. "So an appetizer maybe." She asks the hostess, "Could we have some menus?"

"Certainly."

"Have you an antipasto platter?" Jarleth asks her.

"Yes, sir."

"That'll do nicely. And a glass of dry Riesling."

"I know we have an Austrian Riesling—"

"Lord, no," Jarleth says, "no no no," and rests his hand on his coat, which is draped over the hostess's arm. "The Austrians make music. Not wine."

The hostess chortles obligingly. "Let me send a server over who knows our list."

"No need. I'll take a vodka seltzer."

One might call it a nod, but it's really more of a bow. She absconds. Jarleth unbuttons his suit jacket and sits at the very back of the chair. Then he pinches his trousers at the knees, exposing gray ribbed socks, before crossing his legs. He does this so that the knees don't become worn-looking, though he's never kept one suit long enough for the knees to become worn-looking even if he converted to Islam and knelt for *šalāt* five times a day. "You don't have much time, is it? Are you about to fly home or what."

"I have to be somewhere at seven," Gael says.

"I see. Yes. That's not a rigout for traveling."

He says this, letting his eyes drop to the outfit, which is a work of art to complement the paintings. An off-white long-sleeved heavy-lace top, semisheer with a boat neck and button-back fastening—tiny cotton buttons from the nape of her neck to her lower back. A black bra beneath the top is barely visible; only serves to make the lace richer around the swell of her bust. A pleated black-and-brown polyamide skirt comes just below the knee, but it slinks around her crossed legs and the cushioned chair now. Her dark-brown lipstick draws out the same color in every other fine pleat of the skirt. Her closed-toe sandals are off-white and black leather. The chunky heels are dark wood. Thanks to the hair dryer, she found the slope Guthrie had cut into her black hair, though it's grown out some—the longest bits at the front reach the top of her breasts. She tosses the front part messily across her skull regularly, as if to throw a grapefruit rind into a very smooth martini. The look took five minutes of envisioning, a half hour of very specific searches online and a trip down to the Plaza's front desk to pick up the parcels she'd had delivered.

Jarleth lingers on the gleam of her shin. So it's established he won't avert his gaze from any aspect of her. "I take it that's not how Rose found you," he says. His own summer tan is deep enough to have seen him through the fall and takes a few years off him.

"If Rose is your lawyer, I asked her to send me an invoice."

"Is that so?" Jarleth is trying to find the bite where his molars come most neatly together. Chewing on the question of where the money came from and if there's more of it, no doubt. Why couldn't she have power-dressed in the manner Rose does? Like any woman who understands that to imitate a man is to flatter him and to flatter him is to be on the right side of him. The shadowed side of him, of course. Everything has its place.

"She won't bill you," Jarleth says. "She's already told me details that would contravene our contract, if the client were you. So. It's done." He looks to the oval bar to see if his drink is on its way.

"So I'll bill you for my consent. Since you've gone ahead and con-travened it." Gael says this in a vaguely imitative fashion.

"Don't joke about that, Gael." Jarleth's uncooked spaghetti eye-lashes lower, but only into cold water. Nothing aboil. Nothing doing to soften him. It's disturbing that Gael would have missed what he meant by that—not to joke about consent—if Sive hadn't told her what had happened. What else doesn't she know? The waiter arrives with the vodka seltzer and places what might as well be a thimbleful of nuts before Jarleth. Gael wants to make out with the waiter for this and when she tries to catch his eye, she sees it's someone who had served her several times and who she had generously tipped. A quiet-spoken Latino man in his late forties.

"Ms. Foess, you look exquisite. May I refresh your drink?"

"Thank you, Tobías. On both counts."

The waiter, whose name is not Tobías, takes her glass. Half of Jarleth's glass is drained already and he says he'll also take another. When the waiter is gone, Gael goes to say, Let's not start with the one-upmanship, but Jarleth beats her to it: "He's doing *so* well, you know. Your brother. I'm very proud of him."

Gael huffs so that saliva catches in the back of her nasal passage. "You don't get to be proud." She snorts and swallows. "Where was your pride when he was a fragile little kid and you'd try and bribe me to bully the shit out of him?"

"I intended to protect him, Gael. School isn't a safe place for gentle boys. Their lives are blighted before they've begun."

"So what? No one's life has a safety mode. Don't you *still* fear for his safety? For your own? For mine?"

"It might have spared him heartache. And many visits to Our Lady's Hospital."

"What," Gael says, "and he suffered *heartache* because I wasn't man enough to break him? To toughen him up. A fucking ten-year-old girl?"

"I should never have asked you," Jarleth says. "If you were a boy, maybe."

"No. You should never have wanted it."

The new drinks are placed quietly between them. They go untouched for some time. Jarleth uncrosses his legs and sits forward, elbows on his thighs. "I'm not presuming to know the circumstances . . . but the girl you assaulted to wind up arrested—"

"Woman, Jarleth. We're no longer girls."

"Rose said you and she were friends. As I say, I don't know any-thing about it, but—"

"You've not seen me in four years," Gael interrupts, "and you want to talk about a fight with a friend you've never met?" Jarleth sighs at this. "No," Gael says. "No, you shouldn't have asked me. And you shouldn't have wanted him broken. Anyway, why are you suddenly proud? What's changed? He's a gentle man. Not a gentle boy. Differ-ent noun. Equally corruptible."

"He's found his role in the world. He's confident and capable as a father and Christian and as a—"

"That role, Jarleth, that he has in the world. Tell me: is it a five-talent role or a two, or a one?" There's a jagged gorge between his eyebrows. He can't make sense of this. His brown-green eyes try to read ahead of his daughter's gray-blue ones. "Why don't you want for your son what you want for yourself?"

Now he sees the scripture. She means his abilities. She means that he has said, Well done, son, for performing to the best of your disappointing abilities.

The antipasto platter arrives, but Gael is looking across to the sky, now dark, in the Champagne Bar windows. The lights of taxis awaiting Friday night drinkers. Some time passes like this, because Jarleth is past the phase of life when he feels the need to perjure himself.

"What will your bonus be this Christmas?" Gael asks, turning back to him.

He's taken a toothpick from a silver holder and has set it through an artichoke heart. "What business is that of yours?"

"Just wondering how the institution rewards the very best of its 'value-adders.'"

"Disdain doesn't go well with that outfit." Jarleth takes up a breadstick that has a slice of Parma ham wrapped around the end, like adult candy floss. Before he bites the meat off, he says, "You suspect I'm overpaid, do you? For my abilities."

"No one's *that* able."

Jarleth laughs a little, chewing. Of course he'll eat heartily, no matter how the conversation turns. Gael takes a goat-cheese-stuffed cherry chile pepper. The flavors burst in her mouth so intensely it makes her feel she hasn't eaten in months. She says: "You believe in something so unbelievably fucked up."

"Is that so?" Jarleth says. "I'm on the edge of my seat, Gael, to be told about my puerile beliefs!"

She eats another of the stuffed mini peppers. It's hotter than the last and brings tears to her eyes, but there's no fear they'll be mistaken for the real kind. She washes it down with G&T. Jarleth, too, knocks his drink back. Her mouth full with a third, she says, "You believe you get what you deserve."

"Radical! Absolutely outrageous thing to think. No?" Jarleth holds his arm up and gestures to the waiter, busy with other customers. New drinks. Gael won't have time for hers. He says, "Did they teach you something different at King's, did they?"

"It's not merit that's earned you your wealth. It's having been let in on the rules of the game, thanks to being a straight white guy born into a 'good' family. For good, read rich."

"There must be a mirror in this place," he says, looking around. "If you find one, see if there's a rich white girl in it."

"Woman," Gael says.

"Lady."

"Woman."

"I did my level best to pass along the rules of the game." Jarleth is using the toothpick to relieve an incisor of olive skin. "It's up to you now . . . to participate. To play fairly and to see what you're made of."

Gael shakes her head. "*Fairly's* a myth! That's the point. Ethics don't pay. You *know* that, yet you pretend it's not the case. That's what's fucked. Why not admit to it? Why act like there's such a thing as meritocracy when anyone who gives it a second thought knows it's a sick idea?"

"You were only twelve," Jarleth says, "maybe younger, when I told you to memorize a maxim about the art of business. Do you recall what it was? I told you: commit it to memory and return to it later to see if it pans out."

Gael looks at her father's loosened tie the way she had done as a child when she needed the special focus he demands of you. "Business is the art of extracting money from another man's pocket without resorting to violence."

"Ha-haaah." Jarleth slaps the armchair. "You see? Good. I taught you that part of the game too. I must admit, I half expected you to recite it back to me the next day with my wallet in your hand and a smirk. Thank God you didn't. Take it literally."

"What's the difference," Gael says, "between taking it literally or figuratively? It comes down to the very same thing. Somebody's robbed."

The new drinks arrive and Gael reaches for her handbag. She takes out two hundred-dollar bills and swaps them for her book and phone on the table. Jarleth looks affronted to see that she's leaving. They're having a good time. Like father, like daughter, no? "If things were so simple as arithmetic," he says.

"I'm glad you left us." Gael stands up. Waves the fabric to make sure there aren't crumbs in the pleats of her skirt. "As much as it fucked Mum's career and Guthrie's health . . . and my opinions . . . at least we no longer have to pretend to rely on your abilities. Hold out our hands for talents."

"What do you want, Gael?" Jarleth says. His fingers are turned toward each other on the ends of his wide-apart knees, as if he's recovering from some sport. "For me to be a baddie? To stand around looking cross with a pack of politicless feckless lifelong students in the vague hope that men like me fail?"

Standing over him, she can see that his spoon-shaped balding has widened to a ladle. He's growing older. Whereas the grays in her hair now have black roots. She shakes her head. "No." Takes up her bag. "What I want has nothing to do with you."

Watching the concierge hail her a cab in the evening's cool air, she replays the line over and over. She feels the pack of it in her throat.

III

A fug of people blows smoke outside the gallery with drinks Gael paid for in their hands. When she emerges from the taxi, they stare like she's part of the exhibit. It's not just the outfit. They're staring at her face. It's not just the beauty. They're staring at something more private. Once she squeezes past the flirters in the entryway, takes the emergency stairs (the elevator sounds especially busy) and turns left by the swing (where the desk's been replaced by a coat rack and bar with all-in-black catering staff), she sees the cause of their heeding her. The movable arch wall—that had been positioned in the middle of the gallery, facing the window last time she was here—is now closer to the entrance, just a few feet from the bar and turned to confront guests upon arrival. People cluster round it. Guthrie's beat-up face, in confusingly high definition. Garish pigment. Unframed, the sheet of polycarbonate that overlays it has been smashed with a hammer in the lower left corner, so that it looks like a pellet-gunned window or a vandalized bus shelter. The brilliant icy-blue irises are shattered, too, with bloodshot.

There's an informational panel beside the photograph giving context to the show, but from the prattle Gael picks up, it speaks mostly of the tragic illness and genius-not-long-for-this-world of a teenage Irish rhapsody.

Gael canvasses the room. There's some sixty people. With those outside, seventy. A mixed demographic who all seem to catch itchy-chin syndrome within a painting's vicinity. The angled loft ceiling echo-chambers their voices and Enn is in the far corner by the window contributing an inaudible amelodic lyricless set on DJ decks.

His afro is now dyed to match his jumpsuit: tan with cream piping. A string of small pearls is wound around his neck several times and the long U hangs down his back. It's a pre-dinner drinks party venue, Gael thinks. A well-lit disco. So much for selling paintings.

Already, she's thinking of oboists and other conduits—maybe the art world was never going to have enough business about it—when someone swings her round by the arm as if to tango. Only not to. "Where the hell have you been?" It's M. Gael checks the arm of her white lace top for fingerprints. Her blazer is draped over her purse. "We've been calling you for hours."

"I'm fifteen minutes late. I was chatting to people downstairs. You know? Charm? It sells."

"You're *ninety* minutes late. You were supposed to be here before six. Doors opened at six thirty. Speeches set for seven. People are ready to leave."

Gael looks around. "Hardly." The covens of quirkily dressed extroverts all talking at the same time reminds Gael of bad extras in movies, laughing really hard when no one's lips had been moving and moving their lips when other extras do, going *rhubarb rhubarb rhubarb* with varying levels of enthusiasm because someone told them that looks most like real talk. Everyone's holding a glass. A few people hold several.

M's chest is at Gael's eye line and it enlarges and shrinks like something from Wonderland. Eat me. Bite me. Drink me. "Doing this twenty-six times a year is enough to know when people are about to leave," he says. "They drank too much too fast and need to eat. Trigger mass exodus. Your brother's career in New York is over. No one will show his work if a solo didn't sell one piece on its opening."

"*Jesus,*" Gael says. "What difference does it make if I'm here?"

"Like I . . ." He lowers his voice. ". . . explained in emails and voice mails. Your *speech*. This is how we *do* things. It's our Point of Difference."

"Pfff! Point of difference. MBA-speak in the art world. That's fucking depressing." Gael licks her teeth, which are surely coated in brown lipstick after that sound effect.

"You might have nothing at stake here . . ." M says, "but we do."

Gael feels how narrowly he sees her. An unflattering aperture.

"You're getting handed a mic in sixty seconds. You better know what to do with it."

Gael now effects to wipe his spittle from her cheek. He looks like he's having a chilled enema. "I need to prepare," she says. "Give me a minute. It's been a fucking weird day. I was in jail four hours ago." She actually laughs at this. Now it seems funny.

"You were arrested?"

"Yup." Gael looks at him and throws back her hair.

"For being so unprofessional and ungrateful?" Sweat is beading on M's bald head and his linen granddad shirt clings to his shoulders.

"For occupying Wall Street," Gael says, gazing at his thin lips inside his thick beard. The lips running through a list of things he's not buying. It's palpable now that something needs to happen in the room. She understands.

"You make no sense," he says. Lowers his rutty forehead in a conditional truce. "Sixty seconds." He disappears in the direction of the bar. The whole room has to shift for him to get through, like a man swimming butterfly in a hot pool.

Don't you think she looks like Molly Crabapple? someone says in a group beside Gael, gawping unabashedly. No, the friend says. Gael searches for a painting to stare at so she can think. All she needs is a convincing opener. Something lofty, to live up to. She excuses her way toward the main back wall where six of the paintings hang in a row, distanced generously. As is the way of the paintings, her eye is drawn up to where a long metal pole spans the whole width of them like a huge curtain rod. They're not hung from nails on the wall, but from the rod; from thick metal hangers that travel down the backs of the paintings, hovering an inch from the wall. Lit to cast stark shadows. If you touched them, they would swing. The setup exaggerates their vicissitudes of fragility and brutalism.

Five of the six paintings on this wall are the authentic ones. Four fakes are on the left wall, three on the right and one is hung traditionally on the other side of the movable arch. But this wall is the gallery's statement. The rest is decoration. Periphery. Maybe there is skill in their looking, after all, and M.F.N. was able to tell Guthrie's hand from Xavier's. Gael gets close to one. Squints through a patch of thinner paint for the etchings. For who loves whom.

It makes her jump, the explosion of light and a black barrel pointing her way. She sniffs for smoke. F holds a vintage camera with a telephoto zoom lens and huge antenna flash—a remote clicker in her knotted hand. She lowers the lens so that the camera hangs from its strap and weighs her forward like a pregnancy. Her hair, which is up, might well be wrapped around a femur like Wilma Flintstone, adding a foot to her height.

"We usually do it by the window . . . but stay here. This is good."

The music has stopped and the chatter, quieted. M must have handed Gael the mic because she's holding it. Are the spotlights, too, remote-controlled? A few gins haven't been enough to calibrate her to this world from the paper-bagged-beer world of Zuccotti. With her back to the wall now, Gael is the point of convergence; not the paintings. The arch has been pivoted round so that Guthrie's portrait is facing the crowd. Some look from Gael to the portrait to spot the resemblance. People on the stairwell are returning. She waits for them to settle, or so she makes it look. Crowds are not her thing. Small groups. One-on-one, best. She half expects heckling and imagines how casually Jarleth would shush it, commanding the room as his right. How he wouldn't have to try. How Sive would command it more worthily, but with intention and exertion and effort. Not with words, either. She doesn't make speeches. No, none of the women Gael knows presume to make speeches. And Guthrie?

"When my brother was released from Our Lady's Hospital for Sick Children in Dublin after his first fit . . . we went to the National Museum. It was Mum's idea. A way to focus the mind outward and not in, she said. The mind was—I came to learn—an unsafe place for my brother. He was eight. He fractured his wrist when he collapsed, so he wore a cast. I begged him to let me write on it. He said he liked it plain. But if I really really wanted to, I could draw something. A panda, he suggested. Or a walrus. When go you back to school on Monday, I said, everyone will write on it whether you let them or not. So we settled on X's and O's. He was calmer than I'd ever seen him. It was because of the cast. It made *sense* of the doctor's arrival at school, and how he hadn't come back from the boys' room, and how he'd been surrounded by a pack of spooked adults. He drew smiley faces. Despite what the CT scans said, he had something obviously broken."

People are leaning on one another, listening. They are all still. The gallery has a no-mobile-phones policy, which brings a certain nervous hunger to be in the moment, not normally fed.

"In the museum, our father scolded my brother for resting his forehead against the glass. He was looking at Japanese ceramics. He did as he was told and came away from the glass, but not from the objects. He stood on his tiptoes to see the bowls and jugs spliced through with gold. I stood beside him and read aloud what it said on the panel. Kintsugi celebrates an object's history and damage as part of its beauty. So they were broken? he asked me. And they didn't get thrown out? They got glued back together with gold? Even at eight, he wasn't just drawn to the aesthetic. The thought was equally beautiful. An idea like that could sustain him for weeks. Every day would relate in some way to the idea. Each and every bad experience.

"Waste of gold, our father said, when he saw what we were admiring. It was time to go. He said. He spent most of his career as an investment wanker. Sorry, banker. No, wait, yeah, right the first time."

People laugh and now they are beginning to nod. She describes Guthrie's condition and the auras, without using his first name. The paintings are signed G. Foess and Gael had made M.F.N. add a clause to the contract preventing the use of his first name. Gael had been the one to sign the new paintings, so they aren't really forgeries, per se. And Guthrie will be protected from any media. The idea of him stumbling on a review describing some dozen paintings and his delusional disorder has been enough to keep Gael from entering REM now for weeks. But the rewards of pulling this off would provide enough gold to fill a very large crack in the breastbone.

"I think our father had read the panel in the museum that day that said when Kintsugi first started, collectors would smash valuable pottery deliberately, so it could be repaired with gold seams. Everything our father heard from doctors said that his son's damage had no cause other than a form of psychosis. There was no epilepsy. There was no danger around flashing lights or crowded environments; no reason not to get a driver's license, a degree; no reason to drop himself off the mantelpiece. Our father just Did Not Get how a person could hinder themselves needlessly. Was it a kind of damage fetish?" Gael accuses the audience with this question. Pauses. "That was how he thought. Drugs wouldn't repair his son. Money wouldn't repair him. None of the things my father was willing to provide would repair him. Over the years, out of some rage, our father persecuted him in a thousand ways until he seemed to decide that this ongoing self-harm had rendered my brother useless. The jug had been compromised. Why pour wine into it?" She waits for the crack of silence. "My brother lacked any kind of function our father could understand. Except one. His function as a Christian." Gael pauses again, measures the confession. "So that's how their relationship developed. Desperate for a comforting father amid all the bullying and trauma and physical pain of his disorder, my brother became the best Christian in the village." Gael smiles. There might have been laughter, but for the gleam in her eyes. She swallows so it sounds in the microphone. The patrons in view hold a tension in their mouths that's not wine swilling.

"What I could never come to terms with . . . The enlightenment he'd had as a child always seemed miraculous to me. I didn't have it. I envied it. The true, rapt, awesome admiration of beauty. Not for anything's sake. Not for a cause. Not to *do* anything with it. Just to observe it. Contemplate it. Believe it. After, to produce his own, borne of necessity." Gael can feel them observing her now, closer and closer, spiraling in on the luminous celestial body. "He's never exhibited anything like this collection. He's never painted anything like it. As many shows as he's had for such a young artist, this is the first exposure. When I found the auras stashed in his attic, I saw the almost unbearable harm . . . and its illumination. . . . I'm grateful to M.F.N. . . . I'm honored to bring this experience to you on my brother's behalf . . . and I hope you'll press your foreheads against the glass."

An ecstatic cheer erupts and people clap their thighs one-handed, pressing their wineglasses to their foreheads with the other. Gael responds to this gesture with a wide smile and wet-eyed laughter and looks over the tops of their heads at the lights smoldering in the city beyond like the just-missed fireworks of the New Year, after the kiss. Then a pair of hands shoots up on the right side of the room, near the portrait, and the fingers wiggle: Occupy's hand signal for fervent support of a proposition. The hand signal that had been given just this morning in an equally ecstatic manner. Just before the hands duck out of sight, Gael catches a flash of turquoise and yellow on the wrist. Seconds later, a popping sound announces champagne and Enn, at the decks, has by some means found even weirder music to give volume to—an industrial genre called Japanoise, she's told. Staying and somehow dancing to the nervy, stray drumbeat is an ultimatum tendered to the horde: We've done Truth; now Dare. M is moving through them, pouring champagne from bottles in each hand and F's camera has been given to one of the caterers to do with what he can. When he asks her to stand there and turn this way, Gael warns him that any photograph with the paintings in frame counts as a reproduction, not publishable anywhere without her consent. People are trying to pull her away to talk to her; to have her talk to them, but she brushes them off. Unlikely buyers. "If you shoot any of the paintings, make it these five." She points. "But I still have to approve their publication. So go through the camera and delete any paintings that aren't those five." The guy is a little shocked, given the jubilant mood, and how is this not a success? He says it's not his camera and he can't delete stuff anyway—it's not digital. Gael extracts two bills from her purse and says she'll take the blame if F notices the missing film. "Here." She rubs her hands all over the camera and pushes the notes up the guy's sleeve. "My fingerprints."

"Jeez, Irish. Can't you keep it in your pants for one second?"

Gael turns. Still kitted out in triple denim, Harper is smiling particularly beautifully. Her eyes are heavy sponges. The bruise is caked in concealer. Gael frowns at her. "Did you put a GPS device in me or something? Back in London?"

"Ha! I shoulda."

"Really, though. Harper." Gael's holding Harper's wrist now. The stomach trapezists are in full swing. "How are you here?"

"Just cuz I'm a lit major doesn't mean I can't add two and two. I Googled Foess plus Manhattan. And you're welcome that I got you outta prison."

"What?" Gael leans in, but it's too loud and headachy and they have to shout to be heard. Gael leads Harper by the hand out to the corridor. On the way, she catches someone taking out her phone and detours toward her to deliver a warning.

"I said you're welcome that I got you outta prison!" Harper says, when they've found a spot by the lift. With one hand, she'd swooped two glasses of bubbles from the table as they passed and holds one out to Gael.

"A *lawyer* got me out of prison," Gael says, taking the glass. "But if you want thanks, thank you for getting me arrested. Nice life experience." She takes a drink.

"Just another box I ticked for you," Harper says. "You turned me into Pavlov's bitch."

Gael squints. "What?"

Harper sighs and gives her a defeated look.

"Forgodssake don't sigh at me," Gael says, then finds that her hand twitches by her side, wanting to trace Harper's curves. Wanting to covet her features. Her frank ways. The odd, unrivaled combination of her. Her person as much as the dark finger of cleavage the dungarees force high between the lapels of her shirt. How unstudied she is. How studyable.

"Your story was beautiful," Harper says. "The paintings are beautiful. Your family's beautiful. . . . You're . . ." She brushes her thumb across the part of Gael's forehead with the bump. Lifts onto her tiptoes to do so. Lowers. "It's not just cuz you're so smokin hot. . . . Well, it might be partly mostly to do with the hotness, I'm paying good money to figure that out, but I swear—"

Back pressed against the lift doors, Gael draws Harper's whole body against her and kisses her so deeply she can feel the slip of her mind within her like car tires on black ice, suddenly tractionless. Lightheaded, as though she's spilling blood for every second of it as if gravity is stronger on this section of the globe or at least this part of the room as if something is really badly wrong or just tipping over and it had been just to stop her talking, hadn't it? to stop her saying I love you but now it's not that; now it's not even appetite; it's as if she's never kissed anyone and meant it. At the risk of sinking to the floor, Gael reaches a hand in the direction of the lift call button, but Harper pulls back. Says, "Wait."

It's absurd, where they are, when she opens her eyes. "For what?"

"Wait," Harper says. Her eyes are downcast and welling. "Gael, I love you, and I don't wanna hate you. And I feel like if we're together you're gonna hurt me and I'll hate you. My head will basically break." The line of her cleavage strengthens with her speech, like the volume line of an audio dialogue. "But if we stay just friends then I get to be your friend and that . . . for some stupid *stupid* reason . . . is way more appealing to me than being your . . . nothing. Because it feels like right now is the moment where we're running full tilt at a cliff hand in hand—like a romantic frolicking suicide pact—and I'm laughing but you're just smiling and I totally jump off thinking you're with me but I see halfway down that I'm holding the stump of a hand cut off at the wrist because you had an ax all along and how I didn't pick up on it I don't even know, but you decided that that was the amount you could lose to me so you wouldn't fall with me but so that you wouldn't ruin my fall completely, but it definitely would ruin my fall, Gael, seeing as I'm holding a dismembered hand. And I had that dream a few times and my shrink agrees that friendship might be possible without the cutting."

When Harper lifts her gaze from Gael's shoulder, Gael turns her face to the room and sees how many people have just stopped watching. The back of her head and her shoulders rest against the lift. Harper's hand is on Gael's hip now, feeling for the twisting helix of her.

"I don't need a friend," Gael says, staring at the room.

"That's beyond stupid."

Energy depleted, Gael says, "I've got this far."

"Everyone needs a friend, Gael. Don't be a doofus." Harper pauses, takes back her hand, seeing this logic won't work. Seeing how much further away Gael is from her than she'd thought. "Where would your brother be without you? Huh?"

"Guthrie?"

"Doing all this for him?"

"I get something out of it," Gael says, without modulation.

"Right. That's normal. So you earned a commission."

"No," Gael says. "Not money." Her eyes go out of focus and in, as if someone is toying with her settings. "It's something else."

"Even in the story you told, you were his friend. Reading out the info about the Japanese pots cuz he wasn't tall enough? How adorable is that?"

"I made it all up," Gael says.

"About the pots?"

"All of it."

"Bull. Shit."

Gael doesn't say anything for a while, then, "Exactly." Out of the corner of her eye, she sees Harper shaking her head. The wait staff are beginning to put glasses away into an empty crate. Short party.

"Vegas has a lotta bad acting," Harper says. "My parents once took me to *The Adventures of Pinocchio,* the musical. Worst day of my life."

Gael hiccups a single laugh.

Harper says, "And, whatever you get out of it, whatever Guthrie gets, the patrons get more. Trust me."

"Oh yeah?" Gael looks for M. She wonders if she'll fly home soon, or if she'll make something happen that will decide things. If she can be cocky enough to make it work out.

"I bought one for Mom."

Gael snaps out of it to turn to Harper, who is very much in focus. "Bought what?"

"Whattayathink, a boob job? A *painting,* Gael. We're at a gallery."

Gael closes her eyes and fills her lungs such that the lace on her top stretches to capacity. She squeezes the bridge of her nose with her thumb and forefinger.

"What about it?" Harper asks. "Are you thrilled or what?"

When she opens her eyes again, Gael tips her own glass for dregs, then takes Harper's glass and drains it too. "Which one did you buy?"

"Uh . . ." Harper puts her hand to the side of her mouth to shield what she's saying from the public. "They're all kinda spit and image, right?"

"Was it on the main wall?"

"Uh-huh."

"Was it the one on the far right?"

"No. I dunno. They're all goddamn beautiful. What's wrong with you?"

"This is why I can't have friends," Gael says.

"Because . . . ?" Harper waits for a response, in a frozen show-me-your-cards gesture.

Gael sees M settling up with the catering staff. Some people are getting their coats.

"You've got a one-in-three shot at a Guthrie Foess original," Gael says. "There were only five and it wasn't enough for a show. Guthrie wouldn't do more because he stopped having fits and stopped having sense. Or started. I'm not sure. I hired a guy to make the others."

Harper's blinking at a weirdly rhythmic frequency, like the blinking of a digital watch. She's speechless.

Gael looks at her. Says, "But they're all goddamn beautiful, no?"

Harper's gaze floats rightward, to where M is now standing. Gael's heart hurtles.

"Since you were arrested today," M says, landing his hand on her lower back, "I guess you're good without a helmet? I'll go slow." He's wearing a leather jacket and holds a set of keys to his motorbike. "She coming with?" he asks Gael, who hasn't stopped looking at Harper.

"You're welcome to join," Gael manages to say. "I'm sure M here has a California king."

Harper's downturned mouth is like a child's drawing of a frown, except it's always like that. It doesn't lend her ample cynicism. Gael's brown lipstick had breached its borders. "It's the one in the middle," Harper says. "The one you were in front of."

Gael gives a curt nod. "You've got good instincts, Harper. By and large."

M presses the lift button in a way Gael hopes isn't portending. "Let's take the stairs."

People are muscling past. Gael lifts her blazer from where it straddles her bag with all the togetherness she has in her. All the togetherness she needs. Harper seems to be searching for an Adam's apple in the middle of Gael's marble-white, marble-carved throat, but there is none. There is no flex. No hitting pulse. The skin appears so cool and smooth, you might wipe your finger across it and come away with dew.

Gael wants to wipe her fingers along the creases in Harper's neck like hems; to kiss her cheek; to cripple her with tenderness and see what affections she won't abide. She wants to take her by the hand and go shopping for an ax. She wants to see if laughter is something to live off; if it won't fill her out, so she doesn't hurt Harper with her hollows and edges. But they can't have everything in between.

"You want me to wait outside?" M says.

Gael shakes her head and there's the movement in the throat. "I'm coming." M holds out his hand, but she doesn't see it. She's looking at Harper's wrist. At a welt the cuffs left on her skin, above the silly watch. "Please don't follow me."

Tears stream down Harper's face, but it's a contradiction: "Woolf was probably right," she says. "It's better to be locked out than in."

The wind runs straight through Gael's too-light clothes and her heels feel shaky on the footrests. She has to hold faster to M than she'd like. At least he's warm. The traffic is intimidating. They skirt and lurch through it; pick up speed across the Queensboro Bridge. All this part is new, so it perks her up. It helps to move the mind outward.

At the traffic lights on the far side of the bridge, M tells her there's an artist called Jan Vormann who uses bits of colored plastic, like LEGO blocks, to fill in holes in broken walls. "You find his works in cities all over the world," M says. "There's a couple in Brooklyn. I can take you there." The lights have gone green, but he waits. Cars toot their horns and call out the window and veer around the bike until the lights are back to red. The streetlights gleam off the open visor of M's helmet. It's not what she had expected. It improves him.

"No. Let's just fuck."

M twists the right handle back and the engine revs. "Your call. Your celebration. But maybe go there tomorrow. Take a picture for your brother."

"Celebrate selling his painting to a friend?"

M twists back a little and the leather jacket squeaks like a damp cloth on glass. "Your friend bought the first. Set off a run on the rest. Sold out in under fifteen minutes. It happens, sometimes. People see red stickers go up, they want in." The lights turn green again and this time he takes off. Before tapping down his visor, he says, "You made your brother rich."

9

Diminishing Returns

I

December can be dismally autumnal in Dublin; kids kicking puddle water at one another for want of snowballs. But the day she flies home is so exultantly blue and clear-skied, she doesn't realize the plane is about to hit ground. A thousand feet of cloud typically serve as a warning: a duration of weather you can't hold your breath through. She snatches the next passenger's knee and glances out the window to see the glisten of frostmelt on tarmac. "Buy me a drink first," the woman says. As a laugh escapes her lips, Gael feels it happening already, upon the very moment of contact: the familiar tether slink around her wrist. "The shock of being home, is it?"

If home means Sive and Art's, she isn't headed home. She's headed for Guthrie's. Since that phone call in her very first week in New York, they haven't spoken. But he had offered a kind of truce. He sent a photo of Ronan in A&E with the tiny hospital wristband in shot. The caption read: "Your nephew. Just turned two and already a druggie. Where did I go wrong?" Gael was relieved to find out in an email from Sive that it wasn't anything. Ronan had swallowed a fistful of pills from his father's expired "medication" that, in an effort to help clean up, Art had thrown in the wastepaper basket. At the hospital, Guthrie was concerned that they'd not pumped Ronan's stomach; only had him drink something that made him puke. Was that enough? Poor Ronan. Having to spew the nice sugar pills. On the upside, he might be forever disinclined to eat sweets.

The twins are running rings round a woman seated on the lawn when Gael's taxi pulls up. Although they're running in a circle, it's clear that Soraca is in front and Ronan is chasing in her wake. It's only been a hundred days, but they're bigger. More decided-upon. They're dressed for the ski slopes. Hand-me-downs from some better-off kids who winter in Austria. They don't run to her as she opens the gate, but they do come to a halt and stare with their fingers in their mouths.

"Who's yer one?" the woman says to them, her eyes guarded on Gael. "Who's that one, when she's at home?"

Gael doesn't want to feel the twins' cool reaction to her, or to have to tell some randomer who she is, so she looks to the house. A narrow terraced house on the leftmost end of the block. Pebbledash walls. Flat roof. One of the upstairs tenants is looking out the mesh curtains and he lifts his chin at Gael when he's caught. The reverse nod of the postcrash Irish. She reciprocates. In Guthrie's flat, the living-room blinds are angled open, but it's still hard to make out the room. Could it be a reflection, somehow, or are there really a half dozen people sitting around as at an AA meeting?

"It's nearly over now," the woman says. "One of these days."

"Sorry?"

"Are you the one was in America? Are you their auntie?"

"Yeah. Are you their babysitter?"

"Not really. I'm Monica."

"Gael."

Gael moves toward them and drops her bags. She's brought the empty portfolio back for Guthrie. It seems charmed, now, even though she doesn't go in for that sort of mawk. But maybe he will. All going well. She kneels down on the clumpy grass, facing the house, and invites high fives from the kids. They resume their running game—now around two people—and slap high fives on every orbit. Through the front window, Gael sees that the people in there are all ages and sorts, with bad clothes unifying them. It's weird to see her little brother fraternizing with fully fledged adults. It occurs to her that this is something she hasn't seen much of. But that's not the only reason it's strange. She asks:

"What is it?"

Monica peeks over her shoulder, then back at the twins. "Check-in session," she declares. The way she pronounces them, the words rhyme.

"Check-in?" Gael spots Guthrie among the circle. She'd been looking for his bun, but he's cut it off. Shaved it, even. It's not razor short, but it's not a barber's cut either. She can see that he's talking. "I'm guessing it's not a hotel?"

"Some kind of hotel!" Monica tugs Ronan's trousers up as he passes. "It's more a sort of . . . community service, nothing official. Most lunchtimes, his door's open for a chat. Some of them use and all. You know? On the brown. But the most it's just a mental health ting, you know? Neighborly. Making sure we're all coping and everyting. He cured hisself of his fits. And the wee kids on his own and all. He's a good influence on any of us. Noble sort of person. He has a gift, so he does. Sure you must know that. And you his sister."

A few missed high fives impugns Soraca, who has run to the exterior wall where a casket-sized flowerbed is about to lose its parsley and mint. She grabs one plant in each hand and is getting into a squat position to root them out. Monica's up to stop her. "Seen her da pulling out weeds, so she did," she explains. "That's a living ting, pet, so it is. You can't go murderin. D'y'hear me, Soraca?" Monica addresses Gael.

"Would you ever mind runnin in for me there love? They're gettin antsy. There's Tupperware with sausages and carrots in the fridge."

Gael looks to the house warily. "Sure." But then the front door opens and a handful of people spill out quietly and file straight down the driveway so as not to overstay their welcome. One guy who looks like someone to cross the street from—like the guy who spliced Guthrie's face in Phoenix Park—ruffles Ronan's hair and gives him a pistachio-toothed smile on his way. Ronan clucks, unjudgingly.

"Here we go," Monica says. "They'll get a proper lunch now. Nice to meet yiz anyway."

"Actually," Gael says, "do you mind hanging on for a few minutes? I'll bring out the snacks."

Monica looks unsure and scans Gael's belongings.

"It's just," Gael says, "I owe him an apology and it's easier—"

"Say no more. If he's owed an apolgy, I've all the time you like for that. Come here, Ronan, till we see can we find a shamrock." Monica takes Ronan by the hand and winks at Gael.

The first thing he says, she misses, because of the gaps where his two front lower teeth should be. She'd imagined an implant for the one she knew was knocked out. The other must have followed. It changes his face considerably.

"I'm sorry."

The words hang there and she resists all urges to qualify them. To vocalize the bulk of the debt of which those two words are the interest. To point out that, even a year ago, she would have done some very dark deeds to get what she needed. Look at that for growth. This is, after all, a more generous act than she ever plans to repeat. Guthrie waits, to see if the conditions of the apology will arrive in due course. He doesn't look enraged. He doesn't look forgiving either. He's dragging the four beanbags to line them up along the wall.

An oval coffee table is a new addition to the room. Other than that, there's the couch, tent and playpen. Boxes. Some books and blankets in the built-in shelves. The lingering smell of BO and hangover from the crowd just left. Guthrie looks out the window, with his hands on his narrow hips.

"They're doing beautifully," Gael says.

But he's observing the portfolio; not his children. "You couldn't save even one?"

Gael watches Monica delve through her bag and put whatever she retrieved in her mouth for safekeeping. Then she rolls up one sleeve of her fleece, takes the item from her teeth, unwraps it like a barley and slaps it onto her upper arm. Nicotine. Gael says nothing.

"Why do I feel like you didn't try?"

No wavering on the line taken. "I'm sorry."

Guthrie looks at the crime scene of a carpet. Some moments pass. Then, he turns and says, "Okay. What's done is done."

It occurs to Gael that every single thing her brother says will refer in some way to his violation. And now she's become another of his exploiters. Is this his way of healing himself, though? Tolerating the awful? How much can you write off as sunk costs?

She turns and steps toward him. "Can I say hello?"

Guthrie knits his brow, as if to say, What a question. Gael pounds herself against him in an embrace she's been craving for months. He smells of tree sap. She feels their ribs lace like fingers. The onset of emotion. She presses her eyes into his shoulder to hold it back. That wouldn't be fair. While her head is buried in the recess below his clavicle, she says, "I'm sorry for what happened." This is what she had been sorry for, and only this, but always and ever after, this. "I wish you'd told me. I could have—"

"I heard . . ." He takes her arms and unwraps them from him, but keeps a hold of her forearms, until it slips to just the ends of their fingers, hooked. "I heard you met up with Dad in New York."

Gael nods.

"And you didn't bottle him."

"I got the sense some of the people around us were bodyguards."

He smiles this new unbuttressed smile. "I'm glad."

"Wait, Guthrie. I can't just . . . We can't be . . . Listen. You're the only one I want to be close to. And that means it *has* to be real. We can't just . . . pretend. I can't have been absent for this awfulness in your life and carry on at arm's length from you so you never use me for support or the perspective I can offer because we're on different wavelengths since—" Guthrie unhooks his hands from Gael's and crosses his arms so that his fingers are tucked in his pits, thumbs pointed to the ceiling. "I'm not about to hunt her down or anything. It's you I'm concerned for—"

"I have someone," Guthrie says. Pauses. "Who watches over me, so you don't have to. I don't need your protection. And if that makes you angry, Gael, then yes we are on different wavelengths."

Gael counts down from ten in her head before she speaks. *Ten*-fuckthousand-*nine*-fuckingthousand-*eight*-motherfuckingthousand . . . "You did not get . . . what you deserved." She counts from five this time. "You did not have . . . a guardian angel protecting you." Now from three. "You do not get enlightenment . . . or anything at all fucking *positive* . . . from rape, except HIV."

"I got the twins. And I deserve them."

"There is no such thing as *deserve!*" She's nearly shouting. "It shouldn't be a word! It doesn't mean anything! 'Deserving person'? It doesn't make enough sense to be an oxymoron."

"I don't know what matters to you. Everything's throwaway." He sounds so mature, it's scaring her.

"Not everything."

"It's all irony," he says.

"It's not. I'm not trying to be funny. It's *not* funny. It's massive. It's everything. No one gets what they deserve. He fucked you up to make you think that."

"Listen to yourself! 'Make me think that.' Like I'm a piece of clay."

His cheeks tighten and he glances out the window. "It's as if . . . you think there's something you can do for me. And part of me believes that comes from a good place. But it's also from a selfish place, Gael."

Looking up at the low ceiling, she tries to think of what to say, but there are too many competing lines of argument. Too much argument all together. She doesn't know what substance it is that they're pouring into the scales. But the weight keeps shifting.

"Wait here a sec, will you." He disappears to the kitchen and hurries out the front door with the Tupperware. Monica looks bewildered as he speaks with her. Then he pulls back the waistband of Soraca's ski pants to check her nappy. When he gets back to the living room, Gael notes that the pastiness of his skin has faded since she last saw him. The twins' fondness for being outdoors has freckled him. He looked like the longest one sober from the group of drunks, or whatever they were.

"You look good."

"Thanks," he says. "You look thinner."

"Those teeth, though . . ."

Guthrie minces his jaw. "I'm used to it. And the twins love it when I stick my tongue through."

"That is a legitimate excuse," Gael says. "But what if you discover the perfect job you never knew you wanted in a few years' time and the missing teeth cost you it?"

"Then it wouldn't be the perfect job."

She sighs heavily. "I couldn't mold you if I tried."

Guthrie scratches his cheek and there's the slightest suggestion of his nails meeting stubble. "I don't want to make Monica late for work. She's on a lunch break. Unless you're running off straightaway?"

"Just one thing first. It's important. I'm gonna book us a meeting with an accountant. Is there a time that suits, before Christmas?"

"An accountant? For what?"

She tries to give nothing away. No feeling, triumph or grief. "Your paintings, Guth. They sold."

He looks like he's clamping the teeth he has left, as if he's doing his own countdown. "I don't know, Gael. I don't know if I want to change anything. Things are good, like this. They're tight. It's not like it's easy. The dole's down to a hundred euro a week now, for people my age. But I can't afford to be disqualified from it. With welfare pieced together, I don't have to borrow too much to stay like this till they're in school. Austerity cut subsidies for childcare. So that's not an option. But anyway, I love getting to raise them. And doing what I can with the healing practice and . . . I'm studying for the Leaving Cert."

"*What?*" Gael says. "You're doing your Leaving?"

"Yeah." He dips his head, to conceal his half smile. "Only a couple of subjects this year."

"That's amazing! How the heck—"

"I'm hoping to sit the first set of exams next May. Which seems like ages off, but I only manage an hour before bed and most nights I'm too wrecked to take anything in. May doesn't seem far enough away."

"Do you have any idea how good I am at times tables, Guth? I can *so* help. That's what you do for the Leaving Cert, right? I forget."

Guthrie thumps her arm. "Don't mock me."

"Long multiplication and *Je voudrais aller chez vous*, no? *Quid pro quoi?*"

"Gael."

"Alright, alright. But I do want to help. I mean it."

A few beats of silence play out before he asks, "Does that mean you'll be around?"

Gael considers the serried beanbags at the wall and has an idea. "No. Just for a couple of weeks. I've got job offers to negotiate. But listen, I still want to take you to an accountant. But I have a suggestion . . . of what you could do with the money. Once we've fixed your teeth."

Guthrie shakes his head resignedly. "I take it it's not: bury it in the soil."

Gael smiles. "No." She thought he'd been too young to remember. "Not that."

"Honestly, Gael, I think I need a while. To work through my feelings about it, before anything. I half wanted to just put it behind me." He's distracted again by the twins. They're getting stroppy.

There is one thing she can give him, she has realized. One thing that's less crude than cash. "I get it," she says. "But just in the meantime, to have in the back of your head . . . How does 'The Foess Creative Therapy Center' strike you, for a place to work out feelings?"

Ronan's squawking outside and Monica's playing limbo with them, in a last-ditch effort to keep the peace. Guthrie takes a step back from Gael and looks guarded. "Sounds like three months is enough for the American Dream to catch."

Gael grins. "Think about it. You could combine art and helping people . . . and if it's registered as a charity, then tax stuff would be a cinch—"

"It's a nice idea. Really nice of you to dream it up. I have to get the kids inside now. This is taking advantage of Monica. The temperature's dropping, Soraca needs changing and we all need to eat." He goes to the door.

"Guthrie?"

"It's been a busy day and I'm behind."

"There's enough for a college fund." She pauses. "For both of them. And for you."

He stops, his back to her.

"There's enough to buy a building. You could live upstairs and the center could be downstairs. You could buy it outright. No mortgage. And if it's a charity, it would be a trust fund or something, we can work this out with the accountant. And you wouldn't even have to change anything. If you really do like your life like this."

Those last words resound like ill-tuned timpani. So she jumps in with what she thinks is the right note: "It's four hundred and twenty thousand dollars, American dollars. . . . Give or take."

Guthrie turns and watches her, somehow savagely. He stands there and she stands there for long enough that Monica has given up and the twins have run inside and are now screaming and climbing up their father's body.

"Is it enough then, Gael? Give or take?"

The avalanche of children's needs cascade upon him then and there is nothing to do but to dig and dig and dig for pocketfuls of air despite not knowing which way is up. Stunned, Gael stays and helps. She restrains herself in silent usefulness. The small, measly kind of usefulness that has no lasting effect. But that is what he seems to want from her. She had been wrong, to think it was respect.

Later, in the middle of nonsense child-talk at the two-seater kitchen table, he says that maybe they could donate it to the Epilepsy Care Foundation. Gael holds her fork against her tongue. Hard. Or the St. Vincent de Paul, he suggests, more convinced. Charities have been badly hit in the recession. Unemployment is at thirteen percent. "But thirty percent of people our age, Gael. Are unemployed. One in five mortgages are behind on payments. You know, Niall just told us he found his wife moving food around in the cupboard last night. She was crying so he asked what she was doing. It was so the kids would think she'd bought groceries."

Gael feels her throat contract. "Okay, Guthrie. We'll do some research on charities later." Queasy, she puts her cutlery down and leaves the rest of her sausages and carrot-potato mash.

"I don't want you to think I'm not thinking about your idea, by the way. It's just a shock. I mean, it's very hard to digest. So I'm just trying to . . . Are you not hungry?"

Gael had put her fork and knife together and is helping to interest the twins in putting food into their mouths rather than smearing it around the house like mortar (as if the house weren't already all mortar, too few bricks). "I ate on the plane, so. It'll keep, though, for leftovers. For these monkeys."

They eat the cut-up sausage with their hands and the mash with bright green plastic spoons. The washing machine clatters and wallops from the bathroom like it's cleaning grenades.

Guthrie takes a measure of her. "We're doing fine, Gael. We have what we need. You don't think Dad would let me struggle for the basics? I turn down his money every month. I'm pleased if I'm able to do that."

Gael keeps swallowing, even though her mouth is dry. "Right. No." She takes a piece of sausage and spirals it in the air around Ronan, which must make him dizzy, because he closes his eyes and whinges. She can sense Guthrie's contemplation like an unopened bill in the letterbox.

After a while, he asks: "'The Foess Center for Creative Therapy,' was it?" His expression is drawn. Sharp cheekbones; slender, nostrilly nose; features cut like Waterford Crystal, which happens to have gone into receivership.

"Creative Therapy Center. Therapies. I don't know," Gael says. "Just . . . that way it's not FCCT. Which sounds . . . you know. FCTC is better, I think."

Guthrie stops Soraca from sliding down the high chair, which is getting a little tight for her. He looks changed, now. Brooding in a new way. "You've really thought about this?"

Gael shrugs. For the ten or twenty seconds while she watched him clean up after the support group. In those few seconds, this idea had trumped buy-a-couple-of-properties-while-they're-still-piss-cheap-and-be-a-passive-income-landlord-wanker. "A bit."

"Amen," Soraca adds to the conversation.

Guthrie laughs out of nowhere. "Were you saying your prayers, Sorch?"

"Ya." She pulls her Velcro bib off and starts wiping the tabletop with it.

Gael laughs too.

"Is it because I forgot?"

"You forgot," Soraca says. "Look, Ron!" She holds out the dirty bib to her twin. He takes it and looks grateful. She slaps her freed chest and holds her hands there. "Amen."

"What are you praying for, Sorch?" Guthrie asks.

"I said it."

"What did you say?"

"I said it."

"Are you praying for Daddy?"

"No, Daddy."

"What then?"

Soraca spirals her head around and around, thrilled and annoyed at the attention. She collects her face in her hands and makes it go up and down. "Use the nice voice."

"You want me to use my nice voice?" Guthrie says.

"Ya ya ya ya ya ya ya."

"What's my nice voice?"

"Ya ya ya ya ya ya ya."

"Were you praying I'll say yes?"

"Ya."

"Saying ya is my nice voice?"

"Ya."

"I should say yes?"

"Ya."

"Will I?"

"Ya."

"Ya," Ronan says.

Gael and Guthrie look at each other and burst out laughing. The twins scream and throw their food in delight. The washing machine goes into spin cycle and the whole house shakes so as to guess at an unopened gift.

✦

She asked to borrow the bicycle. She needed to speak with Mum, so would stay at her place. The futon wasn't comfy but at least there was privacy. A door to shut on unwanted questions (Will you stay for Christmas? How much did each painting sell for and *how* and who bought them? What jobs are you up for? Are there friends you'll catch up with while you're home?) and the possibility of Ronan's nocturnal visits. Sive wouldn't be home, Guthrie said. She'd be at rehearsal. She's covering maternity leave for the conductor of a Northside orchestra.

"What? She never said!" Gael beamed. "That's great!"

Guthrie checked himself before speaking. "Yeah. It *is* great."

It becomes clear what information had been withheld when Gael approaches the assembly hall at a dingy technical college in Drumcondra: that this is the kind of orchestra for which "community" is the justification. Oh . . . *my* god, Gael mouths, as she locks up the bike—the clanking of metal links right at home in the concussing soundscape.

The double doors to the hall are shut, likely thanks to a petition by deafened Drumcondrans. Gael sneaks in as discreetly as she can, but several players peer at her because the shaft of light from outside is so conspicuous in the dark, wood-paneled hall, not unlike a confessional (and perhaps better served as one). It's a full orchestra—the whole shebang—arranged on fold-up chairs at the foot of a stage. Sive had said not to come until seven, but Gael ignored her and has arrived at half five, after the rehearsal has begun. She'd wanted to hear them. To watch. Her first impression is that they're warming up, but they're actually halfway through a rendition of *Lord of the Rings* theme music. Resheathe your instruments! For the love of Tolkien! But then the flutes take over the melody from the strings and it's even shriller and accidentally syncopated and like they're blowing into the holes of crutches.

Stood on a timber box, Sive looks all casual elegance in cream chinos and a ribbed burgundy polo-neck. She hasn't noted Gael, busy with so many players having lost their place in the score. Hers are the exaggerated gesticulations reserved for inciting laughter in cranky babies. Macarena conducting. All the bows in the string sections are going in opposite directions, except for the bulk of second violins, who are all airbowing and so can concentrate on whether it should be an up- or downbow. The trombones also have their arms at conspicuously different angles. The first phrase after every pause is barely muttered, until the players gain confidence enough to sound out the notes by the tenth or twelfth bar. The best of the bunch are the trumpets, who have the *Dummmmm-Dummmm-de-de-Dummmmmm* main theme. They're vaguely together and in tune, except that they can only play *forte*. Sive slashes her hands horizontally outward in the universal sign for stop-what-you're-doing, but it takes another twenty seconds for the woodwinds to slide-whistle to silence.

"John."

Sive addresses the French horn player, who is doing well to hold erect the monstrous instrument, given he's in his nineties.

"John," she repeats. He is deaf, it turns out. "What have you got at section D, John?"

"WHERE?" The lungs are robust.

"D. Section D. What have you got at D?"

Gael can tell the color of his eyes from where she's sitting on the floor at the back of the hall, due to his telescopic glasses. He buries his head in the music for a minute, searching for D. Then sits back, bald-faced, and declares with disgust: "NOTHING! SIX-TEEN BARS OF IT."

"That's what I thought. If you've got a rest, John, you've got a rest. Take the break."

John had been playing whatever notes occurred to him. He looks sore at the prospect of missing out on sixteen bars of action. There are only so many bars left in one's life. No time left for wall-flowering.

"We'll go one round through from the start," Sive says, "and then we'll have our tea break. So, with biscuits as an incentive—I think Freya splashed out on Jaffa Cakes this week—I'd like to hear you confidently playing the notes. Together, if you please, and with expression. Intention. This is a dramatic, gutsy piece of music. Give it socks."

"Hobbits don't wear socks," someone says, prompting laughter.

"You're not hobbits," Sive responds. "You're orcs. You're giants. You're men of Gondor. Instruments up. On my count. One, two; one . . ." Cue:

Omnishambles.

The tea break has the atmosphere of a disco. Sive is a celebrity everyone wants to stand near to and warning whispers about the voyeur-down-the-back reach her before Gael does. "That's my daughter," Gael hears her tell them.

Then she's pulled along by arms so that she practically body-surfs the rest of the way to the table, where Sive stands beside the lined-up foam cups—spoonfuls of instant coffee in half of them, tea bags in the rest—several jugs, and a tin can with a coin slot cut out and the word *Kitty* written on masking tape. There are only two kettles, so the tea break is industrious, having to refill and boil the kettles non-stop before the second half cuts off the supply. Gael and Sive hug.

"Ahhh, that's nice," a lady says.

"Lovely," someone agrees.

"Does she play an instrument?" a man wants to know. "Sive, does she?"

Sive laughs. "She plays the instrument of her intellect better than most. And the clarinet, worse than Tristan."

Some of them scream at this and look for Tristan to make sure he heard. He's a great one for taking the mick, someone explains.

"Sandra has a spare clarinet so she does," the lady pipes up.

"Does she?"

"She does! Where's Sandra?"

"Have you the spare in the car, Sandra?"

"Will I get it?"

"Get it now."

"Go!"

"She'll have a go."

"Join in, so she will."

"Course she will."

"Oh yes, you're more than welcome."

"Shove dem seats along over der, Barry, will yi?"

Sive is grinning ear to ear, pouring hot water in a cup and letting Gael fend for herself.

"I don't have my contact lenses in," Gael says. "I couldn't see the music at all, but thanks anyway. I'll just listen."

"You seen the filum, though? You could give it a lash."

"WHAT ARE YOU, LONG OR SHORT?" John asks. "SIGHTED, I MEAN SIGHTED."

Gael takes a Mikado biscuit and scoops out the jam along the center with her pinky finger. The finger in her mouth, she says, "Astigmatism."

"WHAT?"

"I suggest you give your own glasses a wipe, John," Sive says, and takes Gael by the elbow and through the crowd toward the back of the hall where it's quiet. Her skin looks even more craquelured when she smiles, which she's doing more often than ever.

"Well, this is different!" Gael says. "Why did I have the feeling there'd be no going back from Cash Converters?"

Sive tilts her head to her shoulder and studies Gael.

"Did you even *talk* to the NSO about doing the recording?" Gael asks.

She had been in touch with Sive regularly over the past weeks about interest in the oboe concerto. One soloist was very eager to present it to his Artistic Director, but it *had* to be in the form of a recording and Sive had to fly over. Others, too, had asked for a recording. Sive looks back up the hall at the ravenous tea drinkers. "It was very generous of you to spend that time on it, Gael. It was thoughtful and flattering and sweet, but—"

"No! Don't back out now!"

"Let me finish."

Gael throws her hair back out of her eyes.

Sive says, "As you know, I do happen to think the concerto you picked is the most viable. And, God forbid, worthy. But it's been over two years, now, since I left the NSO. And these two years have taught me a lot about what I want at this stage of my life and what's important."

"Let me guess—"

"No," Sive says sternly, casting her gray eyes upon Gael. "I won't have you *guess* at my deepest desires, thank you very much."

Gael feels small for a fraction of a second. She feels the half foot her mother has on her. "Sorry."

"This is what I miss. Conducting." Sive pauses. "Composing I love. But conducting, I've come to realize, I live for."

"That's great," Gael says, a little shyly.

"But I left my job at the worst possible time and, as you said, there is no going back. I'd have to wait for a conductor to die in this country to get back in. And who's to say I won't die first?"

Gael *tsks*. Sive looks up at the group again and sees that they are dutifully finishing up and taking their seats. She checks her watch. "You know, it's peculiar . . ." She breaks off.

"What?" Gael asks, absolutely unable to know what would come next.

Sive glances back at her. "You needn't be on the floor by the way. There are chairs—"

"I've got the bike. I'll cycle back now and see you at home. Is Art in?"

"We'll put the bike in the back of the car," Sive says.

"Oh?"

"The second half is even better. They put brandy in the tea and whiskey in the coffee."

"It's eleven minutes past six!" someone barks: words clearly directed at Sive, who raises her eyebrows and hands Gael her barely sipped coffee. "What were you saying, though?" Gael asks, but her mother is gone. She brings the mug to her lips. Smells peat.

Gael's throat is sore from hysterics and her head is light with respite from thoughts of Harper and Guthrie by the time they slacken their bows and finish up.

In the car, Gael waits for Sive to pick up from where they left off. She takes in the old Dublin streets, with the low splay of cement-colored bungalow town houses and redbrick walls. Corner shops and bookies and Guinness signs and people with walking sticks and steel roller-shutters pulled down on restaurant and café fronts. Two-story Georgian houses with bay windows lining the richer avenues; huge coniferous trees for discretion. Once they've picked their way out of the Bridget's Cross streets, Sive says that Art is open to moving with her. But they'll wait another year, till the twins are closer to school. In any case, it will take her a while to find a decent orchestra. Art will go anywhere, as long as it's not Oklahoma or Bolton. She laughs at something Gael can't know.

"So what's wrong with him?"

Sive glances at Gael charily. Both hands on the wheel.

"How is he . . . so free and easy, to go anywhere . . . when he's jobless, disowned, doesn't drink, doesn't drive, clearly loaded with baggage?"

Sive takes one hand off the wheel and stretches her fingers as if letting something go again and again. Then does the other hand. Calcium deposits crackle. "How much has he told you?"

"Only that he flew in the air force and has a son who lives in Cape Town and won't let him meet his grandkids. That he lived in the States for yonks and got tattoos and that's about it. And I lived with you guys for months. He's almost as good a deflector as me!"

"If we crashed, Gael, your ribs would puncture your lungs," Sive says in a hard voice. "Put your seat belt on properly." Gael does as she's told. Sive takes her time with the wording. Pauses at length between phrases.

"His wife was called Ruth. She died of an aneurysm at thirty-eight, playing tennis. She beat him forty-love. He chuckled when he told me that. As if it was a good line. . . . He'd been a drinker long before she died. But around the time of her first anniversary, it began to spiral. He was in the British air force then. He felt she'd already become blurry and he wanted to have something to pin the forgetting on. He crash-landed a plane and was tested for blood alcohol. They gave him a dishonorable discharge. He couldn't ever fly in Europe again. . . . Not that he believed she was in the sky, but having some distance from the ground she was buried in had been a form of relief. He felt that flying was an essential reminder that it's not about the landing at all. That's not what you're holding out for. . . . A bit like music. You're not waiting for the final chord." Sive turns on the screen sprinkler and the wipers for a moment, until they can read the road markings again. "His father bullied him as a boy, telling him he was color-blind so he wouldn't qualify for a pilot's license. 'See now, you only see red.' He'd go into the clinic for a flu jab and come out to be told by his father they'd detected early-stage diabetes. Another disqualification. An alcoholic himself, his father plied Art with drink and once, as a teenager, he woke up with his cheek to the kitchen tiles. He'd been ticketed for drunk and disorderly conduct, his father said, so that was that as regards piloting."

"What a dick," Gael says.

Sive clacks her tongue. "So he must only have been forty-one or -two when he went to the States. He stayed illegally for fourteen years. He got a job as a crop duster in a farmland. Oklahoma of all places. Snakes and everything, they have. It was risky work too and it didn't get him far off the ground. But it was something. The swooping and turning kept him dizzy. Which he liked. It was a disaster of a plane, I suppose. He flew it half cut. And on top of it all, he started gambling. You see, when the temptation's there on your doorstep . . . He used the plane as a wager more than once, he said, though it wasn't his. When the boss's son found him one morning, slumped and sick in the cockpit, they said if he ever tried to work in Oklahoma again, they'd lend their plane to the police to go after him. He left via Mexico. By the time he got home, his only son was long gone. Auntie Beverly offered to put him up if he'd spend a month in rehab. Which he did. He taught all the patients card counting. And a few of the nurses! He remembered his way with people. Comradeship. What Ruth had loved him for." Sive pauses and checks her rearview mirror, but it's clear. "He needed the counseling, really. Grief is its own addiction and he wanted badly to be sober. His aunt knew grief. How it could be raw and recent even after their scent has left the house. The laundry basket. The silk lining. So he went to her. She was at the age that his presence around the place was relished and needed. He took care of her and she of him. He got a telemarketing job, of all things." Sive says this a little sarcastically. As if she's trying to mask a touch of embarrassment. "Bev had all this money, but he insisted. To remember what it's like to just be in society. Do the things we're supposed to do."

"I get that," Gael says.

"The day you pushed us together in the Tate Modern, he'd come to speak to a curator about Beverly's private collection. She'd given him orders to donate a few pieces when she died. And she had done. Died. He was lonely all over again, but was trying to treat grief in a new way and that was the serendipity of his interest. We were both rebounding. He off a gong. Me off a snare drum." Her words have some vibrato to them.

The tires on the road are calming, though they shouldn't be. "Why wouldn't he tell me all this? Doesn't he think I'd want to know? Or that I have a right to know, even?"

Sive's voice is low, now, and circumspect. "He won't talk about death to people who haven't experienced it. They can't relate and he doesn't want to make them try. That's a generosity. It's the most difficult thing; the existence of life's opposite, hovering over us always as a possibility. Just a flippant iteration of events. You haven't experienced death yet—not of anyone you really knew or loved. But soon you will. Your grandfather. Hopefully."

"Jesus, Mum."

"Well. He's being mocked by his body. Betrayed by his mind. It's harrowing, even to witness." She opens the window to let the cold air brace her. "I wish to God he'd written a will while he was sensible. Given directions to take him to Switzerland, which is what I know he wanted. He hasn't the presence of mind to stockpile his morphine. The rare time we have him home, I leave him in the bathroom for an hour with the cabinets wide open so he might grab a few bottles of what's there. But you can place something in a person's hand and, as irresistible as you think it will be, it's up to them to close their fingers around it. Such is our morality. Anyway, enough of this." She shakes her head. "Art will wonder what you said to me."

They pull up to the apartment, but it's dark now and the lights are off.

II

Gael had asked how Art was free to do what he pleases, but she didn't mean free. She had never believed him to be free, or anything close. She didn't know a single person who was free in the way she understands freedom. A conceit that had stayed with her from King's College (by editing her contractor's essays rather than attending lectures, but however you get your vegetables) was Isaiah Berlin's concepts of positive and negative liberty, from the module Political & Social Philosophy, which, to Gael, might well have been called: Everything.

Negative liberty is definable by what's not stopping us—which doors aren't closed to us. Freedom *from* persecution, harassment, discriminatory barriers. The right *not* to be shot down for what we choose to worship or say or wear. But it doesn't enable us to pursue things. A good education. Scandinavian furniture. A full card of coffee stamps. A Green Party presidential candidacy. The doors open to us are positive liberties. Goals we're free to go after. Or should be.

What Gael had found troubling was how appalled her peers were to discover that the latter liberty was unavailable to them. Firstly, as citizens. That the state can't offer it, because for some to act how they choose and to pursue their goals, others have their freedoms infringed. Newton's third law. His privilege is her restraint. "Freedom for the pike is death for the minnows," Berlin said. (To Gael, the question was clear: how does one become an orca?) The only way a state could enable positive liberty would be to "ascertain" and homogenize the People's desires. Cut to Kim Jong-il. And even if it were possible for a state to facilitate positive freedom, it might not be *desirable* to do so.

But personally, Gael wonders, can you have positive liberty if you can slip around or fit through or dance over the respective constraints? If technically you know your purpose and can realize it—you want to be a ballerina and you're born into an affluent, supportive family, you do all the lunges, audition for Juilliard and get in, put on the tights and so on, *pas de hurrée*—are you then fully, positively free? (Assuming your instructor doesn't say: You're fat; get thin or get out. Taxpayers don't say: We only support extremely pretty ballerinas. Statistics don't say: This isn't a viable career; here's a job in insurance. Probability doesn't break your neck; reciprocity, your spirit.) Assuming absolute rationality and zero external limitations, aren't there other forms of constraint?

How that desire was formed to begin with. Your body type was a harbinger of leotard. Your mother who worked in insurance bought you pointe shoes when you were three. You're a closeted lesbian and ballet was the only career that would let you ogle the female form without having to type your truth into the search bar. Pressure, manipulation, ignorance, repression, false consciousness, weakness, fear.

Art wasn't enslaved by external forces, but by internal ones. He got the license. He was admitted to the air force. He rose above his father's derision. And now he's here, cheery as a bumblebee, with paralyzed wings. The most obvious of Sive's barriers are external, so that's some consolation to Gael. And Guthrie? Alas, Berlin accounted for him, too. "The subject himself can't be the final authority on the question of whether he is free."

✦

There's a photograph on the wall above Sive and Art's dining table that's more expensively framed than the others. It's of Jarleth standing by Guthrie on the altar at the twins' baptism. Jarleth is holding Ronan, and Guthrie has Soraca. They are tilting the babies over the basin, cupping their gauzy skulls. Guthrie looks starkly young, like a child sitting on a hospice bed and being told to take his grandparent's hand. He looks deeply alarmed, too, as if he has been taken straight from the cooling hospice bed to the law firm to discover an enormous inheritance of debt. Gael imagines the artwork label.

> **Title: "They Know Not What They Do"**
> Medium: Baby on doily
> Year: 2009

"Thought I shot a good one there," Art says, "caught your dad looking dead smug. But then his face just stayed that way. Lucky both of you took after your mum, sides your colorings."

Gael drops her gaze to her plate.

It's Christmas Eve. A candlelit supper of meatloaf, boiled chestnuts and string beans, à la Art. It's just the three of them, dreamily calm, but for Bob Dylan rasping out carols in the background.

Sive says, "I think my tolerance for comically bad music is at quota, Art. Do you mind?"

"I'll do it," Gael says, and gets up. Searching through the record collection, she recalls an American composer she'd come across in New York. Frederic Rzewski, famed for his piano composition "The People United Will Never Be Defeated!," which was a series of variations on the Chilean song "¡El pueblo unido jamás será vencido!," which was, at first, a celebration of the socialist Salvador Allende government but later became the anthem of the resistance against Pinochet's regime. Gael finds it on YouTube and plugs the (Cash Converters leaving-gift) speaker system into her laptop.

"What's this?" Sive asks.

"Not sure how to pronounce his name," Gael says. "See if you like it."

Sive pulls a face that warrants a monocle.

They listen. Quietly eat. The plonky scaling sound of it. The distinctive, marchlike opening that leads into a melodic, lullabyish section, frisking around something more historic. The fast progression; prowling agitation. The backing away from; stampeding toward. The discordant statements of class that make the piece increasingly rousing—now antipretentious; now phrenic—as if the simplicity of the introduction and the rallying cry it's based on were never simple or polarizing. That had been just another compromise for the gamut of discontent, which doesn't fit on a stave or a placard. How have we come here, already? From alliterated slogans to this?

By mid-November, Occupy movements worldwide surpassed a thousand. The central conversation had shifted from austerity measures to economic inequality; love and rage the subtexts. It had truly bloomed. And all that blooms must wilt.

On November 15 at lunchtime, a week after Gael had run the New York Marathon, two thousand riot police ringed Zuccotti Park. She was no longer staying there, then, but she saw on the news how the bulldozer had rolled in. How the subway stops were shut down. The Brooklyn Bridge closed. A sound cannon boomed through Lower Manhattan. The library she'd volunteered at was thrown into a skip. She still had Camus in her handbag, which she opened. Later, she read in his *Notebooks*: "It's a kind of spiritual snobbery that makes people think they can be happy without money." It seemed all part of the great contradiction that his writings were going for free in the People's Library.

The music, too, contradicts. There's a crashing sound that makes Sive and Art jump when Rzewski bashes the piano's fall board, as accompaniment for a *sforzando* chord. He plays several triads like this, with huge pauses and the most delicate plucking of high notes in between. He barks, to lend rasp to a chord. A pause. Then, he begins to whistle hauntingly over the music, which gains fluidity and conventional beauty for just a moment, before frenzy recoups the sound and forsakes coherence. Just as it reaches nightmarish havoc, Rzewski diminishes it again to delicate notation and whistling.

The doorbell becomes part of the music, at first. Then, Art casts Gael a strange look. His round green eyes radioluminesce in the half light.

"Was that the doorbell?" Gael asks.

"Yerrit was." He makes no motion to get up.

Nor does Sive, who's trying to dig her fork into a chestnut that keeps crumbling like a floury potato.

"O . . . kay?" Gael says. "I'll get it, then."

Art curls out his lower lip and Sive says, "Could you."

Gael sweeps her hair across from her temple and walks slowly down the corridor, heart bleating. She turns the lock on the front door and pulls it in. A jab of adrenaline to the circulatory system, which sometimes has the effect of making the chest feel stood on.

"*Harper.*"

She is dressed all in black, but not in dungarees or a boxy silk shirt or a hand-knit Christmas sweater. The coat is old and covered in pilling and the black slacks are the wrong size. Tight on the thighs and far too long. She's carrying a travel bag, and a huge brown-paper-wrapped item is propped against her shoulder. A gift? Her eyes are sunken and scorched and unfocused.

"Are you okay? Come in."

But neither of them makes any movements.

Harper blinks and strokes the package's brown paper. "It's Guthrie's painting," she says. "I don't wanna refund, or anything. But Mom died, so." Her chin begins to tremble, but she stills it like a pilot finding less turbulent air. "I don't really wanna see it. And I know he was sad to lose em all, so."

Gael's tears come as a kind of cough. Like a barked chord she didn't anticipate. She steps out to move the painting so that she can embrace Harper, but Harper says, "Don't," and carries the painting in herself. She sets it just inside the hallway against the wall and leads herself into the open-plan lounge where Sive and Art are stood by their places at the table. When Sive sees Gael crying, she covers her mouth and nose in a kind of prayer gesture. They must have known. Art has come round from the table and is holding his hand out to Harper.

"You're shorter than I'd imagined," he says.

Not up to comebacks, Harper hugs him and her muffled words are: "Thanks for everything." This must move Sive because she starts cleaning up plates, which is a rudeness Gael didn't think her capable of. Gael paces up and down the hall, trying to catch a breath; telling herself over and over to get a hold of herself, that this reaction is selfish in the darkest way, but then *stop* Gael *stop* Gael *stoppit stop* is all she can manage. Her breaths thread so many needles. Art and Harper are talking quietly on the sofa and Sive is packing the dishwasher. The cold glare of fluorescent light in the kitchen feels like an incursion on the dark warmth they'd been basking in, their scotopic vision now lost. The dish clattering peters out. Sive clears her throat a few times and blows her nose. Then emerges to introduce herself to Harper.

Harper's voice is hoarse. "Since Jarleth's such an ass, you must be a friggin goddess, to have made Gael."

"Well . . ." Sive says, "you . . ." and tears up, which she doesn't often do in front of strangers, perhaps to protect people from the heavy sorrow she extends. To have broken through to Gael, you must be an angel . . . is perhaps what Sive had been thinking? To have elicited love? "I'm so sorry," Sive says. She tries to stymie this indulgence, putting her hands in her trouser pockets formally, as if getting the body language right means the rest will follow. "I'll make us some coffee."

Art's sitting beside Harper on the couch when Gael comes into the lounge. She expects Harper to look her way and say something impossibly strong, but she doesn't. She's watching Rzewski on the laptop with the piety of a kid watching cartoons. It's now half an hour in and the music has changed tone, as if the left hand can't hear the right and doesn't know they're in different key signatures and, no matter how dexterously and accurately they play the notes, it will never sound of fellowship.

"I can play that," Harper says.

Art laughs, knowing her humor would come. He pats the arm of the couch like a dog.

Sive emerges from the kitchen, a tea towel pressed against one eye. "*Can* you?"

Harper nods. "It's like, the Occupy anthem. Well, Rage Against the Machine was the Occupy anthem. That trumped Rzewski on popularity. But Rage doesn't do piano parts."

Sive stares at Harper, as if at a long-lost sister. "Sugar and cream?"

"Uh-huh," Harper says.

Sive can't know if this Americanism is a yes or no but it's unimportant. She points to the electric piano, which they've moved from the study to the living room, where anyone else would have a TV. "Feel free to tinker around on that thing if it would relax you. Or if you want to go to sleep, you might be jet-lagged . . . Or are you hungry? . . . Anything." Sive dips back into the kitchen alcove and there's the sound of coffee grains being scooped and dropped into the cafetière.

Gael's watching the laptop too, her back against the wall. She doesn't know what's required of her, or what's wanted. Sive's behavior is as much of a shock as the news and the arrival. Gael goes into the kitchen to put biscuits on a plate and she sees Sive leaning on the counter, collecting herself. She starts when Gael lays a hand on her back.

"What is it?"

Sive shakes her head so silver strands of hair fall from her French twist. She doesn't make eye contact with Gael and barely watches what she's doing. "She's just so young." Gael's back is to the counter and Sive is faced toward it. Sive won't look up. "Pass me the tray on top the fridge there, would you."

Harper's six years older than Gael, but her mum had only been fifty.

Someone's hit pause on the video and the static fizz of the dormant speakers fills the room. The forecast anticipated snow and it sounds as if it's come and all the windows are ajar. Harper and Art aren't talking. After a few moments, the first three chords explain their quiet. Gael sets the tray on the counter and glances at her mother before moving into the living room, where Harper is on the picnic-furniture piano stool, hitting the next three chords so heftily, the impulse is to grab her, to protect the instrument. She takes long pauses where there should only be minim rests. Then the next phrases are like brusque rapping on a door and it seems accidental that the notes are right. Are they? Now they're right, surely. She has transitioned into the lighter, sweeter stretch of music, grade-five sort of stuff; melody all in the right hand, bouncy left hand rounding out the chord, a bit of the polka about it. Harper is doing her straight-backed playing Gael had observed in London, with no movement or dynamics. Her coat is off and she's wearing a shapeless turtleneck black sweater, which can't belong to her.

Sive pours whiskey into three of the four cups on the coffee table. Art takes his one.

The left hand kicks into double speed and there are indeed distinctive dynamics. *Fortes* and *pianissimos,* if not much else. Then a pause and a stark bridge into conclusion of the opening section. A longer pause. Then delicate tones, like rain beginning to fall. Tippling from the upper octaves to the lower and the electric piano must not be big enough for the range because notes seem to be missing. The key signature is unreadable, and soon one hand sounds like it's tripping, just a touch, over the other and that they're slightly out of sync, but the gentleness of sound convinces you to keep listening.

Hear it louden. And you listen because of its authority; because it's a story, clearly, not just sounds. There will be a moral and morals are worth all sorts of wretchedness. He will take us somewhere if we concentrate.

Why, then, does it sound made-up? Volatile? If they hadn't just been listening to the composer's recording, they might think the player was losing her mind, in the tidiest, most bourgeois manner possible. And who wouldn't pay to hear how that sounds. Harper makes the motion of turning a page of the sheet music that isn't there, and Gael sees that her eyes are closed and that she is, in fact, losing it . . .

She looks to the keys and catches it again, and it could be the soundtrack from a haunted house or maybe just a normal house where you're pursued by your own demons so you'd better keep climbing the stairs; you'd better pick up speed and suffer the muscle burn because it's life or death, or make-believe, which is analogous. She plays it too fast, now, faster than is possible, notwithstanding your abilities, and her fingers trip and slap and miss. Her hands slide off the keys and hang by her side like buckets.

"Sorry. Mom only liked the first part."

Her head drops forward and Gael rushes to her, as if to catch it. Gael squeezes her and feels the heave and judder of her body, how Guthrie used to convulse in her arms. Except this is a pouring out, not a locking up. Gael presses her mouth to the top of Harper's head and hopes she doesn't feel the trickle on her scalp. The balcony door opens and a chill breeze scurries in. Art stands out there in his slippers, his coffee steaming and fogging the glass. A light snow is coming down. Not enough to hold. But there and beautiful, for the time being.

It feels like seconds, but it must be longer, before Art and Sive are all wrapped up and calling from the hallway.

"Sure you won't come with?" Art asks. "Nice soft snow out there. Gently falling."

Gael feels Harper heave anew at this; her eyes still closed, cheek pressed against Gael's belly. Gael says no. As the door shuts, she thinks she hears Harper say the words *Falling gently,* but that could mean anything.

✦

With her head on Gael's lap, nude on the futon in the study with the duvet across their legs, Harper said that her mother had talked endlessly. Then she corrected herself:

"Not endlessly. *Not* nonstop. I assumed it would be. I begged her to cut it out. I said: 'Is there no tsunami somewhere we can do a minute's silence for?' Then she'd get all hurt and I'd feel bad. What a bitch, hindsight."

From what Harper said, it seemed as if Kendra had wanted Harper to know as much of her mind as could be exposed in the time she'd had left. Even the innermost stuff; the stuff Harper would rather not have known. But all this talk was one of the reasons Harper hadn't expected her to linger on the subject of death: certainly not on how she hoped to experience it.

Years prior, Kendra had attended an introductory seminar on Tibetan Buddhism. She hadn't been ready for the teachings at the time, she told Harper wisely, but they'd all come racing back to her as death neared and, like all things (including how wilted spinach landed on her plate), she took this as a sign.

As Kendra explained it, Tibetan Buddhists believe that in both orgasm and death the self is swallowed up in the intensity of the experience. If a person can succumb to this forfeiture of self, they can experience the freely floating mind—the pristine innermost mind, underlying the conceptual one. All people, they believe, are afraid of this loss and unconsciously resist total immersion in the mind, uniquely available during these concentrated experiences. We fear completely losing ourselves.

Harper spoke:

"'That's all fine for sex,' Mom said, 'it's a pity but it's normal . . . believe me . . . but in death?' She held my hand so tight I thought the whole thing was a setup. That she wasn't really sick! That it was something else! Where'd she get that strength from?" Harper took Gael's hand. "She squeezed my hand like this and said, 'Harper,' she said, 'you don't always like what I believe. But you gotta help me here. To not be fearful in the end, of losing my *self.* I wanna have the *bliss* they talk about. People always say they wanna die in the middle of an orgasm. That'd be a good way to go, they say. Well, the Tibetans think it's possible. Because death and orgasm are the same. Only one lasts longer.'"

Gael laughed. And Harper let go of her hand, lifted her head from her lap and turned on the pillow toward her. Her breasts and tummy weighed down sideways and Gael reached out to bear their gorgeous gravity.

"You're laughing at my dead mom." Her face was spliced all over in red patch-ups, instead of gold.

"She's funny."

"She *was* funny." Harper breathed in intervals. "Truly, she was a hoot." The brown around her eyes looked like eye shadow brushed in the wrong place. "And that was funny, for sure, but it also meant a lot. Because I could respect it. An I never really respected Mom intellectually. She musta known. I hated that she didn't read. I hated a lotta things. But I respect that wish she had. And I respect that she wanted me in on it. And it's hard to be around people you love . . . but don't respect. And I took that out on her, for a long time. So I'm the sucker, really. That I missed out on not finding out sooner."

Harper closed her eyes, because she was too tired to weep anymore. And Gael was there. And Gael's pale lips were there, and the shadows beneath her breasts and the stubborn wishbone of her hips. The diamond hollow where her ribs met. The tongue to slip round the avocado of her sybaritic core. And likewise, but different. Likewise, but fuller and brawnier and all together more forgiving. Those are things that can be lost in and succumbed to and lived on. Later, they can work on the mind. On its presence. For now, the body alone would do. It's what they had.

◆

It's stopped snowing out. Just a very light kiss of it has stuck. Enough to need boots for. Though, she can't risk waking Harper, in her cucumber eye mask, her sore throat clacking on each outbreath.

Opening the wardrobe ever so gently to see if the boots are within reach, Gael recalls Wally's pin. He'd given her quite a scare a few days ago, when it glinted at her like a drunken memory on a too-bright morning. He'd turned up at Guthrie's doorstep, a taxi engine running at the gate. Gael was busy putting toys away when Guthrie had opened the door to him and the voice blared through the house like a severe weather siren.

"Either the Yellow Pages is outdated as I am, or you're Mr. Foess, the great Irish artist. Which of the two?"

Gael had run to the door and embraced him. "Wally!" She had to dissolve the notion that strangers might know about Guthrie before he considered it. "It's the guy from the plane!" she told her brother, who had his son propped on his hip.

"The guy from the plane?" Wally touched his baseball cap and scanned Gael's loosely clad body for a sign of what she was made of. What she had shown him. The blackness of his eye disguised its dilation. "Well, I never been called that before." He chewed on the liverlike flesh of his inner cheek. "But this gal can call me just about anything. You know she got me to wear pajamas? Said she'd